The

September

By

Jim Roan

Memories will flame up from a glowing ember
And rise like the mists of a warm September
(Anonymous)

ISBN: 1-4107-2666-5 (e-book)
ISBN: 1-4107-2665-7 (Paperback)

Library of Congress Control Number: 2003095007

This book is printed on acid free paper.

Printed in the United States of America
Bloomington, IN

Cover by James Michael Roan

Edited by Katherine Osborne Foreman

1stBooks - rev. 07/09/03

PROLOGUE

G T Deane and Isabel Morgan grew up together as brother and sister. When they reached their teens, they found out that their love was not of a sibling nature. During their teens they worked for their fathers, George Deane and Frank Morgan, who strip mined coal. Upon graduation G T announced that he was going to work in an underground coal mine. He and Isabel broke up after that and she started dating Bradley Durham while he dated Veronica Atmore. Bradley and Veronica conspired to marry Isabel and G T and eventually gain control of the Golden Star mines. Olivia Napier whose son Bige was hurt in a mine accident that was blamed on Bradley killed both Bradley and Veronica. Veronica had aborted a child conceived by Bige. The Mists of September picks up where The Fogs of August ended.

The Mists of September
Memories will flame up from a glowing ember
And rise like the mist of a warm September
(Anonymous)

CHAPTER 1

Judge James Constanza made a practice of visiting the prisoners in the Bell County jail before each term of court. This was frowned upon by his fellow jurists, but no one had the guts to check him on it. His purpose was to familiarize himself with the criminals who would appear before him and to assure them that they would get a fair trial. He usually made these visits when the prisoners were taking their break period in the prison yard. He would go into the yard unescorted and had never been threatened.

The yard was enclosed with a cyclone fence with three strands of barbed wire across the top supported on arms standing at a forty five degree angle facing back into the prison yard. This arrangement made it virtually impossible to climb over the fence or at least that was the contention of the designer. The only break in the fence was a walkthrough gate that was used to carry trash through to the alley. It had both a mechanical lock and an electric lock that could only be activated from the guard position on a balcony over the exercise area. During the exercise periods, an armed guard stood on the balcony.

The men and women prisoners took their breaks at the same time, but their yards were separated by another cyclone fence.

Olivia Napier had been a resident of the county jail for almost three years since having been indicted for the murders of Bradley Durham and Veronica Atmore. She and Judge Constanza had become speaking acquaintances during this time. He addressed her formally as Mrs. Napier and she in turn called him Judge or Your Honor. There was no belligerence in their conversations which were never more than two or three sentences long.

She was about three inches taller than he and weighed in at about twenty pounds more. She was a very muscular woman who had kept up the exercise routine she had developed as a young girl. He too had an exercise routine that he followed religiously and from one exercise faddist to the other there was respect.

Not all of the prisoners felt about him the way Olivia did. One in particular was Judy Barnes who was to be tried for bank robbery. She and her boy friend had robbed the National Bank branch at the Forks of Straight Creek, but had been unsuccessful in their getaway. They were both native of Covington, Kentucky and felt it would be easy to knock over a small town bank. They were mistaken.

Prior to the beginning of the September term of criminal court, Judge Constanza made his routine visit. While walking through the women's area, Judy grabbed him from behind and held a shard of glass against his jugular vein. Calling out to the guard, she told him to unlock the gate or he would have a dead judge on his hands.

"Do not open that gate!" Judge Constanza said.

"Open it or watch him bleed to death," Judy responded.

"Let him go, Judy. You'll never make it out of here," Olivia said as she started toward Judy.

"Stay away from me you ignorant bitch or I will kill him," Judy answered.

Olivia could see the point of the shard pressing into Constanza's neck as she slowly moved closer.

"I'm not bluffing, Olivia, stay away," Judy screamed as she backed toward the gate, dragging Constanza with her.

"Let him go, I said," yelled Olivia.

"Open this gate or he is dead," screamed Judy pressing the glass deeper into his neck.

In the process of backing up, she stepped on a large gravel and momentarily lost her balance. That was all it took. Olivia hit her one time and dropped her cold. Turning to Constanza, she asked, "Are you okay, your honor?"

"Yes, Mrs. Napier, I am all right. Thank you for saving my life. I owe you," answered Judge Constanza.

Word of the incident spread like wildfire throughout the area.

++++++

Olivia Napier's trial had been set three times in as many years and Judge James Constanza was getting upset with the continued requests for rescheduling. The first time, Jeff Cawood, Olivia's attorney--requested a continuance for more time to have Olivia examined by a psychiatrist. She naturally took offense at this and cursed a hurricane at Cawood, but Judge Constanza granted the request feeling that it was justifiable and necessary. The second postponement came at the request of the Commonwealth's Attorney, Caron Dell, that the judge recuse himself after expressing to Olivia Napier that he "owed her one." He refused to do so stating that his fairness had never been questioned and he would not let it be this time. The third time, Judge Constanza really got irritated when Theo Shawitz, attorney with Citizen's Rights Group, asked for a change of venue. The judge did not grant the request, but to keep himself in the clear, he reset the trial date to give Shawitz a chance to research the change request which Shawitz didn't do. The Judge had made up his mind that Olivia Napier would be tried during the upcoming summer term or someone was going to jail for contempt.

Judge James Constanza was a Bell County native who had grown up in Middlesboro, Kentucky. He had graduated from high school near the top of his class and gone to the University of Kentucky. His pre-law major was accounting. He was not the athletic type and therefore didn't participate in high school sports; however, he was a martial arts student, primarily to keep himself in good physical condition. The word was that he was very good at it so no one challenged him.

Being small in stature, he carried about 140 pounds that was well distributed on his 5'6" frame. His wife, a pretty blonde woman of the same height and stature, never wore shoes with heels in order to keep from towering over him. He felt that his position merited the wearing of a necktie which he not only did, but he required any male attorney in his court to do. He kept his teeth well-brushed and flossed. Constanza did not smoke, chew gum or tobacco, or dip snuff and did not allow any of that to be done in his court. Some said that he was a martinet, while others said he was what a trial judge should be. His eyes and his voice were his most distinguishing features. His eyes were coal black and looked out from under bushy eyebrows like two sharp knives. His voice was a deep bass with a resonance that sounded as though he was speaking through a bull horn. He commanded due respect for his position and those who did not recognize this often became the victim of his acid tongue. Constanza, serving his second six-year term as Bell Circuit Court Judge after being nominated by his peers from the Bell County Bar Association, ran unopposed both times. It was never clear if he was nominated to keep him out of the hair of other attorneys or because he was such an astute attorney. Either way, no one ever ran against him. His reputation was impeccable. Judges and attorneys throughout the Commonwealth either knew him or knew of him. He had been urged to run for the state Supreme Court, but declined saying he would rather stay where he was. He was fair and honest and one thing for sure was the fact that no matter what she was accused of, Olivia Napier would get a fair trial in his court.

The Bell Circuit Court room was pretty much the same style as other circuit court rooms throughout the state. The judge's bench sat above the rest of the room as it did in all courtrooms. The witness chair was to the judge's left, with the jury box on the same side, but sitting further out into the body of the room. The plaintiff's representative, in this case the Commonwealth Attorney, sat at a table in front of the witness chair and across from the jury box. The defense attorney sat at a similar table in line with the plaintiff's table and to the judge's right. A balustrade with a gate in the center separated the spectators from the court participants. The spectator section, which filled out the rest of the room, was in an arc. Each row was set on a platform four feet wide and six inches above the row in front of it. This allowed all persons to see and hear the proceedings. The auditorium-style seats fastened to wooden runners that in turn were fastened to the floor that was dark and oily from the many maintenance hours spent sweeping it with oily compound. There were four chairs to a section and all of them were uncomfortable.

This courtroom had been the scene of the Dillon-Harp shoot out years ago. Teen-age cousins Savannah Dillon and Augusta Harp had competed in a canning exhibition at the county fair. Savannah's pickled okra had gotten a blue ribbon over Augusta's pickled okra. Joshua Dillon and Boone Harp, their fathers, had gotten into an argument over the judging. The argument had led to a fight where Boone Harp shot and killed Joshua Dillon. Joshua's brother, Jonathan Dillon, had seen the whole thing and was a material witness at Boone Harp's trial. All during the time while Jonathan was on the witness stand, Boone Harp sat at the defense table with the middle finger of his right hand extended in an obscene gesture. In addition to this, Boone grinned all the time. When Jonathan finished his account of what had happened, Boone laughed out loud. It was more than Jonathan could take. He pulled a Colt .44 revolver from under his coat and shot Boone Harp twice before the court deputy could stop him. He fired the other four rounds while he wrestled with the deputy sheriff. All four slugs went over the heads of the spectators, who were lying flat on the floor, and hit the back wall of the courtroom. No one else was injured, but Boone Harp died on the way to the hospital.

The four pockmarks left by Jonathan Dillon's bullets had never been covered up. Every time the courtroom was painted, the presiding circuit judge cautioned the painters to not paint or in any way change the bullet holes. They were left as a reminder of what could happen if proper order was not kept in the court. From that day on, all witnesses and spectators were searched before being allowed to enter the courtroom and in later years, a metal detector was installed.

Jonathan Dillon served twelve years of a twenty-year sentence before a sympathetic governor, who wanted to run for Senator, pardoned him. The governor needed the Dillon vote worse than he needed the Harp vote. This incident had bearing on Olivia Napier's trial. Joshua and Jonathan Dillon were first cousins to Boone Harp, Harp's mother having been a sister to the Dillon's father. Jonathan Dillon was Olivia Napier's grandfather. There had been bad blood before, but the shooting incidents forever closed any doors that may have been open to reconciliation.

Caron Dell, who was to run the prosecution against Olivia, was well-aware of the Dillon-Harp feud. A year younger than Judge Constanza and a year behind him in high school at Middlesboro, Caron Dell had a beautiful voice and quite often sang in church and at funerals. She stayed a year behind him all through college and law school at the University of Kentucky. Her pre-law degree had been in political science, which made her a very astute politician. Her shoulder-length auburn hair set off her brown eyes and heart shaped face, which together with her 125 pounds on a 5'7" frame, made her a very attractive woman. She was dramatically statuesque with perfect posture and dressed in expensive designer clothes, which she wore well. Her poise, good looks and nice looking clothes gave her a decided advantage over her opponents, especially when addressing a jury that was predominantly male.

Jeff Cawood, Olivia Napier's attorney, was a Pineville native who had also attended the University of Kentucky. His pre-law degree had been in business management, but he had worked for a building contractor one summer and loved it. The practice of law was his vocation, but building construction was his avocation. He formed his own construction company and did most of the work himself. He didn't like to admit it, but his business degree greatly helped him with his construction company. His father had been in politics for years and had alternated between county court clerk and sheriff for twenty four years. He was in his third term as county court clerk. He didn't want Jeff to get into politics, but he did want him to get a degree in something besides building construction. Jeff was a nice-looking young man with dark brown hair and brown eyes. He was built along the same proportions as Judge Constanza, slight, but wiry. He wasn't married, but he dated Caroline Moss, who was the court reporter. They had discussed marriage, but discuss was all that they did. Though he was a very competent lawyer, he sometimes got involved in his contracting business to the point that he overlooked details in his law practice. Such was the case when he asked for the second continuance on Olivia Napier's trial.

Theo Shawitz, who was the other defense attorney, was a decidedly different cut from the rest of the attorneys in the case. He was the son of a Russian immigrant couple from St. Petersburg, who had come to America at the end of the Cold War and settled in Rochester, New York. His father, Ivan, was an engraver, who did beautiful work. He had once engraved a meat platter that the Governor of New York gave the President of the United States. He had gotten a letter of appreciation from both the governor and the president that he had framed and hung on the dining room wall. Both Ivan and his wife Darva were what you would call nice people, but Theo resented his parents being immigrants. That coupled with his 5'4" stature gave him a very antagonistic and aggressive attitude. His black curly hair and his black eyes bespoke his Russian heritage and made him even more belligerent. He had gotten his law degree from New York University with a pre-law degree in social sciences. He was not a particularly good student, but he made good grades by using other people's work. Upon graduation, he had gone with the Citizen's Rights Group, a supposed advocacy organization. His social science degree along with his law degree made him appear to be a champion of the down trodden. He wasn't. He had gone with CRG to gain experience and notoriety and he had become one of their leading attorneys. Theo had read about the Olivia Napier case in a law periodical and it interested him, primarily because he felt that he could make a mockery of an eastern Kentucky court and get his name spread over all the tabloids. He figured it would be sensational and bring him a large amount of publicity.

The notoriety preceding the impending trial gave it the aroma of a Roman circus. The possibilities for chaos were countless, and the whole county awaited the opening date with glee.

CHAPTER 2

G T Deane had graduated magna cum laude from the Engineering College at the University of Kentucky with a perfect 4.0 standing all the way through both Southeast Community College at Middlesboro and UK. He had been inducted into several honorary fraternities including Tau Beta Pi, the engineering honorary. Upon graduation, he enrolled in law school at UK. Due to his grades, the law school was delighted to have him and made room for him that it is doubtful they would have made for an applicant of lesser standing. Before he graduated, the dean of the Civil Engineering department offered him a student assistant job, but G T turned it down. Thanking the dean, he explained that he wanted to do some practical hands on engineering. Several engineering firms offered him jobs and he finally took one with Banner Engineering in Lexington, which specialized in mining permits. His past experience at both underground and surface mining made him a valuable asset in the preparation of mining permits. The company made arrangements for him to work when he didn't have classes.

Of all the engineering applications in the preparation of permits, G T enjoyed the design of siltation ponds and diversion ditches the most. When he and Isabel Morgan, his girlfriend, were teen-agers they had worked summers for their fathers on a surface mine job and they had built several ponds. Frank Morgan had explained to them that the purpose of the ponds was to contain the water that ran off from the surface disturbance until the silt in the water could settle out and not muddy the creek or river that was the final recipient of the runoff. He explained to them that the principal spillway, a length of culvert pipe that extended through the dam, was set at a point that would let the clear water on top of the pond run out, or 'decant' as it was referred to.

"The pond's principal spillway, that piece of culvert pipe, is designed to take a 10-year, 24-hour storm," he had told them pointing to the galvanized culvert pipe in the dam.

"What does that mean?" Isabel had asked.

"That is the amount of rain calculated to fall in storms at 10 year intervals and don't ask me how they know because I don't know. Scientists have figured it out and you'll just have to take their word for it," her father had answered. "The emergency spillway, which is a trough or swale on the top of the pond dam, is designed to take a 25-year, 24-hour storm," Frank had gone on. Its purpose is to allow the water to run over the top of the dam if the principal spillway can't handle it. It's riprapped to keep the water from cutting into the dam. "

"I still don't know how they know that it will rain that hard every 10 or 25 years," Isabel had said.

"Let it go, Isabel. We'll just build the ponds the way the engineer designs them and won't worry about why they are designed the way they are," G T had said.

Frank had showed them how to dig the dirt out of the backside of the pond site and use it to build the dam. He also showed them how to dig the keyway to control seepage and how to compact the dirt so that the dam would be solid. They built several ponds that summer, being ever cautious to not get caught by an inspector because they were too young to do that kind of work.

Everybody got a good laugh when Jerry Hoag, a reclamation inspector, complimented Frank on the ponds. "Have you got somebody new building your ponds, Frank?" he had asked. "They sure look a heap better than what you have put in in the past."

This kind of background had made G T an authority on silt ponds. He had done a number of permits for several coal companies and had never had any problems. His work was so well-done that quite often the permit reviewer would not even check his calculations, so it was understandable why G T was perplexed when he got back a permit that he had submitted for White Pines Coal Company. A permit reviewer named Rebecca Holton had done the review. The name rang a familiar bell from somewhere, but he couldn't place it. Calling the Department of Natural Resources, he asked for her.

"Good afternoon, Rebecca Holton speaking. How can I help you?" came a sugary voice over the telephone.

"Good afternoon, Ms. Holton. My name is G T Deane and I recently submitted a permit for White Pines Coal Company, which you reviewed and sent back. I'd like to know what was wrong with it so that I could make the corrections and return it to you. The company needs that permit as soon as they can get it or they are going to have to lay some people off," G T explained.

"Well if it isn't old Four-Point-0 Deane who never has a permit sent back. How's that bitch girl friend of yours?" Holton answered.

It suddenly came to G T who she was. He remembered Isabel talking about a girl who was in her suite her sophomore year. They had had a knock-down drag-out cuss fight over the pros and cons of surface mining. Rebecca Holton had moved out at the end of the semester.

"Well, Four 0, you are going to have to redo those ponds to take a 15-year principal spillway and a 30-year emergency spill way," Rebecca continued.

"Those ponds were designed in conformance with the Department of Natural Resources specifications," he answered.

"Those ponds were designed in conformance with the old standards. You'll have to redo them and resubmit them in accordance with the new specs, Four 0," Rebecca retorted.

"I haven't received any notice of a change," he said.

"You have now," she countered.

"I'll be back with you," G T said as he hung up the phone. He then dialed the Department of Natural Resources again, this time asking the receptionist for Barry Foreman. Barry Foreman and G T became friends during G T's senior year. Barry was a graduate assistant who had G T in a lab course. He was impressed with G T's attitude and knowledge. He had been the person who recommended G T to the dean as a graduate assistant. Barry had grown up in Haggard, Kentucky where his father worked for the postal service. He was smaller than G T, but had been a pretty fair athlete in high school, playing football, basketball and baseball. His black hair and black eyes set off an olive complexion that hinted at Mediterranean ancestry. He had obtained a Bachelor of Science degree in Civil Engineering from UK and was working on his masters while he worked for Natural Resources. He was biding his time and gaining experience while waiting to hear from a job interview that he had with an international engineering company. He had applied for a job in Nepal that he had found advertised in an engineering magazine and had told the interviewer that he would have his Masters in the spring of the coming year. Hopefully he could get his Masters and the job at the same time. Being unmarried with no family responsibilities, he could pick up and go on a minute's notice.

Answering the phone, Barry asked G T what the problem was.

"Who in the hell is Rebecca Holton that she can raise the standards for principal and emergency spillways just because she wants to?" asked G T.

"Settle down, G T. She is from the Environmental Protection Agency and has full sway over the design of silt ponds, diversion ditches and impoundments," Barry answered.

"Where did she come from and how can she change the standards?" G T asked.

"If you remember back several years ago, there was an impoundment failure that just about flooded the world. The EPA got involved in it and that wimp who was governor at the time signed an agreement that gave them full authority over the design of silt ponds, diversion ditches and impoundments. We have had two or three of their people in here who were real easy to work with, but then along comes this witch who changes all of the game rules. She is pretty sure of herself, because the first time the director braced her about upping the spillways she told him that it was her prerogative to set any reasonable standards and he buckled under."

"But she can't change the law. That can only be done by the legislature," countered G T. "Who is her supervisor? I'll call him."

"Phillip Banks is her section supervisor. Now, I've got to go G T. We'll talk about this another time," Barry said as he hung up.

G T remembered Phillip Banks. He had reviewed G T's permits before and had always been complimentary of the way they were done. G T didn't think he was a native Kentuckian or at least he didn't talk like one. Actually he was a medium-height redhead from Omaha, Nebraska. He had gotten a civil engineering degree from the University of Nebraska and his MBA at Tennessee Tech, and from there he came to the Kentucky Department of Natural Resources. How he got from University of Nebraska to Tennessee Tech was a story no one knew. He would never discuss his part in the Vietnam War and his resume had a four year blank place in it that he labeled "Vietnam." When asked about it he would answer, "I was there." He never gave a military unit or any other pertinent information. He was more of a shadow than anything else, but a very nice person to do business with.

G T called for Phillip, but he was not available. He had gone to a seminar in Atlanta. G T was thoroughly upset and frustrated by the whole thing. Going to the president of Banner Engineering, Arthur Banner, he explained his problem.

"Arthur, I've got a problem with a permit for White Pines and there seems to be nothing that I can do about it," he explained. "They have a person from EPA in Natural Resources who has changed the groundrules on ponds. Her name is Rebecca Holton."

"I've heard of Ms. Holton and the word is that she is tough and sure of the ground she is standing on," replied Banner. "You'll just have to work it out."

This made G T even madder and he promised himself that he would get her fired or moved, one or the other, and maybe quit Banner along with it. It didn't appear that Arthur was going to help him and didn't care whether he worked it out or not.

CHAPTER 3

During her four years at the University of Kentucky, Isabel had become a very close friend with Sandy Deiss who had shepherded her through the entire time. Isabel had called Sandy when she and G T got engaged and Sandy had planned to have Isabel in her wedding, which never did occur. Her fiancé, Marc West, had broken it off for no reason. Isabel had heard from other girls that Sandy was too smart for him and it made him feel inferior. She also heard that he had another girlfriend that was dumber than a coal bucket, so in Isabel's opinion, Sandy was too smart to marry him anyway. It had been a trying time for Sandy and Isabel had stood by her. When Sandy took a crying spell, Isabel took one.

Isabel had obtained her degree in journalism and with encouragement from Sandy, she was pursuing her Masters, which she would get in the fall. Sandy was working at the *Lexington Journal* and had gotten Isabel a job working with her. Isabel found the job exciting and interesting, but she didn't particularly like the interviewing. She classified it as being nosy. The two girls had worked together on several stories for the paper and the news editor, Sam Eldridge, had complimented them on their coverage. The toughest story they had done was a house fire where six elderly people lived. One couple had not gotten out in time; they were found hugging each other. Both died of smoke inhalation. It broke Isabel's heart when she saw them, but she wrote the story up and turned it in. The memory of the scene stayed with her for days and kept her awake at night. She finally overcame it and knuckled down to the work at hand.

Sam called both of them into his office one morning.

"Isabel, aren't you from Pineville?" he asked.

"Yes sir," she answered.

"I would like for the two of you to go to Pineville and cover the trial of this woman who allegedly killed a man and woman and put them in the bathtub. This is going to be a sensational trial and it would be good experience for both of you," he said, "One of the attorneys for the defense is Theo Shawitz from the Citizen's Rights Group. He is a very flamboyant lawyer and thrives on upsetting both the judge and the prosecution. The judge is James Constanza and he is a hard-nosed, but fair judge. It will be a tug of war between Theo and him, and I want our readers to see the whole thing. Interview as many as you can who have any attachment to the proceedings. You can call the stories in and a desk person will take it down for you. The company will pay all of your expenses. You will have a front row seat to see 'King Kong meets Godzilla' when Judge Constanza and Shawitz lock horns."

All the time Eldridge was talking, Isabel had her hands folded in her lap and her head bent down as if she was looking at something she was holding. When he finished talking, she raised her head and tears were streaming down her face.

"Mr. Eldridge, please don't ask me to interview people. I will be glad to go with Sandy and introduce her around, but please don't ask me to write about the trial. I dated the man who was murdered and my fiancé dated the woman. My fiancé saved the life of the son of the woman who is accused of the crime. I am just too involved to be objective.

"Okay, you can show Sandy around and introduce her to people. I can see where you would have a hard time discussing testimony with acquaintances," Sam said.

Isabel and Sandy left the next morning for Pineville. Isabel had called Sarah Morgan, her step-mother, and told her that she and Sandy were coming home to Pineville, and asked if it would it be all right for Sandy to stay with them. Sandy had remonstrated with her about it, but to no avail. Sandy told Isabel that since the paper was paying their expenses she felt that the least she could do was to pay Sarah. Isabel blew her stack at the suggestion. She told Sandy that Sarah would get fighting mad if she so much as mentioned paying for her stay. Sandy finally let the matter drop.

On the way to Pineville, Isabel told Sandy all about Bige Napier and how G T had rescued him during the cut-in accident. She told Sandy that she had heard that the reason Olivia Napier had killed Brad was because he was responsible for the cut-in and caused Bige to be crippled. Then she had killed Veronica because she had had her pregnancy by Bige aborted.

"It sounds like Olivia caught them together and avenged both incidents at the same time," Sandy said.

"Olivia has a bad reputation for fighting. G T and I went to grade school with Bige at Holly Tree and the other children wouldn't run around with him because of her. He and a neighbor kid got into it one day and the kid's mother broke it up. Olivia told her to keep her hands off of Bige or she'd burn her house down. The woman had her put under a peace bond and she settled down for a while. She is plain mean, although she likes G T. She thanked him for saving Bige's life and told him that she owed him one. I don't know what she meant, but I don't think she is G T's type," Isabel said with a laugh.

"Tell me about Veronica," Sandy said.

"I didn't know her too well. I remember when she was in high school, she had a bad name. People said that she did anything any boy asked her to do. She was really pitiful. She had waited on me several times when I went in Carboones where she worked and she was as nice as anyone could be. She was really a beautiful girl with shoulder length blond hair, blue eyes and hour glass figure, but she wore too much makeup. She never had a chance. Her mother and father divorced when she was small and she stayed with her mother, which was a mistake. People say her mother was worse than she was and had a new boy friend each week. Veronica started chasing G T about the same time that Brad started asking me out. G T and I never could figure out what the deal was, but that's behind us," Isabel said.

"What about Olivia? What do you know about her?" Sandy asked.

"Well, it's like I told you, she was mean as a pit bull. There was a tale that went around about her that I don't know to be true, but one of the fellows that G T worked with at the mine told him and G T said that the man knew what he was talking about. Olivia had bragged about it to this man's wife. Please don't say where you heard it. Promise?" said Isabel.

"I promise," said Sandy.

"She came from a big family of six boys and two girls. She was the oldest girl and the third oldest child. When she was about nine years old, the oldest brother molested her and kept it up for five or six years. G T said that is what made her so mean. She didn't play little girl games like hop scotch or jump the rope. All that she ever did was exercise. She lifted weights and built herself into a super woman. She could whip any boy her age and was the scourge of the playground. She also picked up the habit of chewing tobacco.

"One night about dusk, she waylaid the brother with a baseball bat. She knocked him unconscious and while he was lying there on the ground, she methodically broke both of his legs at the knee joint, both of his ankles, and his left arm at the elbow and the wrist. She then hit him in the groin two or three times. She told the man's wife that she spat tobacco juice in his eyes and told him 'he wouldn't mess up no more little nine-year-old girls that were afraid to tell on him.' Two of the other brothers found him and took him to the hospital. The doctors said that it was a miracle that he was still alive. She had fractured his skull with the first blow and he never got over that. He is a physical and mental cripple today and has to use a wheel chair. G T says that the brother recognized her because every time she comes close to him, he starts crying and making sounds in his throat. " Isabel drew a breath.

"Why did she break his left arm, I wonder?" asked Sandy.

"He was left-handed," said Isabel.

"What about Olivia's husband? Where is he in all of this?" Sandy asked.

"He works for the railroad. His name is Clyde Napier and is a real nice person from what little I have seen of him. The story I have always heard is that he had a good job where he could be home every night, and he bid down on a lower paying job that kept him on the road all of the time so he could get away from her," said Isabel.

"Why didn't he just divorce her and get it over with?" Sandy quizzed.

"Most people say it's because he didn't want to leave Bige. Besides that I think he was scared of her," said Isabel.

"You have to wonder why he ever married her," said Sandy.

"That's another story that G T told me," said Isabel pausing for a minute or two.

"Well, don't leave me hanging," said Sandy, "tell me about it."

"Olivia's sister was named Dorothy and she was dating Carson Napier, Clyde's brother. They decided to get married after she found out that she was two months pregnant. They got Clyde and Olivia to go with them to Tennessee and stand up for them while they got married. The four of them bought a case of beer and drank most of it before they got to the Justice of the Peace that was going to marry them. After the ceremony was over, they had a round of beers to toast the new couple and the JP. He had a couple of beers with them and then told them that he would marry Clyde and Olivia at no charge since they had been such nice customers. They took him up on it and got married.

"She settled down after that and made him a pretty fair wife. They bought a house and she completely redid it. She made new curtains, painted all the walls and woodwork and really put her heart into making it a home. The abuse she suffered from the brother resulted in her not being able to have any children.

"What about Bige?" asked Sandy.

"I'm coming to that," said Isabel. "It seems that the four of them were going fishing one Saturday afternoon over at Norris Lake and as usual they bought a case of beer. Olivia was driving. Just before they got to the place where you turn down to go to the dock, she rounded a curve too fast and got over into the gravel. The car slid over the bank and went into the lake. Clyde had the window down on his side and he got out. Dorothy was holding Bige, who was only six weeks old, and Olivia reached over the seat and grabbed him. She swam out the open window with him. The car must have shifted or something because Clyde told people that he dove back in, but couldn't help Dorothy or Carson. Later on Clyde and Olivia adopted Bige."

"Then Olivia isn't Bige's mother, is she?" asked Sandy.

"No, she's his double aunt and his adoptive mother," answered Isabel.

"She's his what?" queried Sandy.

"His double aunt. She's his aunt on his mother's side and his father's side," said Isabel.

"I've never heard of that before," said Sandy.

"When brothers and sisters marry sisters and brothers, their children are double cousins, and the aunts and uncles are double aunts and uncles," explained Isabel.

"Isabel, you are making that up," laughed Sandy.

"Well, it makes a good explanation, doesn't it?" laughed Isabel.

Sandy had been to Pineville before, but she had never been in Frank and Sarah's home. When Isabel pulled into the driveway, Sandy couldn't believe her eyes. It was really palatial. The grass had just received its first trimming for the summer. Flowerbeds of pansies and tulips were lying down to make room for marigolds and geraniums. Several dogwood trees in the front yard had shed their white cross blooms and were showing their new greenery for the summer. The redbuds had done the same. The driveway was lined on both sides with junipers that had yard lights hidden in the needles. A large stately oak stood to the left of the drive and looked down on its realm of smaller trees and bushes as if to say, "I am here to protect you."

The warning signal light that blinked when a car entered the driveway had come on and Sarah on seeing it went out on the front porch. She had stayed home from work to greet the girls when they came home. Both girls unloaded their bags and carried them up on the porch. Sarah hugged Isabel and then gave Sandy a "Welcome to our home" hug.

Once inside, Sandy was even more impressed.

"My, what a beautiful home you have," she said to Sarah.

"Thank you. It's a little more than we need, but it is ours and we love it. I hope you will be comfortable while you are here. Frank and I are delighted to have you," said Sarah as they walked into the entrance hall.

"Isabel will show you your room. If you all want to freshen up before supper, go ahead. We will wait on Frank and probably go to the Lodge to eat," continued Sarah.

Sandy couldn't get over the luxury of the house. The thick plush carpeting made her want to take her shoes off and walk barefoot.

Isabel took her to a bedroom across the hall from hers. The solid cherry queen sized bed was already turned down. Sandy set her suitcase on a stand at the foot of the bed and hung her clothes bag in a cedar lined closet across from the bed. She retrieved a dark green summer pantsuit from it and went into the bath where she took a quick shower and changed her clothes. Meanwhile, Isabel did the same. When they finished, they went back down stairs. Sarah had fixed a pitcher of iced tea and had four glasses sitting on the coffee table. Pouring each of the girls and herself a glass of tea, she began to quiz them about the trial.

"I am supposed to do color type stories about the people involved in the trial, such as the lawyers, the defendant and others," said Sandy, "and Isabel is supposed to introduce me around."

"I begged off on interviewing," said Isabel. "I felt that I was too close to the trial to be objective".

While they were talking, they heard Frank's diesel truck come up the driveway. Parking in back of the house, he came in through the back door, took off his muddy boots and walked on into the living room. Leaning over Sarah, he kissed her first, then he hugged Isabel who had gotten up. Sandy was standing beside her chair and he hugged her, welcoming her to their home.

"What do you have planned for supper?" he asked Sarah.

"I thought we would go to the Lodge," she responded.

"That's fine with me," he said. "Let me take a quick shower and change clothes and we will go," Frank answered her as he left the room and went to the bath.

"How do you think the trial will turn out, Mrs. Morgan?" Sandy asked.

"To you, I am Sarah," Sarah said before continuing. "I have very mixed emotions about it. From all I have heard, Olivia Napier is guilty. In fact, it is my understanding that she made a confession to Jacob Gibson and John Talbert. Two wrongs don't make a right and her killing the two of them wasn't right, no matter what they did. On the other hand, Bradley Durham was no account. He endangered an entire crew of men, our G T being one of them. One of them died and another was crippled. As for Veronica, I feel that abortion is the same as murder. I realize that at the time she was young and scared, but that still didn't make it right. Like I said before, Olivia's killing them was not right and she should be punished for it; however, I can see how a person would be filled with hate and seek vengeance for the things Bradley and Veronica did."

Frank came into the room and asked them if they were ready to go eat. Isabel said that she was starved and she was sure that Sandy was. Sarah said that she also was ready to eat, especially since she didn't have to cook.

On their way to the Lodge, Frank drove them to the Lone Pine Lookout where he had proposed to Sarah. The view was awesome to Sandy who had never been in the eastern Kentucky mountains. The Cumberland River looked like a silver ribbon as it meandered its way along the floor of the valley past Pineville and on to the northwest toward Barbourville. The variety of trees that lined the riverbanks had the appearance of green levees as they were viewed from the height and distance of Lone Pine. Sandy had heard about the Lodge from Isabel, and she was anxious to see if Isabel had over done the description, which she hadn't. A waitress seated them beside a window and took their order.

"Order the fried catfish," Isabel told Sandy. "It is delicious."

Frank and Sarah both said the same thing, so Sandy ordered the fried catfish. While the others chatted, Sandy was overcome by the view of the Clear Creek Valley that stretched for miles to the southeast away from the Lodge. A soft blue haze had settled in over Clear Creek, giving the impression that it was being viewed through pale blue glasses. Everything was so peaceful and quiet that Sandy found it hard to realize that the purpose of her being here was to cover a murder trial.

Getting up from the table, all four went to the salad bar. While they were serving their salad plates, three men came in the door to the dining room and a waitress seated them at a table across the room from Frank and the three women. As soon as she sat down, one of the men came over to the table and spoke to Sandy.

"I thought that was you, Sandy," the man in a deep blue sports shirt said.

"Well, hi," she responded as she looked up to see who had addressed her. Motioning to the others at her table, she introduced them to Bill Minter, reporter for the *Washington Herald.*

"I'm no longer with the *Herald,*" said Minter. "I am now with an international news service known as Reporting Service International or RSI."

Bill Minter was born and raised in Duluth, Minnesota, the son of the CEO of a large appliance manufacturing company. His father had become quite wealthy over the years from prudent investments. He always received a bonus at the end of the year, but he was quite different from most people in his category in that he did not take his bonus until his employees had all gotten theirs and his was the same amount as theirs. He was a firm advocate of the equal share theory which resulted in his never having any labor problems. His firm had been approached about a buy out, but he refused it. His stock holders were very happy with the way he did things. Bill had gone to a two thousand-student high school in Duluth where he was editor of the school newspaper. His father felt that Bill was no better than the people who worked for him and though he could have sent Bill to any private school in the country, he elected to send him to a public school. Bill had a knack for journalism that his teacher discovered and made use of. His senior year he had been selected as editor of the yearbook, a very prestigous assignment.

His parents had encouraged him to study journalism and he graduated in the top five percent of his class at the University of Minnesota's College of Journalism. Upon graduation he took a position with the Cincinnati Journal and had worked there for a couple of years when he heard of an opening on the *Washington Herald.* He jumped at the opportunity. A year after he started with the Washington paper, he broke a story on a gambling ring that involved several well-known congressmen. It led to a commendation by his paper and nomination for a Pulitzer Prize. He didn't get the Pulitzer, but he got national publicity for it. Bill was a tall, good-looking man with unruly sandy hair and blue eyes. His hair was his attraction. He parted it on the right and it more or less lay to the left, actually seeming to do pretty well what it wanted to do.

After Sandy's introduction, Minter returned to his table and seated himself in a position where he could look at Isabel. The other two men with him were Theo Shawitz and Chris Evans, another Reporting Service International reporter.All through dinner, Isabel had a feeling that someone was staring at her. Finally she turned around and saw Bill Minter looking straight at her. He smiled. For an instant it reminded her of Bradley Durham and his actions at Otis Hensley's funeral. She didn't return the smile, although she did think he was attractive.

Sandy explained to the others that she had spent a year of journalism internship with the *Cincinnati Journal* and during that time she was Bill Minter's gofer. He was a very nice person to work with, ever professional, yet with a good sense of humor. From where Sandy was sitting she could see Minter's intense gaze at Isabel, thinking to herself, "This is going to be interesting."

CHAPTER 4

Thelma Durham, the mother of Bradley Durham, was hurrying as fast as she could to get ready to go to Olivia's trial for the second day. She wanted to see Olivia get the death penalty for killing Brad and Veronica. She had heard that Olivia had already confessed to the crime and she didn't see why they had to have a trial. She had eaten a bowl of cold cereal for breakfast and removed the chain lock from the back door to let Jemjelf Tinsley in. Jemjelf had been cleaning Thelma's house for years. She was a very beautiful black woman who had sent four children to college. Fred Tinsley, Jemjelf's husband, was a foreman at Golden Star mine, having worked for Ed Durham from the time he was twenty years old. Jemjelf didn't really need the money now that the children were out of school, but she continued to come help Thelma because she felt Thelma needed the company. She was much more than Thelma's housekeeper, she was Thelma's friend.

Thelma always removed the chain lock from the back door first thing in the morning to let Jemjelf in. Jemjelf had a key, but Thelma was a firm believer in chain locks.

Thelma had taken a shower and fixed her hair and was in the process of dressing when the front door bell rang.

"Drat," she said putting on her housecoat, "why do people come visiting early in the morning when you are trying to get ready to go somewhere?"

After Ed died, Thelma got real security conscious and had "peep-holes" put in the front and back doors. Looking through the peeper she saw a middle-aged man and a young girl standing on the porch. Cracking the door, but leaving the security chain lock in place, she asked them what they wanted.

"We are sorry to bother you, Mrs. Durham, but we are from the Tennessee State Police and we are looking for an escaped convict that we thought might contact you," the man said as he held up a TSP badge.

"Can you come back another time? I am in a big hurry to go someplace and I need to get ready," Thelma replied.

"We feel that it is very important that we talk to you, Mrs. Durham, we feel that your life may be in danger," the man answered.

"Let me see both of your identifications," Thelma demanded.

Holding their badges and ID cards up to the crack in the door, she studied them. Satisfied herself that they were what they said they were, she removed the chain lock and let them in.

"As I said, Mrs. Durham, we are very apologetic about bothering you, but we have reason to believe that the escaped convict, Curtis Bradley, may try to get in touch with you," said the man.

"Who did you say?" Thelma asked.

"Curtis Bradley. Let me start from the beginning," the man said as he seated himself,

"My name is Martin Wallace and this is Ms Jennifer McComb. We are both detectives with the Tennessee State Police. Three days ago a man by the name of Curtis Bradley escaped from the Brushy Mountain State Prison at Petros, Tennessee. We questioned the man's cellmate and he told us that Curtis said he had a bastard son named Durham, who lived in Pineville. We checked and found that you are the only Durham living in this area. We would like to have all of the information that you can give us on Bradley."

Martin Wallace was in his fifties and beginning to show it by the gray streaks in his black hair. He had good posture and held his 180 pounds on a 5'11" frame. His ruddy complexion was due to spending most of his spare time in the outdoors either hunting or fishing. He never killed anything and seldom caught any fish. The peaceful quiet of the woods and the lake were his reason for spending so much time in fruitless hobbies. At the time he had enlisted in the U. S. Marines, he was engaged to a local girl who died while he was in Korea. He never seemed to adjust to this and was somewhat of a recluse in his off the job time.

His partner, Jennifer McComb, was young enough to be his daughter and he treated her that way most of the time. She was a pretty young woman with natural blond hair and fair complexion. The eyes were a deep blue that complimented her hair. Her small stature was deceiving. She was a graduate of the Eastern Kentucky University Law Enforcement School and a very proficient martial arts student. She had acquired a reputation for being a hard case when it came to making an arrest. She tolerated no foolishness and the culprit was smart to do just what she said. This was the word on the streets of Knoxville. She liked police work because it gave her an opportunity to help people who had been mistreated.

"Well, as you said, 'let me start from the beginning'," said Thelma, "As a young girl I was not at all attractive. In fact, I was homely and age has done nothing to improve me. I was going to the University and since my father was very wealthy, I felt that I would be a shoo-in to be asked to join a sorority. I was wrong. I was not a good dancer nor conversationalist. In fact, the only social grace that I had was an ability to consume large amounts of alcohol. My husband often referred to me as having a hollow leg. When I was snubbed by all of the sororities, I started running with a group of girls who lived in the dorm. They called themselves the 'wild bunch' because they loved to party and drink.

"One night we were all invited to a fraternity house for a party. As usual I sat by myself and watched the others dance. I loved the music and I would fantasize that some time a nice looking young man would come up and ask me to dance. That particular night, a nice-looking young man did come up to me, introduced himself as Curtis Bradley and asked me to dance. I almost fainted, because no one ever asked me to dance. We danced a couple of sets and then he asked me if I would like to get some fresh air. By that time I was so enamored by him that I jumped at the chance to be alone with him. There was a garden behind the house and we went out there. He offered to go get me a glass of punch if I would like it. Of course I said yes. He went back in the house and came out with two glasses of punch. Mine tasted funny, but I drank it anyway. The next thing I knew, I woke up lying on the grass with all of the boys and girls standing around me, laughing. I don't need to tell you what had happened. I have never been so humiliated. I left the University and never went back. Two months later I found that I was pregnant. My father arranged for me to marry a man who was working for him. The man's name was Ed Durham. When the child was born, I named him Bradley Durham so that I would never forget who his low-life father was. Years later I found out that Curtis had bet his fraternity brothers that he could seduce me. I was so bitter about all of it that I made Ed Durham's life a misery. I am very ashamed of that now that I can't do anything about it.

"Ed Durham was a good man and he made Bradley as good a father as I would let him. If I had let Ed have his way, my son might still be alive today. Three years ago a woman killed my son and her trial started today. That was where I was preparing to go when the two of you came to the door. I lost track of Curtis Bradley. My son grew up to be quite like him. He was handsome and loved the young ladies. He was a roué and I knew it, but I didn't care. I spoiled him rotten and it wound up costing him his life. That is about all that I can tell you about Curtis Bradley. Now it is your turn," Thelma concluded.

"Before I start to tell you about Curtis Bradley, let me say that I belonged to that fraternity and I was there that night, although I didn't engage in the hilarity that surrounded your mortification," said Martin Wallace. "After that episode, I went to the Dean of Men and told him about what happened. He said he would expel the fraternity, but he never did anything about it. The word got out that I had gone to him and the fraternity shunned me. I left the University after that semester and was going to transfer to another school when the war broke out in Korea. I enlisted in the Marines and spent three years in that mess. I am terribly sorry about what happened, Mrs. Durham, and if I could have prevented it, I would have.

"Curtis Bradley came from a small town north of Knoxville, Tennessee named Trenton. His grandfather was a large landowner in that area and when the Tennessee Valley Authority was created, he made a fortune selling a part of his property to the government to inundate for Norris Lake. When he died, he left everything to his only child, Curtis' father, who was the pattern Curtis followed as he grew up. Curtis' mother tried to make something out of him, but he was cut out of the same cloth that his father was. He was a woman chasing party boy and a good-looking young man that carried 175 pounds on a 5'11" frame. His dark brown hair and brown eyes, very correct posture and winning smile made him a lady-killer.

"His father gave him a car when he was fifteen years old and before he was eighteen, he had wrecked it and three more. The only serious injury that resulted from his recklessness was a crippling injury to a young man named Harvey Stone, who had his left shoulder and back broken in one of the wrecks, and neither injury healed properly. He walked with his back hunched over and his left arm swinging useless at his side. Although he could grip with the hand, he couldn't lift the arm. He was slightly retarded and ran with Curtis because he didn't have any other friends. Curtis used him as a flunky. When Curtis went to college, he got his father to hire Harvey and keep him around doing odd jobs so he would have someone to wait on him when he came home. Harvey was an orphan with no place to go, so he lived on the Bradley farm. We interviewed Harvey and he told us that he hated Curtis, but he needed the income. He also said that if he ever got the chance, he would kill Curtis.

"Now the word around his hometown was to the effect that no respectable young woman would go out with Curtis. That didn't bother Curt since he was looking for the other kind anyway.

"He was not the athletic type although he took great pride in his physique and exercised religiously. With Harvey's help he had transformed the old barn behind the Bradley house into a very up-to-date gym. It was outfitted with all the latest muscle-building and toning equipment, including a weight machine, stationary bicycle, treadmill and slider. The gym occupied two-thirds of the front part of the barn while a garage for Curtis' car took up the other third. The doors to the garage looked like standard eighteen-foot barn doors, but they weren't. They were located to the right of the center of the barn, allowing direct entrance into the garage. Their composition was barn wood on the outside backed with one-quarter inch sheet metal. The operating mechanism that opened the doors was voice-actuated, attuned to his voice and a certain phrase that he used.

"Behind the gym and garage were Curtis' living quarters. This area consisted of a large living room, bedroom, bath and kitchenette. These were unbelievable! The living room was outfitted with eight large overstuffed recliners and four full-sized overstuffed sofas arranged in such a way as to allow excellent viewing of a large television set. Television hadn't been in existence too long when he built the room, but over the years he updated his set each time a larger, more improved one became available. An exhibition-style pool table was at one end of the room and a large open fireplace at the other. Between the two was a six-place gaming table complete with chips and unopened decks of cards which were marked in such a way that only Curtis could read them. The entire room was lighted by cove lighting, fitted with a dimming switch. To augment the cove lighting and provide for those who wished to read, tall floor lamps were set by each chair.

"The pool table had two large floodlights over it and the gaming table had a single floodlight over it. In the center of the ceiling was a strange looking fixture that had what appeared to be cameras projecting from it in four different directions. There were no windows in the room, which left the walls to be treated with wildlife prints done by a famous Kentucky artist. The basic wall color was a deep crimson with a small wildflower design spread throughout. The same color carried over to the plush wall to wall carpeting.

"The bedroom was fitted with a king-sized bed headboarded against one wall with a walk-in closet on the adjacent wall to the left, with doors to the bath and living room on the adjacent wall to the right. The walk-in closet still has Curt's suits, coats and shoes in it. Drawers were built into the closet wall that provided storage space for socks, shirts, underwear and other wearing apparel. These were all filled to the brim with his belongings. The room was done in soft mauve wallpaper with a small geometric design running through it. The headboard of the bed accommodated reading lamps and shelves for books and magazines. The walls were tastefully done with wildlife prints similar to those in the living room. Evidently Curtis' mother had had a hand in the decor of the rooms, hence the wildlife prints instead of 'girlie' paintings.

"The bathroom was luxurious in its furnishings. A six-place Jacuzzi occupied the corner of the two walls that didn't have doors in them. A double-sink lavatory together with an enclosed shower sat along one of the Jacuzzi walls, while a walled-off commode was sited on the other wall. A medicine cabinet with a mirrored door was in place above each lavatory. All of the fixtures were an off-white in color which coordinated with the off-white walls and white ceramic tile floor. It had the sterile appearance of a hospital emergency room. As with the other rooms, the cove lighting was dimmer-controlled, with the exception of a shaving light over each of the medicine cabinets.

"The kitchenette wasn't quite a full kitchen, but it had all that was needed to cook a meal. An electric stove complete with two ovens, one large with a rotisserie and the other a smaller warming oven was located on the back side of the aisle behind the serving counter. Two counters the size of the stove were located on its either side. These both had solid maple wood tops for placing hot dishes and pans that came from the stove. A wide under-the-counter refrigerator with double doors allowed storage of a large number of perishable foods and beverages, while a smaller freezer was located next to the refrigerator. A six-place countertop provided eating space, each with a barstool in front of it. A number of accessories including a blender, a can opener, a small hand held mixer and a juicer occupied spaces above the two serving counters on either side of the stove. I didn't mean to get so involved in the description of Curtis' place, but we went through it on our way up here looking for him and it was fabulous. It has been kept in real good shape by his sidekick, Harvey.

"Curtis graduated from the University's law school and went into practice in Knoxville. After two years of working for someone else, he founded his own law firm. He took in two other University graduates as junior partners. They practiced corporate law and over a very short period of time, became quite successful. As the practice grew they took in a young lady named Deborah Haley who had also graduated from the University. She was a beautiful girl who had won a number of beauty contests and Curtis became infatuated with her. He tried on several occasions to date her, but she refused, saying that she didn't think it a good practice to date the people she worked with. He became quite insistent and she finally took a job with another firm. This infuriated Curt so that the night before her last day with his group, he went to see Deborah to try to convince her to stay. He had been drinking heavily and she evidently didn't realize this until after she had let him in. He pled with her not to leave, but she adamantly refused to stay with his firm and asked him to leave. Curtis hit her and knocked her down. As she fell she hit her head on the corner of a coffee table and fractured her skull. He called an ambulance and went to the hospital with her. She died on the way. He was tried and convicted of manslaughter and was sentenced to ten years at Brushy Mountain.

"During his imprisonment, Curtis kept up his physical appearance by exercising regularly. In addition to that, he took up martial arts, becoming a black belt in Karate. He had served five years of the ten-year sentence, had been a model prisoner and was up for parole when he got into a fight with another prisoner over a package of cigarettes. The prison guards broke up the fight, but a couple of days after that Curt caught the other prisoner unawares and broke his neck. This was cold-blooded pre-meditated murder and he drew a life sentence for it.

"Three days ago he slipped into a milk delivery truck at the prison and by holding a homemade knife against the side of the driver, he escaped. He forced the driver to take him to Jacksboro, where Curtis bound and gagged him, leaving him in the truck. He stole a car, which was found abandoned on Highway 63. We assume that he stole another car, but as yet we haven't found it. That is why we are here, Mrs. Durham.

"I apologize again for taking up so much of your time and keeping you from the trial of your son's killer, but we felt it of great importance to tell you about Curtis' escape and warn you about his possibly coming here."

"I can't seriously believe he would come here. I never did try to keep up with him and I am surprised that he even knew about Bradley. I thank you for coming to see me and if I hear anything from that lowly bastard, I will certainly let you know," Thelma said as she accompanied them to the door.

Thelma had heard Jemjelf come in while Martin Wallace was talking, except that Jemjelf didn't come in by herself. As she had opened the back door, a burly white man grabbed her and put a knife to her throat.

"Don't make a sound and I won't hurt you," he said.

"Jemjelf, was that you that came in?" Thelma had asked

"Answer her," he whispered.

"Yes ma'am, it's me," answered Jemjelf.

Jemjelf Tinsley was a beautiful Afro-American woman. Tall and statuesque, she carried herself like she was royalty, which she was. Her great-great grandmother was a Nigerian princess who was kidnapped by a rival tribe and sold into slavery. Her betrothed lover was the chief of another tribe who avenged her kidnapping by massacring the rival tribe, including men, women and children; however, he was too late to save his bride-to-be. He felt that there was nothing left for him after she was taken away, so he sold himself into slavery and followed her to America. He was every bit a king as she was a princess. Once he was landed in America he searched for her by word of mouth and eventually found her. Her owner, not knowing what was going on, bought him and put them together.

Jemjelf's husband, Fred, had worked in one of the captive mines of eastern Kentucky from the time he was fourteen years old. He didn't have the royal background that she did, but he was considered one of the best coal miners in the region. He got bossing papers when he was young. Ed Durham, who had heard about him, sent him word that he had an opening if Fred was interested. Fred took him up on it.

Fred and Jemjelf had four children, two who were successful college graduates and two who were still in college. The eldest, a girl named Sarita, was a doctor in a clinic in Nashville, Tennessee. The second child was a boy named James who was a lawyer with a very prestigous law firm in Lexington. The third child was also a boy named Curtis who was still in college and playing basketball at the University of Kentucky. The "baby" was a girl named Margaret who was a freshman at Eastern Kentucky University where she was studying to be a nurse anesthetist.

CHAPTER 5

Three months after Ed Durham's funeral, Betty Smith and John Talbert got married. It was a very small wedding that was held in the Gibson home. Jacob Gibson stood up with John while Rosemary Gibson was Betty's matron of honor. Father Jerome Hogan and Reverend Pomeroy Jones performed the ceremony. Gerry and Sarah helped Rosemary get everything in order while Emma Caldwell of Pretty Posy Flower Shop did the flowers, which as usual were beautiful.

Thelma Durham was there in all her glory. Since Ed's death she had become a lot friendlier with everyone and she had started attending the Holly Tree Baptist Church. It wasn't the same with Randy Hall not there, but she liked his replacement, Paul Nolan. John had gotten Emma to make a corsage for Thelma, which he had pinned on her when she came in. Big tears came in her eyes as he hugged her. She thought how much she would have liked to see Brad marry some nice girl, but that was all gone now. She needed a son and although John was almost as old as she, she looked on Jacob, Randy and him as hers.

Both John and Betty had advanced in their jobs since they got married. John had been promoted to lieutenant and put in charge of the Fugitive Warrant section. It was an easy job that didn't require his being away from home over night very often. Betty had become a personal assistant to the governor. She had been just another clerk in the Vital Statistics Department of the Kentucky State Police until one day she answered the phone. It was a Mexican laborer who wanted to know how to become a naturalized citizen. His English was very broken and difficult to understand. Betty had put him at ease by asking,

"Habla espanol, senor?"

The man became overjoyed and kept repeating, "Si, si senorita."

She continued to converse with him in Spanish and her supervisor, Anne Quinlan, heard her. After she hung up Anne asked her, "Do you speak fluent Spanish?"

"Si, senorita," Betty answered laughingly.

"Do you speak other languages?" asked Anne.

"I speak French, German, Spanish, Vietnamese, and three dialects of Chinese," Betty said. "I don't speak Japanese, but I understand it pretty well. I listed only French and Vietnamese on my application, but I do understand and speak, somewhat haltingly, the others."

Anne reported Betty's skill to her department head, who in turn reported it to the State Police Commissioner. "The governor has been looking for an interpreter," the Commissioner told the department head. "He has representatives from a lot of countries that are looking for plant sites and he has to depend on the people they bring with them to tell him what they are saying. I am going to report this to his aide and he may want Betty to come in for an interview." Two days later Anne Quinlan got a call from the governor's office, telling her that a trooper would be coming for Betty to take her to the governor's office for an interview. Betty tried to demur, but Anne told her that there was no way out.

"I'm not dressed for an interview with the governor's aide," Betty said.

"I wouldn't worry about that," Anne answered, not telling her that the interview would be with the governor and not with his aide. A Kentucky State Police trooper walked in the office and asked for Betty Talbert. She had gone to the ladies room and fixed herself up as best she could. There was nothing she could do about the jeans, blouse and flats that she had on so she acted like it was nothing, thinking all the time that it would be an aide that would talk to her. When she got to the capitol building, the trooper escorted her to the governor's office. She was still under the impression that her audience would be with an aide of the governor. Betty seated herself in a chair next to the door in the waiting room. She had no more than sat down when the door to the governor's office opened and he came out. She had seen him a time or two on television so she recognized him immediately.

Governor Albert Martin was a medium-sized man of about 6 feet. He had done a hitch in the Marines as a helicopter pilot in Vietnam and from that had developed a very straight posture. He still wore his hair in an almost burr as his widow's peak didn't lend itself to long hair. He was a very smart dresser, his suits always matching his shirts, socks and ties. He had made Kentucky a good governor. Though he was a politician, he ran his office for the betterment of the people of the state. His last legislative session had resulted in a strong anti-litter bill that had been opposed by the soft drink and beer bottlers, but had gone through anyway. One legislator commented that if Martin had been Moses, there would have been an eleventh commandment saying, "Thou shalt not litter." His wife, Margaret, had been his childhood sweetheart as they grew up in Berea, Kentucky. She had waited on him to come out of the Marines and graduate from law school. They had one son, Austin, who was becoming a problem. He had been an asthmatic in his childhood days and as a result his mother had spoiled him. He had graduated from the University of Kentucky with a degree in pharmacy and worked in a Frankfort drug store. He was on the edge of being a problem drinker and his parents were pretty much disturbed about it. Coming over to where Betty was sitting, he asked,

"Are you Mrs. Talbert?"

"Yes I am," she said, wishing she could hide her blue jeans and flats.

"I am Governor Albert Martin and I am very glad to meet you, Mrs. Talbert. Will you please come into my office where we can talk?"

Betty got up and followed him into his office where he offered her a chair. "Please have a seat, Mrs. Talbert and put yourself at ease. My wife wears blue jeans most of the time and I would too if I could get away with it," he said.

"Oh Lord," she thought, "he's read my mind.

"You are John Talbert's wife, aren't you?" he asked.

"Yes sir, I am," she answered.

"John and I go back quite a ways. I was in the Marines and he was my drill sergeant when I was at Parris Island. He had a reputation for being the toughest drill sergeant in the Corps, but he made survivors out of us. His trainees had the fewest number of causalities in Nam.

"How is he? I haven't seen him in quite a while," Governor Martin said.

"He is getting along just fine. He likes his new job," Betty answered, feeling more at ease.

"Let's get away from the formalities if you will. I am going to call you Betty and you can call me whatever makes you most comfortable," he said.

"Thank you, Governor," Betty answered.

"Betty, I have a problem that I hope you can help me with. From time to time I have foreign dignitaries call on me and quite often they do not speak English. I don't speak it too well myself, but that is beside the point. They usually bring an interpreter with them, but then half the time I don't know what the interpreter is saying. I have also gone to several foreign countries trying to set up some trade relations with them and again I have been at their mercy when it came to the language barrier. I would like to have someone available that I could call on from time to time to meet with me when these visitors come. I would make arrangements with your supervisor to allow you to come to my office when I need you. Your part in this would be to listen to the person speaking and then listen to the interpreter to see if I am being told the truth. A nod of your head would tell me. You would also listen to my response and let me know if the interpreter passed it on correctly. I would let you know at least two days before I would need your help. Will you help me?" he asked.

What could she say? Here was the Governor of Kentucky asking her to help him. "I'll do what ever I can, sir," she said.

"Occasionally, I have to go to these foreign countries to shore up our trade relations with them. I would like for you to accompany me the next time I go. The state legislature insists that I have a state policeman as a bodyguard so I will arrange for John to go with us. It will be a nice trip for the both of you. I also have...."

Loud talking in the waiting room outside his office interrupted him. Opening the door, he saw a state policeman and the receptionist each holding the arm of an Asian woman, who was obviously pregnant and scared to death.She was slight in size and had she not been pregnant, one would have taken her for a schoolgirl. Her long hair was black as jet and done in a long pigtail that was greasy dirty. Her face was dirty and tears had streaked her cheeks like chalk marks on a slate board. Her clothes, which were dirty, looked like they hadn't been washed in weeks and smelled like it had been longer than that. The knee-length coat she wore was heavily brocaded with figures of horses and butterflies. To Betty it looked as though it was very expensive. The strap sandals on her feet were threadbare and almost falling apart.

"What's the problem?" asked Governor Martin.

"She doesn't understand you, sir," answered the receptionist.

Betty had come to the door to see if she could help. Addressing the woman in Vietnamese, she asked her what she wanted. All she got for an answer was a quizzical expression that indicated the woman didn't understand her, but she recognized that Betty was speaking in an Asian tongue. Betty tried again in one of the Chinese dialects she knew. There was a glimmer of recognition in the woman's eyes, but still she didn't understand what Betty was saying. Trying another dialect, the woman became ecstatic and began to talk to Betty. Betty asked her questions and got long answers. Finally turning to her audience of the trooper, the receptionist and the governor, she told them:

"She is Chinese and her name is Wing Fu. She and her escort are from Beijing and they paid a man to smuggle them into the United States. Her escort is a farrier and they had heard that Kentucky was a place where there were a lot of horses so they paid a man in San Francisco to get them a plane ticket to Lexington. They had a little money left when they got to Lexington and they rented a trailer in a run-down trailer park while he looked for work. They had asked the man in San Francisco what to do if they had a problem and he told them to go see the governor. Her escort left four days ago and she hasn't heard from him since. He speaks some English and has been the one who did the talking, but she doesn't speak any at all. The trailer park manager evicted her because they hadn't paid their rent. She hasn't had anything to eat for two days and she is afraid she is going to lose the baby. She is eight months pregnant. She caught a ride with a woman truck driver on the outskirts of Lexington and got off at the first Frankfort exit."

"Ask her how she knew to come to Frankfort if she couldn't understand English," said Governor Martin.

When Betty asked her, she pulled a dirty piece of paper out of her pocket and handed it to Betty. Printed on it was "how to go francfort see guvnor." Her escort had given her the note when she asked him what to do if he didn't come back. "She says that she would show this to people and they would point. That's how she caught a ride out of Lexington. She showed the note to a woman truck driver in a fast food place outside of Lexington."

"I have some more questions, but you had better take her to the cafeteria and get her something to eat before she passes out on us," said Governor Martin. He then told the trooper to file a missing persons report on her escort, and asked Betty to come back to his office after they were finished at the cafeteria.

Betty explained to Wing Fu where they were going as they left the waiting room and went to the cafeteria. She cautioned her not to eat too much or too fast, even though she was starved. Helping her through the line at the cafeteria, Betty got her a moderate amount of food that was full of vitamins. Watching her closely to be sure that her bites were not too big and that she chewed her food well, Betty led her through her meal. When Wing Fu finished, she thanked Betty, explaining that she didn't have any money to pay for it. Betty told her to not worry about it, that she had already paid for it. When they got back to the governor's office the receptionist, Karla Matheson, was very complimentary of Betty's handling of the incident. Betty and Wing Fu had a seat while Karla buzzed the governor and told him that they had returned from the cafeteria. He came out and escorted them into his office, asking Karla to come in also.

"We need to work out some kind of arrangement for Wing Fu to have a place to stay. We also need to get her examined by a doctor and have a hospital lined up to take her when the time comes. I wonder what has happened to her escort, as I am sure both of you do. For him to be gone four days doesn't sound good. Karla, will you please call Dr. Ralph West and ask him to take Wing Fu as a patient and tell him I will foot the bill personally. Betty, I am very impressed with your ability. Will you take Wing Fu to the shelter for abused women and get her set up there?" Governor Martin asked.

"If it is all right with you, sir, I will take her home with me and see that she gets a good hot bath and some clean clothes. I'll get John to take us to Lexington and we will get what little she has at the trailer park," Betty said.

"That is certainly nice of you, Betty," Martin said.

"Well, if you can get her medical attention, the least I can do is give her a place to stay," Betty answered.

Since John usually took Betty to work in the morning and picked her up in the afternoon, she called the dispatch and asked them to call him and tell him not to stop by for her, that she would explain it all to him when he came home. Then the governor ordered the trooper who stood outside his door to take Betty and Wing Fu to John's and Betty's apartment.

After they had left, Governor Martin buzzed Karla and asked her to come in.

"What do you think of my interpreter?" he asked.

"I am very much impressed. She will be quite an asset to your team," Karla answered.

++++++

John came in from work not long after Betty and Wing Fu arrived. Wing Fu was in the shower, that Betty showed her how to work. Then Betty got some old clothes that were loose-fitting on her and should be just about right for Wing and laid them out on the bed. When Wing Fu undressed, Betty noticed a birthmark on her left shoulder blade. At first she thought it was a tattoo, but on looking closer she saw that it was really a birthmark. It was a bear with its mouth open to devour a butterfly that was flying above it. This rang a bell in Betty's head but she didn't know where from. She didn't ask Wing Fu about it and she decided not to tell John until she knew what it meant. Betty knew that John had a bad taste in his mouth for the Chinese due to the part they played in the Korean War, so she wasn't sure how he would react to Wing Fu's presence. She took him through the whole day's events including her new position as the governor's aide. When she came to the part about her bringing Wing Fu home with her, she faltered. He beat her to the punch.

"You said that Albert set her up for medical attention and so that you wouldn't be bested, you brought her home with you. Am I right?" he asked.

"How did you know?" she quizzed.

"Male intuition," he laughed.

"When she gets out of the shower, will you take us to Lexington so we can get what little she has in that trailer?" asked Betty.

"I'll be glad to, Mrs. Big Heart," he laughed.

Wing Fu came out of the bathroom, looking like a different person. She had washed her hair and it was hanging loose almost to her waist. The clothes Betty had laid out for her were a little big everywhere except the waist, which was sort of snug. Betty introduced her to John who told Betty to tell her she was most welcome in their home. After the introductions, Betty showed her the spare bedroom where she could stay. Then Betty told her they would go get her things in the trailer where she lived.

When the three of them got to Lexington, Wing Fu showed Betty a piece of paper that had the trailer park address on it. Betty gave it to John, who said that he knew where it was. Pulling up in front of the manager's trailer, John got out and went up to the door. A fat, greasy looking man wearing an under shirt and pants, but no shoes, came to the door and asked him what he wanted.

"We would like to get in the trailer where this girl lived," John said.

"You ain't getting into nothing until she pays me the fifty bucks she owes in back rent," Greasy said.

"We would appreciate it if you would let us in the trailer," John repeated.

"Don't you hear good, mister? I said she wasn't getting in there until I get my fifty dollars," Greasy snarled.

Reaching into his rear pocket, John got out his wallet and flashed his badge and ID card. "You let us in her trailer now or I'll have the Lexington building inspector out here in about five minutes and you will be out of business," John said very quietly.

"Look buddy, I don't want no trouble," Greasy said. "Let me get the key."

The inside of the trailer was as clean as Wing Fu could get it. The furniture in the front room of the trailer was an old sofa that had springs sticking out of it and a straight back chair. The kitchen was no better. The propane stove was rusted around the burners and the oven didn't close tightly. The sink was rusted where the enamel was chipped around the drain. Opening the refrigerator door, John was greeted with a totally empty space that was as warm inside as it was outside. There was not so much as an ice cube in the freezer compartment. Going into the bedroom, Betty and Wing Fu got what few clothes she had. There were two porcelain figurines on an orange crate that served as a dresser. These she wrapped up in her clothes and put in her zipper bag. One was a bear and the other was a butterfly. The bed was an old mattress lying on the floor with no springs under it. When they went into the bedroom, a rat ran out through a hole in the wall. Betty elected to not go into the bathroom. She could only imagine what kind of filth she would find there.

Looking around the bedroom, John could not see any evidence of a man having lived there. There were no clothes, no shoes, no shaving material nor any other normal male accessories. Turning to Greasy, Talbert asked him, "Where is the man that was with her?"

"I don't know. She left here two days ago and not long after she left, he come back and got his stuff. He said that she would pay me and like a no-brain, I believed him," he told John.

"What kind of a damn fool do you take me for?" John asked. "You wouldn't buy a story like that. Now tell me the truth."

"He give me three joints to let him in the trailer and I did. He cleaned out all he had and left out of here in a car with three other Chinamen and a China woman driving. That's the truth."

Betty had heard all of this, but she didn't tell Wing Fu. She loaded her guest's bag with its meager contents in the trunk, and they went back to

Frankfort. On the way, John radioed the Lexington Police Dispatch and sicced them on Greasy's trailer park.

When they got back to Betty and John's apartment, Betty sat Wing Fu down in a chair and told her she wanted the whole story. Wing Fu began to cry as she asked Betty if she was going to go to jail. Betty told her certainly not, but she needed to be up-front honest about how she came to Kentucky.

"I come from a small province in China, north of Beijing and the Great Wall. It lies in a very deep valley and only has a few villages in it. The entrance to the valley is a very narrow opening in the canyon wall. It is large enough for only two horses abreast at a time. All of the people in my province depend on raising and selling horses. Our horses are the fastest in the world. They have raced against both Arabian horses and your thoroughbreds and have won quite easily. Your country has never heard of us because we raised horses only for the Emperor of China. He gave each of the officers in his army one of our horses, and they cared for them as if they were their children. When the communists took over my country, they quit buying the horses, but we managed to sell some to the Saudi Arabian princes. The communists want to stop our sales, but they are afraid to come into our valley. There is always a very thick cloud cover that completely blocks out any view from the sky or the mountains that encircle the valley.

"My escort, Lin Chou, and I came to the United States and Kentucky to try to set up a sales agreement with one of the horse breeders who live around here. We believe that the communists will allow us to continue raising horses if we sell them in the United States. They want very much to show your country that they allow free trade even if they don't."

"Why did you come here if you were expecting a baby in a month or two?" asked Betty.

"I am the province princess and it is my responsibility to see that my people continue to live as they have for centuries," answered Wing Fu.

"What happened to your clothes and other things that you brought with you?" asked Betty.

"I brought Lin Chou with me because he had learned to speak English before he moved into our province. We allowed him to stay because he is an excellent farrier. He bought tickets for both of us to fly to your country. When we landed in your California, our baggage was stolen, or at least he said it was. He also told me that he was robbed and only had a few dollars. We still had our tickets to Kentucky so we came on. He rented that filthy place where we stayed. I now believe that Lin Chou is in the employment of drug dealers, who would like to have our province for the raising of opium poppies. I feel that he has been sent into our province to spy on us. I think he abandoned me so that I would not have any help in the birthing of my baby and we would both possibly die in childbirth. The communist government of our country would also like to have our province. Our mountains have reserves of very high quality coal that are unbelievable.

"If my mission here fails or if I die before this child is born, then the communists or the drug dealers will starve my people into moving out of our valley. If I die a violent death, then my province will be unattainable to either group; however, if I starve to death or die in a natural way, then my province will be left unguarded. Both groups are afraid to try to come into our valley because of what happened centuries ago when the Mongol leader, Bear, tired to conquer us.

"I apologize for being so filthy dirty, but I didn't have any choice. There was no water in the trailer and the bathroom didn't have a bath or shower. Lin Chou carried water from a spigot in the middle of the trailer park to flush the commode. After he left I was afraid to carry the water so I just went dirty. I want to thank you and your husband for letting me stay with you. I feel clean for the first time in days.

"My country's government knows that I am in your country and they will come looking for me. The drug dealers also know that I am here. I am safe from assassination by either group, but I must avoid capture. If they find me they will take my baby and put me in a prison. They will starve both of us to death and leave my people unguarded. I must take the chances I am taking for my people. They trust in me as they have all of my family before me. I do not have a husband like you do. I select a man to sire my children, but he does not live with me or marry me as you do in your country," Wing Fu said as she began to cry again.

"You have had a tough day," said Betty as she turned down the bed for Wing Fu. "Go on to bed and get some rest. We will talk more tomorrow."

"What was that all about?" asked John.

"Wing Fu was telling me about how she came to this country. There is still something that she isn't telling me. I have heard of her home province and I can't remember what it was that I heard. I'm going to the UK tomorrow and talk to a professor of Asian history that I know."

CHAPTER 6

Ever since Pete Kelly absconded with the two million dollars, Jack Colbert had been pretty quiet. He sensed that some of his PSK board felt that he might have had something to do with it since he had gotten three post cards from Pete. A mailroom is always a hotbed of gossip and the higher the executive, the hotter the gossip. They had had a ball since Pete left. The first postcard was a photograph that came from France. It showed Pete standing between a man and a woman with his arm around each. Written under it was the sentence: "Guess which one is mine." The people in the mailroom at PSK really got a charge out of it. The second was a picture of a bullfight, mailed from Spain. Written under the scene of the bull ring was: "Wish you were here." It stayed in the mailroom for three days while the mail clerks tried to make something out of the message. Pete Kelly had made the message cryptic in order to stir up the mailroom people who he knew would try get some meaning out of it. The third card came from Berlin. It was a beer hall scene of a group of young men drinking beer. The only message under it was the word "Bonanza." One of the braver clerks made a photocopy of the card and passed it around the offices. If Colbert had found out about it, he would have fired someone.

Each card made Colbert furious. They were timed to come just a few days before a board meeting and he stayed in a bad humor for a week after he received one. The entire company was laughing at him behind his back and he knew it. The last one came just a few days before his spring board meeting, so he went into it with a big chip on his shoulder.

"Good morning ladies and gentlemen," he said. "Welcome to our spring board meeting. I have a surprise for you and I hope you will accept it with the same anticipation of its success that I have. A couple of years ago, I made a proposal to hire a man who I felt could streamline our company and make it one of the front-runners in the utility business. About the same time our Mr. Pete Kelly absconded with about two million dollars and left our company with a feeling of distrust for its management by the stockholders and general public. During all of this I was visited by the SEC who could find nothing wrong and gave me a clean bill of health. These occurrences made me somewhat gun-shy of trying anything new, so I shelved the idea for the time being. I feel that the time is right for us to move to another level of efficiency and so without any further ado I would like to introduce to you Mr. Al Jamison, who will be our new Personnel Director."

The door at the other end of the conference room opened and Al Jamison made his appearance. Whitley Rogers nudged Harry Baker with her knee. Jamison was a short fat man in his late fifties. What was left of his once blond hair was turning gray and his face was flushed from too many noontime martinis. His eyes were bleary from the same martinis. He was wearing a white shirt that badly needed ironing, while his brown plaid suit looked more like something a racetrack tout would wear. It was wrinkled as if he had slept in it. The red, white and blue tie he wore by no means matched anything else he was wearing and he was in bad need of a shave. These were things that he could do something about, but he was also very bowlegged. The absolute topper was the toothpick he was sucking on when he came into the room. He removed it when Colbert called his name. His personal appearance was not that of a highly paid executive, but more like that of a down-at-the-heels bum. He walked with a decided limp that he told people was the result of an injury he suffered during a covert encounter when he was a Green Beret. This was a bare-faced lie. He got drunk and was thrown out of a Mexican bordello, at which time he broke his leg. The closest he ever got to the Green Berets was watching a John Wayne movie.

Colbert continued with his flowery introduction of Al Jamison. "He is a man who will put this company on the front burner and advance it into the next millennium. He comes with credentials that are impeccable. He has a long string of accomplishments that verify his being called one of the foremost management consultants in the industry today. We are most fortunate to have Al come aboard and make us beneficiaries of his talent. We fully expect everyone to cooperate with Al.

"We will tell you now that there will be cries of anguish among some employees who are being laid off. They will be given good buyouts that will far surpass their needs. You can well expect to have friends, relatives, politicians and others hit on you about Joe Blow's job. You will have to take the heat or get out of the kitchen, as one former president put it. Please don't waste your time or Al's or mine calling in here asking for favors about Joe's job. They will not be given. We are going to make this the most efficiently-run power company in the world. This will be reflected in the increase of our stock dividend. Hang tough and enjoy the fruits of the labors of a shrewd businessman. That is all we have on the agenda today so we will adjourn," Colbert said, without giving anyone a chance to challenge his decision to hire Jamison.

Everyone shook hands with Jamison and wished him well, offering to help him anyway they could. Little did they know that he was about to turn Public Service of Kentucky into a sad joke.

Whitley returned to her office to attend to some papers she had left on her desk when her inter-office buzzer sounded. Picking it up, she answered, "Whitley here."

"Whitley, this is Mr. Jamison. I need for you to be in my office at 1:15 this afternoon. There are some very important things I need for you to do for me and I want to go over them with you," he said.

"I'm sorry, Al, but I have a previous appointment that will keep me the rest of the afternoon. I have a vacancy on my calendar for 8:30 AM day after tomorrow, if you would like to come in then," she responded.

The answer she got was a click of the phone as he banged up the receiver.

Getting her coat, she left, telling the secretary that she would see her in the morning. Whitley made her way to her car in the company parking lot, got in and drove straight to her condo. When she got home where she felt secure, she called Joe Barnes. The receptionist answered and transferred her call to Joe.

"Well, what do you think of Mr. Jamison?" she asked Joe.

"First off, I'd say he is a rum soak, then I'd guess that he is a woman chaser and no girl in the building will be safe from him. On top of everything, he's so bowlegged, he couldn't hem a sheep in a ditch. That's not his fault, but it takes away from his management stature. I usually don't make quick evaluations of people, but I'll bet that I'm right about this one," Joe said.

"Right after the meeting, he buzzed me and said he wanted me to come to his office at 1:15. He used that old superiority routine of referring to himself as Mr. Jamison and me as Whitley. I replied that I had an appointment for the rest of the afternoon, but I had a time on my schedule for the day after tomorrow. He hung up in my ear. I believe that I am on his hit list, probably in first place," Whitley said.

"Don't you fool around and get yourself fired," Joe advised, "'cause then I'd have to either adopt you or marry you."

After she finished talking to Joe, she called Harry Baker. When he answered the phone, she started purring. "And what did the banking vice-president think of Mr. Al Jamison?" she asked.

"Sleaze," answered Harry. "He looked like he had just come off of a weekend drunk. I'll wager that he is a 'heavy hitter' from the looks of that red face and watery eyes."

Whitley told him about Al demanding her presence at a certain time and his addressing her as Whitley while referring to himself as Mr. Jamison. They talked about some other things and Harry asked her if she was busy the next night. She said she wasn't.

The next morning Whitley's buzzer sounded not long after she came in. It was Jack Colbert. "Whitley, can I see you for a minute?" he asked.

"Yes, sir, Mr. Colbert," she responded, thinking to herself that Jamison hadn't wasted any time. Tapping gently on Colbert's door, she waited a few seconds and then went in.

"Shut the door and have a seat, Whitley," he said as he got up from his chair in a gesture of good manners.

"What is your first opinion of Mr. Jamison?" he asked.

"I have always spoken my piece, Mr. Colbert, and this is no exception. Just to be perfectly honest with you, I think Mr. Jamison needs to spruce himself up. He may well be the high powered executive that you say he is and I don't doubt your word, but he needs a real good grooming," Whitley answered.

"That was what I wanted to hear," Colbert said. "If you had answered differently I would have known you were not being truthful. I am impressed by your response. I haven't asked you lately about Brad Durham's replacement. What kind of progress have you made?"

"To be perfectly honest, Mr. Colbert, I haven't looked too hard since you backed off on the hiring of Al Jamison. However, now that he is on board and it appears that we will be going ahead with your original plan of merger with CEG, I will intensify on that."

"I think you should. The merger will take some time and that will give you the opportunity you need to break in a new one," Colbert said.

Whitley left Colbert's office in a daze. "What is his game?" she mused to herself. She had criticized his new pet, Jamison, and he complimented her for it. Now he was beating on her to get Brad's replacement. Two years ago when Colbert had first mentioned this to her, she had searched high and low, but couldn't find the type of young man she wanted. Now she was starting all over. She knew that Cam Good, the human resources director, had looked through his records to no avail. He had taken early retirement after Jack Colbert made the public statement that Al Jamison would take his place. This was a year before Jamison showed up. The HR department of PSK had been in a shambles ever since Cam's departure. Whitley's problem now was how could she get into the personnel files without going through Jamison. There was bound to be another way and she had to find it.

On her way home that evening, she stopped at the supermarket and got two choice Angus filets, together with two potatoes for baking and the ingredients to make a walnut-orange salad. She had a small charcoal grill that she set out on the balcony of her condo that overlooked the parking lot. She put the potatoes in the oven and set the timer for forty-five minutes, planning to put the steaks on when the timer went off, leaving fifteen minutes for the potatoes to get done while the steaks were cooking. She then made the salad, leaving out the red onion slices that really made the salad good but didn't enhance romance. Once she had all of that done, she took a shower, put on her sweatsuit and fixed her hair. She got Harry's combined UK-UL sweatsuit out of the closet and laid it out on the bed. All of this was in preparation for soliciting Harry's help in finding Brad's replacement.

Harry was punctual as usual. She met him at the door and gave him a big hug and kiss.

"What kind of trouble are you in this time?" he asked with a laugh.

"I'd be ashamed," she answered, feigning hurt feelings. "Someone invites you to spend a nice romantic evening with them and you think it has some kind of hook in it."

"I apologize. I hadn't heard from you for a week or two and I thought that maybe I had made a miscue of some kind," he said.

"I really do need your help, but it can wait until after we eat. Your sweats are in the bedroom. While you change, I will mix us a martini," she answered.

The meal was cooked to perfection. Everything came done at the same time and after they finished their martinis, they ate. The single life had left Harry with a secret yearning for something homecooked. Vera tried, but somehow it didn't come out like it should. Harry mused on the thought of what kind of wife Whitley would make. That was all that he did. The quickest way to end a beautiful friendship was to get married, he decided.

After finishing their meal and quickly cleaning up the mess, she poured each of them a snifter of brandy and they retreated to the comfort of the couch.

"What's the problem?' he asked.

"Jack Colbert called me into his office this morning and asked me for my opinion on Al Jamison. I didn't use the term 'slob,' but I intimated as much. He evidently felt the same way because he agreed with me. Then he asked me where I was with finding a replacement for Brad. I am at a total loss as to what kind of a game he is playing. It's a no-win situation for me. If I don't find someone, he is going to do it for me. If I do find someone, then in a short time I will be out on the street. If I could find a similar job, I wouldn't mind leaving because I think the whole company is going to take a fall after Sleaze gets through with it. My question is, where in blazes do I find someone?"

"I've thought about Brad's replacement several times and I don't know offhand where you could locate such a person. I think I would try the Mining Engineering College at the University first. I realize you did this a couple of years ago, but the people have changed since then. Who knows, your quarry may be sitting by the phone awaiting your call," Harry answered. He was anxious to get on with other things besides finding her an assistant.

++++++

Scott Senters had grown up in the western Kentucky coal town of Sturgis. He was the eldest of five children and, like a lot of young people his age from a large family, he hadn't had the money to go to college right after graduation, so he went to work in a coal mine nearby his home. He liked coal mining and he wanted to stay in it, but he also wanted some things in life that the mine pay would not afford. He saved his money and with the help of a mining engineering scholarship, enrolled in the engineering college at UK. He had been a good student in high school, as well as being a good athlete, and he was a good student in college. Now a nice-looking young man in his middle twenties, he wore his brown hair close-cropped in almost a burr. His brown eyes matched up with the hair. He kept his person clean and neat. His nails were trimmed and he brushed his teeth after every meal. When he was working underground, he had chewed tobacco, but his stint at the university had pretty well gotten him away from that. To offset the lack of sunshine of his underground work, he had used a tanning bed periodically. His high school athletics had left him with a nice physique. He was what could be described as a "clean-cut kid".

While Scott was a college sophomore he had been friends with a young man named Thomas Wilder, who was a senior in the Mining Engineering Department. Just before Tom graduated, the vice-president of Public Service of Kentucky in charge of fuel procurement, had interviewed him. He was very much interested in the job and thought he had it when all at once he was notified by the vice-president, Whitley Rogers, that the job was no longer available. The day after Whitley's little cookout with Harry, Scott happened to call Ms. Rogers and told her that if the job ever came open again he would be very much interested in making application. Much to his surprise Whitley told him that the job was once more open and he could come by the PSK offices and get an application, which he did. Scott turned in his application the day after he got it. For references, he gave an engineering professor, the engineer of the coal company where he had worked and a United States Congressman from Kentucky, who was a neighbor.

Jack Colbert had been very emphatic in his instructions to Whitley that he wanted to talk to any prospect in which she was interested. This had bothered Whitley, but there was nothing she could do about it. She had managed to get three other applications out of the Human Resources files. They were all three good prospects. One of the three was a young woman. Whitley hadn't realized this when she made her selection, but she didn't think a girl would be a good replacement for Brad; however, she contacted all three and had them come in for an interview, along with Scott Senters. The girl had the best grades of the four, but Whitley felt that two women running the coal procurement section would have a negative effect on the dealings with coal operators.

Buzzing Jack Colbert's office, she told him that she had four applications if he would like to look over them. He told her to bring them in, that he would like to look over them before she made a selection. Gathering the applications together, she went to his office.

"Which of these is your choice?" asked Colbert after looking over them hurriedly.

"I think the Senters fellow is probably our best choice. He should know his way around the mines and should be pretty well up on what our needs would be," she answered.

"I agree," Colbert responded. "Let's get him in and see what he has to offer."

This shocked Whitley. She would have bet her next month's salary that he would not agree with her. She had toyed with the idea of using a reverse psychology approach and telling him she preferred one of the others, but she had decided against that and once more he took the opposite of what she expected. This was beginning to upset her.

Going back to her office, she called Scott Senters and told him to come in for an interview the next day at 10:00 AM.

CHAPTER 7

The trial of Olivia Napier for the murder of Bradley Durham and Veronica Atmore had finally begun. The jury selection had been a long and arduous task for all concerned. Judge Constanza had made a point of reminding the jurors that they were under oath before he asked for any of them that were as close as second cousin to Olivia or related to the Harp family to stand aside. Out of one hundred fifty prospective jurors, a panel of four men and eight women with two male alternates was selected. This took three days. Caron Dell asked similar questions regarding the Napier family, like whether they had any kin who worked at Golden Star or had ever been injured in a mine accident. Jeff Cawood was a little easier on them, only asking if they were kin by marriage to the Harps.

Prior to seating the jury, Judge Constanza had all four attorneys into his chambers for pre-trial instructions. This was a formality that he usually put all attorneys through. It was his way of laying down the groundrules for trials in his court.

"Mr. Shawitz, these other people have practiced in my court before and they pretty well understand my way of doing things, so in order to not put you at a disadvantage, I feel that I should tell you what I expect. I will not have witnesses harassed. I will call your hand if it appears that you are doing this. If I sustain an objection, it is sustained. If I overrule an objection, it is overruled. In either case, I expect my ruling to be accepted. I expect good courtroom manners from both sides. I do not want law practiced in the newspapers, tabloids or other news media. I expect you to address me as 'your honor' and in return, I will address you as 'counselor.' If all of you understand me, then we will proceed with the trial of Olivia Napier," Judge Constanza concluded.

Following his instructions to the attorneys, Judge Constanza seated the jury and asked the prosecutor to make her opening statement.

"Ladies and gentlemen, the prosecution intends to prove to you without the shadow of a doubt that this woman, Olivia Dillon Napier, brutally murdered Veronica Atmore and Bradley Durham. We will also prove by her own admission that she planned this gruesome deed over a period of several years, which makes it premeditated murder and warrants the death penalty. Thank you," Caron said as she returned to her seat.

"The defense may now present their opening statement," Constanza said.

Before Jeff Cawood could come out of his seat, Theo was already up and in front of the jury. Leaning his left arm on the balustrade in front of the jury box, he put on his best act.

"Ladies and gentlemen of the jury, yours is an awesome responsibility. You and only you will have the life of this woman in your hands. We will show you that she was coerced into making a confession to the aforesaid murders and before you can convict her of these heinous crimes, you have got to convince yourselves that she did them. No matter what the judge says, you are the ones who decide. Thank you."

Caron then called her first witness, Joan Carter, Veronica's co-worker at the store and the person who found the bodies. After being sworn in and giving her name, Joan seated herself in the witness chair.

"Mrs. Carter, please tell the jury how you came to find the bodies of Veronica Atmore and Bradley Durham," Caron said.

"Well, Veronica hadn't been to work for three days, poor little thing, and since she lived only two houses down the street from me, I felt it my responsibility to check on her. Well, I told my husband that I was going to check on her and he called me a busy body. Well, anyway I went to her house and the screen door was unlatched so I opened it and there was a key in the door. Well, I knocked several times, but no one came to the door so I opened it and went in. Well, there was a terrible stink in the house and that kind of upset me so I went back home and got James, my husband. Well, we went back to the house and he went in. He told me to stay outside, but I didn't want to stay out there by myself," Joan said.

"Judge, make her get to the point. We don't have all day to sit here and listen to all this drivel about 'poor little Veronica,'" Shawitz said.

"Continue with your testimony, Mrs. Carter," Judge Constanza said, ignoring Shawitz's rude interruption.

"Well, like I was saying, Jimmy, before that man interrupted me, we went into the house me and James, you know my husband James, don't you, Jimmy, well, we both smelled a bad stink. James was in front of me. Well, he went into the bedroom and told me to go back outside, but I stayed right behind him. Well, I saw all of that blood and I started to get sick. James went into the bathroom and told me not to come in there, but I went anyway. Well, when I saw that man and poor little Veronica in that bathtub, I fainted. The next thing I knew I was sitting on the front steps with a wet cloth on the back of my neck. That's how I came to find them, Mrs. Dell," finished Joan.

"Thank you, Mrs. Carter. Now, Mrs. Carter, have you ever seen that woman over there in or around Veronica's house?" asked Caron Dell pointing to Olivia Napier.

"Well now, Mrs. Dell, she came to my house about three or four years ago and asked if she could get some hot water. She said that she was cleaning up the house after some people had moved out and there wasn't any hot water. Of course I let her have it. Well, I asked her who was moving in and she said she didn't know. I was home that day from work and I told her I wouldn't be home the next day and she…"

"Judge, make her come to the point, we ought not to have…"

"All counsel approach the bench," Judge Constanza boomed out. He didn't try to talk in low tones to keep the spectators from hearing him. "I explained to you before this trial started that I would not tolerate harassment of a witness and I meant what I said. Now you go back to your seat and keep your damn mouth shut or I will cite you for contempt of court," Constanza growled.

"I plan to file an appeal in this case and your cursing me will certainly be a part of it," Theo said turning and going back to his seat.

"You can continue with your testimony, Mrs. Carter. I apologize for the treatment you just received. I promise you that it will not happen again," Judge Constanza said in a much more civil tone.

"Well, like I was saying, Jimmy, I told the lady that I would be at work from now on. She said that she had turned on the water heater and she would have hot water, but she thanked me for helping," Joan concluded.

"Mrs. Carter, what kind of employee was Veronica?" Caron asked.

"She was just as sweet as anyone could be. Everybody liked her. She was always on time and would work over when asked to. I know that during Christmas season it was nothing for her to work anywhere from twelve to sixteen hours a day," Joan answered.

Shawitz started to say something, but Judge Constanza glowered at him and he thought better of it.

"Do you have any idea why someone would want to kill Veronica, especially in such a gruesome manner?" Caron asked.

She hadn't said the last word when Shawitz came out of his seat."Objection, Judge! That is purely conjecture and has no bearing on why the woman was killed," he said.

"Overruled," said Judge Constanza. "You may answer the question, Mrs. Carter."

"Thank you, Jimmy. I have no idea why someone would want to kill such a sweet girl who never did hurt anybody," said Joan Carter.

"That should be stricken from the record," Shawitz screamed.

"All counsel, approach the bench," Constanza demanded. They did so. Looking Shawitz square in the face, Judge Constanza put on his most effective low voice. "One more outburst from you and I will have you removed from this courtroom," Constanza said. "Now, go back to your seat and keep your damn mouth shut until it is your turn to speak."

"That is the second time you have cursed me during the course of this trial. I fully intend to report this to the Kentucky Bar Association and demand your removal from the bench in addition to disbarment," Shawitz said in a loud enough voice for the entire courtroom to hear him.

"Bailiff," Constanza called out, "please stand ready to remove Mr. Shawitz from the courtroom and escort him out of the courthouse." Turning to the courtroom, he apologized to the spectators for what had taken place and told Caron Dell to proceed with her witness.

"I have no further questions, your honor," she said with her face twitching to laugh, but knowing better than to do it.

Nodding his head toward the defense table, he told them it was their turn. Before Jeff Cawood could get on his feet, Shawitz was up in front of Mrs. Carter. "Do you have any children, Mrs. Carter?" he asked.

"Yes," she answered.

"How many?"

"Two," she said.

"Are they married?" he asked.

"One is and one isn't" she answered.

"Do you have any grandchildren?"

"Two," she said.

"How old are they?

"One is ten and one is eight," she said.

"What would you do Mrs. Carter, if someone killed one of your grandchildren and crippled one of your children?" Theo asked.

"Well, I really don't know. I never really thought about it," she answered.

"Would you kill a person who did that to your children, Mrs. Carter?"

"I can't say. I don't think people should kill other people. The Bible says that 'vengeance is mine, saith the Lord' and I believe what the Bible says is ri..."

"We don't need a Sunday school lesson," Theo said slowly walking away and then wheeling around he pointed his finger at Mrs. Carter. "Did you know Veronica before she went to work at the place where you work?"

"No, I didn't," she said.

"Had you never heard of what a bad reputation she had?" he asked.

"No, I hadn't" Joan Carter answered.

"Do you mean to tell me that you had never heard the stories about 'Sweet littleVeronica' sleeping with every man in town?"

"No, I hadn't. I don't gossip," she said.

Pointing his finger at her he yelled, "You are lying. Judge, I want this woman indicted for perjury," he screamed.

"That did it. Bailiff, please escort Mr. Shawitz out of this courtroom and this courthouse," Constanza said.

Percy Hatfield, the bailiff, was a hulk of a man. He stood about 6'3" and weighed in at about 215 pounds. He had played linebacker at Morehead State University in his younger days and was drafted by the pros his junior year. Nobody wanted to tangle with him, especially in Constanza's courtroom. Shawitz had gathered his papers and put them in his brief case by the time Percy got to him. Stalking out of the courtroom, he started to make a parting remark to Judge Constanza but thought better of it.

"If anyone else would like to leave the courtroom, now is the time," said Judge Constanza.

Bill Minter, Chris Evans and Sandy Deiss went out along with Theo Shawitz. Isabel stayed where she was. She was watching Bige Napier and it just about made her cry. He was sitting right behind Olivia and spent the entire proceedings leaning up in his seat to be closer to her.

With Shawitz's exit, the courtroom returned to the model of decorum that it was supposed to be.Once he was outside the courthouse and Percy was out of hearing range, Theo set in on Judge Constanza. "Self-important judges like him should be removed from the bench. He thinks he is God and reigns supreme over all he sees," postulated Theo, "I will file a formal petition to ask the State of Kentucky to remove him from the bench. People of his ilk should not be allowed to sit in judgment in a court of law."

While Theo was vilifying Judge Constanza, Bill Minter asked Sandy where she was staying. Sandy told him she was staying with Isabel's father and stepmother and though he didn't ask, she told him where they lived and how to get to there.

Going to a pay phone on the corner of the courthouse square, Sandy called her paper and related the day's happenings to the desk person. She finished her report at about the same time Isabel came out of the courthouse, so they went home together.

Isabel had been crying and Sandy asked her what was wrong.

"I feel so sorry for Bige Napier that I can't hold back. No matter what she has done, to him she is his mother and he loves her. To sit there and hear her be accused of the crimes is more than he ought to have to take. I don't remember my mother, but I would feel the same way about Sarah," Isabel sobbed.

CHAPTER 8

Back in Lexington, G T had studied about the White Pines Coal Company permit and how he was going to get Rebecca Holton to back down. He needed to know more about her, so he called Barry Foreman and apologized for blowing up on him the day before.

When Barry answered the phone G T told him who he was.

"I'm sorry I blew up on you the other day, Barry, but I still don't see how that bitch can change everything just because she wants to. Let me buy you a steak while you fill me in on who she is and where she comes from," G T said.

"I didn't pay any attention to your getting upset yesterday; I've known you long enough to not let your blowing off a little steam bother me. I'll take you up on that steak," responded Barry.

"I'll meet you at that new steak house on Nicholasville Pike tomorrow night about seven o'clock if that suits you," G T replied.

"I'll see you then," said Barry.

G T got to the steak house about five minutes before Barry. He waited in the parking lot while leaning up against his car. Barry pulled into a parking space beside G T and got out. They went into the eatery and got a booth in the no-smoking section. They both ordered the house specialty, grilled T bone with onion rings, a baked potato and tossed salad with bleu cheese dressing. Barry ordered a beer and G T got a glass of iced tea.

"Who is this girl that she can change the ground rules on permits?" asked G T.

"Like I told you, she came to us from the EPA after that impoundment failure. She has a chip on her shoulder as big as a saw log and she dares anyone to knock it off. She's not bad looking and has a pretty good sense of humor about most things, but she is as serious as a heart attack about ponds and impoundments. She comes from West Virginia, and from all that I can find out her daddy was hurt on a surface mine job and she is going to make the world pay for it," said Barry.

"How did he get hurt?"

"He was shot man on a strip section. He put off a shot that he was too close to and it had a lot of fly rock in it. A piece of it hit him in the back as he was running to get away. It was his own fault and a fellow that was working on the section told me that he wasn't hurt that bad. He comped out on the company and went home to sit. Rebecca thinks that all strip miners are demons from hell. Uh oh! Guess who just came in the door?" said Barry.

"Who?" asked G T.

"None other than the present subject, the Wicked Witch of West Virginia, Rebecca Holton," said Barry, "and she's with Austin Martin, our governor's illustrious son. That explains a whole lot of things, including why we can't get her moved."

"Did she see you?" asked G T.

"I don't think so. They went on into the back part of the building. You ought to be able to see them. She has on a light blue pantsuit," said Barry.

"I see them," said G T. "She's sitting with her back to me. I don't believe I have ever seen her before, but Isabel said that she was a heller when it came to the subject of surface mining."

Their meal came and they both ate like they were starved. They talked about careers and how to get into something that would be worthwhile and pay well. Barry told G T about his interviewing with an engineering company that had some governmental work going on in Nepal. G T said he sort of envied him, that he would like to get something like that, but he didn't feel that he ought to go away and leave George and Gerry. He was also thinking about Isabel, but he didn't tell Barry. They finished their meal with a large nut-filled brownie topped with vanilla ice cream and hot fudge sauce.

Just as they were getting ready to leave, they saw Rebecca and her date go out. It appeared that they were arguing about some thing. G T told Barry that he wasn't a "drink counter," but he had seen the waiter take at least four rounds of single drinks to the table. Evidently Austin had drunk his meal while she ate hers. G T and Barry let them get out before they paid their check and left. When they got outside, Rebecca and Austin were standing behind his car.

"I am not going with you unless you let me drive," they heard her say.

"Nobody drives my car but me. Now shut your damned mouth and get in or I'll go without you," he threatened.

"You are too drunk to drive," she said.

"My old man is the governor of this state and nobody is going to arrest me," Austin bragged.

"I'm not worried about getting arrested," she said, "I'm worried about getting killed. Now give me the keys, Austin," she said taking hold of his arm.

That was a mistake. He swung around and backhanded her, knocking her sprawling on the pavement. He got in the car and scratched off out of the parking lot, leaving Rebecca lying on the pavement. She began to cry.

Barry and G T were parked several spaces away from where Austin had been. Barry told G T that he would get back to him in a day or two, that he was going to follow Austin in case he got picked up or even worse, had a wreck. Then G T went over to where Rebecca was sitting up. She had torn a big hole in her trousers and had skinned her knee. He got a clean handkerchief out of his pocket and, rolling up her pants leg, bandaged the wound.

"Thank you very much," she said. "Now if you will help me into the steak house, I'll call a cab."

The sudden realization came to her that she had placed her purse under the front seat of Austin's car when they went in to eat and she didn't have any money on her. She started to cry again. "That sorry bastard ran off with my purse and I don't have any money," she said.

"I'll be very glad to drive you home if you will tell me where you live," G T told her.

"I live in Frankfort and I couldn't let you do that," she responded.

"Look miss, I am unmarried, sober and have a full night ahead of me. I would be glad to help you. Now if you will accompany me, we will be on our way," G T said reaching down to pick her up off the pavement. Easing her into his truck, he went around and got in the driver's side and started to Frankfort.

"This is certainly nice of you…I didn't catch your name," Rebecca said.

G T had thought about what to say when she asked him his name. He first thought he would give her some fictitious name, but then he thought better of it. "I am G T Deane, Ms Holton," he answered.

There seemed to be hours before she answered him. "This has really been my night. First my date gets drunk on me, then he knocks me flat in the parking lot and runs off and leaves me. Next, a man that I have insulted rescues me. Am I ever the born loser? Okay, Four 0, I am at your mercy. Preach to me about your ponds," she said.

"I don't play unfair. You are at a disadvantage, so I'm not going to mention the ponds. When you get back on your turf, then we will fight out the pond issue," he answered. "Let's just talk about something else."

The thirty-minute trip to Frankfort was mostly her talking. He had asked her how she got mixed up with Austin.

"I met him at a legislative mixer one night and he asked me for a date. I told him to call me and I gave him my phone number. I inquired around about him and most people said he was a fair sort except that he drank too much. I thought I could handle that. I had dated several people around Frankfort who had been nice, so I thought I would give him a try. Boy! Was that a mistake! I'll not go out with him again. I ought to send him a bill for this pantsuit, but it wouldn't do any good. That kind would never pay."

Rebecca gave G T instructions on how to get to her apartment. He pulled into a slot in the parking lot, got out, opened her door and put her arm around his shoulder. Her knee had stiffened up during the ride from Lexington and she had trouble standing on it. He helped her into the apartment building and up to her apartment. She had another key hidden under a mat which he got out for her and unlocked the door. She thanked him again for his assistance and bade him good night. She didn't ask him in, for which he was glad. After she went to bed, she thought about how nice G T was. She wasn't used to that kind of treatment. She didn't blame Isabel for fighting for him. He appeared to be well worth it. She just might give old Isabel a tussle for him.

The next morning, G T called Rebecca at work. "Good morning, Ms Holton, how is your knee this morning?" he asked when she finally answered.

"It's sore, but I think I'll live. I want to thank you again for being so nice to me, especially after the way I had talked to you," she said.

"That's okay," he said. "You have a job to do and I have one too. The only problem we have is that I see it one way and you see it another." G T felt sorry for her. It was really pitiable to see someone as bitter as she was about something that she undoubtedly knew was her father's fault. Yet she was going to make the mining industry pay for it. G T was also smart enough to know that one swallow didn't make a summer and his helping her wouldn't change her mind about the ponds.

"I have a philosophy that the steeper the slope, the bigger the pond should be. You know as well as I do that the 10-year, 24-hour storm doesn't fit all mining conditions. On a steep slope the runoff is faster and therefore it carries more silt. If a pond is built to accommodate a 10-year storm on a steep slope, it will fill up faster and the silt will not have time to settle out. Instead, it will discharge siltated water," Rebecca argued.

"I don't have any problem with what you are saying, but we both know that the governing factor in pond design is the pond capacity. We both also know that the purpose of the pond is to allow the silt to settle out of the water. If the pond is configured to hold the runoff of a design storm, then that is what its size should be," countered G T, "besides that, the slope is too steep to accommodate a 15-year pond."

"That is not my problem," smarted Rebecca.

"I think visiting the pond sites on the ground would change your mind," said G T.

A light went on in Rebecca's head. "If Issie sees me with him, school will sure be out as far as a soon-to-be-wedding is concerned," she thought.

"Try me," she said.

"What do you mean, try me?" he asked.

"Just what I said. Take me to see the ponds," she responded.

G T thought for a minute. "The mining is in Red Oak Hollow which is just three hollows up from Holly Tree. I could take her home with me, stay one night at Mama's, see the ponds the next day, stay another night and then come on back here."

"How about this weekend? We could go to Pineville on Friday and come back Sunday. I could show you the ponds Saturday," he suggested.

"Suits me," Rebecca quipped.

G T called Gerry and asked her if it would be all right for him to bring Rebecca home with him. He explained the circumstances. Of course Gerry agreed, but she didn't like it. She was afraid that G T and Isabel were drifting apart and this other girl was not going to make the matters any better.

After G T called Gerry, he called Isabel. She didn't answer. He hung up and said to himself that he would try again.

CHAPTER 9

One of Isabel's favorite home "menus" was beef roast, mashed potatoes, glazed carrots and broccoli casserole. It went without saying that Sarah's gravy accompanied the meal. For dessert, Sarah usually made a chocolate pound cake with peanut butter-flavored chocolate icing, a recipe she had gotten from Gerry. It was Isabel's favorite and had been for years ever since the Sundays when they would eat dinner at Sarah's. She fixed such a meal for Isabel and Sandy. Eating out once in a while was fine, but she really preferred to cook. It was homier.

When Isabel and Sandy came in, Sarah fixed a pitcher of iced tea and they went out on the patio to drink it. Frank came home while they were talking about the trial.

"Daddy," Isabel said, "what is Bige doing about working? I would say he needs the money."

"George and I took care of that, honey. We offered to let Bige take off and we told him we would pay him, but he said that wouldn't be fair to other employees so he swapped places with another man and he now works the second shift. He needed to pay the lawyers so we let him borrow the money and we tore up the note, but he doesn't know that we did that. Bige asked to be moved to a surface section about two months ago and we transferred him. He is a born equipment operator and planner. We didn't know that until he had been on the section a while. One day the foreman was off and Bige took over for him. I went on the section with him to cover him since he didn't have surface foreman's papers. I watched him all day and he is a natural. I don't know where he learned it, but he sure knows how to keep all of the equipment moving. There are no wasted moves in his plans. As soon as he gets his time in and takes the foreman's test, we want to find a section for him."

"That is really nice of you and Mr. Deane," said Sandy.

"Please don't put that in the paper," Frank asked.

"Oh, no sir. I wouldn't do that, but I do think it is nice of you all," Sandy replied.

Sarah called Isabel to come set the table and told Frank to go wash his hands so they could eat. Seated at the table, they held each other's hand while Frank returned thanks.

"Bige is an excellent employee," Frank said continuing the conversation that Sarah had interrupted by calling them to dinner. "He really cares about his job and looks after the company's equipment as though it was his own. We are lucky to have him."

While Frank was talking, the phone rang and Isabel went to answer it. It was G T. "I'm going to do something you aren't going to like, but I have to do it," he said.

"If you know that I won't like it, why are you going to do it?" she asked.

G T explained to her about the ponds and Rebecca Holton. "I have to get the ponds approved so the permit will pass and showing her the pond locations is what it is going to take."

"If you want to take that bitch up in the woods, why ask my permission? Go ahead, I don't care. Call me sometime when you aren't busy pond hunting with Rebecca," Isabel snarled as she hung up in his ear. Going back into the kitchen where the others were eating, Isabel was sulled up like a poisoned toad.

"Who was that?" Frank asked.

"It was G T. He called to tell me that he was bringing that witch of West Virginia home with him to look at some ponds." Isabel was so mad that she wanted to cry, but she held back. She had gotten her composure when the front door bell rang. Since she was still standing up, she went to the door. It was Bill Minter.

"Good evening, Ms Morgan. Am I interrupting your dinner? If I am I can come back at another time," he said.

"No, not at all," Isabel said. "We were just finishing up."

"I wanted to talk to your father," Minter said, still standing in the door.

"Come on in. We had finished eating and were sitting at the kitchen table talking," Isabel said.

Following her down the hall to the kitchen, Bill couldn't help but notice how attractive she was. She was a nice figured girl who walked like a cat. Her shoulder-length blond hair undulated as she walked and her hips moved from side to side as though keeping time to some fifties love song. In anybody's book, she was a beautiful woman.

On entering the kitchen, Isabel told Frank that Bill wanted to talk to him.

"I apologize for barging in on you this way, but I had some questions I wanted to ask you about mining, Mr. Morgan," Bill said.

"Here, have a seat," Isabel said as she moved a kitchen chair between where she was sitting and Frank. "Would you like some chocolate cake and ice cream?" she asked. Sarah had gotten up and cut everyone a piece of cake. Isabel went to the refrigerator and got the ice cream, putting a big dollop on each plate and serving everyone.

"If you and I are going to talk about mining, we are not going to start off by you calling me 'Mr. Morgan'," Frank said. "I am Frank to all that know me."

"Thank you, Frank, that makes it much easier. Theo Shawitz, Mrs. Napier's attorney, keeps referring to an accident known as a cut-in. What does this mean?" Bill asked.

"As deep mining is done, maps are kept up showing where the mining has taken place. Periodically these are updated and sent to the Department of Mines and Minerals in Lexington where they are kept on file. The purpose of this is to make anyone mining nearby aware of the presence of the old works. In the case of the cut-in at Golden Star, which is what I figure you are making reference to, there were evidently two sets of maps. One set was earlier than the other and showed a sufficient barrier between the old works and the mining plan. The other map, which was done much later, shows the barrier to be approximately fifty feet thick if the mining was carried out as planned. Bradley Durham had submitted a mining plan based on the older map, although he undoubtedly knew better. Sometimes there are areas where mining is done and the map has not been updated. This, in all probability, was the case where the accident occurred. When the miner cut into the thinner barrier, it gave way and released thousands of gallons of water. This is ground water that accumulates over the years and is nasty, to say the least. It is black, cold and stinks to high heaven," Frank said, taking a bite of cake.

"How is the coal mined?" asked Bill.

"We use a continuous miner. Briefly, this is a large rotating drum mounted on hydraulic arms. The surface of the drum is covered with spike like bits that cut into the coal as the drum rotates. The cut coal falls onto a pan under the drum and is gathered in by a set of arms mounted on the pan. At the back of the pan is a conveyor that carries the coal to the rear of the miner where it is dumped into shuttle cars. These are rubber-tired, electrically-driven, wagon-like machines with conveyors in the center, that transport the coal to the head of the conveyor system that moves the coal outside. It is dumped there and the car goes back for another load."

Bill was taking notes all the time that Frank was talking. When Frank stopped, Bill started on his dessert. "This cake is delicious, Mrs. Morgan," said Bill.

"Stop right there," Sarah said. "Like his name is Frank, my name is Sarah."

"This cake is delicious, Sarah," Bill repeated.

"Thank you, that is much better," Sarah laughed.

"What is the story behind Olivia Napier and the murders?" Bill asked.

"Isabel can tell you more about that than anyone else," said Frank. "She and G T probably knew Brad and Veronica better than anyone."

Isabel told Bill Minter all that she had told Sandy on the way to Pineville from Lexington. He made notes about all items that had entered into Olivia's personality. Isabel got tears in her eyes when she talked about Bradley and also when she talked about Bige. Some of the items she asked him not to have printed, and he said he wouldn't

"I believe that I have enough to make a good story, so I will again apologize for interrupting your dinner. Thank you for your help and the delicious cake," Minter said getting up from the table.

"I'll show you out," Isabel said as she also got up.

"This is really going to be interesting," thought Sandy Deiss.

When Bill Minter opened the front door and went out on the porch, Isabel followed him.

"Sandy told me that you were engaged," said Bill.

"Well, yes, in a way, I guess that I am, but I don't have a ring and there has not been a date set," replied Isabel.

Not being one to have to have a brick wall fall on him, Minter took the hint.

"Would I be out of line if I asked you to have dinner with me some evening?" he asked.

"Ask and see," said Isabel.

"Would you have dinner with me some evening?" Bill asked.

"Yes," replied Isabel, "if you will let me pick the place."

"Where would you like to go?" he quizzed.

"Cumberland Falls," said Isabel.

"I never heard of it," said Minter

"That figures," said Isabel. "Cumberland Falls is the largest water fall east of the Mississippi river with the exception of Niagara, and the only place in the world where there is a moonbow, with the exception of Victoria Falls in Africa. It is a beautiful place."

"What is a moonbow?" asked Bill.

"It is the same thing as a rainbow except it is only seen when the moon is full and there is no cloud cover. It spreads out over the falls and is formed from the mist that comes off the falls," Isabel said.

"Sounds very romantic," said Minter.

"It is," said Isabel. "The moon is full tomorrow night and the weather report says that it will be clear. See you about 5:00 PM?"

"You sure will," said Bill.

"Now, G T Deane," said Isabel to herself, "how do you like them apples?"

CHAPTER 10

Jemjelf wanted to warn Thelma, but the knife against her throat made her think better of it. Thelma let the two police officers out and went into her bedroom to put on her clothes and go to the trial. Pulling on the pants to the suit she planned to wear, she slipped on a blouse and started into the kitchen as she buttoned it.

"Well, if it isn't my old flame Thelma, the mother of my son. Don't you recognize me, Thelma dear?" the man asked.

"Who are you?" she queried.

"I am Curtis Bradley," the man answered.

"What do you want?" Thelma asked.

"Well, for starters, I need a change of clothes. That skinny little milk truck driver's clothes are killing me. Get me a pair of pants, a shirt and some socks. We will go on from there," Curtis said.

Thelma started out the door into the dining room when he called her back.

"Not so fast, sweetie pie. First we tie up this good-looking helper of yours. Find me something here in this kitchen to tie her up with," Curtis said.

Thelma rummaged through several drawers in the kitchen cabinet, skipping over a roll of duct tape. He was looking over her shoulder and stopped her when she passed over the tape.

"Hold up right there, Thel, that ought to do the trick," he said as he grabbed the ball of tape. "First thing you do is tape her mouth up," he commanded.

"I'm not going to do it," Thelma responded.

"Thelma, listen to me real careful 'cause I'm only going to tell you this once. I am an escaped murderer. I have killed two people and one more won't make any difference. Now, you tape her mouth up and then tape her hands to the arms of that chair she is in, or I am going to slit her throat and then I won't have to worry about her getting loose," he directed.

Thelma wouldn't have had anything happen to Jemjelf for the world so she did as he told her. Once she secured Jemjelf, she went back into the bedroom to find a pair of pants and a shirt that would fit Curtis who was about Ed Durham's size. She turned around to start back into the kitchen and he was right behind her. Handing him the pants and shirt, she started to leave while he changed.

"Oh no, you don't. You stay right here 'til I get changed," he said.

Turning her back to him, she waited until he had changed. She finished buttoning her blouse and put on the jacket to her suit. She had fixed her hair before the two Tennessee officers arrived, so she was now dressed.

"Look, Curtis, why don't you just leave us and we won't tell anyone you were here," she said.

"What kind of damn fool do you take me for? I wouldn't be out the door before you'd call the police. Do you have any money?" he quizzed.

"I have about fifty dollars in my purse that you can have," she answered.

"Do you have one of those automatic teller cards?" he asked.

"Yes," Thelma said.

"Good. Now what about your car? Does it have a full tank of gas?" He kept asking questions without giving her a chance to answer.

"It's in the garage and full of gas," she said.

"Let's go," he commanded.

Thelma led the way to the door between the kitchen and the garage, stopping to pat Jemjelf on the knee.

"I'll be all right," she said as she read the anxiety in Jemjelf's eyes, "I hope I didn't get that tape too tight."

Jemjelf responded by shaking her head, "No."

Curtis had swapped the shiv he used to coerce the milkman and Jemjelf for a butcher knife he found lying on the counter in Thelma's kitchen. Then, holding the knife at Thelma's back, he ordered her out the door to the garage. "Give me the keys," he demanded.

"Are you going to drive?" she asked in wonderment.

"No. You are going to drive, but I'll give you the keys when I get ready for us to leave," he answered.

Thelma got in on the driver's side and Curtis went around and got in on the passenger side. Moving the seat back as far as it would go, he hunkered down in the floor. Holding the knife with the point against her stomach, he gave her the keys.

"Now Thelma, don't try to be heroic and do something stupid. I don't want to hurt you, but if you make one false move, I'll rip you open like a gutted hog," he warned.

"Where are we going?" asked Thelma as she opened the garage doors and started the car.

"We are going to my home in Trenton, Tennessee. You've been through there enough on your way to Knoxville so I don't need to give you directions," Curtis said as he adjusted his position to get more comfortable for the trip.

"On our way out of town, stop at that money machine in the bank parking lot and withdraw five thousand dollars," he told her.

"The maximum I can get is two thousand," lied Thelma.

"Then get that," Curtis responded.

Pulling into the automatic teller, she put her card in the slot and punched in a withdrawal of two thousand dollars. In accordance with bank policy, the teller notified a supervisor of the withdrawal of over one thousand dollars.

"Did you make a withdrawal of two thousand dollars, Mrs. Durham?" asked the supervisor over the intercom.

"Yes, I did," she answered.

"Thank you," the supervisor replied as she matched Thelma's voice with a voice tape.

"What is that all about?" asked Curt.

"They do that to make sure it is you. If I had let you try to get the money the machine would not have let you have it," explained Thelma. Which is what I should have done, she thought.

Curtis told her to turn off on Bradley Drive after she passed through Trenton, which she did. Next he told her to go straight to the end of the road where she would come to a gate. There she should blow her horn four times and the gate would open, which it did. He then told her to drive straight to the barn, pull up beside a post that stood outside the barn, and roll down her window. After she followed all of his instructions pulling up beside the post and rolling down the window, Curtis raised up from the floor and called out, "Open doors. Your master, Curtis Bradley, wants in."

To Thelma's surprise, they opened. She drove in and the doors shut behind her. Reaching over her, Curtis took the keys out of the ignition and put them in his pocket. He got out of the car after telling her to not move until he told her to and walked around to her side.

"Get out," he ordered. She did, then shut the door and asked him what he intended to do with her.

"I haven't made up my mind about you yet, so don't get anxious," he said.

Walking up to a door at the end of the garage, Curtis addressed it in the same manner he had used on the garage door. The door opened into a luxurious room that was just as Martin Wallace had described it. Motioning Thelma into the room ahead of him, he shut the door behind him.

"In case you are thinking of doing something stupid, Thelma, I think you ought to know that the doorknobs do not work. For anyone other than me to open the door from the inside, it is necessary to have a key. Harvey Stone, my helper in times past, has one, but he stays up at the house with my old man. I need to do some things and I don't trust you running loose. Open the drawer on that end table in front of you and get out those handcuffs. Fasten one cuff around your left wrist and the other around that floor lamp," he instructed.

"Curtis, if you don't mind, I need to go to the bathroom and the handcuffs would be terribly inconvenient. If this place is so well secured, why must I wear the handcuffs?" she asked.

Giving thought to her question for a minute or two, he showed her the bathroom door and told her she didn't need to wear the cuffs. Going into the bathroom, she didn't shut the door completely, leaving a half-inch opening. Quietly she flipped the lock on the door between the bedroom and the bath, leaving the door into the living room as the only access to the bath.

Suddenly she heard a knock on the living room outside door and heard a man's voice call out, "Curtis, is that you, old buddy?" he said. "This is your friend Harvey. Can I come in?"

She remembered Martin Wallace telling her about Harvey, and Curtis saying he had a key. Peeking through the door crack, she saw Curtis standing on a small platform that was connected to a long pole that extended into an attic above the ceiling. The platform was the strange-looking fixture that she had seen in the center of the ceiling that appeared to have cameras in it. While she was looking, Curtis gave an inaudible command that sent the platform with him on it through the ceiling into the attic above. In the blink of an eye, he was out of sight and the ceiling returned to normal once more.

Two seconds later, the front door slowly opened and a small hunched-back man came in. She was reminded of the Hunchback of Notre Dame, Quasimodo. His eyesight must not have been too good because he squinched his eyes. He was wearing a dirty tee shirt that had a large orange letter T on the front. His bib overalls almost covered the Tennessee Volunteer initial, but enough was visible to make out what it was. He had a full beard that was mottled in color between brown and gray. The old tennis shoes he was wearing were the cheap canvas type that were already broken out at the edge. All in all Harvey was not a fashion ad but he had one unmistakable accessory: he held a pistol in his right hand. His left arm hung limp at his side. He came on into the room and kept calling out for Curtis. He eased over to the bedroom door and cautiously opened it, holding the pistol in his left hand at his side. Once he had cracked the door, he reached over with his right hand and took the pistol out of the left hand. Suddenly giving the bedroom door a hard push with his shoulder, he jumped into the room, scanning the room with the pistol at the ready.

Thelma wasn't sure what he intended to do if he found Curtis, but she didn't want to be mistaken for him. She was afraid that Harvey would jump through the bathroom door and seeing her, might think that she was Curtis and shoot. She didn't have anything to defend herself with as she looked around the bathroom. Harvey had come out of the bedroom and was walking slowly toward the bathroom. Thelma became frantic for something to arm herself when her eyes fell on the porcelain lid on the water tank at the back of the commode. Quietly she removed the lid and positioned herself beside the door in such a way that Harvey would have to come in the bathroom to see her. Holding the lid over her head, she waited. He came to the door and called again for Curtis. When he didn't get a response, he pushed the door open as he had done the bedroom door. Coming into the bath, he turned his back to where Thelma stood. That was his mistake. She came down on his head with the water tank lid and sent him sprawling in the floor of the bathroom. Quickly she took the gun out of his hand and stepped over him and out of the bathroom, shutting the door behind her. It occurred to her that while she was armed, Harvey was still capable of coming after her when he awakened from his water tank nap. Looking in the drawer where Curtis had put the handcuffs, she found two sets. One set she put in her pocket, the other set she took into the bathroom and cuffed Harvey's arms around the base of the commode. He was still unconscious so she rifled his pockets and found a set of keys. Putting these in her pocket, she backed out of the bathroom and left him lying on the floor. When she turned around, she saw Curtis descending on the platform to the living room floor. Pointing the gun at him, she told him to lay down on the floor.

"Now look, Thelma, I didn't harm you when I could have, so you shouldn't harm me," he said.

"Lay down on the floor, Curtis, and put these cuffs on," she demanded as she threw the cuffs on the floor in front of him.

"Now look, Thelma…" was all that he got out of his mouth when he heard the pistol report and saw the bullet plow through the rug between his feet.

"I said lay down on the floor and put those cuffs on or the next shot may be higher," she warned.

"I can't believe that you would shoot me," Curtis moaned.

"Well, you'd damn well better believe it," she said.

"I could easily kill you and no jury would convict me. You said yourself that you were a convicted murderer. Now for the last time lay down on the floor and put those cuffs on," she said as she cocked the pistol.

Realizing that Thelma had a longtime hate for him and seeing what a good shot she was, Curtis obeyed her order and put the hand cuffs on. He fastened his left wrist first and started to snap the other cuff on the other wrist, when she stopped him.

"Fasten that other cuff around the base of that floor lamp just like you were going to have me do, but before you do that take the car keys out of your pocket and pitch them over to me. As you told me, don't try anything heroic. I don't want to kill you, but if you force me to, I will," she warned.

Following her instructions, he pitched the keys toward her.

"Now, put that other cuff around the base of the floor lamp like I told you," she said, "and don't get up. If you start to try to get up, I'll kill you. Like you said about Jemjelf, it would be a lot simpler for me if I did."

He had figured she would lean down to pick up the keys and when she did he planned to jump her. She was smarter than he thought. She kicked the keys across the room. He fastened the cuff to the floor lamp and she walked across the room to the keys. She stooped down and picked them up, never taking her eyes off of him and holding the gun on him all of the time.

CHAPTER 11

The trial was getting underway for the second day and Caron Dell was to present her last witness, John Talbert. As soon as the courtroom settled down, Judge Constanza called both sets of attorneys to the bench. In very clear tones, he warned Shawitz: "I want it understood that you will conduct yourself in a decorous manner for the remainder of this trial or, so help me, I will have you locked up. I do not want to do this, Mr. Shawitz, but if you force me to, I will. I want this trial conducted strictly by the book and properly. As I have told you, I will not tolerate the harassment of witnesses. Now, ladies and gentlemen, let's proceed with the trial of Olivia Napier."

John Talbert and Jacob Gibson had been summonsed as witnesses for the prosecution and therefore were not allowed in the courtroom. They had been allowed to go to the dispatch room and out around the courthouse grounds. Caron Dell had John summoned from where he was sitting in the dispatch center and after being properly sworn in, he seated himself. Going through the formalities of his name, his employer and his duties, she began the questioning.

"Lieutenant Talbert, have you ever seen that woman sitting over there, the defendant in this trial?" she asked pointing to Olivia.

"Yes," John answered.

"Please tell the court on what occasion you met the defendant?" she asked.

"Trooper Jacob Gibson and I went to the defendant's home with a search warrant in an attempt to find a weapon we suspected was used in the murder of Bradley Durham and Veronica Atmore."

"Why did you go to the defendant's home in your search?" queried Caron.

"The interrogation of a suspect gave us sufficient cause to obtain a search warrant," said John.

All the time John was testifying, Judge Constanza was listening intently while at the same time conducting a stare down with Shawitz. The judge won. Theo broke his stare and started sorting through his papers.

"Did you find such a weapon?" Caron continued.

"Yes, we did," answered John.

"Did you find other evidence that gave you cause to believe that the defendant had committed the murders?" asked Caron.

"Objection!" shouted Shawitz. "My client is being tried for these crimes. The witness is not the jury to decide that she is guilty."

"Sustained," said Constanza. "Rephrase your question, counselor."

"Was there other evidence?" Caron asked.

"Yes, there was," John answered.

"What was this evidence?" Caron continued.

"We found a toboggan type ski mask that had blonde hairs in it. The laboratory in Frankfort matched the hairs to those of the defendant. We also found threads under the Atmore girl's fingernails that matched those taken from the ski mask. This evidence is what we used to obtain an arrest warrant for the defendant," said John.

Handing John Talbert a copy of the confession that Olivia had signed, Caron Dell asked him, "Lieutenant, is this your signature as a witness to the defendant's confession of guilt in this case?"

"Yes, it is."

"I have no further questions, your honor," Caron said to Judge Constanza as she returned to her seat.

"Your witness, Mr. Cawood," Constanza said.

Jeff Cawood knew perfectly well that Theo would beat him to the witness stand, so he didn't try to race as Theo strutted to the stand.

"Lieutenant Talbert, who was the suspect that you questioned who gave you sufficient information to lead to the arrest of the defendant?" Shawitz asked.

"I'm not allowed to divulge that information," said John.

"What you are telling me is that you and Gibson were running out of time to find someone to arrest, so you picked the defendant's name out of the phone book and pinned the charge on her, just like you do to a lot of innocent people. Isn't that right, Talbert?" asked Theo as he walked toward the jury.

"No, that is not right," said John. "We had evidence to substantiate her arrest.

"Come on, Talbert, tell us the truth. We all know how you troopers operate," Shawitz said.

"Approach the bench, counselors," boomed Constanza.

"I have had all of this harassment that I will tolerate. You, Shawitz, go back and sit down and let your co-counsel resume the questioning of this witness. If you can't conduct yourself in a decorous manner, then you can leave. Any further actions by you could easily result in your spending the night as a guest of the county," Judge Constanza said.

Turning to the bailiff, the judge told him to stand by to take Theodore Shawitz to jail. Jeff Cawood resumed the questioning.

"Lieutenant, did the defendant have legal counsel present when she made this confession?" he asked, handing John the confession.

"Yes, she did," answered John.

"And who was that counsel?" asked Jeff.

"It was you," John answered.

Theo hit the floor, screaming at the top of his lungs,

"This is the greatest travesty of justice, I have ever seen. This whole legal group is in collusion to railroad this poor woman…"

That was as far as he got. Percy Hatfield had him by the arm and was leading and dragging him out of the courtroom. Sandy and Chris Evans followed them. Bill Minter, who was sitting next to Isabel, stayed.

"I have no more witnesses," Caron Dell told Judge Constanza, who declared a recess for fifteen minutes.

"Lieutenant, you and Trooper Gibson are excused," Caron Dell said to John.

John and Jacob left the courthouse together. John hadn't been back to Pineville for some time and even though he frequently called Thelma, he hadn't seen her.

"Let's go see Thelma and give her a thrill," John told Jacob.

"I saw her last week and she said she would be at the trial, but I haven't seen her. Have you?" he asked John.

"No. That's why I wanted to see her while I was in town," John answered as he got into Jacob's cruiser.

Pulling up in front of Thelma's home, they saw a dark blue four wheel drive pickup truck with a Golden Star decal on the door and a Tennessee state police car parked in the driveway.

"Wonder what's going on?" John asked.

"I don't know," Jacob answered.

As they walked up on the porch, the front door opened and a pretty young woman wearing a Tennessee State Police badge let them in.

"I am Trooper Jennifer McComb of the Tennessee State Police and you are…..?" she quizzed.

"I am Lieutenant John Talbert and this is Trooper Jacob Gibson. We are of the Kentucky State Police," John answered.

Letting them into the living room, Jennifer introduced them to Martin Wallace, Fred Tinsley and Jemjelf Tinsley. Jacob knew Jemjelf and Fred and he shook hands with Fred.

"Mrs. Tinsley, tell these gentlemen what you told me about Curtis Bradley and Mrs. Durham," Martin said.

Jemjelf told John and Jacob about Curtis forcing his way in and making Thelma drive him somewhere, but she didn't know where.

"What is your best bet about where he has gone?" John asked Martin.

"He couldn't have much money, if he has any at all, so that means he would have to rely on her to pay his way. He has a place outside of Trenton where his father lives that would probably be the first place he would go to. He may have money stashed away there, so that is where we are going to look first," said Martin.

"Trooper Gibson and I would like to accompany you. We have a vested interest in Thelma," said John.

"Jemjelf and I would like to go along too, if it is all right. We have a vested interest also," said Fred.

"I believe it would be best if Trooper McComb rode with Trooper Gibson and I rode with you," John said to Martin. "That way we would both have authorization to be in Tennessee."

"Jemjelf and I will take my truck," said Fred.

Martin and John left first, followed by Jacob and Jennifer, and then Fred and Jemjelf.

"I recall seeing a fugitive warrant cross my desk last week advising that Curtis Bradley had escaped and might be coming into Kentucky, but it didn't occur to me that he was the father of Bradley Durham. I doubt that I would have connected him with Thelma anyway," John said.

"He is one more bad character," said Martin as he went on to explain Curtis' past. "I really fear for Mrs. Durham's safety if he has her as Mrs. Tinsley said."

"Thelma is pretty tough herself," answered John, "I wouldn't be too sure of Bradley's safety if she gets the upper hand, which she is sharp enough to do."

Jacob and Jennifer had gone several miles before he spoke.

"Did you go to the Tennessee Police Academy before you became an officer?" he asked her, as he tried to make smalltalk.

"Yes," she said, "all of us have to go there for our training before we start on the road. I graduated from the Eastern Kentucky University School of Law Enforcement before I went to the Academy," she said.

"I took some courses at Eastern while I was going to the Kentucky Academy. I really liked the school. I had a scholarship to play football there when I graduated from high school, but I became a trooper instead. I finished two years at the Southeast Community College in Middlesboro this past spring and have enrolled at the University of Kentucky to get a degree in accounting before I go on to law school. After I finish law school I plan to make application with the FBI," Jacob said.

"I would like to go to law school and work for the FBI," Jennifer said, "but I'm supposed to get married next spring."

"I'm kind of engaged, too," said Jacob, "but I haven't talked to her in about two weeks. I guess she is mad and I don't know if I care."

Here he was telling this perfect stranger all of his inner problems. Why was he doing this, he asked himself. "Do you know where the Bradley place is in Trenton?" he asked her to kind of change the subject.

"Yes," said Jennifer, "we stopped there on the way up. I'll show you where to go in case you lose Martin."

"How long have you been a trooper?" Jacob asked.

"A little over three years," she answered. "Why?"

"I just wondered. You look pretty young to be a detective. I always thought they were bald-headed old men," he said.

"You mean like Martin and your boss?" she asked laughing.

"Who are you engaged to?" Jacob asked.

"He is another trooper. He works out of Franklin, Tennessee and I don't see much of him except on weekends. We went to the Academy at the same time and started dating while we were there. Since we've been apart for a while, I'm not too sure it's what either of us wants to do," she said with a slightly sad tone in her voice.

"Martin is turning down that lane on the right. Is that the way to go?" Jacob asked her.

"Yes," she answered.

As Jacob turned down Bradley Lane, Jennifer unholstered her pistol and checked it. She sat with it in her left hand as they drove toward the barn.The three vehicles stopped in front of the barn. All four officers got out of their vehicles and moved very quietly toward the barn door. Fred and Jemjelf got out of his truck and stayed a little behind the others as all six moved toward the barn.

When Martin and Jennifer searched the place on their way to Kentucky, Harvey had given Martin a spare master key that overrode the audible commands and unlocked all of the doors in the barn. Standing back away from the door, Martin called out in a loud voice, "This is the Tennessee State Police. Open this door."

Getting no response, he cautiously moved to the door and unlocked it. Signaling to the others, he jerked the door open and jumped back.

"That's Thelma's car," Jemjelf said to Fred.

Moving slowly, all six entered the garage and approached the door into the living quarters. Inserting the master key into this lock, Martin unlocked the door, shoved it open and fell to his knees all at the same time. The other three officers acted accordingly. Fred and Jemjelf stayed behind Thelma's car.

Martin looked to his left into the barrel of Harvey's pistol that Thelma was aiming at his head.

"Good evening, Detective Wallace, I have been expecting you," Thelma said in her usually calm voice. "You are running a little late, aren't you?" Wheeling around, she aimed the pistol at Curtis as he started to try to get up,

"One more move and I'll blow your damned head off," she told Curtis.

After handing Curtis' keys and pistol to Martin, Thelma hugged Jemjelf, Jacob and John all at the same time.

"Are you all right?" Jemjelf asked her.

"Yes, honey. I'm sorry I had to tape you up like I did, but I didn't have much choice." Thelma said as she reached out to Fred and hugged him.

Turning to John and Jacob, she asked in a mock hurt voice, "Where are you two when I need you?"

They stumbled over each other trying to alibi why they hadn't checked on her more often.

"That's all right," she said hugging them again, "I love both of you. You have always been there when I needed you."

"You need to check the status of that man in the bathroom. I hit him in the head with the commode water box cover and I may have hit him too hard. If I did, I am sorry, but it was me or him." Thelma said to Martin.

Jennifer opened the bathroom door. Harvey had his eyes open and seemed to be rational as he asked what happened to him. After unlocking the handcuffs, Jennifer told him to get up, which he did. He was still pretty wobbly when he stood up, but he managed to walk out of the bathroom.

"Hi, Curtis, it's your old pal Harvey. Ain't you glad to see me? I'm glad to see you. You'll be going back to do the big house now, won't you. I saw you and that woman drive down here and I come down here to tell you that the old man died last week. I had him cremated since you weren't nowhere's around. I took his ashes to the lake and spread them out on it. I guess the fish eat them. He had it coming, he's eat enough of them. He wrote up his will here a while back and left this farm and all he had to me. You didn't get one penny of it. Ain't that funny? You ain't never gonna get outta jail. I'll be the richest farmer in this county and you'll be the poorest prisoner in the pen." Harvey said to Curtis as Jennifer led him out of the barn.

"We really don't have any cause to keep him, Jennifer, so he can go back to his big farm. Looks like Curtis paid for all the grief he caused some people," Martin said. "Thank you, Lieutenant. We appreciated your help."

There was a round-robin of hand shaking. John asked Thelma if she didn't want one of them to drive her home.

"Certainly not. I got down here by myself and I can get home by myself. I wouldn't care if you came by to see me and told me about the trial," she said, with a twinkle in her eye.

John looked around for Jacob, but he couldn't find him. Martin said he saw Jacob following Jennifer out to the Tennessee cruiser with Curtis in tow. Looking out the barn door, he saw Jacob standing beside the cruiser talking to Jennifer.

"If you aren't sure you are engaged and I'm not sure that I am, maybe I could come to Knoxville some evening and take you to dinner," he said.

"I think I would enjoy that," she answered handing him her calling card with her home phone number written on the back.

CHAPTER 12

Scott Senters arrived at the PSK corporate offices at exactly 9:30 AM on the morning of his scheduled interview. Punctuality had become a virtue with him ever since the morning he overslept and the mantrip went in the mine without him. The three-mile walk in 50-inch coal to get to the work place plus the loss of pay for the time he was absent had definitely made a believer of him. He was never late again.

On this day he was dressed in what he considered a casual manner, wearing a brown tweed sport coat and dress khaki pants, with the traditional blue oxford cloth button down collar shirt and a red tie. He had seated himself in a leather-upholstered chair next to the receptionist's desk. This was somewhat distracting to her, but she managed to keep her mind on her business since she was married. She had buzzed Whitley and told her Scott was here when he came in. Whitley let him cool his heels for about fifteen minutes before going out and introducing herself.

"I am Whitley Rogers and I believe we talked on the phone yesterday," she said.

"I am very glad to meet you, Ms. Rogers," he answered. "I am Scott Senters and here is my resume."

Taking the resume in her hand, she beckoned to him to follow her as she went back to her office. "I see where you worked in the Western Kentucky coal fields," she said.

"Yes, I worked there four years to make enough to go to school. My home is in Sturgis which is in the heart of the coal country. I have also served in the National Guard for the past six years," he said.

Whitley picked up on Scott's non-use of the word "ma'am". This could mean that he was putting her on the same age level as himself or he could be resentful of a woman boss. Time would tell.

"I worked there for a few years before I came to PSK. I especially liked the engineering part of coal mining. The projections, the estimates, the plans and all of the other mathematical problems, but I was closed in as far as advancement went, so I left. " she said.

"I enjoy the engineering part of it also. To me that is the meat and potatoes of coal mining," Scott answered as he seated himself in a chair in front of her desk.

Scanning his resume, Whitley asked him some questions about his grades, how he spent his time after work, whether he was married or engaged and most important of all, his ambitions.

"I like mining engineering and I want to get my masters. After that I want to find a job that has good benefits, a bright future, an open path for advancement and meritorious pay incentives. Am I shooting too high?" he asked.

"I don't think so," Whitley responded. "If you don't have ambition, you don't have much to live for."

The small talk continued for at least forty-five minutes. Scott was very concise in his answers and as respectful as an employee should be when talking to his supervisor. Finally Whitley told him that Mr. Colbert wanted to talk to him, as she buzzed Jack's office. "Mr. Colbert, I have Scott Senters in my office anytime you want to talk to him," she said.

"That's fine, Whitley. Give me about five minutes to clear my desk and send him to me," Jack said.

Whitley followed his orders and sent Scott to see the president of PSK. She would have given her eyeteeth to hear the conversation, but she settled for waiting for a better time. She hoped to make this young man loyal to her. She returned to her office and about fifteen minutes later, Scott tapped on her door. Before she could answer it her intercom buzzed. It was Colbert.

"I believe you have found a good replacement for Bradley. Let's put him on the payroll, if you agree," he said.

This dumbfounded her. She had thought that he would at least want to discuss Scott's qualifications before hiring him, but once again he left her confused. Going to the door, she found Scott waiting in a chair."Come in, Scott. When can you start work?" she asked.

"Whenever you want me to," he responded.

"Day after tomorrow is the first of the month so why don't we make it then and that would put everything on an even starting date," she said.

"That's fine with me, Ms. Rogers," he answered.

"I will be your supervisor, Scott, but I prefer that you call me Whitley. Ms. Rogers sounds too old."

"It would take more than that to make you old, Whitley," Scott said.

The receptionist, who was overhearing all of this since the door to Whitley's office had been left open, almost swallowed her chewing gum, thinking to herself, "Oh boy, is this ever going to be interesting."

Whitley went home and followed her usual procedure of taking a shower, putting on her sweats and relaxing before fixing something for supper. She had just sat down when her door buzzer sounded. "Who could that be? I'm not expecting anyone," she thought as she answered the intercom. "Yes?" she said.

"Whitley, this is Scott Senters. Could I see you for a minutes?" he asked.

"Why certainly," she answered.Releasing the door latch, she waited with the door open for him to get off the elevator.

"What is the problem, Scott?" she asked after pouring both of them a soft drink.

"I couldn't talk to you at the office, but I felt that I needed to tell you about my conversation with Mr. Colbert," Scott said.

"Go right ahead. I promise you that it will go no further," Whitley answered.

"Well, I don't know exactly how to ask this except to come right out and ask. Is he gay?"

Whitley almost choked on her Coke.

"Why do you ask?" she queried.

"Well, I'm not and if that is part of the job then I will look some where else. I've been in the National Guard and I have been around a little bit and I can recognize the approach." Scott said. "I really don't like it. I also don't like being told to report on my supervisor's comings and goings. If that is the kind of job I'm being hired for then I would like to withdraw my application."

"In answer to your question, he reportedly is gay. Being a woman, I've never experienced the 'approach' as you call it. Spying on me is not part of your job, but you will have to tell him something. My advice is play it cool and fend him off as best you can," Whitley said. "I do appreciate your loyalty, although you haven't even started the job. Thank you for coming to see me. I promise you it will not go unrewarded."

Letting Scott out, she shut the door and leaned up against it. She couldn't believe what he had told her. What about that lecher Colbert hitting on a new employee on top of asking him to spy on her? She made up her mind. It was time for her to go to greener pastures.

As soon as Scott got back to his apartment, he called Jack Colbert.

"She took the bait, hook, line and sinker," Scott said.

"Good boy, Scott. I can see that you are going places in this company," said Colbert.

As he hung up the phone, Scott said to himself, "If I can play that fag against her then I ought to have her job in about six months, but I've got to keep him at an arm's length. Ticking him off could mess up the whole deal."

Scott's first week was spent going over coal analysis from Golden Star and Big Sky, a coal company in Wyoming. Whitley had him match up the sulfur, ash and moisture contents against the provisions of the contract for the plant where the coal was to be burned. She watched him and came to the conclusion that he pretty well knew what he was doing.

She had just gotten home and taken her shower when her phone rang. "Hello," she said, "Whitley Rogers here."

"Ms. Rogers, my name is Timothy Patterson and I am employed by Daniel Winston, Management Consultants. We look for personnel for various companies. We got you name several years ago and started to call you, but then the employer got in touch with us to tell us that the job was no longer open," said Patterson.

"How did you get my name?" she asked.

"The founder of our company, Mr. Daniel Winston, had a World War II friend named Ed Durham. Over the years, they had kept in contact with each other and a few years back, we got a client who was looking for a coal buyer. Mr. Winston called Mr. Durham and after they went through Normandy together again, on the phone, he told Mr. Durham what he was looking for. Mr. Durham highly recommended you. We ran an investigative report on you and found that you are pretty much what our client is looking for. If you are interested in interviewing with us, we will talk further. If not then I apologize for having bothered you," concluded Patterson.

"Give me a number where I can call you back in a few minutes. I have just stepped out of the shower," said Whitley. Writing the number down, she matched it against her caller ID, waited about five minutes and then dialed it.

"Daniel Winston, Management Consultants," said a feminine voice.

"May I speak to Timothy Patterson, please," said Whitley in her nice voice that she used with receptionists.

"Timothy Patterson speaking," answered the voice on the phone.

"Mr. Patterson, Whitley Rogers here. Can we resume our conversation?" she asked.

"As I told you, we have a client who is looking for a coal buyer. At this time the client does not want their name revealed. When we interview you, we would divulge to you the client's name. Our offices are in Pittsburgh. We would like to talk to you in the near future, if possible. Actually, the sooner, the better. Are you still interested?" Patterson asked.

"I could leave Lexington tomorrow morning and be in your offices by mid-afternoon if that would be agreeable with you," Whitley said.

"That would be excellent, Ms. Rogers. We will make reservations for you at the Pittsburgh Marriot, which is located at the airport. A shuttle will take you from the airport to the hotel and from there you can catch a cab to our offices. If this all meets with your approval then we will see you around 3:00PM tomorrow. Until then, au revoir," said Timothy.

As soon as she hung up, Whitley called the airport and made reservations for a nine o'clock flight out of Lexington to Pittsburgh. She then packed her clothes for at least a two-day stay. Whitley had her good points, one of which was being a classy dresser. She chose a navy blue pantsuit, a light tan pants suit and a cocktail dress just in case. Naturally she packed shoes, blouses and other items that went to make a nice-looking outfit look nice.

She got up at six the next morning, took a shower, dressed and fixed her hair and got ready to leave. Whitley called the office as soon as she thought Scott was in and told him she had to go out of town for a couple of days on personal business. She also asked him to tell Colbert, who never came in before 9:00 AM.

The flight to Pittsburgh was uneventful. After going through baggage check, she got her bags, found the shuttle and went to the Pittsburgh Marriot. After checking in, she went to the coffee shop and got a sandwich. Before eating she bought a *Wall Street Journal* and checked on PSK stock. It was staying pretty level at 24 so she read other items, one of which was an ad for Daniel Winston, Management Consultants. It was a rather exclusive ad that seemed to say something to the effect that they only interviewed prime people. That made her feel good.

Having finished her sandwich, she returned to the room, brushed her teeth, put on some lipstick and went back to the lobby. Looking at her watch, she saw that it was 2:15 PM, so she went out and hailed a cab which she had take her to the offices of Daniel Winston. After checking the directory in the lobby of the office building, she went to the fourth floor to the Daniel Winston offices. Going to the receptionist's desk she announced herself. The receptionist responded by buzzing Timothy Patterson, who emerged from one of the offices situated around the receiving area.

"Ms. Rogers?" he asked. "I'm Timothy Patterson. How very nice to meet you. Please come into my office where we can talk."

Patterson led the way into his office where he offered Whitley a chair. The interview consisted of the general run-of-the-mill questions: Was she married or engaged? Did she live alone? What was her base salary? Did she receive bonuses at the end of the year, and if so, in what amount? Then came a group of questions that she was not familiar with. Did she speak any foreign languages? She said that she had two years of German in high school and two years in college; however, she did not speak it fluently. She understood it fairly well. Next. Did she have any problem about living overseas? To that she responded no, that she would like very much to live outside the United States for a while.

The interview had lasted two hours but Whitley was still fresh as a daisy. As she was preparing to leave, Timothy Patterson asked her if she had any plans for the evening. "I don't know anyone in Pittsburgh so I planned to eat dinner and read a book," she answered.

"Would you have dinner with my wife and me? The dining room at the Marriot has an excellent menu for dinner. Their chef is from France and does wonders with lamb," he said.

"I would like that very much," Whitley said.

"Would six o'clock be a suitable time?" Timothy asked.

"Yes," answered Whitley. "I will see you then.

Returning to the motel, Whitley showered, donned her cocktail dress and fixed her hair. She had just finished her hair and added a trace of cologne when her phone rang. Answering it, she found that the Pattersons were in the lobby.

Timothy met her as she came into the lobby and introduced her to his wife, Casey, and a man standing with them.

CHAPTER 13

G T drove to Frankfort and picked up Rebecca at her apartment. She was wearing a very nice looking maroon pantsuit with matching shoes. She had bought both items just for this occasion.

"You're not going to look at those ponds in that outfit, are you?" G T asked.

"Of course not," she snapped. "I have blue jeans and boots in my rucksack. I didn't want your mother to think I didn't know how to dress like a lady, even though you don't think that I am one."

"Get off it, Rebecca," G T said. "I was just kidding. You sure are touchy."

"I'm uneasy about going to your house and meeting your mother and daddy. I've never been to stay at a boy's house before and I don't want your mother to think I am some kind of a tramp that you picked up on the side of the road," she answered with her voice quivering.

"That's not saying much for me that you think I would pick up just anyone and take them home with me. I respect my mother more than that," G T answered.

"Look, if we are going to argue all the way there, then let's call it off and fight the pond problem out in court. You can take me back to my apartment," she said.

"I'll back off if you will," G T said holding out his hand to shake. Taking his hand in hers she gave him a hearty handshake.

"Let's be friends, G T," she said.

"I would like for it to be that way," he said. "Tell me about yourself, so I'll know if there are any subjects I should avoid."

"Well, let's see. I was born in Beckley, West Virginia. My father was a blaster on a strip job. He put off a timed shot that had a shorted hole in it and it ignited before it was supposed to. He got hit in the back with a piece of fly rock and it partially paralyzed him. He was on compensation for a while and finally the company cut him off. They said that he didn't set the delays correctly on the shot and that it was his fault. The drill operator sided with my dad at first and then changed his story and said that Dad stood too close to the shot. Dad had been putting off timed shots for years and he knew better than to stand too close, but the company lawyers made him out a liar and he lost the case. His back hurts him something terrible when it rains. I guess that it's arthritis. My mother had never done anything but keep house, so when Dad got hurt it fell to me to find a job and support them as best I could, since I am the only child. I got a job after school working in a fast food place that paid the minimum wage. I was fourteen and in the eighth grade, but I had matured fast and even though I was too young, I looked older, so I lied about my age. I had a fake driver's license and that's what I used as an I D.

"There was a boy in my room at school that I kind of liked and he would come to the hamburger stand about quitting time and walk me home. I appreciated it until he got to thinking that I owed him something for doing that and we broke up. Not too many boys were interested in hanging around until 11:00 just to walk a girl two miles up a dirt road, so I gave up on romance. It was a little tough at first to see the other girls in my class get voted cheerleader or homecoming queen candidate, but I got used to that too. I had always been somewhat of a loner so being outside the cliques in school didn't really bother me. Dad got a small social security check and we managed to make it. He owned our home and even out of that pittance of a check he saved some money to give me to go to school."

"Where did you go to high school?" asked G T

"I went to a big high school in Beckley. I did pretty well and graduated in the top ten percent of my class. I wanted to be a home economics teacher, but so did everyone else. I was going to have to get help to go to college, while girls whose mothers were home ec teachers somehow got preferential treatment and took all of those scholarships. The only thing I could find was a scholarship from a conservationist group that offered a full four-year, all-expenses-paid ride for studying environmental engineering, provided I would be an environmental activist and oppose surface mining once I graduated and went to work. I signed a pledge to fight surface mining, not paying any attention to the fact that they would dictate to me after I graduated. Dad also signed off on it and I don't think he read it too close. Anyway I have always loved the outdoors so I took them up on it. I went to a small college here in Kentucky and got my first two years there. It is a very good school and I liked it. I then transferred to the University of Kentucky to get my engineering degree because they have a top notch environmental engineering program.

"After I got my degree here at UK, the Group, as it was called, got me a job with the EPA. Here again they told me that I was to fight hard against surface mining and do whatever was legal or illegal to force the issue. There was that horrible impoundment failure the year after I graduated and the Governor of Kentucky signed an agreement with EPA to give them full authority over the design of impoundments, silt ponds and ditches. Someone in the Group got me assigned to the Department of Natural Resources as a permit reviewer. I liked the work, but I began to get pressure to turn down surface mining permits and fabricate reasons if necessary. They were the ones who pushed the 15-year and 30-year pond requirements on your permit. That is pretty much the story of the trials and tribulations of Rebecca Holton," she concluded.

All the time she had been talking, G T noticed that she looked straight ahead. Even though she was talking to him she seemed to be in a trance. When she started talking about her teen-age job, she got tears in her eyes. "If you don't agree with the things this Group is telling you to do, why don't you just tell them to stuff it?" he asked.

"That paper my dad and I signed had a clause in it that said they could take my family's house if I didn't do what they told me to do," she answered.

"I don't have my law degree yet, but I can tell you for sure that they can't force you to do something illegal." he said, "Besides, how do they know whether or not you turn down a permit?

"There is someone in the permit section who is a member of the Group and they see if I have turned one down," she went on.

"Who is it?" he asked.

"I don't know," she continued. "It is a secret and I am not in on it."

"Are you telling me that you turned my permit down because you were afraid that someone in Natural Resources would blow the whistle on you to the Group and you would lose your job, along with your mom and dad losing their home?" he asked.

"That's pretty much it," she answered. "They don't want the White Pines property mined. Don't ask me why because I don't know. Please don't tell anyone what I have told you. I shouldn't have done that. My mom and dad don't know any of this."

"Can't I even ask Barry some questions about who might be the person that is a member of the Group?" he asked.

"No, please don't, G T. I know Barry is your friend, but he might also be a member of the Group," she begged.

"I know Phil Banks and Barry, but I don't know any of the other people in your section. Who are they?" asked G T.

"Well, there is Jerry Hoag who is Phil's boss, and of course there is Edwin Lee who is the Assistant Commissioner, and then there is Commissioner Adam Lawson," Rebecca answered, "They are all pretty nice people except Edwin Lee."

She then gave G T a quick run-down on the three men. Jerry Hoag was an older man who had been a Natural Resources Inspector. He had been a field supervisor, but had been moved into the Office of Permits at his request. He had taken a pay cut to move. His thinning hair had been brown before it began to turn gray. His ruddy complexion came from many years in the field, and with his steel blue eyes made one think he had been a nice-looking man in his younger days. He was a medium 5'10", 150-pound chainsmoker. He spent a lot of time on the telephone answering questions about permits. Edwin Lee was the "office snitch." Everything that he heard went straight to the Commissioner. He was a weasely looking little man that wore gold rim glasses and suspenders. He had the very disgusting habit of picking his nose in public. He had come from the Division of Water and knew nothing about mining. Rebecca didn't care for him and showed it, which was not to her advantage. He returned the dislike. Adam Lawson, Commissioner of Natural Resources, was a political appointee. Governor Martin had put him in as a favor to the party chairman. He didn't need the job having retired from the United States Army Quartermaster Corps as a Lieutenant Colonel. Unfortunately Lawson tried to run Natural Resources like it was an army unit.

Rebecca's presence didn't set too well with the upper echelon of Natural Resources, but there was very little they could do about it since she was there as the result of an agreement between a former governor and EPA, and Albert Martin, the incumbent governor wasn't going to change it.

"Do you suspect any of those people you have named as being the one spying on you?" G T asked.

"Like I said, G T, I have no idea who it is that is telling on me," she said, "and please don't make any waves, cause it would just make it hard on me and my family."

The conversation ended with them pulling into the driveway of G T's home. Gerry came out to meet Rebecca, whom she hugged and welcomed to their home. G T also got a hug after he got their bags out of the back of his truck. Gerry and Rebecca left G T to carry the bags in the house and upstairs to the spare bedroom where Rebecca was to stay.

Since it was afternoon when they left Lexington, they were both hungry. George had come in from work and had cleaned up and was ready to eat supper. G T introduced him to Rebecca as they sat down at the table. Gerry had fixed one of G T's favorite suppers of pork roast with gravy, mashed potatoes, greens and a vegetable salad. She had baked a huckleberry pie for dessert. There was a lot of smalltalk while they ate, but it was steered away from the subject of surface mining. G T had told Gerry that it was a sore subject with Rebecca and that was why they were home in the first place. She had cautioned George and he did what she told him.

Early the next morning, after eating a hearty breakfast, G T and Rebecca set out to review the location of the sediment ponds for the White Pines Mining Company. Gerry fixed them four bologna sandwiches and put them in a cooler along with four soft drinks.

"I haven't done this since George was working third shift at Golden Star. I'm glad I don't have to do it every day," Gerry said.

"That's an awful lot of trouble for you to go to, Mrs. Deane," Rebecca said.

"Nonsense, child, it brings back some real nice memories. Besides, that my name is Gerry," she answered.

"After eating that big breakfast, I probably won't be hungry on up in the day," said Rebecca as she tried to make smalltalk with Gerry.

G T had come into the kitchen and was putting on his boots while the conversation was taking place. He picked up the cooler with the lunch in it and went out to put it in the truck. Coming back in the house, he got George's .22 pistol out of a drawer and strapped the holster on his belt.

"Getting snakebit once in a lifetime is enough for me," he told Gerry and Rebecca.

"You be careful with that, G T," Gerry said.

"I don't know what time we will be back, Mama. There are ten ponds that Rebecca wants to see and that will take a while," G T said.

Driving out of Holly Tree Hollow, G T turned right and went on up Straight Creek to Red Oak Hollow. Turning up the gravel road that led up the valley, he began explaining the geographic lay out to Rebecca.

"Red Oak is a long Y valley that splits about two miles up. The hollow to the left is called Red Oak Left and the hollow to the right is called Red Oak Right. Red Oak Right butts up against White Mountain and has a common property line with Golden Star. The stream that runs out of the hollow is called Right Branch. I guess the people who named the creek thought Red Oak Right Creek was too much of a mouth full to say. The area that was to be mined was cleared of the merchantable timber before any mining was done. There were some beautiful hemlock and oak on the property and, you won't believe this, but they took seeds from the healthiest trees and had a forestry man put them in a nursery. They did this at least four years before they started logging. After the logging and mining were completed they used the seedlings to reclaim. They left a twenty-foot berm all the way around the mining area in such a way that you couldn't see the mining operation in process. I am going to brag now and tell you that they got the idea of mining this way from Dad and Frank. There are some real responsible people in the mining business.

"The mountain top to be stripped is the ridge between Red Oak Right and Left. It is a good-sized piece of property. The White Pines people plan to strip the Haggard 12, 11, 10, 9 and 8. There are five ponds on either side of the ridge. We will go up the right side first. The other side of the hollow in both cases has been mountaintopped and the upper seams have been contour mined. You will notice as we go up the hollow that there are ponds at the base of the slope in the drains that come down from the top," G T said. "I designed those ponds and used the 10 year, 25year criteria.

"That doesn't look to me like it has been contour mined," said Rebecca.

"White Pines does a good job of reclamation. They have received first place plaques from the Governor's Reclamation Committee," said G T as he pulled to the side of the road and parked. "The last pond in this hollow is just a little way up the road, but the road narrows down to a path just around that bend."

They got out of the truck and walked up the path to the location of the last pond. A mother elk and her calf were standing in the pond. When she saw G T and Rebecca, she gave them a dirty look and turned and walked up the mountain into the woods with the calf following her.

"White Pines plants a lot of autumn olive bushes and other plants that animals eat," G T continued. "They do this to give food to the deer and elk. The elk are pretty new in this area. There have also been some black bears reported in the area, but I never have seen any. The Fish and Wildlife people brought some elk in from Wyoming and turned them loose two years ago on White Pines and Golden Star. The coal companies sowed the flats left by the mountain top removal in orchard grass and fescue. They stock it with cattle that they take to market every year. The proceeds go to a foundation that the two companies have put together. The foundation takes applications from groups like the Boy and Girl Scouts, Salvation Army, Red Cross and others and gives the money out that way. It does a lot of good. At the same time they have been negotiating with a company that makes computer elements to build a plant on one of the flats. Mama and Sarah are Golden Star's members of the foundation and the wives of the president and vice-president represent White Pines. The president's name is Jason Strick and his wife's name is Margaret. Her maiden name was Perkins.

"Jason is a very domineering and quarrelsome man. His wife has left him on three separate occasions. They don't have any children and I've heard that she said that she would divorce him except that she was afraid of him. He is local and grew up on the Right Fork of Straight Creek. He got to be president of White Pines by brown-nosing and cheating. He is not a likable person, but his wife, who is from Harrodsburg is a real nice person. In all honesty, he doesn't deserve her. The vice-president is Bryan Fuson and his wife is a girl that Isabel and I went to school with, named Avaline McGill. Bryan is a mild-mannered sort of fellow who does as little as possible to get by. He lets Jason push him around and does whatever Jason tells him to do. He is not a local person. In fact I don't know where he came from. He married Avaline after he came to Pineville. She is a real pleasant girl who always has a smile on her face. I've heard that the company sent him in here to keep check on Jason, but that is wasted time. He is not the coal operator type to me nor is he the type to ride shotgun on the likes of Jason. The only thing he and Jason have in common is the fact that they are both claustrophobic and will not go underground no matter what. They have never developed any deep mines and that is the reason.

"A conglomerate corporation out of Boston owns the company. They seem to pretty much leave Jason and Bryan to run the company as they see fit. A couple of years ago they bought all of the property in fee simple from the Aser Land Company on Jason's recommendation and since that time their reclamation has fallen off. All of their coal goes overseas. They sell exclusively to an international power supplier in Germany named Electrique Internationale. The plant that the coal goes to is in China."

Rebecca looked at the site of the last pond and agreed with G T that the slope was too steep to support a 15-year, 30-year pond. She even made a comment to the effect that it would be hard to get a 10-year pond in the proposed location.

"Isabel and I built some ponds on slopes this steep and they have held for at least seven years," G T said, "but I am afraid that a 15-year pond would blow out in a real heavy down pour."

After viewing the right fork of Red Oak Hollow, they got back in the truck and drove around to the left hollow.

"There isn't a road up Left Branch so we will have to walk," said G T. "White Pines had a rough road in here when they mined the section on the left that these ponds protect, but they let it grow up after they finished. There is a path up the side of the branch that we want to look at, so we will go up it. They try to leave everything pretty much as it was when they began."

They started up Left Branch with G T in the lead. He had cut a couple of sassafras saplings and trimmed them down to make walking sticks which were handy to keep back the bushes and weeds. Just to be extra cautious, he loosened the holster on George's .22 in case he ran into a snake. As he walked up the path that ran along the side of Left Branch, Rebecca followed close behind. The creek banks were lined with rhododendron, laurel and ferns. It was a picture book setting. Small minnows darted around in the little pools of the creek and tiny blue flowers stuck their heads out of the beds of moss that housed them. The smaller dogwood, sassafras, pawpaw and redbud were along the path, but back from the creek a little. The larger trees such as the hemlock and oak had been there for quite a while as they formed a canopy over the smaller trees and shrubs. It was a pristine scene.

"This is the site of the first pond," G T said as he stopped in a little draw. "There isn't any water in the drain, but it has had some as you can see by the bent down weeds. It's as steep as a cow's face and it would be tough to get a 10-year pond in here, much less a 15-year."

"Let's stop this charade, G T," Rebecca said. "You and I both know that you can't get a 15-year pond in this place, but what am I going to do? If I don't find some reason to deny the permit then both my family and I will suffer. I can't quit and walk away or I would still be in trouble. Now you tell me what to do."

She sat down on a nearby fallen hemlock and began to sniffle. It wasn't a put-on exhibition to garner sympathy from G T, but a true combination of fear and sorrow. Sitting down beside her, G T put his arm around her. That was all it took. She opened up and began to cry her heart out. She wasn't the caustic, brassy, overbearing hussy he had first pictured her to be. Instead she was a scared little girl who all of a sudden realized that she was in a corner and didn't know what to do about it. The rock-hard veneer that she had coated her personality with had disappeared.

"G T," she said, "I have a confession to make. I conned you into bringing me home with you to make Isabel jealous. It has backfired on me. I have never had a boy be nice to me like you have been. You haven't made a pass or tried anything and I am most sorry for having caused you and Isabel any trouble. Please forgive me."

After wiping her eyes, she put the tissue in her pocket, turned around and kissed G T. It caught him completely off balance, but he reacted accordingly.

Later she said, "Now tell me how to get out of this bind that I am in."

++++++

The ringing of the phone irritated Jason Strick who was reading the *Wall Street Journal*. After answering the call with a gruff, "Yes," the voice on the other end started in without an introduction.

"We've got problems with that permit. I thought that Holton girl had turned it down, but now I find out she and that G T Deane have gone to look at the ponds in the field and that might mean she will approve them," said the caller.

"We don't have a problem, you have a problem. Now hear me loud and clear. I do not want that permit approved for at least a year. By that time, White Pines will have lost their contract with Electrique Internationale and I can get what I want," said Strick.

"I don't know how to keep it from being approved. Deane does a good job of putting the package together and the only way to stop him is to raise the pond standards. She did that and then he sweet-talked her into going to look at them. You know what that could lead to," said the caller.

"I don't give a damn if they go up in the woods and play games," said Jason, who was getting angry, "but I don't want that permit approved. You do whatever you have to do to get her out of the way, but do not let that permit get approved. I repeat, do not let that permit get approved. I pay that damned Group of tree huggers that you are so wrapped up in enough to make it worth their while to see to it that I get what I want. If the Holton girl has an accident then that's too bad. Do you understand me?"

"I don't want to be a part of nothing like that. You get you somebody else to do that sort of thing. I'll slow up a permit, but I won't kill nobody," the caller said.

"You will do what I tell you to do. Now you call the home office of your outfit and tell them what the problem is. They will take care of it for you. Don't call me anymore at this number," Strick said as he slammed down the receiver.

The White Pines property had a good boundary of coal on it, somewhere in the neighborhood of twenty million tons of proven reserves in both surface and deep mines, but the only interest Jason Strick had was in an ancient mine opening that was at the head of Left Branch. According to an old map he had, there was a Civil War treasure hidden in the cave. The cave was actually a "dog hole" in the Haggard #4 coal seam which was only 38 inches high at this point. Randy had told G T one time that he had worked in the #4 when he first started mining and it was about 32 inches high further back, but as it got closer to the outcrop, it thickened. It was a very high BTU coal that was heavily mined in the 1920s and '30s. The stream that ran down beside the path had its beginning in the opening. When G T scouted the area in preparation of the permit, he had found arrowheads and other artifacts that indicated there had been activity in the area in centuries past. There was nothing to cause him to think that there may have been a village or burial ground in the immediate area where he had proposed to put a large valley fill, so he didn't report his findings.

++++++

Jason's great-great-grandfather, Burl Strick, had been a member of a guerrilla band known as the Tri-Staters that had raided throughout Western Virginia, Kentucky and Tennessee during the Civil War. Most of their attacks had been against banks and payroll carriers. It made no difference to them which side the money belonged to or where it was going. Both the Union and the Confederacy had rewards offered for the capture "dead or alive" of the members of the Tri-Staters. The Tri-Staters, however, avoided capture in a novel way. Half of them wore complete Union uniforms, while the other half wore Confederate uniforms. If they raided a place sympathetic to the Confederacy, the group dressed as Union troops would do the killing and looting. If they raided a Union bank, the "Rebel" group would perform. After a very lucrative raid on a Confederate bank in east Tennessee, the "Union" group had headed back toward Kentucky. Unknown to them, their Confederate counterparts had been apprehended by a troop of real Union soldiers. Most of those Tri-Staters were captured and executed on the spot. However, when Burl and his brother Samuel, together with Cyrus Hoag and his brother Ezekiel, met up with the same regiment of Union soldiers, they were handily mistaken as Union troops on a different mission. In other words, they had escaped with all of the loot. Their plan was to hide the wealth in the vicinity of Pineville and escape into Mexico. Each of them had two saddlebags of silver coins together with a pack mule that carried four more saddlebags of the same. This made a sizable treasure of twenty-four saddlebags of silver coins. After the war, they planned to come back and retrieve their loot, returning to Mexico to live in luxury. They figured that the silver had a value even if it was Confederate money.

They were on their way to Pineville where they planned to follow the Cumberland River to its juncture with the Mississippi after they hid the treasure. From there they were to board a steamboat and travel to New Orleans and eventually cross Texas into Mexico. They were coming down the Right Fork of Straight Creek when the lead man spotted Union soldiers encamped on Breastworks Hill near the confluence of Straight Creek and the Cumberland River at Pineville, known at the time as Cumberland Ford. They had retreated up the Left Fork of Straight Creek to Red Oak Creek and went up it, turning up Left Branch. They supposedly hid their moneybags in the old mine opening at the head of Left Branch. In a double-cross, Burl and Samuel Strick killed, or thought they killed, Cyrus and Ezekiel Hoag. Then Burl killed his brother. He drew a map of the location of the treasure and hid it in his boot. As he came out of Straight Creek, he was captured by a troop of Union soldiers who hung him and didn't even bother to bury him. The blue uniform didn't fool them that time.

Cyrus Hoag turned out to be as sly as Burt Strick. During the ride up Left Branch he had filched three coins out of the moneybags that carried the loot. He put these in a tobacco pouch that he carried in his shirt pocket. When Burl shot Cyrus, the slug hit the coins in the pouch and didn't even break the skin; however, the force of the bullet knocked Cyrus down where he played dead. Burl had been so busy murdering his brother that he didn't realize that he hadn't killed Cyrus. Getting on his horse, Burl scared the other horses and pack mules out of the hollow. They had cleared the mouth of the hollow when the Union cavalry caught him. Cyrus played dead until dark, when he finally got up. He dragged Samuel's and Ezekiel's bodies into the narrow mine opening and put both of them across the moneybags as though to guard it. He then very carefully rigged a deadfall of rocks near the entrance in such a way as to cause a roof fall if it were disturbed. Next he drew a map of the area. He had a faint idea where he was since he had been raised in the eastern part of Tennessee, but he was confused about where Red Oak Creek was. He mistakenly mapped the hollow above it, Dog Star Hollow, that was also a long Y hollow like Red Oak. He stayed in the woods as he went down the creek to where he saw the body of Burl Strick hanging from a tree limb. "Serves ya right, ya murdering sonuva bitch," he muttered as he crept further down the hollow. Little by little he made his way through Cumberland Gap into Tennessee and down the Powell River to his home in Crasset, Tennessee. Cyrus Hoag waited fifteen years after the end of the Civil War to come back to Straight Creek and look for the treasure. He followed his map and his memory, but to no avail. He had mistakenly mapped Dog Star Hollow, which was the hollow above Red Oak.

The Shawnee Indians had used Dog Star as a place to make arrow heads just as they had used Red Oak. They had dug some coal out of the Haggard #4 in the head of the left fork of Dog Star and had left a small opening. For someone who hadn't been there for fifteen years, Cyrus thought he was in the right place. He had crawled back in the opening for about six feet, but found nothing. He should have missed the skeletons of Samuel and Ezekiel, but time and rotgut whiskey had taken their toll. Cyrus finally gave up and went home, but he told his grandson Jefferson Hoag about it and swore to him that the treasure was there, even though he couldn't find it. Jefferson Hoag told his son Abraham about it and the legend was passed down from father to son, although none of them had been able to find it.

Jason Strick's great-grandfather, Burl Strick's son, died in 1957 at the ripe age of 99. As a small boy living at the Forks of Straight Creek, he had watched the Union troops hang his father and had no regrets about it. Muttering to himself after the troops left, "That's the last time he'll tie me to a tree and whip me." He stole the boots, the map in them and a wallet that was in the other boot. He hid the map in a family bible and forgot about it. Years later he found it, but didn't pay any attention to it. He gave it to Jason, who as a child treasured it and vowed to someday find the treasure. He kept the map hidden and in later years explored the area. Although he found the small mine opening, he wouldn't go in it as he had a fear of caves and underground mines. He shone a light in, but didn't see anything except bats hanging from the roof of the mine. He overlooked a coin that was lying in the creek.

Jason Strick was in a bind. Although he was afraid to try to get the silver out, he couldn't trust anyone to go in the mine and get it for him. He was also afraid of getting caught and the Boston Company laying claim to the treasure, which was rightfully theirs. His only chance to get the treasure was to own the property. Once he owned it, he could open up the mine and claim the silver. He was wealthy enough and devious enough to be able to buy it from White Pines if they had to sell it. He could then retrieve the treasure and sell the property to Golden Star, which could mine the substantial coal reserves. Jason didn't need the silver for its monetary value, since he was wealthy enough as it was, but finding it had been an obsession with him since he was a small child.

Most of all, he was afraid that if he didn't stop the permit, White Pines would force him to put a valley fill-in over the cave and it would be lost to him forever. He was not about to let Rebecca Holton or anyone else stand in his way. He had done all he could to keep from developing the property on Left Branch, but the people in Boston insisted on it being done. He had retained Banner Engineering to do the permit, but he had made arrangements to get the permit turned down—or so he thought.

++++++

G T and Rebecca walked on up the path to the head of the hollow where Left Branch came out of the mountain.

"If you approve the permit, then you may be able to see who is trying to keep you from doing it. Once you know who it is then we can blow the whistle on them. I'll help you every way I can and I'm not doing this just to get the permit approved," he said, as he walked on toward the mine opening. When I scouted this area for the permit, I found some arrow heads. There were no other signs of Indians having inhabited this area, so I didn't note it on the permit," G T said.

"Isn't this a strange looking place?" Rebecca asked. "It makes you wonder what went on here."

"I would say that the Indians made arrow heads here," said G T, "That creek bottom is real hard and from the way it is shelved, I figure they must have chipped off pieces of it. They had the coal to build a fire, and cold water to drip on the rock after they heated it to make it chip off."

"What is that shiny thing there in the creek?" she asked.

"Probably a piece of aluminum foil or a chewing gum wrapper," G T said, not bothering to look down at what Rebecca was referring to.

Getting down on her hands and knees, she reached down in the creek and picked up the shiny silver coin.

"Look at this, G T," she said, holding the coin up to him.

"This is a piece of Confederate money," he said as he held it up and scrutinized it closer. "That is Jefferson Davis' image on the front of it and on the back it has CONFEDERATE STATES OF AMERICA with the date 1863 at the bottom. A large 1 is in the center, I guess to show that it is valued at one dollar. Wonder where this came from?"

"Do you think it has any value?" Rebecca asked.

"It may be worth something to a coin collector. We will check when we get back to Lexington, which is what we need to be doing," he said.Reaching down he took her hand and helped her up. When he did, she put her arms around his neck and kissed him again.

"I could fall in love with you in a heart beat," she said. "If you and Isabel ever break up for keeps, let me know. I'd play second fiddle to her any day."

Leaving the old mine, they walked back down Left Branch to the truck, got in and went home. It was late afternoon when they got back to Gerry, who was a nervous wreck. Isabel and Bill Minter had been by, and she was scared to death that G T and Rebecca would come in while they were there. She didn't tell G T that they had been there. Carrying water on both shoulders was getting to her. She was about to adopt a "don't give a damn" attitude, but she wouldn't call it that.

They got up early Sunday morning and after G T vowed to Gerry that he would start going to church on Sunday, they started back to Frankfort. G T was racking his brain to determine who was putting the hit on Rebecca about the permit and why. It had to be some environmental nut who wanted the area to stay the way it was. This didn't make any sense because both White Pines and Golden Star had mountain topped the ridges on both sides of the proposed area and there hadn't been any objection. There was more to this than just an environmental issue. They arrived at Rebecca's apartment in mid-afternoon and she invited him to come in. He graciously refused, but did ask her to go out to dinner one evening in the upcoming week. He walked her to the door of her apartment and kissed her goodbye.

All the way back to Lexington he was confused. Rebecca was really a nice girl that seemed to have her head on straight, but was bitter about the way she had grown up. He was still in love with Isabel even though he was mad at her. When he got back to his apartment, he noticed his answering machine blinking which indicated that he had a message waiting. Playing it back, it was from Rebecca asking him to call her immediately.

When Rebecca answered the phone, her voice was shaking.

"G T, I've got a message on my answering machine that scares me. Let me play it back to you," she said.

"Either deny the White Pines permit or you and your family will have a bad accident. I hope they don't get caught in the fire when their house burns. And be sure to fasten your seat belt," the tape said.

CHAPTER 14

Olivia's trial jury had been sequestered and they were still out when Bill Minter called Isabel. "Are we still on for this evening at five o'clock?" he asked.

"Yes we are," she answered. "Could you come about four? I'd like to take you to meet someone who is very dear to me."

"I'll be there whenever you say," Bill responded.

Promptly at four o'clock, he rang the front doorbell. Isabel was sitting in the living room waiting on him. She really did look nice. She was wearing a lime green pantsuit with a white blouse under it. She had pulled her hair back in a ponytail in the back. Bill Minter had been a lot of places and seen a lot of pretty women, but she put him in a state of awe.

"Before we start, let me say that you are a very beautiful woman. You could easily grace the cover of any women's magazine. I am completely overcome by your beauty," he said in all seriousness.

"Let's go before my head swells up to where I can't get in the car," said Isabel.

"Where are we going?" Minter asked.

"I'll show you," she answered giving him directions on how to get to Gerry's house.

After parking in Gerry's driveway, Bill got out and went around to open Isabel's car door. Bradley had done this, but G T had never bothered. Aware of what he was going to do, she sat still. On opening the door, he took her hand and helped her out, not that she needed it.Gerry had seen them pull in the drive and she went out to meet Bill and hug Isabel.

"Bill, this is my foster mother, Gerry Deane. She raised me to be what I am today. She is also G T's mother," said Isabel as she hugged Gerry.

"I am very pleased to meet you, Mrs. Deane," Bill said, "or should I call you Gerry, which seems to be the proper way to address people around here."

"I am Gerry to you, Bill, just like I am to all of Isabel's friends," Gerry said turning to Isabel. "And how is my little girl?" she asked.

"I am all right, but I am disturbed about Bige. I don't believe I have ever felt as sorry for someone as I do for him. He looks like a whipped puppy. He has spent the entire trial sitting right behind his mother. Every now and then he leans up and whispers something in her ear. Judge Constanza started to say something to him the first time he did it, but he backed off. I think he feels as sorry for him as I do," Isabel said.

Turning to Bill, Gerry asked him how he felt the trial would turn out.

"I would say that Mrs. Napier would be very lucky to avoid the death penalty," he answered.

"I guess we'd better go. I wanted Bill to meet you since you and Sarah are my mothers," said Isabel. Gerry didn't mention G T and Rebecca having been there and she prayed that Isabel wouldn't find it out.

Getting in the car, Isabel and Bill left for Cumberland Falls. For a long period of time Isabel didn't say anything. Finally Bill said, "A penny for your thoughts."

That slammed Isabel like a bucket of cold water in her face. Bradley had said the same thing to her at Sun Valley. Once more she was measuring G T against another man. The holding the car door open had started her thinking. "I was thinking about Bige and the torment he must be going through. He is a very humble fellow and from what my dad says, he is a good worker. They offered to let him off for the trial and pay him just the same, but he wouldn't do it. He said it wasn't fair to the other employees," she said.

"I would say he will take it pretty hard when the jury comes in Monday," Bill said.

Isabel changed the subject. "Tell me about yourself. Don't tell me that you have a wife and six children back in Duluth. Are you engaged? Have you ever been married? Do you have any illegitimate children? Where are you going from here?" She rolled it out like it was a tape recording.

"Hold on!" he cried. "Give me a chance to defend myself. I am not married. I do not have any illegitimate children. I am not engaged. I am not gay. I have never been married or engaged. At this time I do not have a serious relationship with anyone, although, I am beginning to think about one with you. You are most attractive, but I am sure you are aware of that."

"Thank you for the compliment, but please keep your eyes on the road," she said.

"I thought you were driving," he bantered back, breaking the stalemate they had reached in the conversation. "Now it is your turn. Tell me about the beautifully illustrious Isabel Morgan, champion of the down-trodden."

"My mother died when I was three years old and my dad got Gerry to keep me while he worked. G T and I grew up together like brother and sister. When he was born, he had a twin sister that died at birth. I sort of filled that void for Gerry. We played together and he watched out for me all the way through school. He even got bitten by a copperhead for me once. I don't know whether to take him as a lover or a brother. Enough about him. Tell me about your childhood," she said.

"I grew up in Duluth. I didn't have any siblings and very few friends. We lived in a neighborhood that was sort of posh and I didn't care for any of the kids that lived nearby. I often wondered why my mother and father lived there because they are both very down to earth people. I had somewhat of a knack for writing and as a result I went to journalism school after high school. I first went to work for the *Cincinnati Journal* and from there to the *Washington Herald.* As you well know, I now work for Reporting Service International and I enjoy that more than any other job I have had," Bill explained.

"That sounds interesting," said Isabel. "Where do you go next?"

"I don't know," Bill said. "The Service will pick up on a story somewhere and send Chris and me information on it. They deal primarily in very sensational stories. Don't get me wrong, they are not a tabloid or a publication, but more of a wire service similar to Associated Press or other worldwide news services. Would you like to work for them?"

"I might be very much interested after I get my Masters in the fall. Right now I'm having to concentrate on that," Isabel said.

"Tell me more about this area," Bill said.

"It is really very historical," she started, "Cumberland Gap is just thirteen miles to the south. Through it came Daniel Boone and the Long Rifle people. The Shawnee Indians were the inhabitants at that time. Today the Cumberland Gap is a National Park. If we have time before you have to leave, we will go through it. It is right in Middlesboro," said Isabel.

"I think that is where Chris and Sandy were going today," answered Bill."Daniel Boone was the first white man to come into Kentucky, wasn't he?"

"You studied the wrong history book," Isabel said. "Dr. Thomas Walker was ahead of Boone by about seven years, but he never did get credit for it. In 1931 an ancestor of his lobbied Kentucky Governor Sampson to have a festival in Dr. Walker's honor. This materialized to be the Kentucky Mountain Laurel Festival, which is held every year on Memorial Day weekend. Aside from the festival held during the Kentucky Derby, the Laurel Festival is the oldest festival in Kentucky. A queen candidate is sent from each Kentucky college or university and they compete for the honor of being Queen."

"What is laurel?" asked Bill.

"The mountain people call it ivy and they call rhododendron, laurel," answered Isabel. "Both plants are members of the heath family and are native to Kentucky. The laurel blooms are smaller and pinkish, while the rhododendron is much larger and almost white. Plus the laurel blooms before the rhododendron, usually in late May. Rhodies don't bloom until June."

Coming to an exit ramp outside of Corbin, Isabel told Bill to exit and turn right at the end of the ramp, which he did. "Now follow old 25W until we see a sign that says 'Cumberland Falls'," she directed. Bill followed her directions until they came to DuPont lodge. Pulling into a parking slot, he stopped, got out and went around to open her door. This particular action made her heart bounce a beat. She got out and thanked him.

"Let's have dinner and then walk down to see the moonbow. It will probably be around 11:00 before it will be evident," she said as they walked toward the lodge.

After eating dinner, they went to the gift shop which had the usual "See Kentucky" items for sale, most of which had a "Made in China" tag on them. From the gift shop they ambled down the path to the falls. A long period of rainfall had made the water flowing over the falls very plentiful.

"This is beautiful," exclaimed Bill. "I would have never guessed that a place such as this existed."

"G T and I came here several times when we were in high school, but it has been a while since we have been back," she said.

"What is the problem between G T and you? Whether you realize it or not, almost every sentence you utter has him in it somewhere," Bill said.

"He is the only boy I have ever been serious about. I guess I love him, but somehow we just don't seem to be able to get on the same track. He is a home body. I want to travel. He would be satisfied to live in Pineville all of his life and I'm not sure I would be. He is nice to me, but sometimes he has the manners of a hog. He doesn't drink or smoke. I'm not sure if he still dips that smokeless tobacco or not. He is about the best-looking man I have ever seen, present company excepted. I'm just real confused about how I feel about him. There you are. You asked and now you know," Isabel said.

"I believe your problem lies in the fact that neither of you have ever had a serious relationship with someone else. In essence, you and G T got married when you were three years old. It's not natural for you to reach the age you have reached and have never kissed another man. The same holds true for him to have not kissed another woman. You need to turn each other loose and live for a while, then talk about marriage and settling down. As I have told you, Isabel, you are beautiful, have personality, are intelligent and have other attributes. You could go on to be whatever you want to be," Bill told her.

There was a long silence as they went down the steps to go under the falls. Finally she turned and looked him square in the face.

"Kiss me," she said.

"Why do you want me to kiss you?" he asked.

"I want to see what it feels like," she answered.

Complying with her request he took her in his arms and kissed her. Though she wouldn't say so, bells and whistles went off in her head. It was different from kissing G T and here again she was making a comparison between them.

"It's almost time for the moonbow. We had better get back up on the falls level or we will miss it," she said.

Bill was very impressed with the moonbow. He had done some research on it the night before so that he wouldn't be too ignorant of it. Sure enough, Isabel was impressed with his knowledge of Cumberland Falls, the proposed power plant that was to be above the falls, but never came about, the DuPont family's part in the development of the park and generally the history of the Falls and its place in southeastern Kentucky's past and future. On the way home, there was a long period of silence. Finally she broke the ice by asking him what he thought the jury would bring back on Olivia.

"It's like I told Gerry Deane. I believe Olivia will be lucky to escape the death penalty. Her attorneys may cut a deal for 'Life without parole,' but I can't see Theo accepting that. In my opinion, he didn't do a very good job of defending her. Her local attorney, Jeff Cawood, did much better. Theo's getting the judge ticked off didn't help matters any," Bill said.

Isabel had scooted over close to him. He could feel her against him as he was talking. This could lead to things he wasn't sure he wanted to happen. He could very easily fall for her, if he hadn't already. At the same time, they hadn't known each other but a few days and he didn't want to hurt her or on the other hand, get hurt. He had no doubt that she would someday be either a famous model or a movie star. If she ever got out in the wide world, G T would be very lucky not to lose her."May I come see you tomorrow night," Bill asked.

"I would like that," Isabel said.

The next morning, Sandy went to church with Isabel, although she wasn't an every- Sunday regular. Reverend Owen Thomas had learned long ago that the mind couldn't hold more than the butt could and his sermons were usually relatively short and to the point. To the girls' surprise, Bill and Chris were at the service, though Isabel and Sandy sat with Frank and Sarah. After the service, Isabel introduced Sandy, Bill and Chris to Reverend Thomas. He was always glad to see Isabel because she seemed to light up the church when she came in.

Sarah had put a roast in the oven and surrounded it with carrots, potatoes and onions. She had made a broccoli casserole before church that she put in the other oven and set the timer for it to cook while she was gone. She had a banana pudding for dessert. Realizing that she had more than enough, she invited Bill and Chris to dinner. Both men accepted in a hurry. It was very seldom that they got a chance to eat a home-cooked meal. The table conversation dealt primarily with the trial and the anticipated outcome. No one would be surprised if Olivia was found guilty, since by her own admission she was. Fred Tinsley had told Frank and George about Thelma's being kidnapped and how she knocked Harvey Stone unconscious with the commode waterbox cover. Isabel almost had hysterics. Her three guests didn't know Thelma so they didn't get the charge out of it that Frank, Sarah and Isabel did. It broke the tension that had built up in Isabel over Bige.

After dinner, while Frank talked to Bill and Chris, Isabel and Sandy helped Sarah with clearing the table and putting the dishes in the washer. Both reporters were interested in knowing more about coal mining. Frank offered to take them on the strip job and underground if they wanted to go. They accepted his invitation for a later date. The afternoon wore away pretty fast. Sandy and Chris seemed to be getting up a case, as Isabel referred to it. Chris' intelligence was not on a par with hers, but he could pretty well hold his own.

Isabel told Bill more about the history and geology of the Pine Mountain area. She explained that Pine Mountain was the result of a thrust fault that occurred eons in the past. She told him about Turtle Back and how the surface had been eroded in such a way that it resembled the back of a turtle. About Shelter Rock, which was an overhanging rock ledge that provided the kind of protection from the weather that a lean-to offers, and where boys chiseled the names of the girls they loved in the top of it. She explained about Chained Rock and how the chain was dragged up the mountain by two teams of mules. She told him about Lone Pine which had been made into an overlook that covered the chiseled names of many boys and girls, and about Rock Hotel that was similar to Shelter Rock, but much larger. Isabel seemed in a trance when she talked about these places.

Bill asked her if every rock in Pine Mountain had a name and she got a laugh. She dwelled on the good times she and her friends had in their teenage years, how they drank out of the spring under Turtle Back and how they spent nights in the summer camping out on top of Rock Hotel, how Frank and Doctor James had chaperoned them and then gone to sleep while the boys and girls courted all night. All the time she was talking, she had a misty look in her eye as though she had gone back in a time machine and was reliving the happiest days of her life.

On Monday morning, Isabel and Sandy got up early and hurried down to the courthouse. The door to the circuit court room was unlocked and they went in. Bige was already in place immediately behind Olivia's chair at the defense table. Isabel got a seat right behind him. She didn't know why, but she felt that she needed to. Sandy took her usual seat in the press row with Bill and Chris. The courtroom filled up fast and at exactly 9:00 AM Judge James Constanza took his seat at the bench. After calling for order he instructed the bailiff to bring in the jury. Addressing the jury foreman, Judge Constanza asked if they had reached a verdict. The foreman, Mary Ann Taylor, responded that they had.

"Will the defendant please rise?" Constanza said to Olivia.

With Theo Shawitz on one side and Jeff Cawood on the other, Olivia stood up. Bige started to get up too, but Isabel put her hand on his shoulder and he stayed seated.

"Will the jury foreman please read the verdict?" the Judge asked.

"In the case of Bradley Durham, we the jury find the defendant guilty of murder in the first degree. In the case of Veronica Atmore, we the jury find the defendant guilty of murder in the first degree."

"Thank you, ladies and gentlemen," Constanza said. "Sentencing will be delivered on Wednesday of this week at 9:00 AM. This court is adjourned."

Bige leaned across the balustrade that separated him from Olivia and hugged her before the deputy sheriff handcuffed her and led her out of the courtroom. Bige started to cry, so Isabel leaned across the seat and hugged him.

"Thank you, Isabel," he said. "You and G T are the best friends I have. I'm sorry for what Mama did and I know she should be punished, but I still love her. She is all I ever had. Daddy was always good to me, but he never was home. She was mother and mostly daddy to me. Do you think she will go to hell for what she did to Veronica and Brad?" he asked.

"That's not for us to say," Isabel said. "God is very merciful and He is the only one who will judge your mama. We need to pray to Him for her."

"Mama never did go to church or make me go, but every night before I went to bed, she read the Bible to me and made me say my prayers," Bige said, "She was good to me, Isabel."

"I know, Bige," Isabel answered as she began to cry.

"I wish G T was here. He's always been there when I needed him real bad," Bige said as he started crying again.

"I'm sure he will be here, Bige," Isabel said.

Sandy, Bill and Chris were waiting on her outside the courthouse.

"If this doesn't end soon, you'll be out of tears," Sandy said.

"I can't help it," Isabel said, wiping her eyes with a tissue. "I feel so sorry for Bige, but there is nothing anyone can do."

Bill Minter had been around enough to know that now was not the time to further any romantic endeavors, so he just stood back and let Sandy and Isabel talk.

"Bige asked me if G T would be here for the sentencing. He said that G T and I were the only friends he had. That's pitiful, you know it?" she said.

"Let's the four of us go have a picnic. I think I need to get away from thinking about Bige and his mother," said Isabel. "Sandy and I will go get a bucket of fried chicken and some potato salad. You two can get the soft drinks and come pick us up at about six. Is that is all right with everyone?" Bill and Chris were very agreeable and left.

"Are you giving G T a hard time?" asked Sandy.

“Not really. I think he and I need time to think about things before we make a mistake,” Isabel answered as they got in the car and left the courthouse.

“I need to call in and give my story to a copywriter,” said Sandy.

“I need to call G T and tell him to come home, that Bige needs him,” said Isabel.

When they got home, Isabel let Sandy call first. After she had finished, Isabel called G T at work. “G T,” she said when he answered the phone, “the jury found Olivia guilty on both counts of murder in the first degree. She is to be sentenced day after tomorrow at 9:00AM. Bige broke down when she left the courtroom and told me that he wished you were here, that you were always there when he needed you. Do you think you could come home for the sentencing?”

“I’ll be there,” he said, “You and I need to go to the Misery and have a long talk about us.”

“I think you are right. I’ll see you in the courtroom Wednesday. I love you,” Isabel said.

“I love you, too,” he answered.

CHAPTER 15

While Olivia Napier's trial was underway, Betty Talbert called Dr. Ralph West and asked him when he could see Wing Fu. His receptionist made an appointment for 10:00AM the next day, which would be Tuesday. Then Betty called her supervisor, Anne Quinlan, and asked her if she could take two days vacation, one to go to UK to see Dr. Tao Chang, a professor of Asian history, and the other to take Wing Fu to the doctor. Anne asked her if her taking off had to do with the Chinese woman who came to the governor's office the day Betty was interviewed and Betty told her it did.

"I have strict orders from Governor Martin himself, to let you off any time you ask, particularly if it has to do with your house guest, Wing Fu," said Anne. "This time off is not chargeable to your vacation."

Betty explained to Wing Fu that they would be going to the doctor's office the next day to make pre-birth arrangements. Wing Fu got a worried look in her eyes and asked Betty if the doctor would abort the baby. "Absolutely not," said Betty. "The doctor will make arrangements for you to go into the hospital and have your baby when the time comes. He wants to examine you to be sure that no problems are going to come up unexpectedly." Wing Fu didn't look too convinced, but told Betty that she would take her word for it. Betty had explained the TV to her and how to turn it off and on. She also told Wing Fu about going to Lexington, but that she should be back by lunchtime and if Wing Fu got hungry to help herself to what was in the refrigerator.

Leaving Wing Fu, Betty drove to the University of Kentucky. She had taken a course in Asian history several years ago from a nice Chinese professor named Dr. Tao Chang. Dr. Chang was a small man who wore his hair in a pony tail and sported a goatee, complete with accompanying mustache. There were only two other students in the class she took and they had all conversed in Chinese. Arriving at the UK History Department, Betty went to Dr. Chang's office. He was very glad to see her and began to question her in Chinese. She responded accordingly. Finally getting through the small talk, he asked her the nature of her visit. She didn't tell him about Wing Fu, but she asked him about the bear and butterfly birthmark. He got a strange look on his face.

"Where did you hear of this?" he asked.

"I had read about it years ago but I couldn't remember what it was. I recently read a magazine article that mentioned it and it stirred up my memory," Betty said crossing her fingers to correct for the white lie she had told.

"My dear, you have asked me about the Shuai Province, which lies in a very deep valley in the northern part of China near the Mongolian border. Its people have long bred and trained horses. Its climate is a phenomenon. The annual year round temperature is 72 degrees. It very seldom gets above 80 degrees or below 50 degrees. It has a very dense overhead cloud cover that hangs on the mountains that surround it. There is an opening in this cover that admits sunlight, but closes if it is violated by some man-made object such as an airplane or balloon. The only entrance to the valley is through a narrow opening in a cliff wall. The opening will accommodate only two riders at a time, or a small vehicle such as the Jeep used by this country's military. The entrance is somewhat of a tunnel that is about two hundred feet long.

"Some of the fields are used as vegetable gardens. The Shuaites do not eat meat and they raise their own food. They use the cows they have for milk, and the chickens and geese they use for eggs only. They raise bees for the honey and the wax, which they use to make candles. They heat their homes with a very high grade of coal that is dug from the mountains around the province. It is basically a self-sufficient commune. All the food goes into a central storage area and they rotate their crops so as to not wear out the ground. Their fields are long and, though narrow, are spacious and verdant. Red clover is the predominant groundcover. For centuries the province supplied the Emperor of China with horses for his officers. It was considered a very great honor for a person to be given a horse by the Emperor. This practice was abandoned when the communists came into power. From birth the horses are exceptionally fast, competitive and fearless. They would go headlong into battle as if they enjoyed it. Their riders who never reined them gave them their heads.

"A woman known as the Butterfly Princess rules the province in a very firm but gentle manner. The throne is handed down from mother to daughter. The Princess does not marry but somewhat like the queen bee in a hive, has suitors she selects from the province. She may have several children, but only one of the girls will be born with a birthmark on her left shoulder blade. This is the mark of sovereignty. It depicts a bear standing on its hind legs with its mouth open and one paw raised in the air with a butterfly overhead.

"There is a legend that tells the story of a Mongolian chieftain named the Bear who decided to take over the province and raise the horses for his troops. He was warned by the Butterfly Princess to stay away. Not paying any attention to her he led his troops into the valley. There was no opposition to his entry and the villages were abandoned. When all of his troops were well within the valley there was a sudden onslaught of millions of butterflies. They completely covered the men and their horses. The

Mongols had no way to fight them off. The butterflies smothered them, getting in their eyes, mouths and noses. Some of the troops and horses suffocated. Others slashed blindly with their swords killing their own comrades. Finally the Bear withdrew in total defeat and returned to his northern home, vowing as he left that he would return one day and eliminate the Shuai province.

"The story of the Bear and the Butterfly is the first story the children of this province hear. It is taught in the schools where the dialect that you and I are speaking is taught. The Butterfly Princess always has in her possession two small porcelain figurines, one of a Butterfly and one of a Bear. In fact, there is a song the Shuaites sing to their children. I guess you could call it a form of a National Anthem. It goes something like this," Dr. Chang said as he began to sing.

The Bear came down from the icy north, the Butterfly's land to pillage.
"Do not come near, leave our home alone, tread you not on our peaceful village".
"Who are you?" said the scornful Bear, "to threaten one as great as me."
"Stay away from us," said the Butterfly, "or our vengeance you will see."
The Bear came on with his Mongol horde, to trample the peaceful life,
But no one was there to counter his purge, to engage in resistive strife.
When suddenly from out of the woods, came the roar of uncountable wings.
They completely engulfed the astounded troops, their horses, their swords and their slings.
The Bear left the scene in total defeat, back to the north he did stumble.
"I'll return again," said the angry Bear, "and for this I will make you humble."
"There will always be a Butterfly and a price you'll be made to pay.
"So stay away from our peaceful home, don't come again as you did this day"

"Present day Shuaites see the communist regime of China and its determination to eliminate their province as the return of the Bear. My family came from Shuai. They left there years ago to come to Kentucky to train horses. I was never told the complete story of why they left because a Chinese child does not question its parents. When I was twenty-two years old, my father got a message from the Butterfly Princess requesting that I come back to Shuai to father a child by her. She was devoted to my family and there was no way that I could refuse. You may not understand this, but I did what I was supposed to do. I was later notified that I was the father of the Butterfly Princess of today. Her name is Wing Fu.

"While the Princess is within the confines of the province, she leads a charmed life. Once she has a daughter that is marked to succeed her, both she and her daughter are safe as long as they stay within the confines of the province. However, if the Princess leaves the province, she is like any other person. If she is killed before another girl is born with a sovereign birthmark, then the mountains will fall in on the entire area and it will be blotted off of the face of the earth. If she dies a natural death before a sovereign girl is born, then the butterflies that guard the entrance will all die and the entrance will be open.

"The area has long been sought as an ideal place to raise opium poppies, but all of China is afraid to try to enter the province. This includes the military and the drug dealers. If a person tries to get into the area without permission from the Princess, butterflies smother them. I know that this sounds like something out of a science-fiction magazine, but it is the truth. China is a land of mystery and this is one of them," concluded Dr. Chang.

Betty had sat through the entire dissertation in complete awe. She knew that there was something that Wing Fu had not told her and it was the fact that she was the Butterfly Princess. Thanking Dr. Chang for all the information, she left and started home.

On her way back to Frankfort, she played Dr. Chang's talk over in her head. It suddenly dawned on her that Wing Fu was in danger of being kidnapped, if anyone knew that she was with Betty and John. That must have been the reason she was so apprehensive of going to see Dr. West. Betty upped her speed past the limit in order to get back to Wing Fu as soon as possible. The next question was how to keep her presence a secret and how to guard her when she and John were at work.

Pulling into her parking space at the apartment, she hurried to the elevator and pushed her floor button. Once the elevator door opened, she half-ran down the hall. Betty could see before she got there that the apartment door was open. Going in she called out for Wing Fu, but got no answer. Wing Fu was nowhere to be found.

CHAPTER 16

Whitley was surprised that Timothy Patterson and his wife had "blind-dated" her, but she didn't mind after Timothy introduced her to Kurt Holtz, the president of Electrique Internationale. Being the suave European that he was, Kurt took her hand and bowing low at the waist, kissed it.

"I must tell you, Ms. Rogers, that I eavesdropped on your interview with Timothy this afternoon. In view of your past experience and education, I am prepared to offer you a starting salary of twice what you are presently making with all the usual benefits and other perks. I realize that this is neither the time nor the place to make you a job offer, but I wanted to set your mind at ease so that we could enjoy the evening. Only one question remains and that is, When could you start?" Kurt said.

Whitley almost fainted. Now she could tell that pinhead queer who hated her guts to take it and stuff it. She planned on giving him two weeks notice, which is more that he or that jerk Jamison would do for her. All of these things flashed through her head as she tried to be nonchalant about the offer.

"I accept your offer, Mr. Holtz. I feel that I should give my present employer two weeks notice. I would like another week to settle my affairs in Lexington and prepare to move to my new home, where ever that is."

Kurt Holtz was every bit a Prussian general from an old World War I movie. The only things missing were the monocle and the dueling scar on the cheek. He was very gallant and handsome to boot, with ramrod straight posture. His head was covered with a thick, slightly wavy mat of gray hair that looked as though a beautician had just set it. His steel-blue eyes pierced whatever he was looking at, and he had the healthy tan of someone who played a lot of golf or tennis in faraway places

"I'll bet he is a heller when he gets mad," thought Whitley.

The dinner was fabulous. Kurt had made the declaration that it was his party as he ordered a bottle of twenty-year-old champagne. He selected a menu that blew Whitley's mind. It began with a cup of vichyssoise that was delightfully cold. Next came a garden salad that consisted of a bed of romaine lettuce nesting broccoli florets, asparagus spears and slices of avocado, with a walnut-raspberry vinaigrette. The main course was peppercorn-encrusted roast lamb marinated in a mint sauce and covered with a gravy made from the marinade. Accompanying this was half of a baked potato that had been scooped out, mashed with sour cream and chives, stuffed back in the shell and covered with melted sharp cheddar cheese. A generous serving of small spring peas with mushrooms and baby onions finished out the main course. Kurt selected a dinner wine with which the waiter kept each glass filled.

The dinner conversation was primarily about Kurt and his company. He had the equivalent degree of a Master of Science in electrical engineering with a similar degree in business administration, both of them from the University of Hamburg. He had grown up in Hamburg, Germany, the third child of a beer parlor owner. His siblings were a brother younger than himself and a sister who was older. He had been a super soccer player in his youth and at one time considered going professional. Upon graduation from the university, he had taken employment with an electric energy distributor. He was a hard worker and a tyrant of a supervisor. He put in long hours and he expected his employees to do the same. Unknown to the community, his father and mother had hidden Jewish refugees during Hitler's purge. One man, whom his father had helped, remembered this and came back to repay the debt. Kurt's father had died after the war, but the refugee he had helped took Kurt under his wing. The man was a large stockholder in a company named Electrique Internationale. He secured a place for Kurt and boosted him along. With his work ethic and his inside help, Kurt rose meteorically in the company. He was not married, which made it easier for Whitley to further her off-the-job ambitions.

The evening ended with Kurt escorting her back to her room and kissing her hand again as he said good night. He told her he would be in contact with her within the next week and they would work out the details of her job.

Whitley was on cloud nine all the way back to Lexington. She had caught an early flight that would put her home about 11:00 AM. She played over in her head what she would say in her letter of resignation. In spite of the fact that she would like very much to walk into Colbert's office and tell him point-blank to go straight to hell, she planned to be very gracious and polite. On the other hand, she was going to relish telling that fat, bow-legged slob of a Jamison to jump off of a high bridge. Just thinking about him gave her the creeps. She felt obligated, which was a new feeling for her, to tell Joe and Harry about the job before she told Colbert.

When the plane landed at Bluegrass Airport, she got her luggage and went to her car. She went straight home and unpacked, then she called Joe Barnes. When he got on the line, the first thing he asked her was where had she been.

"If you are going to be in for a while, I'll come by and tell you all about it," she said.

"I'll wait," Joe said.

When she got to Joe's office, she went through the usual niceties of greeting his secretary and then waiting while she buzzed Joe. He came out to meet her and usher her into his office. Seating herself, as she usually did, she began to relate the events that had taken place the last couple of days.

"Do you mean to tell me that you are going to pack up and move out on me?" Joe asked.

"If I don't move now, Colbert and that pig he's brought in will move me," she answered.

"I believe you are right," said Joe, "but I will have to say I hate to see you go. You kept things stirred up."

"I am afraid that Public Service of Kentucky has seen it's best days. By the time Jamison gets through, there won't be enough left to bury. I hate to leave you and Harry, but I believe I had better take this offer because I may never get another," Whitley said as she got up. She hugged Joe and gave him a goodbye kiss like he had never had before.

Going back to her apartment, she called Harry. When he heard her on the other end of the line, he asked the same question that Joe had asked about where she had been for the last two days.

"I got a job offer that I am going to take. I went for an interview and I just got back. I have already told Joe Barnes and I wanted you to know before I handed in my resignation," Whitley said.

"I hate to hear that, but I don't blame you. After Colbert picked up on our little game I figured he would make it hard on you, which I think he will yet do," said Harry, "I'll see you again before you leave."

At work the next day, Whitley got on the elevator just as Al Jamison did. He was smoking a foul-smelling cigar and puffed on it while the elevator was filling up.

"He is a real horse's ass," thought Whitley as she nodded her head in reply to his "Hello." They got off on the same floor and as she started toward her office, he stopped her.

"I need to have you come to my office at 8:30," he said.

"I've been out of the office for two days and I need to catch up on my mail. You can see me at 1:30 in my office," she curtly replied.

"Look," he said, "I am the Personnel Director and I can cause you all kinds of grief if you don't do as I say. Now, you be there at 8:30 or I'll go to Jack about it."

"You can go to Mr. Colbert about me any old time you want to and I still will not be in your office at 8:30," she said as she walked into her office and shut the door.

Her first order of business was to type up her letter of resignation, which she did. She was almost unctuous in her reference to Jack Colbert, but it wouldn't hurt anything to be nice about leaving. If he wanted to show himself over her leaving, that was his business. She finished the letter after editing it no less than five times. Folding it neatly, she put it in an envelope and buzzed Colbert's office.

"Yes?" Colbert answered.

"Mr. Colbert, this is Whitley and I wondered if I could talk to you for a few minutes," she said in her oiliest voice.

"Why yes, Whitley, come on in," he said.

Checking her makeup to be sure she was at her best, she knocked gently on Colbert's door.

"Come in," he said as he got up to welcome her."Have a seat, Whitley."

"Thank you, Mr. Colbert," she answered as she placed the envelope with her resignation in it on his desk.

"What have we here?" he asked as he picked up the envelope and withdrew the letter. Very carefully he read it, a word at a time. Finally looking up, he folded the letter and eyeballed Whitley. "Where are you going?" he asked.

"My future employers asked that I not reveal this until after I have signed a five-year contract with them," she lied as she returned his stare.

"Is Bradley's replacement ready to take your job?" he asked.

"I feel that he will be pretty well able after I work with him for a few more days," she responded.

"Does this job pay more and have as good or better benefits as the one you presently have?" he asked.

"It pays considerably more and the benefits include a housing allowance for as long as I work for the company," she answered.

"Is that the reason you are leaving?" he queried.

"Not really," she retorted. "I feel that the hiring of Al Jamison is a mistake, for one thing and I also am uneasy about the company's future, what with all of the forced mergers and other problems. I like the company and I have enjoyed working here, as I said in my letter, but there are also some bad memories, such as Mr. Marlowe's death, that I would like to shake. I think moving will help to erase those."

"I hate to see you leave, Whitley, but it appears that you have your mind made up so all that I can do is wish you well. I would appreciate it if you would give young Senters as much training as possible in the next two weeks. If you would like a letter of reference, I would be glad to give you one," Colbert said.

Whitley thought she was going to vomit over his hypocrisy. She knew he was so glad to see her leave that he would probably take a day off to celebrate. Getting up, she thanked him again for the "nice" association and left the room. She no sooner cleared the door than Colbert buzzed Al Jamison.

"Come in here," he bellowed into the phone.

Looking his usual uncouth self, Jamison sauntered into Colbert's office and took the chair that Whitley had just vacated.

"I thought you had connections that would keep that witch from leaving," Colbert said as he handed Jamison her letter of resignation.

"I do," Jamison said as he read the letter.

"Then find out where she is going and put a stop to it. If she gets out in the general public and tells what she knows about this company, we will never be able to pull off what we have planned," Colbert warned.

"Don't get so worked up. She can't stop us," said Jamison, getting up and leaving.

The two weeks went by real fast for Whitley. During that time she had Harry down for a meal and some recreation, went out to dinner with Joe Barnes and showed Scott Senters the "ropes" of PSK. Kurt Holtz called her and told her that her contract was in the mail. When she got it and read it, she was very well pleased. The corporate offices were in Bern, Switzerland and Kurt had rented a nice condo for her at the company's expense. When she told Will Hoskins, her half-brother, about her job, she thought he was going to cry.

"What am I going to do?" he asked.

"Will, you are a grown man and it is time for you to quit depending on me for everything," she said. "Get out and find some nice girl and get married."

On her last day, she stuck her head in Colbert's office and said goodbye. He wanted to kill her, but he would wait for another time. She cleaned out her desk, put a few mementos in her brief case and left.

Kurt had sent the Electrique Internationale corporate jet to Lexington and had come with it. She was glad to see him and he seemed glad to see her. She had sent all of her clothes and other small belongings to her condo in Switzerland. She was going to like this. On the flight to Bern he explained to her that he was negotiating with the Chinese government about building and operating a power plant for them in a small province near the Mongolian border. It had millions of tons of high grade coal that would more than last the proposed fifty-year life of the plant. He also told her that his primary supplier in the United States, a company by the name of White Pines, had fallen behind on their deliveries and he had heard that they were having permit problems. Once she got settled in, he wanted her to look into both items and give him a report.

"What is the status of PSK?" Kurt asked.

"What do you mean?" responded Whitley.

"I have studied a number of companies in the United States for a possible merger or adverse take over, if necessary. PSK is one of my target companies. Would it be ready for a foreign suitor to make overtures as to a merger and if so, what would be the attitude of the stockholders relative to such action?" he said.

Whitley told Kurt everything that had taken place at PSK. She told him about Joe Barnes, Harry Baker and all of the ins and outs of Colbert's plans.

"Give Al Jamison another month and he will have that company so torn up that it will be easy to take over," she said.

CHAPTER 17

When Bill and Chris pulled into the Morgan driveway promptly at six o'clock on the day of Olivia's verdict, Isabel and Sandy were waiting on them.

"Why don't you let me drive," said Isabel, "since I'm the only one who knows where we are going."

"Okay," said Bill getting out and holding the door open for her. There it was again! That holding the door open got to her in a way she didn't understand. Chris and Sandy got in the back seat of the rented Chevrolet while Bill went around and got in the passenger seat next to Isabel.

"Where are we going on this outing?" asked Chris.

"I'm going to take you to one of the most serene places you will ever see," responded Isabel. "We are going to the Tunnel."

Driving out Clear Creek Road like she was going to the Lodge, she pulled off the road at the Clear Creek Baptist Bible College and parked in front of the chain that blocked any travel down the old railroad bed.

Isabel turned tour guide. "This used to be the railroad on up Clear Creek to Davisburg and Chenoa, but that was a long time ago. The CSX people took up the track and turned the right-of-way over to the land owners. It has made a nice walking path. It used to be the L & N railroad, but they merged with the CSX, whoever they are."

They walked down the path until they came to the old trestle that crossed Clear Creek. The trestle had been built in the early 1900s with rocks hewn from the surrounding mountain serving as abutments. Like all railroad trestles, creosoted timbers had been used for the underpinnings and cross members. Even though the construction had taken place many years ago, the smell of creosote still permeated the air on a hot day. The creek that ran beneath the trestle was running full from a recent rain. It made a rippling sound as it jumped from rock to rock. Little depressions in the rocks made ponds for small minnows that would eventually get big enough to jump out and join others in the schools that filled the creek.

They walked the next half mile as Isabel gave them a history lesson about a man named Murph Sharp who had logged all of the watershed of Little Clear Creek, bringing his logs to a railhead on a dinghy railroad that ran for miles up Little Clear Creek. The logs were dumped beside the L & N track at the railhead and loaded into coal cars by a crane for transport to a mill somewhere far off. The logged-over area had long since regrown the timber that had been removed. As they walked along the old roadbed, Isabel was still thinking about G T and Bill, Bill was still thinking about Isabel, Sandy was thinking about both Chris and Mark West, her erstwhile fiancé, and Chris was thinking about Sandy. It was the kind of day and place that would bring such thoughts to mind. It was what a poet would call a romantic time. As they rounded the last bend in the path, the tunnel came into view. Just in front of the tunnel was another trestle that was exactly like the one they had previously crossed.

"How long has it been since any of you have seen a real live, honest-to-goodness railroad tunnel?" Isabel asked, breaking the silence.

"A long time," said Bill.

"I never have seen one except in books or movies," said Sandy.

"I'm like Sandy, this is my first one," said Chris.

Isabel came to a halt. "There used to be a cabin over there where those foundations are," she said pointing to her right. "The people who owned it spent the summers there. I don't remember them, but daddy once told me that he knew them. All of the children grew up and moved off and the place just died a death of neglect."

Turning back to look at the tunnel that was cut through a massive cliff of sandstone, she put the cabin behind her. Crossing the trestle first, Isabel ran into the tunnel, ducking to avoid the water that dripped from the roof. The others followed suit. Going over to the right side of the tunnel about twenty feet from the entrance, she rubbed her hand across the wall until she found what she was looking for. Carved into the rock with a chisel was: G T LOVES I M.

"We used to walk up here from the other end of the track when we were teen agers," said Isabel as she walked on through to the other end, "and we would go swimming in a deep hole further down the track that we called Blue Hole. The creek was real clean then. We would play tag and have water fights, and sometimes when it was dark the boys would skinny dip, or at least they said that they did."

The dome-like tunnel opening had the appearance of the entrance to a cathedral. Its sides were craggy but still had the aura of majesty. The tunnel had been built in the days before high-speed air compressors and drills. The drilling had been done by a steam drill that could be elevated to position by a crank and chain mechanism and impact was provided by steam from a boiler on a railcar that was pushed ahead of the engine. When the proposed location was set, the drill would put a hole in the center and then be turned to drill other holes at various angles. Once a series of holes had been drilled to a prescribed depth, they were loaded with dynamite and the rock blasted out. It was moved away from the mouth of the tunnel by mules hitched to the large sandstone boulders. The smaller rock was put into a wooden box that was mounted on runners and dragged away. All of the stone that came from the excavation was piled beside the creek, raising the roadbed to a level with the floor of the tunnel.

The finished tunnel was approximately 150 feet long, 25 feet wide and 20 feet high. The perfectly-arched roof was a beautiful job of engineering and construction know-how that was accomplished without the aid of computers. Groundwater dripped into the tunnel along the walls and the entrance. Ditches on both sides of the roadbed caught the water, leading it out of the tunnel and into the creek. The roof of the tunnel was black from the many steam engines that had passed through it on their way to load coal and timber and then return to various markets.

Exiting the tunnel, Isabel ran down a path on the right side of the railroad embankment until she got to the creek bank. Sitting down in the sand, she waited on the others. The bank was sandy for four or five feet back from the creek, but from the edge of the sand back to the foot of the mountain, a distance of about twenty feet, there were mostly blossomless laurel and rhododendron along with some smaller shrubs and the ever-present poison ivy.

"Let's eat," said Isabel as she spread a tablecloth that Sarah had given her. Reaching into the backpack that she had laid down, she got out four complete fried chicken dinners and handed one to each of the others. Bill had carried a small cooler that had four cold soft drinks in it. It was not like one of Sarah's meals, but it tasted good and let Isabel think about something besides G T, Bill and Bige.

"Where does this path go?" asked Sandy with a mouthful of chicken, pointing to a path that ran beside and up the creek through the brush

"It follows the creek around that bend and back to the trestle on the other side of the tunnel. Why?" asked Isabel.

"Chris and I are going to walk around it. We'll wait on you all on the other side," said Sandy as she put her empty chicken box and pop can in Isabel's backpack.

"Okay," said Isabel as she watched them go off down the path.

"You really love this area, don't you," said Bill.

"It's all I have ever known, but I want to see other places to see if there are any I would rather live in than this," she said.

"What about G T?" fished Bill.

"We agreed to break off the engagement and date other people to see what it is like to like to be with someone besides each other. Does that make sense?"

"I think it makes a lot of sense," said Bill.

"I believe that Chris and Sandy are getting up a case," said Isabel, changing the subject before it got too involved.

"I believe you are right," answered Bill, taking the hint to drop the romantic talk.

"We'd better go before it gets dark," said Isabel picking up the empty food cartons and pop cans and putting them in her backpack, and then washing her hands in the creek.

"You were right, Isabel, this is a very serene place. I had never known that there were places like this in the world. You are very fortunate to have been able to grow up in this kind of surroundings," said Bill, "I envy your childhood."

"It wasn't all peaches and cream," she said, climbing up on the roadbed. "There were some rough spots."

When Isabel and Bill came out of the tunnel, they saw Chris and Sandy wading up the creek with their shoes hung around their necks. Sandy stumbled a little on purpose, giving Chris an opportunity to put his arm around her.

"Are you all having fun?" asked Isabel.

"What do you think?" responded Sandy.

Climbing up the rock ledges that held the trestle, they sat down at the top and put their shoes on. All four started back up the track to the car, playing over their dreams of the day.

++++++

The next morning Isabel, Sandy, Chris and Bill were already in the courtroom for Olivia's sentencing when G T got there. Isabel had saved him a seat beside her where she sat behind Bige. Sitting down in the seat she had saved, G T leaned over and patted Bige, who turned around and hugged him.

Judge Constanza came in and everyone in the courtroom rose. After he was seated, everyone sat back down. The jury was seated in the jury box, with Olivia seated between Jeff Cawood and Theo Shawitz, while Caron Dell sat by herself at the prosecution table. The whole room was as quiet as a tomb.

"Will the defendant please rise?" said Judge Constanza.

Olivia stood up, with Jeff and Theo on either side.

"Olivia Napier, you have been found guilty of the murder of Bradley Durham and Veronica Atmore in the first degree. This court now sentences you to imprisonment for life without parole. May the Lord have mercy on your soul," Judge Constanza announced solemnly.

Olivia didn't move a muscle. Bige started to cry, but she turned around and told him not to do that, that he was a man now and he needed to act like one.

Theo couldn't stand it. He had to show himself.

"We will file for appeal immediately. This court is a travesty of—"

"Shut your damn mouth, you little fart, There ain't gonna be no appeal," Olivia snarled, as she wheeled on him. "I did what they said I did and I am sorry for the hurt I caused other people, but those two had it coming and I was proud to do it."

Judge Constanza had raised his gavel to command order, but he hesitated since Olivia had expressed his views exactly, using words he wanted to use.

Bige leaned across the balustrade and hugged her. "I love you, Mama, no matter what you did," he sobbed.

"I love you too, baby. You take care of yourself and be a good boy. Don't judge me too hard for what I've done or what I do in the future," she said.

"I won't never judge you, Mama," he said as the deputy led her away.

Turning to Isabel and G T, he hugged both of them at the same time. "Thank you all for being here when I needed you. I'm sorry for what Mama did, but I still love her," he said.

"We know that you love her and you should," said G T, "and you always will.

The three of them walked out of the court room together with Bige in the middle.

"Come go home with us and eat, Bige. My mama has fixed a big dinner," said G T.

"Thanks G T, but I better get home," Bige said. "Daddy is supposed to be in on that five-thirty train from Norton and I need to fix him some supper. I have to get on the section for the night shift at six."

As Bige left, Bill, Chris and Sandy came up. Isabel introduced G T to Bill and Chris, whom he shook hands with, and then he spoke to Sandy.

"We thought we would go up to the Lodge and eat supper," Sandy said. "Won't you all come with us?"

"I don't guess I'd better," G T answered. "Mama has fixed chicken and dumplings for me and I can't miss that."

"I'd better go with G T," Isabel said as she looked at Bill Minter, "since I haven't seen him in a while. He can take me home after we eat."

They all parted company as G T and Isabel drove to Gerry's.

"We're here, Mama," G T said.

"Thank the Lord that you two are together. I can't stand it when you all are mad at each other," said Gerry.

"We're going up to the Misery, Mama," G T said.

"I'll call you when supper is ready," Gerry answered.

As they walked up to the Misery, they both had memories of past days they had spent together, but neither of them spoke. They passed under the pin oak where they had gone squirrel "hunting" with two broomstick guns. They passed the rock where they spread the walnuts out to dry for Gerry.

They came to the Misery where the two chairs that George had made for them were still where they had left them years ago.

"Remember the copperhead, G T?" Isabel asked. "You saved my life."

"Mama had told me to take care of you and I couldn't let that snake bite you. She would have killed me if I had," he said.

"Remember the first time you kissed me?" Isabel said as she laughed at the thought.

"I was kind of slow, wasn't I," he laughed. "You kissed me, I didn't kiss you."

"Do you really love me, G T?" she asked in all seriousness.

"I do, but I'm kind of confused," he said.

"I think we are both confused," she answered.

"Let's hold off on the engagement until we have tried other relations," she continued, "but still hold on to the prenuptial sex agreement."

"That's fair enough. After we have both dated other people, maybe we will find out that we are meant for each other. Then again, we may find that we aren't as well-suited as we thought we were. You and I can take this, but I don't know about Mama," G T said.

"Look at me, G T," she said looking him square in the face with big tears in her eyes. "I will always love you. Will you be my dearest friend?"

"I will always be yours if you will always be mine," he answered. "Pucker up, Isabel, like you've eaten a green persimmon."

"That's my line," Isabel said as she began to laugh and cry at the same time.

G T took her in his arms and kissed her. There were bells and whistles in her head which meant that the feeling was still there.

++++++

Driving back to Lexington after Olivia's sentencing, G T was bone-tired. He wanted to go straight to bed, but he thought he should call Rebecca and find out if she had received any more threatening phone calls. She said that she had gotten another one while he was gone. She sounded pretty shaken up. He asked her if she would like to go out to dinner and see a movie the next night about seven o'clock.

"I would like that very much," she said, "Thank you for checking up on me, G T. That means a great deal to me."

"Strick's Silver Mine," G T said as he sat bolt upright in the bed. "That's what it's all about."Looking at the clock, it said 2:00 AM. It was too early to call Rebecca, but he knew that he had found the answer.

All of his life he had heard about Strick's Silver Mine being somewhere in the mountains of southeastern Kentucky. He even got so interested in it that he went to the library and checked out some books on it. According to the legend that he had always heard, there was a Union payroll officer that was attacked by guerrillas during the Civil War and in order to save the payroll, he hid it somewhere around Pineville. Some people had a different idea and thought it was a silver mine where you dug for silver, while others thought it was a silver mint that coined Confederate money. At any rate, it was a tale that had lived for years and all of a sudden he had stumbled on it. G T began to put two and two together when he hit on the name of Jason Strick, president of White Pines Coal Company.

"That couldn't be it," he said to himself. "That is too far fetched. Still it would be worth looking into. If that is what it is and he is responsible for putting the pressure on Rebecca, then it needs to come to light. I should go home and take a look. I also need to check on Bige and see how he is doing."

As soon as he got to work that morning, he called Rebecca to be sure they were still on for dinner and the movie. She assured him that she was. He told her he would pick her up at her apartment at seven o'clock. All through the day he kept playing over in his mind the things that he knew about the White Pines permit. There had been no problem with the hollow fill that he had designed to go into Left Hollow, which would have covered the mine entrance. Why then was the Group picking on Rebecca? She must be the only person in permits that they had control over, or at least thought they had.

G T left work at five o'clock and went to his apartment via the law school. He had done a paper for his class in torts that he needed to turn in. While in the building he ran into Oliver Barton, an attorney who taught classes on environmental law. He started to ask him a hypothetical question about Rebecca's signing the Group's contract to do whatever they told her, but he thought better of it, fearing that Professor Barton might be a member of the Group. G T told himself that he was getting paranoid about Rebecca's persecutors.

Seven o'clock saw him running a little late as he took the first exit off of Interstate 64 into Frankfort. Keeping within the speed limit, he parked in front of Rebecca's apartment, not paying any attention to the black Ford Marquis in the parking lot. Its tinted windows precluded anyone seeing the two men sitting in it.

He hurried in and went up to Rebecca's apartment. When he rang the door bell, she came to the door, looked through the security peephole and even then asked who was there.

"It's me, Rebecca," G T said.

Opening the door, she had a scared look on her face.

"What's the matter?" he asked.

"That black car has been sitting in the parking lot ever since I got home. It has two men in it that I don't recognize, but it pulled in right after me. I don't know if they followed me home or what, but I am getting real shaky about all of this," she said as she began to cry.

Reaching out and hugging her, G T told her that she was probably imagining things, and a good meal and movie would dispel all of her fears. Picking up her clutch bag, she went out the door as G T held it open for her. When they got to his truck, he opened the door for her and after she was seated went around behind the Marquis and wrote down the license number. The car was from Tennessee. As they pulled out of the parking lot the Marquis did also, except that it turned toward downtown Frankfort as G T turned toward Lexington.

"See there," he said. "They weren't following you. It was just a matter of coincidence."

In the Marquis, the man on the passenger side dialed his radiotelephone. "Deane made the car and wrote down the license number. Someone needs to pick them up at the I-64 exit," the passenger said as he described G T's truck.

Turning onto I-64 toward Lexington, G T noticed a black Toyota Camry parked on the side of the road. As G T passed, a man was out acting as though he was checking his tires. Hurriedly getting in the Camry, he pulled into traffic trying to keep G T in view. G T watched him in the rearview mirror until he got blocked off by two tractor-trailers that were passing.. Topping a small rise that would put the Camry out of sight for a moment, G T pulled off on the side of the road.

"What are you doing?" asked Rebecca.

"That car parked on the side of the road as we came off the exit ramp is following us. I plan to lose him."

The two tractor-trailers went thundering by, with the Camry tailgating the Margo Mover truck in the left hand lane. As soon as they passed, G T pulled into traffic. At the next median cross over, marked with a big EMERGENCY ONLY sign, he swung across the median and started back toward Frankfort. The driver of the Camry was watching G T in his rearview mirror and not paying attention to the Margo Mover tractor-trailer that was still in front of him in the left lane. A car in the right lane ahead of the Landon Trucking tractor-trailer suddenly cut over into the left lane in front of the Margo Mover that was passing. Hitting his air brakes, the Margo Mover trucker skidded his vehicle, cussing the driver in front of him at about the same time the Camry rear-ended him. The Camry driver hit his brakes too late and ran up under the trailer. The driver and the passenger were both killed instantly. From the shape their bodies were in, some forensics expert would really have a tough time making any identification. The Camry stayed stuck up under the trailer until the trucker pulled over on the right shoulder of the road and stopped.

Crossing the median again at the next crossover, G T proceeded back to Lexington. He slowed down as he passed the accident scene. Rebecca looked real hard as they went by but she didn't recognize the car. The license was from Ohio, but she couldn't get the numbers. On reaching Lexington, G T went straight to his apartment and parked in back. There were no suspicious vehicles in his parking lot, but he wasn't taking any chances.

"What are we doing here?" asked Rebecca in a questioning voice.

"I want to make a phone call," G T said.

Once in his apartment, he went straight to the phone and dialed the Golden Star offices. Gerry answered the phone.

"Mama, I want to bring Rebecca home and let her stay for a few days. I'll explain to you later. Please look up Howard Gibson's phone number," he said.

Gerry had learned years ago not to slow G T up asking details when he said he would explain later. Looking up Howard's phone number, she gave it to G T who said goodbye and hung up. When he dialed the Gibsons' number, Rosemary answered. With a real quick hello, G T asked her how to get ahold of Jacob.

"He's right here," she said, handing the phone to Jacob.

"Jake, this is G T and I need two favors. First I would like to know who this vehicle is registered to. It is a late-model Marquis," he said as he read the license number to Jacob. "Second, there was an accident about an hour ago on I-64 between Frankfort and Lexington. A black, late-model Camry rear-ended a tractor-trailer. I need to know who the Camry is registered to and who the occupants were. I'm on my way to Pineville now and I will play all of this over with you when I get there."

Going into the bedroom, he got two pairs of old jeans, four sweatshirts and four pairs of socks and put all of them in a backpack. Coming out he grabbed Rebecca's hand and went out the door.

"Where are we going?" she asked.

"I'm taking you home to stay with my family until we get this thing straightened out," he said.

"What about work?" she asked as they pulled out of the NO PARKING zone in the back of the apartment building..

"Forget it. You can't work if you are dead," he said turning off Richmond Road and getting in the southbound lane of I-75. "Tomorrow morning we'll get Mama to call in and say that you have had a bad accident and you will be hospitalized for several days," he continued. "Now, Isabel, let's think about—"

That was as far as G T got when Rebecca interrupted him. "Damn it, G T, I am Rebecca, not Isabel. If you can't keep your mind on who you are with, then turn around and take me back to Frankfort. I'll take my chances with the Group rather than be insulted," she said as she started to cry.

"I'm sorry, Rebecca. I apologize. Please forgive me," G T said with his face as red as fire. "Let me start over. Let's think about this problem. Somebody wants that permit stopped bad. Why? It appears that they don't mind what extreme they have to go to in order to stop it. Why? Who would profit by the permit being held up? We don't know. No one has objected to the area being surface mined before, so why all of a sudden do they want to stop it. The only person in the Division of Permits who can be leaned on is you. The only things you can put pressure on are the ponds or ditches. That leaves us with the question of we don't really know if it has to do with the ponds. It could just as well be a hollow fill," finished G T.

"I can't answer any of your questions," Rebecca said.

"Did you ever hear of Strick's Silver Mine," asked G T.

"No, I haven't," she said. "I know that Jason Strick is president of White Pines and is about the rudest man I have ever had the misfortune to have any dealings with. He jumped on me about two days after I had gone to work in permits. I had returned a submittal because the ditch calculations were wrong. I've forgotten who the engineer was who did the design, but he had made some real bad errors that I pointed out when I returned it. Strick called me up and gave me a round house tongue-lashing over sending them back. He said that he would go to the commissioner if he had to and he would make sure I would not check any more of White Pines' permits. Commissioner Lawson called me into his office and asked what the problem was. I explained the errors and he agreed that I did the right thing, but he would rather I didn't check any more of White Pines' work."

"Do you think Lawson is the Group's contact?" asked G T.

"I don't know," she replied. "I know that I got your work to check while he was out of the office, so he must not have told my supervisor to keep White Pines' work away from me. I guess I should have turned it down, but I really didn't think things would get this complicated. There was a note attached to the permit package directing it to me, but there was no signature on the note. Someone other than my supervisor sent the package to me. What about Strick's Silver Mine?"

G T went into great detail explaining about the mine, its whereabouts and what its contents might be.

"I still have that coin I found when we were there," she said going on to ask him if he thought Jason Strick was the person putting pressure on her to quash the permit.

"I don't know, but it's a good possibility. As it stands now, if the permit is approved, the hollow fill in Left Branch will be one of the first moves made. That will cover the old mine entrance once and for all. If Strick is the one behind all of this, then he would have to try to get the treasure out, if there is one.

"If his parent company, Garbon Ltd., found out about it, they could lay claim to it and he would lose it. His only chance to get at the treasure is to own the property. If he is stymieing the permit in hopes they will not have sufficient mineable coal to fill their orders and have to sell the property, then he could buy it through an anonymous buyer and recover the treasure. Once he had recovered the treasure, he could sell the property to Golden Star. Does that sound far out to you?" G T said.

"I think it is terribly far-fetched, but plausible," said Rebecca.

The conversation about Strick's Silver Mine had occupied most of the time the trip took from Lexington to Pineville. G T pulled into the Deane driveway and parked beside Gerry's truck. Pulling the backpack from behind the driver's seat, he went around to the passenger side and opened Rebecca's door. Helping her out, they went to the back door that Gerry was holding open for them. G T took the backpack up stairs and put it in the room where Rebecca was to stay.

Coming back down stairs, he went out in the kitchen where Gerry and Rebecca were seated.

"Please tell me what is going on," Gerry said in a very disturbed tone.

G T started at the beginning about Strick's Silver Mine, the pressure being put on Rebecca to turn down his permit, the Marquis in the parking lot and the Camry accident."I was afraid for her to stay in her apartment after all of the happenings that had taken place. The only safe place for her was here. I brought some old clothes of mine for her to wear while she is here," he said.

"G T, your clothes would cover her twice," his mother said. "I have some jeans and sweatshirts that she can wear. I'll go to town tomorrow and buy her some underwear and other necessities."

"Where is Daddy?" G T asked, noticing that it had gotten dark and George wasn't home yet.

"He, Frank and Sarah went to Boston the day before yesterday. They are due back sometime tomorrow," Gerry answered, waiting for G T to question why they went.

"Went where?" he quizzed.

"To Boston, Massachusetts," she answered, still waiting for him to ask her why they went.

"What in the world did they go to Boston for?" asked G T, finally taking the bait.

"They are looking into the possibilities of buying White Pines," Gerry answered.

"I've told you all about our secret, now you tell us about their deal," said G T.

"Three weeks ago, a Patrick Flannery, president of Garbon Ltd, called Frank and told him they would like to discuss the possibilities of selling White Pines to Golden Star. Two days later Frank received a package in the mail that had copies of all of White Pines core logs, maps, permits, contracts and other pertinent information. He and George went over it with a fine tooth comb for another two days and came up with an amount of proven reserves that was somewhere in the amount of thirty million tons. All of White Pines coal is dedicated to an overseas conglomerate named Electrique Internationale. Frank called Calvin Marks at Piedmont Bank in Spartanburg, North Carolina. He has been in the office several times wanting to make some big loans to Golden Star. Frank asked him to come in and talk to them. Mr. Marks said he would be in the next day, which he was. They had a long discussion and Piedmont agreed to lend Golden Star the money to swing a deal of so much at a very enticing rate of interest. The top limit never was revealed, but he gave Golden Star a letter of credit that would cover the sale."

"Why is Garbon Ltd. so anxious to sell all of a sudden?" asked G T.

"You and Rebecca both realize that this is all very confidential, don't you?" asked Gerry.

"Yes, Mama, we realize that. Now go on with your story," said G T.

Gerry was interrupted by the sound of George's diesel truck pulling up into the driveway.

CHAPTER 18

Betty Smith Talbert was beside herself. She called out for Wing Fu several times, to no avail. There was nothing missing from Wing Fu's bedroom except the two figurines of the bear and the butterfly. Recalling Dr. Chang's conversation she remembered his saying that these were the mark of sovereignty. She went to the phone and called John.

"Wing Fu is gone and I can't find her. The door was open when I got home and the apartment was empty. I am scared John. What should I do?" she said, her voice beginning to quaver.

"Shut and lock the door. Don't open it for anyone. I'll be right home," he told her.

What was normally a fifteen-minute drive from his office to the apartment turned into a five-minute drive with the help of the blue light on the dashboard of his car. Running from the parking lot to the elevator in the building was another two minutes. The ride up in the elevator stretched his time from when Betty called to when he got in the apartment to ten minutes.

"Tell me exactly what happened," he coaxed her.

Step by step, Betty went through her day from when she left Wing Fu, through her conversation with Dr. Chang till when she called John.

"Did you tell this Dr. Chang that Wing Fu was staying here?" he asked her.

"No," said Betty, "I did ask him about the birthmark and he told me the same thing that Wing Fu had told me. Oh, John, I am sure he wouldn't divulge her where abouts even if he knew," said Betty. "She is his daughter."

"Whoever has taken her must have come in right after you left, so they knew she was here before you went to see Dr. Chang," John said as he went into Wing Fu's bedroom, "and I have an idea where they found out."

Looking around the room, he noticed that the venetian blinds were slightly ajar as though someone had been peeking out of the window. He also noticed that her sandals were beside the bed so she must be barefoot. That would mean that she couldn't go far. He checked all through the apartment, opening all of the closet doors and even looking under the beds. All was to no avail. In the hallway outside the apartment, he walked down to the maintenance closet door. Opening it, he almost missed seeing Wing Fu as she hid behind a large trash container. Betty, who was right behind John, spoke very softly to Wing Fu and told her that it was all right, that no one would harm her. Then Betty reached over and took the girl's hand. Next putting her arm around her shoulder, she reassured the girl that no harm would come to her as they walked back to the apartment. Wing Fu told her that she had peeked out of the bedroom window to watch Betty leave. As Betty pulled out of the parking lot, Wing Fu saw Lin Chou with two other Chinese men and a Chinese woman, who was her half-sister, Ching Lee, get out of a car and start walking toward the building. She grabbed the figurines and ran out of the door, shutting it behind her. She ran down the hall to the maintenance closet and went in and hid. She heard the group discussing her as they walked up and down the hall. One of the men opened the closet door and looked in, but didn't see her. She told Betty that her half-sister, who was older than she, had always been jealous of Wing Fu because she was the Butterfly Princess.

"What are we going to do, John? The people who are after her know that she is here and as soon as we leave they will try again to take her," asked Betty.

"I have an idea," said John. Picking up the phone, he dialed the governor's office. When Karla Matheson answered, John told her who he was and asked to speak to the governor. Karla knew that anytime John Talbert called the governor she was to put him through, no matter how busy Martin was. Buzzing the governor, she told him that John was on the phone.

"Good afternoon, Sarge. What can I do for you?" he asked.

"Good afternoon, Governor. It's 'Lieutenant' now thanks to you," John said.

"What's the problem, John?" the governor asked in seriousness.

"Betty and our roomer need to talk to you. Will you have the secured entrance to the capital garage cleared for me to drive into? I'll be there in about fifteen minutes," Lieutenant Talbert said.

"It and the secured elevator to my office will also be waiting for you," said Governor Martin.

Betty had gotten together Wing Fu's simple possessions and put them in a backpack, being sure that the figurines were in it. John went out and got the car, bringing it around to the back door. That way anyone who was watching the front of the building would not be able to see Wing Fu get in the car. John figured this would give him a head start, which was all he needed.

Clicking on his blue light, he headed for the capital. He hit his siren at the first red light and went through. The car following him had to stop. Making a right turn, two lefts and another right put him back on track to the capital, but thoroughly confused the car behind him.

At the secured entrance to the capitol, the door opened and Talbert drove in as planned. A state policeman who was guarding the entrance showed them to the secured elevator. Pushing the "GOV" button, they were taken straight to the governor's suite. The door opened and Karla Matheson welcomed them into the reception area. Governor Martin came out of his office and shook hands with John, giving him a very smart salute. Speaking very politely to Betty and Wing Fu, he ushered the three of them into his office.

"What is the problem, Sarge?" he asked.

"Betty will fill you in. I need to make a phone call," answered John.

Betty began to tell Governor Martin all that had happened since Wing Fu showed up at his office three days earlier. Meanwhile,John went into Karla's office and called the bar on Short Street in Lexington, where Booger hung out. When the bartender answered, John asked to speak to Booger.

"Hullo," was Booger's response.

"Booger, this is Sergeant Talbert," John said.

"You got no cause to roust me, Talbert," Booger whined.

"I'm not rousting you, Booger. I need a favor," said Talbert.

"You're asking me for a favor?" questioned Booger.

"Yes. Now listen close. There is a fat, greasy slob who runs a trailer park in the lower end of Lexington," said Talbert.

"I know where it is," said Booger.

"Okay. I want you to go out there and persuade 'greasy' to tell you if he told that Chinaman that owed him the fifty bucks who I was and who was with me. Anything else you get out of him is a bonus. I'll pay you the going rate," said Talbert. "I'll call you tonight for some answers."

Back in the governor's office, Talbert asked Governor Martin if he could still fly a chopper.

"As you well know, I was one of the best," said Albert Martin with a grin.

"Could you fly the three of us to Pineville and let us put Wing Fu in the hospital there?" asked Talbert.

"I sure can. I'll have to take a trooper with me, but I've got a real good one who is a pilot and a bodyguard," said Governor Martin.

"What I have in mind is having her put in isolation at the Pineville Community Hospital until she has that baby. Then I'll get Thelma Durham to let her stay at her house until Wing Fu is able to travel. When she gets well enough to travel we will have to make some more plans," said John.

"I've been thinking and I believe I can talk Abdullah Savig in going back to her province with us to see about buying some horses. He owns that big spread outside of Lexington on Old Frankfort Pike named Oasis Farms," said Albert.

"The only thing left that I need to do is to get Dr. Stephen James to admit her and confine her in isolation. So I'll call Thelma Durham, fill her in on what is going on, and get her to call Dr. James," said Talbert picking up the Governor's private phone and dialing Thelma's number.

When Thelma answered, he told her real quick what he wanted. She said that she would call Dr. James and she was sure he would accommodate Wing Fu. She also said that she would be glad for Wing Fu and the baby to stay with her for as long as necessary.

"We're ready when you are," said Lieutenant Talbert to Governor Martin.

Just as they were about to leave, Karla buzzed Governor Martin on the intercom."I'm sorry to bother you sir, but this is the Chinese consulate in Washington," she said.

Picking up the phone, Albert answered it.

"Governor Albert Martin speaking," he said motioning John to another phone. "May I help you?"

"A special envoy from the People's Republic of China requests a meeting with you tomorrow to discuss a very important issue that is straining the relations between both of our countries," said the consulate. "She will be in your office at ten o'clock tomorrow morning. Thank you."

Hanging up the phone, Albert Martin buzzed Karla right back. "Karla, have that called traced," he said.

CHAPTER 19

Jamison put together his first committee that was to begin the tear-down of PSK. He had interviewed at least a hundred or more, before he began. His first committee was made up of office clerks and secretaries because they were the ones who knew all of the company gossip and were also the ones who had quite often been passed over in the review process. He selected at least one from each of the twenty districts that comprised PSK and the General Office. The total count of the committee was thirty-eight. This was a very large committee, but he would pare it down after the first meeting. With all of the committee members in a large conference room, Jamison gave them a pep talk. Each was seated at an individual desk similar to a school desk.

"You people are the backbone of this company. You are the ones who do the most work and get the least credit and that is why I chose you. Together we are going to get rid of the deadwood in this company and make room for some advancement of you people who have never had a chance. I interviewed all of you, but I am terrible at names, so I will just point my finger at you if I want a response. Actually it will be easier on me if I don't know your names.

"I am going to give you a questionnaire that I would like for you to fill out. I want you to do this all on your own without anyone else seeing what you have done. The questions will probably shock you to a degree, but remember we are here to change this into an efficient organization. We all know that you have to break eggs to make an omelet. Don't put your name on the paper or in any other way identify yourself. There is a number in the upper right hand corner of the desk where you are seated. Please put that number in the upper right hand corner of your sheet. These responses will be kept confidential, but you never know when that may be breached, so don't identify yourself. Take your time. I want these questions answered to the fullest of your knowledge. Don't hold back. Say what you think. Remember, we are here to streamline this company and we can't do it with out your being dead honest on these questions."

"After this first meeting, the committee will be narrowed down to a more workable group. If you are not selected to be on this first committee, don't feel that you answered your questions incorrectly. To be up-front honest with you, I will select five people for this committee by putting the numbers in a hat and drawing them out. I cannot match your number against your name so I will send the list of numbers out to all areas for posting on the company bulletin boards. You will check the boards to see if your number has been selected. If it has, you are to respond to my office and give your name."

All the time Jamison had been talking, he had had another employee who was looking through a one-way window, make a seating chart of the numbered desks and the people seated at them.

Handing out the questionnaire, Al Jamison began the methodical dismantling of Public Service of Kentucky. The questionnaire was a "hate" sheet in itself: What is your supervisor's name? Do you like/dislike him/her? Give reason for your answer. Do you want his/her job? Can you do it better than he/she? Were you given an increase after the last evaluation? If not, why not? Do you think your supervisor is having an affair? If so, with whom? Do you think your supervisor is dishonest? If so, can you prove it? Do you think the company would be more efficient with you as a department head in place of your supervisor? How would you change things? What other departments need new supervisors? To reduce your department by 50% who would you layoff? Why would you lay them off? To reduce your total district employees by 50%, who would you layoff? Why? To make the company more efficient, who would you layoff? Why?

The filling out of the questionnaire took most of the day but he broke up the meeting in time for all of the members to get back to their homes. He didn't want them to stay the night in Lexington and have the opportunity to get together and discuss the questionnaire, at least not this time. After taking the questionnaires to his office, Jamison went through them. Employees who had said that they liked their supervisor went into one pile. Those who didn't went into another pile. He then separated the two piles into four piles, depending on how they answered the last question. If they listed ten or more for layoff, he put them in one pile. Those of less than ten he put in the other pile. He wound up with five employees who didn't like their supervisor and listed ten or more for layoff. This was the group he intended to call back for another session. Jamison repeated this "game" over a period of three weeks until he had culled the satisfied employees from the dissatisfied. He wound up with a core group of twenty employees who not only didn't like their supervisors, but would collectively layoff over half of the present employees.

Al called a meeting of his committee to begin the layoff procedure. Gathering them into a conference room, he made his pitch.

"This committee is the nucleus of the future PSK. From it will come the recommendations to get rid of some of the deadwood. I have a list of persons who you people feel need to go. This is not a "hit list," as some of you may believe. It is a very business-like approach to a serious problem that is hampering this company's growth. It is a program that has been put in operation in a number of big companies that are suffering from the same lethargic output that this company is suffering from. I am going to read you some of the comments that were put on the questionnaire that was filled out by over a hundred of your fellow employees. These are all direct quotes as follows:

'My supervisor is a slob. He doesn't do anything but drink coffee all day.

'The next time my supervisor pats me on the butt, I'm going to knock her flat.

'Why does my supervisor make more than me when I do all of the work?

'My supervisor and her boss are having an affair. I caught them in the act.

"These are the type of people we want to get rid of. They have been here too long and they don't appreciate the good company they are working for. Don't be afraid that the company is going to put them out with nothing. They would never do that. They will be offered a buy-out of $10,000 for every year of service up to 20 years. That's almost a quarter of a million dollars. They can take early retirement if they are eligible. This is a pretty sweet deal."

What Jamison didn't tell them was the fact that he made up the responses he had just read to them, plus the buy-out sounded good, but they would have to pay their own medical insurance and one open-heart surgery could cost $150,000. Basically the laid-off employees were going to be shafted and didn't know enough about it to realize what was happening.

"Now we are going to get down to the nitty-gritty of this operation. I am going to give you a list of fifty supervisory employees. I want you to divide these into five groups of ten to the group. Those you feel should go first, put in the first group. Next, put the ones to go after them, et cetera. If you don't know a person, leave that name blank."

What he was saying was he would fill in the blanks and get rid of whom he wanted to, while the committee would get the blame. It was a sure thing that before this was over, most of the committee members would wish they had never heard of Al Jamison.

++++++

The week following the committee meeting, the first and second groups were called into Lexington and given the buy-out pitch. Twelve of the twenty said they would take it. The other eight didn't like it. One supervisor named Candace Bingham said she was going to fight it. She had an uncle who was a state legislator and she called him. She hadn't been one of those who were on the committee and she told him it was a kangaroo court type of thing. Elmer Bingham, Candace's uncle, was a big worker in the local Democratic party in the town of Barmore and a close friend of the governor.

He had never done anything but be a politician. He had served two terms as jailer of Bannon County, of which Barmore was the county seat, and then went on to greater things. He was a tall, thin, stoop-shouldered man with gray hair and a gray beard that was stained with tobacco juice. He talked real slow and thought real fast. From all outward appearances, you would think he was another dumb cluck who fell into it, but you would be wrong. He was as sharp as a tack and people who knew him, knew that.

Elmer called Governor Martin and told him what was going on. Governor Martin in turn called Jack Colbert and asked him what PSK was doing. After he explained to Colbert that Elmer Bingham's niece was being laid off, Colbert said that he was sure that there was some mistake; he would check into it and get back to the governor. Then he called Al Jamison into his office and told him to shut the door.

"You damned fool, do you know what you have done? You have laid-off one of our people who has an uncle in the legislature and who is one of the governor's best friends. Now you get on the phone and call the office in Barmore and tell Candace Bingham that there was a mistake and she was not one of the ones to be dismissed," Colbert said.

"You don't call me a damned fool or I'll walk out that door and leave you with a real mess," Jamison retorted. "That broad was the top one on the list to go. Everyone on that committee voted to boot her out. She is the most disliked employee you have and she was a unanimous choice to be the first to go. You're going to tear this all to hell if you keep her, but it's your baby so you are the one that has to change its diaper."

"Okay, I'm sorry, but we do need to be more careful. I don't want this to be a bigger problem than it already is," Colbert said, thinking to himself, "I'll get rid of you quick when this is over."

A few minutes later, Jamison called the Barmore office and asked to speak to Candace Bingham.

"Candace, this is Mr. Jamison and I'm sorry, but there has been a bad error made. Your name was mistaken for another employee and the company wants to withdraw its offer of early retirement and payment for the thirteen wonderful year's service you have," Jamison lied.

"That's a bare-faced lie and you know it," she responded. "My uncle called the governor and he called Colbert and Colbert called you in and chewed you out. So now you have to eat crow and you don't like it. I'll tell you something else while I'm at it. I'm going to tell everybody I see what happened and you are going to get your tail in a great big crack."

Candace was a woman of her word. The layoff was the topic of conversation in every group where she was present. She called Jamison every kind of a "lyin' sonuva bitch" that she could lay her tongue to. He definitely hadn't heard the last of her.

CHAPTER 20

Whitley had gotten settled into her new accommodations in Bern. She had been there for six weeks and she really loved it, especially the late summer weather. She missed the companionship of Harry and Joe, but she felt she could fill that need in the very near future. The people she worked with made her feel wanted, although they also made her feel lacking in some respects. They all spoke German, French and English, while she spoke only English. Learning French was on her calendar of things to do.Her apartment was actually a small chalet that sat on a hill side at the edge of the city. It had a living room, a kitchen-dining area, a large bed room and a bath. The entrance was a narrow natural stone walkway that connected the house and the sidewalk. A connecting garage housed the new Mercedes that was her company car.

The living room had a vaulted ceiling with exposed beams of rough hewn lumber. The floors were wide board with wood pegs polished to a glossy sheen. There were windows on each side of the door and two at one end of the room. They were double-hung clear thermopane glass at the bottom and fixed thermopane stained glass at the top. The floor had a large shag rug that left sections of the highly shined floor visible. A large fireplace occupied the other end of the room, with a wood rack full of oak and ash wood stood next to it. Ventilators installed in the chimney warmed the room when the fireplace was active; otherwise, there was an electric heat pump that heated the house in the winter and cooled it in the summer. The furniture was of local design, being made of sturdy oak. There was a large couch along one wall with two wing back chairs across from it. These were all overstuffed and very comfortable. End tables accommodated reading material and floor lamps provided lighting at the side of each chair and both ends of the sofa. A stairway up one side of the room ended at a walkway to a balcony that was on the end of the room with the fireplace. From it one could view the Aare River that bordered the city and on a clear day, the Bernese Alps.

The kitchen-dining area was pretty much the same as she had in Kentucky. A stove and refrigerator filled one side of the room while a sink together with dishwasher and china cabinet filled out the other. A broom closet type cabinet stood next to the china cabinet. This provided storage space for canned goods. A drop leaf table sat in the middle of the room with two chairs placed at it. Four more chairs were at the end of the room, providing seating for six when the table had both leaves extended. Cabinets, in place above the stove and sink, held spices and other necessities for cooking. Under the sink, which contained a disposal, was a cabinet that housed a garbage can and cleaning supplies. The counter tops and floor were covered with ceramic tile.

The bedroom walls and ceiling were done in a light green, with matching wall to wall carpeting of a deeper shade. A king-size bed sat against one wall with a dressing table, mirror and chair against the other wall. A small fireplace was used for heat in the winter. A walk-in closet was fitted along one wall, next to the bathroom entrance. The bedroom was situated next to the bath, which was almost as big as the bedroom. It had the usual fixtures such as commode, lavatory, shaving cabinet with mirror and an enclosed shower. It also had a four-person Jacuzzi that Whitley really loved. Wall decorations such as pictures and other hangings were not present in either bedroom or the living room. Kurt Holtz had told her when he showed her the chalet that those items were to be of her choosing.

A shopping mall was located within walking distance of the apartment area and Whitley found that she could supply just about all of her needs by visiting it. She did most of her shopping in the mall after work. One evening while she was buying groceries, she saw a familiar face. She was in a position that kept the target from seeing her. She stared until her eyes hurt and, sure enough, it was Pete Kelly. He had grown a beard which made him look different, and he looked as if he was sick. He was pale and gaunt as though he had lost weight. She couldn't believe it. He was going through the checkout lane so she hung back, taking a can of peaches out of her cart and leaving the rest of her purchases in the buggy. Hurrying through the line, she exited the store in time to see Pete walking down the street. She followed him as he walked two blocks to a chalet- type condo, similar to hers. Unlocking the door, he went in. Hurriedly she wrote down the address and returned to the grocery store to finish her shopping.

When she got to her chalet, she put the groceries away and sat down to the telephone. She had a company calling card that Kurt had told her to use in any way she wished. Following the instructions that he had given her, she began to dial Joe Barnes' office, not realizing that while it was 5:00 PM where she was that it was 1:00 AM tomorrow where Joe was. When she didn't get an answer, she came to the realization that there was a time change, so she dialed his home. Sleepily Joe answered in a very gruff voice.

"Guess who this is," she teased.

"I don't know, but if I don't find out pretty quick, I'll hang up," he groused.

"Why Joe, you wouldn't hang up on Whitley, would you?"

"Where are you?" he asked.

"I am in my condo in Bern, Switzerland and it is five o'clock in the afternoon," she said, "and guess who I just saw."

"I have no idea," Joe answered.

"I was in the grocery, which is not far from here, and standing in the check out lane was Pete Kelly. I hung back so he wouldn't see me and when he left the store I followed him. He is living in a condo about three blocks from me. What do you think I ought to do?" she said.

"There is a $10,000 reward on his head," Joe told her.

"I remembered that, but I don't really need it right now. I think I will send Colbert an anonymous letter with Pete's address on it and tell him to give the reward to the Special Olympics or some other fund," Whitley said. "It would be worth ten grand to watch the fireworks when Colbert catches up with him."

"Give me your phone number so I can call if anything happens," Joe said.

Giving him the number and instructions on how to call, Whitley told him good bye and hung up.

The next morning on her way to work she mailed the anonymous patchwork letter to Jack Colbert, giving him Pete's address and instructions on what to do with the reward. Then she drove to the office in downtown Bern and parked in a place marked for her in the garage. She took the elevator to the floor where EI's offices were located. Her first job was to review the contracts that EI had for the purchase of coal. There were two mines in Russia, one in Germany, one in China and one in the United States, White Pines by name. All of the coal that was mined in those countries supplied power plants located within a two-hundred-mile radius of the mines, with the exception of White Pines. Its coal at present was being shipped to the plant in China that was located three hundred miles east of the Shuai province. It was Kurt Holtz's intention to build a 500-megawatt plant in the Shuai province and supply coal to it and the other Chinese plant from mines located within Shuai. He also wanted to acquire Public Service of Kentucky and supply its generating plants with coal from White Pines. All of the mines were captive only in a contract sense. The mining was done by independent companies such as White Pines.

Before ever hiring Whitley, Kurt Holtz had looked at Public Service of Kentucky and Commonwealth Electric and Gas as possible entrees into the power market in the United States. He had done his homework on Jack Colbert and Bill Carson, President of Commonwealth Electric and Gas, when he had attended a power company executive's seminar in Acapulco a few years back. Colbert, Carson and a man named Al Jamison had been sitting in a booth next to Kurt in the hotel bar. All three had gotten pretty well oiled up and he heard Jamison brag that he could bring PSK to the point of merger with CEG in less that three months. Colbert had told him he was hired and when he got back to Lexington, he would make his board approve the hiring of Jamison. Kurt didn't know what happened, but he never heard any more about it. Little did he know that his newly hired coal buyer had queered the deal.

Two weeks after Whitley had gotten set up in Bern, Kurt Holtz stopped in her office one morning. "The Bern Symphony Orchestra is in concert at the Casino Hall tomorrow evening. Could I have the pleasure of your company for dinner and the concert afterwards?" he asked her in German.

Taken completely off guard, Whitley blurted out, "I would love to," in Kentucky English.

"I will come for you at 6:00 PM. The concert is at 8:00, so this would give us time for you to see the city," he responded again in German.

Thinking fast she answered in broken German, "I will be ready."

The next day dragged on like it would never get to quitting time, although it finally did. Rushing home, she showered, fixed her hair and donned a beautiful maroon evening dress, cut low in the back, but decently low in the front. Six o'clock found Kurt at her door. Asking him in, she went through the martini routine that she always went through with Harry. Kurt graciously accepted and seated himself on the couch. Pouring the martinis, she served Kurt and seated herself next to him. She was completely enamored by him. He was wearing a plaid jacket tuxedo together with cummerbund, black patent leather shoes, and an off-white ruffled shirt with a maroon bow tie. He looked like something out of a magazine ad.

After finishing the martinis, they left for dinner. On the way he showed her the bear pits near the Nydegg Bridge. Pulling into a parking space set aside for the viewing of the bears, he got out and went around to open her door. He had a sack in his hand that she couldn't imagine what it contained. At the fence that surrounded the pit, he opened the sack and gave her a bunch of carrots. Seeing the carrots, one bear reared up on its hind legs and begged like a dog.

"Throw her a carrot," Kurt said.

Responding to his directions, Whitley threw the bear a carrot, which she caught in her mouth and immediately ate. A smaller bear that was obviously her cub, stood on its hind legs and begged as she did, getting the same result from Whitley.Finishing the bunch of carrots, they went back to the car and drove to the restaurant where Kurt had made reservations.

"We are right on time," he said as they passed the 700-year-old clock in the town square.

Dinner was "fabulous," to use her terms. They had roast duckling with baby new potatoes and asparagus with a delightful cheese sauce. The salad was a congealed fruit and vegetable salad flavored with champagne. Dessert was a very light lemon chiffon pie with lemon zest sprinkled on the meringue. Again Kurt selected the proper dinner wine as he had done in Pittsburgh. Talk during dinner was mainly smalltalk. He gave her a rundown on his life, his love of the company and desire to make it grow into the world's largest supplier of electrical energy. He had never been married, but had had several serious relations. Something always seemed to happen that interfered. Then Whitley told him about her life, especially while she was at PSK. She told him about Colbert's plan to up the dividends by reducing expenses and jiggling the books then merging with CEG. He listened intently while she talked. He didn't tell her he knew all of this from the bar talk in Acapulco. He wanted to see if she would tell the truth to him, which she did.

Suddenly realizing that the time had crept up on them, they hurried to the concert which she thoroughly enjoyed.

CHAPTER 21

George Deane came in the back door of his Holly Tree Hollow home, dropped his suitcase in the bedroom as he went by, and went on into the den where Gerry, G T and Rebecca were waiting for him.

"How was your trip?" G T asked.

"I've been places I didn't even know were on the map," said George after he went over and kissed Gerry. "We landed in Boston and got settled in a hotel at the airport. Sarah had checked on the planes out of Boston to Portsmouth, so we cleaned up and flew to Portsmouth to see Alberta and Dewayne, who were both in real good health. We didn't stay long and came back to Boston. The next morning we ate early and went to see Patrick Flannery, President of Garbon, Ltd. He told us that they wanted to sell White Pines so they could invest in some other projects that they thought would give them better return on their money.

"He asked us what we thought of Jason Strick, so Frank told him that what dealings we had had with him were friendly enough, but that he kept himself pretty well away from the local scene since he lived in London, Kentucky which was some fifty miles away. Flannery said that Strick was the primary reason they had to sell White Pines, that Jason kept putting up excuses to not mine the ridge between Right and Left Branches of Red Oak Creek. We told him that we had heard that White Pines had been having problems with getting a permit approved to mine that area, but that we didn't know anything about what the problem was. Flannery told us that they had a contract with a European company named Electrique International for all of the coal they could mine, but they were about to lose it because their production had fallen off and EI, as he called it, was going to void the contract. He had gotten approval from EI to sell to us. He said that they weren't going to tell Strick about the sale until they had completed it.

"He made us a price and we took him up on it and signed the papers. We now own White Pines Coal Company, but we are going to keep operating it under that name instead of having to move everything over to Golden Star which would mean we would have to repermit everything. Flannery is coming to Pineville tomorrow for a few days to break the news to Strick. He said that he didn't have any problem with Bryan Fuson, except that he didn't have too much initiative and the company directors didn't feel that he had the get up and go needed to run the company. He pretty well let Jason run it. He said that they had a place in the company that Bryan would fit into very well and they would move him out in the very near future. Flannery kind of has a feeling that Jason had some hidden reason for not wanting to mine the ridge in Red Oak, but he couldn't find out what it was."

G T and Rebecca had listened to George very intently until he finished.

"Daddy, do you remember me looking for Strick's Silver Mine when I was in junior high school?" G T asked.

"Yes, but what has that got to do with the White Pines permit?" asked George, a little piffed that G T had changed the subject.

"We believe that we have found it and that is why White Pines can't get their permit approved," said G T.

"You're crazy, G T. What is the connection?" he asked, still perturbed that no one wanted to hear about his trip.

G T started from the beginning when Rebecca turned down his permits and went through the whole thing clear up to the Camry wreck. George was courteous enough to listen. He had learned years ago that G T figured things out pretty well before he started to talk about them.

"Tomorrow morning I'll get two lights and hard hats and you, Rebecca and I will go look into your silver mine which I still think is a fairy tale," said George.

"Can we put it off a day? I would like to check on Bige and get Mama to call in sick for Rebecca," G T said.

"Okay. I forgot that I told Patrick Flannery that I would pick him up at the Middlesboro airport tomorrow morning," answered George.

The next day was a busy one for George. He met Flannery at the Middlesboro airport and drove him to Pineville. Patrick sent the corporate jet to Knoxville for refueling and layover while he got things straightened out at White Pines. He told the pilot that he would call him and give him instructions on when to come back to Middlesboro. Patrick Flannery was a very affable man whom George described as being as Irish as Patty's Pig. He was of medium build with black hair and black eyes. He had nice straight teeth that shined when he smiled, which he did quite often. He had been born and raised in Boston and had gotten a degree in business from Amherst University. He furthered his education by getting an MBA at Massachusetts Institute of Technology. He was a student of people and he sized them up pretty fast, but he had failed miserably when he selected Jason Strick to head up White Pines.

George felt that it would be best if he and Frank were not present when Flannery gave Jason Strick his walking papers, so he got a company truck for Patrick to use and told him how to get to the White Pines office. Gerry asked Rebecca if she would like to go to town with her and get some personal things, but G T vetoed it.

"I don't know who knows Rebecca and who doesn't, but I sure would hate for her to be found out. We've come this far without telling anyone where she is so let's not spoil it now. Also, Mama, we need you to call the Natural Resources office in Frankfort and tell them that Rebecca has had a bad accident and will be in the hospital for several days. Be sure to use a pay phone so they can't trace the call," G T instructed. "I'm sorry, Rebecca, but I don't want to take a chance on that black Marquis finding you, which reminds me, I told Jake I would call him when we got here."

Then G T picked up the phone and dialed Howard Gibson's residence. "Rosemary, this is G T, how are you?" he asked

"I'm fine, honey. Here is Jacob," Rosemary said, handing the phone to Jacob.

"How's it going, G T and where are you?" asked Jacob.

"I'm at Mama's," answered G T.

"I don't know what you are into, but I have some info on those two items you asked me about, and if you'll stay there for a few minutes, I'll come tell you about them," said Jacob.

Jacob was as good as his word and ten minutes later he pulled into the Deane's driveway.

G T met him at the back door and led him into the living room.

"Everybody here knows about the Marquis and the Camry so you can talk freely," said G T, as he hurriedly introduced Jacob to Rebecca.

"I will after you tell me what this is all about," said Jacob.

G T proceeded to fill Jacob in on all that had happened to Rebecca including Strick's Silver mine and the entire permit hassle. Then it was Jacob's turn.

"The Marquis was a stolen vehicle from Nashville. Not long after you called me it was found burned up on a back road off of the old road to Shelbyville. It had been wiped clean. Whoever stole it cleaned it out. The spare tire was gone as well as the tools. The hot wire job was professional. The Camry was out of Ohio. It also had been stolen. The two fellows in it were messed up so bad that the forensics people couldn't get a make on them until they had run their prints through the FBI files. They didn't have anything on them to identify them. Neither had a wallet or even any change in their pockets. Each of them had a .357 on him and there was a sawed-off shotgun in the floor. I think that Rebecca is fooling with some very dangerous people and needs to stay out of sight until we get a better handle on this."

As soon as his explanation was finished, Jacob had to leave in response to a call from dispatch. G T told Gerry to go to a pay phone and dial the Natural Resources offices in Frankfort. When the receptionist asked her who she wanted, Gerry was to ask for Rebecca's supervisor, Phillip Banks. When she got him, G T told her to tell him that Rebecca had been in a bad automobile accident on I-64 near Frankfort and had been taken to Lexington in an ambulance. The two men with her had been killed and Gerry thought she was taken to ICU in critical condition. She was to say that the ambulance was from Metropolitan Emergency Services and she didn't know which hospital she was sent to. Before he could ask her who she was, Gerry was to tell him that she was a friend named Polly Wilson and hang up.

Gerry went to a pay phone at the Chevron Service station in Pineville and did as G T had told her. Banks didn't seem too disturbed that Rebecca had been hurt and didn't ask Gerry to which hospital she had been taken. He acted as though he didn't care. After she made the call she went on to the mall to get Rebecca some clothes and personal items. When she got back home, she parked beside Jacob's cruiser that was in the driveway. When she got in the house, she put Rebecca's things on the kitchen table and went into the living room. G T, Jacob, Bige and Rebecca were all in there. Bige was crying. G T motioned Gerry into the kitchen.

"Jacob came by and got me to go to Bige's strip job with him. Olivia slashed her wrists this morning in the bathroom at the jail. She took one of the fluorescent bulbs out of the overhead light and broke it. She cut both wrists and bled to death before they found her. One of the other prisoners saw blood on the floor in the stall where Olivia was and called the turnkey. She had locked the door and the turnkey had to break it open to get to her. They took her to the hospital, but it was too late," he said.

While he was talking, Isabel came in the back door.

"What happened?" she asked.

G T went through the details again. She went on into the living room where Rebecca was consoling Bige. He was sitting on the couch and Rebecca was sitting next to him. When he looked up and saw Isabel, he started crying again. Isabel sat down on the other side of Bige and put her arm around him.

"Do you know Rebecca?" Bige asked Isabel.

"Yes, we were roommates for a while," she answered as she asked Rebecca how she was.

What had the possibilities of being a very stilted situation, if not ugly, was friendlier than G T had expected. He breathed a sigh of relief. The only thing that bothered him was the fact that two more people knew that Rebecca was at the Deanes' house. He knew that neither Bige nor Isabel would blow the whistle, but it still concerned him.

Bige got his composure and arose from the couch. "I guess I'd better be getting to the house. I want to be there when Daddy gets in. We'll have to go to the funeral home and make arrangements. Do you think Randy Hall would have Mama's funeral, G T?" he asked.

"I'll call him if you want me to," GT said.

"I sure would appreciate it," Bige answered. "I guess we would have it tomorrow if Randy can get here."

"Rebecca and I will take Bige home," Isabel told G T, who almost fainted.

Getting into Isabel's car with Rebecca in the back seat, they drove Bige home, leaving G T standing with his mouth open. When he recovered, he went inside to dial Randy Hall, who was attending the seminary in Louisville. Randy answered the phone.

"Randy, this is G T," G T said waiting for Randy to answer him.

"Hi G T," he answered. "What is going on?"

"We need a favor," G T told him.

"As always, I'll do it if I can and it is honest," he said.

"Olivia Napier committed suicide this morning and Bige asked me to call you to see if you would have her funeral," G T said.

There was a silence while Randy let what G T said soak in.

"When would this be?" Randy asked.

"Circumstances being what they are, I'd say that the visitation will be tomorrow evening with the funeral right after it. Back when Bige got hurt, she told me that they had burial plots in the Napier cemetery on Greasy Creek, so I guess that's where she will be buried. Jacob told me that she wrote Bige a letter, which the jailer gave to Jacob to give to Bige. I don't know what is in it, but it might give you some idea what to say. I'm not trying to tell you how to do it, I'm just giving you information that you might need. To the best of my knowledge, she didn't belong to any church so I guess the funeral will be at the funeral home."

"I have a class tomorrow morning, but I will leave right after it. I should be there sometime after lunch and I will get with Bige and his father to see what they have in mind. Thanks for calling me, G T. I appreciate the opportunity to help Bige. I'll see you tomorrow," Randy said as he hung up.

After Bige asked G T to call Randy, Jacob got to thinking about Thelma and what a hate she had for Olivia, so he decided to go tell her that Randy was being asked to conduct Olivia's funeral. After pulling up in Thelma's driveway, he got out and went to the door. Jemjelf answered the door and let him in. Jacob stood up until Thelma came in the room and gave him a great big hug.

"How is my favorite state trooper and student?" she asked.

"Better than ever," he said.

"And to what do I owe this pleasure?" she said.

"Well, it's not really a pleasure call," Jacob answered. "I need to tell you something and get your feelings about it."

"This sounds serious," she responded taking a seat on the couch and offering him a chair.

Sitting down on the edge of the chair, he started talking,

"Olivia Napier committed suicide this morning," he said.

"That isn't particularly bad news to me," Thelma responded cooly.

"Her son, Bige, asked G T Deane to call Randy Hall and ask him to conduct her funeral. I know how you felt about her and I know how you feel about Randy, and I thought I ought to run it by you before you heard it from someone else," Jacob said.

There was a long silence as Thelma sat with her head bowed. Finally looking up at Jacob, she told him, "I hated that woman for killing Bradley and I can't say that I am sorry she is dead, but Randy is a minister and funerals are a part of his job. I certainly can't feel ill toward him for doing what is the right thing. I think it is what Randy should do. Maybe someday the Lord will forgive her for what she did and forgive me for the way I feel. I do feel sorry for that son of hers because from what I hear he loved her and is a fine young man. She must have been a better mother than I was or Brad would have turned out like her son. I hope no one minds if I go to the funeral. Randy's sermons always make me feel good."

As soon as Jacob left, Thelma called Randy and told him she had an extra bedroom and she would like for him to stay with her. He thanked her kindly and accepted the invitation. Thelma had no sooner hung up the phone from talking to Randy when John Talbert called her on the governor's secured line. She told him about Olivia, but he said that he couldn't make the funeral, although he would be in Pineville the next day.

"I need a favor from you," he said as he went on to ask her to call Dr. James.

Thelma called Dr. James as soon as she got through talking to John. She asked him to take Wing Fu as a patient and to put her in isolation. He questioned the confinement, but Thelma said this had been requested by the state police. When she told him that, he said he would do it.

++++++

When Sarah Morgan called Isabel to tell her about Olivia, Sandy opted to stay at the Morgans'. She told Isabel that she would feel out of place at the Deanes' since she didn't know Bige or any of the other people. Bill Minter called the Morgan home while Isabel was gone and Sandy told him about Olivia.

"I guess that pretty well wraps it up," he said.

"Where do you and Chris go from here?" she asked.

"I'm not sure. There is a rumor going around the international news circuit that there is a renegade Chinese woman seeking asylum in Kentucky. We hear that the Chinese consulate has contacted your Governor Martin and asked him to turn her over to them. We may stick around for a day or two to see what comes out of this, if it is true," Bill said, "Besides that I would like to go to Mrs. Napier's funeral. I understand that the minister who is to conduct the funeral was the foreman when G T and Mrs. Napier's son were flooded. I find that very heart warming. I guess I have a certain amount of curiosity also."

Meanwhile, Isabel and Rebecca drove Bige out to his home. His father's car was in the driveway so he thanked them and hurried in. Rebecca got in the front seat and Isabel pulled out of the driveway. Isabel broke the ice.

"I believe that I owe you an apology that has been a long time coming. I have a very smart mouth and a very sharp tongue and I would like to be friends with you," she said.

"I will accept your apology if you will accept mine. I also have a smart mouth and a sharp tongue and I would like to be friends with you," Rebecca answered.

"I guess you know that G T and I broke off our engagement for the time being. We both felt that we should see other people and if it was meant for us to marry, it would happen," said Isabel.

"I think he is one of the finest people I have ever met and by far the most polite. I've never had a boy open the car door for me and help me in and out. You have done a good job of training him," Rebecca said.

Isabel got quiet for a minute as she thought, "I'll pull his damn hair out the next time I get him alone," but she went on and changed the subject. "What's going on with you all?" she asked.

Rebecca started from the beginning with her turning down his permits and what had happened since. She finished just as they got back to the Deanes' house. "I would appreciate it if you wouldn't tell anyone that I am here. The people who are after me must be pretty dangerous from what Jacob said and to be truthful about it, I am scared to death," Rebecca said. "I'm sorry I can't go to Bige's mother's funeral, but I'm just plain scared to. He seems like a nice fellow and is very humble."

"I don't believe I would go if I were you," Isabel said getting out of the car.

They went inside where Gerry was talking to Sarah on the telephone. She told Sarah that the girls had come in and she had better go as she hung up. Isabel gave Gerry a hug and a peck on the cheek. Then she went out, got in her car and drove home to change clothes for Olivia's funeral.

++++++

Randy Hall came in early the next afternoon and went straight to the funeral home for the visitation prior to the service. Bige and his father were there along with Clifford Steele, the funeral director.

"I have a letter that Mama wrote me before she did what she did. If you would like to use it or some of it in your sermon, you are welcome to," Bige told Randy, handing him the letter. Clyde Napier, Olivia's husband, told Randy that he really appreciated Randy agreeing to conduct the funeral. While they were talking Isabel and Sandy Deiss came in.

"Randy, Sarah and Daddy would like for you to stay at our house while you are here," Isabel said.

"Thank you, Isabel, but I have already accepted an invitation from Thelma Durham," Randy answered.

Turning to Bige and his father, Isabel told them that Sarah was fixing some snacks for them and she would bring them in a few minutes. She went up to the open coffin and said a little prayer for Bige and his daddy.

As the afternoon drew on, more people came in. Most of them worked with Bige or his daddy. Two of Olivia's brothers came and some of Randy's old crew came to see him since the word was out that he was there. Sarah came in about four o'clock with a big tray of fried chicken, a bowl of potato salad, a dish of baked beans and a chocolate pound cake with Gerry's famous peanut butter chocolate icing. Bige first said that he wasn't hungry, but then he began to nibble and finally got a plate and sat down. Isabel and Sandy sat with him.

"That Rebecca sure is a nice girl. She talked to me and we prayed together and she really was nice to me," Bige said to Isabel.

"Don't tell anyone that you saw her. She's not supposed to be here. She and G T will be in big trouble if some people find that she is here," warned Isabel.

She had already explained Rebecca's presence to Sandy, whom she swore to secrecy. While she and Sandy were talking to Bige, Thelma Durham came in the funeral home. You could have heard a pin drop. She introduced herself to Clyde Napier and spoke to his father whom she met after Ed Durham's funeral. Then she went over to the table where Bige, Isabel and Sandy were sitting. When Bige got up and dropped the napkin that was in his lap. Isabel reached over and picked it up.

"Young man," Thelma said, "I hope you don't mind my being here."

"Oh no, Mrs. Durham, I really do appreciate your coming," he said. "I want to apologize to you for what Mama did and I hope you and me can be friends."

"Damn if I haven't heard it all," thought Sandy Deiss. "These people beat anything I have ever seen. It's no wonder Isabel loves mountain people. No matter what you do, they will forgive you in time if you will forgive them."

Clifford Steele gently called the gathering together for the service. As usual, Emma Caldwell had made the casket piece that was beautiful. There weren't many flowers, but enough to be presentable. Ginny Grace, who was seated at the organ, had been quietly playing various hymns. Bige had asked G T, Jacob, Jeff Cawood, Frank, George and Percy Hatfield to be pallbearers; Clifford brought them in and seated them. He next brought Randy in and led him to the dais. While Clifford closed the casket, Ginny sang "Amazing Grace." Then Randy stood up to the microphone. His homily was based on forgiveness. He read from scripture how Christ forgave the thief on the cross and the woman caught in adultery, then he read Olivia's letter to Bige.

"Dear son. Please forgive me for the many bad things I have done. I was not a good mother, but I loved you and wanted to protect you. I hope you will become a good man and find a good girl to marry and have children with. You were not my blood child, but no mother could love a son any more than I loved you. I ask you to forgive me for never taking you to church. I should have. I hope you will start going to church. I hope you will ask Mrs. Durham to forgive me for what I did to her. I am sorry. Thank Jeff Cawood for being my lawyer. I wasn't much of a client. Thank Isabel and G T for being your friends. I guess you have asked Randy Hall to say my funeral, so please thank him for me. It was a lot to ask of him. There are a lot of other people I want to thank, but I don't know how. I am ready to do what I am doing and I hope you will forgive me for this. Tell your daddy I loved him even though I never showed it. Goodbye. I love you. Mama."

There wasn't a dry eye in the place. Bill Minter and Chris Evans had come in and were sitting on the back row. Both of them had tears in their eyes. Randy's voice broke as he read the letter and finished his talk.

The funeral procession to the cemetery was not very long. The cemetery was on a knoll not far from the blacktop road to Williamsburg, about ten miles north of Pineville. Some of Bige's friends from the strip section had dug the grave which was in a clay bank. After the graveside service, Bige tried to pay Randy who refused to take anything from him.

"You always did what I asked you to do for me, so it's only right that I do what you asked me to do for you," Randy said.

CHAPTER 22

Albert Martin hadn't lost his knack as a chopper pilot. He took off from the helipad on the capitol building without a hitch. As soon as he got airborne, he headed north toward Louisville rather than southeast toward Pineville. John complimented the governor on his ability, and before John could question him Martin explained that anyone watching them would think they were going to Louisville and would react accordingly.

From her office, Karla had successfully traced the phone call from the Chinese consulate and, sure enough, it came from the Chinese Embassy in Washington, D.C.. As Martin had instructed, she scheduled an appointment for the special envoy at ten o'clock the next morning. He expected to be back from Pineville well before then.

The flight to Pineville was very uneventful, but it suddenly dawned on Governor Martin that he would need Betty in case the envoy didn't speak English, and at the same time she was the only person who could communicate with Wing Fu. He finally decided that the envoy would have to get across to him what she wanted without Betty's help. Martin had suddenly gotten involved in an international incident and he loved it. Like John Talbert, he didn't have any love for the Chinese either, but he felt sorry for Wing Fu. Since she had come to him for help, he was jolly well going to give it to her.

He set the helicopter down on the helipad at the Pineville Community Hospital where an ambulance was waiting to transport Wing Fu from the landing site to the emergency room. Dr. James was waiting with the ambulance when Albert set down. The Kentucky Governor's helicopter wasn't hard to recognize, with a big replica of the state seal on both sides of the fuselage. Always the politician, Governor Martin hopped out of the plane and shook hands all around. The hospital staff had been "host" to VIPs before, but having them come in the governor's chopper with him at the stick was a bit unusual to say the least. He told Betty and John to stay with Wing Fu while he would take care of the consulate. John thought to himself, "I've trained him well."

"As soon as I get rid of them, I'll call you, Sarge," Martin said as he got back in the helicopter and took off. His trip back to Frankfort was as uneventful as the trip down. His copilot, Trooper David Wilson, who had also flown in Vietnam, was very complimentary of the governor's flying skill. He didn't ask what was going on. He knew that Governor Martin would tell him what he wanted him to know.

Once he was in the Pineville Community Hospital, Lieutenant Talbert called Booger at his "office" in the bar on Short Street in Lexington. When

Booger got on the phone, John asked him how it went with the mobile home park manager.

"Them greasy fingers are hard to pull out of the socket, Talbert. I ought to charge you double, but this one is on the house," Booger said. "This guy paid off like a slot machine after I disjointed only two fingers. Seems that the China man is with some other China men that are dealing in pot. Their boss is the China woman that come and picked him up the day you were there, or so Greasy says. They've got some local fellow raising the pot, harvesting it and drying it in an old house up one of them creeks. He told me the guy's name and I think you asked me about him back when that man and woman got killed in the bathtub. I'm not sure, Sarge, but I think it was Smith. When I asked him how they got by the coal company, he said that the fellow that ran the company was in on it. He said that they cured the stuff and packed it in fifty-five gallon oil drums and shipped it with the coal that goes to China. They mark the barrels 'Samples' and it goes right through.

"Thank you, Booger, I owe you one," said Talbert.

"Just don't never tell where you heard this. Hey, Talbert, did you ever see somebody shoot the bird with the finger sticking straight up and their hand flat? It's what you call a reverse bird. Go look at Greasy, it'll crack you up," said Booger, laughing so hard that he was almost unintelligible.

++++++

The Chinese special envoy was very prompt and appeared in the governor's reception room at exactly 9:58 AM. Karla announced Ching Lee and her companions to the governor. Albert was ready for them and asked Karla to show them in, which she did.

Ching Lee didn't look a thing like Wing Fu. She was tall, with her hair done up in a bun on the back of her head. Dressed in a pale gray suit that was two sizes too small, she wore a gray pillbox hat that was definitely out of style and seemed to define her character. She was wearing spike heels that made her even taller than her constituents, and it was obvious that she was not used to them because she turned her ankle twice before she sat down. She was just plain tacky and that was all there was to it. Her nails were longer that necessary and painted a brilliant orange. There was a look about her that was hard and mean. Her associates were no better. The clothes they wore were of a cheap brand and looked like they had come from a hand-me-down store. She introduced them to Albert, but she had just as well talked to the wastebasket for all the sense it made to him.

Albert offered Ching Lee a chair and her cohorts seated themselves. He then buzzed Karla and asked her to come in and take notes. With everyone in place and seated, he asked the nature of the visit.

"I am a special envoy of the People's Republic of China and we are greatly concerned with the fact that a renegade has come into your country under the guise of being a person of royalty known as the Butterfly Princess. I am the Butterfly Princess and I have the Bear and Butterfly tattoo that is my sign of sovereignty to prove it," Ching Lee said as she slid her blouse down to the point where the tattoo could be observed. "The impostor is a dangerous woman. She is planning the overthrow of our government and we must capture her and take her back to our country before she puts her plan in effect. She will be tried for treason and imprisoned for life. We will take custody of the child she is carrying and it will be put in a government home for orphan children. We have reason to believe that she is being harbored by persons in your employment and we demand your assistance in apprehending her."

Governor Martin looked her squarely in the face and replied, "I have no idea what you are talking about or who in my employment would be doing such as you say. In my state, no one demands anything from me except the state legislature, and they aren't in session."

"We have enlisted the aid of your federal government in the search for this woman and I have a federal search warrant that authorizes us to go through your office and look for anything that might tell us that she has been here," Ching Lee warned as she pulled a folded piece of paper from her purse.

"I am governor of this state and I will have you arrested and jailed if you so much as act like you are going to search my office. This meeting has just ended and I will give you and your henchmen exactly five minutes to get off the premises of the Commonwealth of Kentucky. Before you go, let me have that search warrant," Albert Martin said, as a door, different from the one they entered, opened and four armed state policemen entered the room with drawn pistols. Ching Lee's accomplices were armed and had moved in a threatening manner. The troopers disarmed them and searched them for other weapons. In the process, they took the piece of paper she held in her hand. It was not a search warrant, but only a blank piece of paper. Governor Martin told the troopers to take them to their car and then escort them out of Frankfort. He also told them to put the pistols in the trunk of their car, but to not give them back to them. The troopers did as they were told and the last they saw of Ching Lee and her friends, they were headed toward Louisville.

As soon as the room cleared, Albert Martin called John Talbert at the hospital. "How's it going, Sarge," he asked, realizing that he was once again taking orders from Lieutenant John Talbert, even though he was the Governor of Kentucky.

"We have a winner," John said. "We no sooner got in the hospital than she went into labor. She had a beautiful little girl weighing seven pounds-ten ounces. The mother is doing exceptionally well. She gave the baby the

Chinese name for Alberta in honor of you. The daughter has the mark. How did it go with the woman?" John asked, still avoiding the use of names and still talking in veiled references.

"I kicked her and her associates out of my office and had them escorted to the interstate. She said she had a federal search warrant for me and I blew up on her. I didn't have the room debugged because I wanted her and her friends to hear what I had to say. If any of the four of them show up here again, I'll have them arrested. Do you read me loud and clear, Madam Special Envoy? I'll see you day after tomorrow, John," Albert said as he hung up.

John cracked up on that. He could just picture the four of them pulled off in the rest stop between Frankfort and Louisville, listening to Albert's part of the conversation on the bug that one of them had put under the arm of his chair. They had screwed up royally and would be called to task for it. For all of their efforts they couldn't make out where Wing Fu was.

Talbert's picture was accurate. Ching Lee and her gang were listening in from a rest stop. They pulled back out on the interstate and drove into Louisville, then on out to the airport where they rented a helicopter. Ching Lee told the owner that they would need it on a minutes notice and they would pay him around the clock, but he must be ready to take off when they told him. Unknown to the gang, an unmarked state police car had picked them up at the Shelbyville exit, where the officer that was tailing them dropped off. Trooper Margaret Callahan followed them all the way to the Louisville airport. She parked her car some distance from theirs and watched them go to the heliport. As a plain clothes detective, they didn't pay any attention to her. After they left she went to the owner of the chopper, showed him her identification and got a rundown on what they told him. She cautioned him not to tell them that she had been there or that there had been any inquiries about their business.

Callahan went back to her car and called the governor. When Martin answered the phone, she told him where they were and what they had done. He thanked her for the information and asked her to check on Ching Lee the next day at about ten o'clock and then call him back.

The next morning, Albert Martin put his own plan into action. With everything ready, he and his co-pilot, David Wilson, took off from the heliport on top of the capitol. As he had done the previous time, he headed toward Louisville.

"I'll make it easy for them," he told Trooper Wilson.

Five minutes after he took off, Trooper Callahan called him. "Governor, they forced out the owner of the chopper and took it over. One of the Chinese is flying it and he is headed toward Frankfort."

"Looks like they are going to want to play games, David," Albert told his co-pilot.

"There they are at one o'clock, sir," Trooper Wilson told him.

"I see them, David," Albert said as he swung the chopper around and headed back toward Frankfort. "I guess the best thing to do is to let them follow us to Haggard. They will have to land at the airport also and when they do, I'll have them arrested. They are hell-bent on kidnapping that Wing Fu and her baby, and I'm just as determined to prevent it."

All during the trip, the Chinese stayed well behind Albert and David. Calling the Haggard State Police Post on his portable radio, Albert told them who he was and then told them that he was being followed by some dangerous people in a helicopter. He said that the chopper was stolen and he wanted the people in it arrested when they landed. Martin also cautioned the dispatcher that they might be armed.

From the time they left Louisville, Ching Lee and her comrades had bickered about who was to blame for not finding Wing Fu when they went to John and Betty's apartment. The one who was second in command after Ching Lee and pilot of the plane, blamed the other two who were flunkies. Ching Lee listened to it as long as she could stand it, and finally told them to hush. She didn't know the area they were in and she could only guess where Albert was headed.

"The direction of his flight is toward London, Corbin, Pineville and Middlesboro. This map shows a hospital in each of those towns, but which one," she mused half out loud. While she was thinking, Albert turned north. This really confused her until she consulted her map again and it showed a hospital in Haggard, Kentucky.

"That's it," she said, showing the pilot where to go.

"Take a short cut and beat them to the airport. We can get out of sight before they land. We'll steal a car, find the hospital, get in it, take Wing Fu and the baby, if she has had it, and get away before that stupid helicopter pilot knows what happened," she laughed.

When Ching Lee broke off the chase and turned toward Haggard, Governor Martin told Trooper Wilson that he would slow down and let them get ahead of him. He figured that they were going to try to beat him to Haggard, so he would just let them. When they landed, the state police would arrest them.

CHAPTER 23

Jamison's run-in with Candace Bingham hadn't slowed him down. He let a couple of weeks go by and then came up with the brilliant idea of closing the Barmore office. Colbert had given him full authority to do whatever it took to put this merger together as soon as possible. He called Roy Seevers, the manager of the Barmore office, and told him to come to Lexington. Roy was aware of the conversation between Jamison and Candace Bingham and he figured he was going to catch it over that. He wasn't far from wrong.

Roy Seevers was as loyal an employee as Public Service of Kentucky had ever had. He had started out as a meter reader after he came back from Vietnam. He had progressed from that to serviceman, service foreman and then manager. He knew his district like the back of his hand and he knew just about every customer in it. Seevers was a small man with an almost bald head, but with a full moustache and beard that he trimmed daily. His eyes were pale blue and his hair was a deep brown. Unknown to most people, he had a small tattoo on the underside of his left arm: a heart with "Debbie" in it. She was his wife, whom he had married before he went into the service. He was a very personable man and most people considered him very humble. He was that, but he was also a fighter as his Bronze Star and Purple Heart signified.

He settled himself in a chair in the reception area outside Al Jamison's office. He didn't like being called into Lexington and he didn't know whether to blame Candace or Jamison. He whiled away his time by thumbing through a magazine he found on an end table beside his chair. He read an article about a power outage in northern Michigan that resulted from a squirrel getting electrocuted in a substation. There was a picture of the charred squirrel carcass and some hickory nuts lying on the top of the transformer that had faulted.

The Barmore District of PSK was neither the largest nor the smallest district. It covered the town of Barmore and several small settlements in the outlying area where it abutted the Pineville District. The primary source of income for most of its customers was farming, the biggest crop being tobacco. The Amalgamated Tobacco Company had a large warehouse on the outskirts of town. During the fall of the year after the farmers had cured their tobacco, they brought it into town and sold it to ATC. From time to time, some of the smaller farmers would ask Roy to tide their bills over until they got paid for their crop. He never refused one and he never lost a dime on it. The accounting department fussed at him about it, but it rolled off him like water off a duck. Jamison had picked up on this during his search through the Barmore records and this was what he was going to use as an excuse to close Barmore.

Coming to the door of his office, Jamison yelled to Roy, "Hey, Seevers, come in here."

Being called by his last name had always rankled Roy, but he let it slide this time as he got up and went into Jamison's office.

"Get you a chair there. You and me need to talk," said Jamison in his usual rude manner. "We're going to close that office of yours. We've found a lot of things that are against company policy in that district and since we need to close some offices, we had just as well start with yours."

"Is this because you had a run-in with Candace Bingham?" asked Roy.

"Nah. I don't pay attention to little broads like her. She could be replaced by about any streetwalker you could find, if Barmore was big enough to have street walkers. We found where you had let some customers slide on paying their bills and the company doesn't approve of that. You have been sent a bushel basketful of cut-off notices, and none of those bill moochers has had service discontinued. The company doesn't like that, either. We aren't in business to provide free electric service to a bunch of pan handlers."

"What happens to my people?" asked Roy, whose temper was getting up.

"We'll layoff the office force with retirement if they have been here long enough to get it; otherwise we'll let them collect their unemployment money. That will carry them for six months and that is more than most of them are worth. Service people, we'll keep most of them 'til we get the uproar settled and then we'll thin them out. You'll get a job as meter reader if you want it with a cut in pay, but if you don't want it you can take retirement or you can quit. It's entirely up to you," Jamison said, leaning back in his chair and lighting one of his foul-smelling cigars.

"What about health insurance and employee stock options, what happens to that?" asked Roy.

"They are on their own for health insurance. The company will buy their stock for three percent less than what it is on the market, which is a good deal for them. A broker will charge them six percent," Al said.

"In other words, you don't give a damn what happens to those people, do you?" asked Roy.

"Look, Seevers, I've laid it out for you. You can leave now. I've got work to do," Jamison said as he got up from his desk, hiked up his pants in a threatening manner and walked around to where Roy was seated.

Roy got up from his chair and in the same motion, dropped Jamison with a right cross square in the mouth. He fell like a polled ox. He started to get up, but Roy was standing up over him, waiting for him.

"That was a bad mistake, Seevers. You didn't know that I have a black belt in judo," bragged Jamison, spitting blood and teeth as he talked.

"I don't give a damn if you have a red bandana in Alabama. If you get up, I'll knock your fat ass off. You haven't heard the last of this. The word is out on you, you sloppy, sleazy, bandy-legged little bastard," said Roy as he left, slamming the door behind him.

"You'll get a bill for $4000 for my bridge work," Jamison whimpered.

++++++

At about the same time that Seevers knocked out Jamison's teeth, the mail courier delivered a letter to Jack Colbert. There was no return address, but the stamp indicated it came from Bern, Switzerland. Opening it, he found a patchwork letter put together with words cut from a magazine: "Pete Kelly lives at 1728 Montmarte Street Bern Switzerland, give the $10,000 to the Special Olympics." Colbert first flew into a rage, then settled down and began to think. The more he thought, the more determined he became to go to Switzerland and confront Pete. Picking up the telephone, he dialed a travel agency and asked them to get him a flight to Bern, as soon as possible. He left the next day.

Arriving in Bern, he immediately went to the hotel where the agency had made his reservations. When checking in, he asked the desk clerk if he had a map of Bern. The clerk gave him a map with an advertisement for a beer company and told him he could have it. When he got to his room, Colbert unfolded the map and found that Montmarte Street was only three blocks from where he was staying. It was a long street, but he felt he could walk that far even though he had a cold that had been hanging on for some time. He decided to wait until dark since he didn't want anyone seeing him go into Pete's apartment. The jet lag had screwed up his timing, but he finally figured it out. It would be about three hours until dark, so he lay down and took a nap. He was bone-tired.

Waking up at 8:00 PM Bern time, Colbert took a shower and put on some old clothes he had brought. He uncovered the .32 caliber pistol he had smuggled in with his clothes and attached the silencer that went with it. "I'll kill that little bastard and leave tomorrow," he thought as he pocketed the pistol and left.

He walked until he found Montmarte Street and looked at the street number of the first building he came to. It was 1624, meaning that he only had about a block to walk. The air had a chill to it as a stiff breeze came in off the nearby mountains. He was breathing hard when he finally reached Pete's condo. Two cars passed while he was looking around, so he lit a cigarette while he waited for them to get by. Once he was sure no one was watching him, he walked up the steps, moved quietly into the foyer and rang the bell. Poor stupid Pete didn't ask who was at the door. He just opened it.

"Hello, sweetheart, long time no see," said Colbert, sticking his foot in the door.

It took Pete a second or two to recognize Jack and when he did he tried to shut the door. He was too late. Colbert pushed the door open and went in, closing it behind him.

"Aren't you going to welcome your old buddy?" asked Colbert.

"What do you want?" demanded Pete.

"For openers, I want what's left of that two million you stole," Jack answered him.

"It's all gone," Pete said coughing into a handkerchief.

"Well you've had a good time out of it, so you won't mind me killing you since none of the money is left," Colbert told him.

"Go ahead. You'd be doing me a favor on account of I don't have much longer anyway," coughed Pete.

"What's the matter?" asked Colbert.

"I have lung cancer or worse," answered Kelly.

"You have what?" yelled Colbert.

"You heard me."

"How long have you had it?" questioned Jack.

"I found out about a month before I left PSK," Pete said as he started laughing. "That's when I decided to withdraw the money in the special account I had and go live it up."

"What's so funny?" asked Colbert.

"You smoked more than I did, so I'll bet you have it too or something else," he said.

"Did you send me a letter telling me where you lived, just so you could get me over here and tell me that you have cancer?" asked Colbert, ignoring Pete's remark.

"No, I didn't and I don't know who did," said Pete. "Now go on home and leave me alone so I can die in peace. I'm ready to go. I've had a ball. I had all kinds of friends as long as I had money. After it was gone they drifted away, but I didn't care. It was fun while it lasted."

Taking Pete's advice, Colbert pocketed the pistol and left. When he got to the hotel, it dawned on him that someone in Bern had blown the whistle on Pete, but he couldn't figure out who it was. Whoever it was had probably watched him go in Pete's condo so he was glad he didn't kill him even though he would have liked to.

Elsewhere in the city that night, Kurt and Whitley left the concert and started to her condo. "If he makes a pass I'll accept it," Whitley thought as he drove slowly up Montmarte Street. "If he doesn't, then I won't either and I will wait until another time." As they passed Pete's condo, she saw Colbert standing in front of it as he lit a cigarette. She was dying to see what went on, but she couldn't without telling Kurt about it and she didn't want to ruin a perfect evening, so she let it go.

When they got to her place, Kurt got out and opened her door. Asking her for her key he held her arm as they walked up the steps and entered the foyer. He opened the door and held it for her.

"Will you come in and have a snifter of brandy for a night cap," she asked in her best German.

"I don't believe I'd better. Tomorrow is a workday and I always like to get there early. I have some questions I would like to ask you, but that can wait," he said. Taking her right hand in both of his, he kissed it.

"Thank you for a lovely evening," she said.

"And thank you for a lovely evening," he answered as he turned and went to his car.

"Whitley, old girl, you have landed in a bed of roses with no thorns, at least that can be seen," she said to herself as she shut the door, locked it and proceeded to get ready for bed.

CHAPTER 24

Two days after Olivia's funeral, George got a call from Pat Flannery about 7:30AM.

"Jason Strick didn't like getting fired one little bit," Pat reported. "He made some threatening remarks about you and Frank, so I wouldn't turn my back on him if I were you. He cursed me, you, Frank and a girl named Rebecca Holton. He said that we had cheated him out of his birthright. I don't understand what he is talking about, do you? I spent a whole day going over the books and getting what I could out of Jason."

"I'm not sure what his birthright is, but if I ever find out I'll let you know," said George. "If you are ready to go back to Boston, I'll go to the airport with you and bring the truck back. Our house isn't hard to find. Just go like you are going to the White Pines mines and turn up Holly Tree Road. We live in a white house with black shutters on the windows. The shutters have hearts cut in them. Turn up the driveway and I'll be watching for you."

Fifteen minutes later, Pat Flannery turned in the driveway. George went out and invited him to come in and meet his family, which he did.

"What happened to you?" George asked as Flannery got out of the truck, his shoes and pants covered with mud.

"I had a flat on the way to White Pines and had to change the tire," Flannery said.

When George introduced Rebecca, Pat remembered Jason's cursing her.

"Young lady, keep your head down and your powder dry, because Jason Strick is mad as a hornet at you and the Golden Star people. I don't know what your part is in this and I guess I don't want to know, but I would beware of him if I were you." He then turned to Gerry and G T. "I am very glad to meet you, Mrs. Deane, since I have talked to you on the phone. I always like to know the people I am conversing with. And I've heard of you, G T. I believe you prepared the permit that Jason didn't want approved. They tell me that you are a graduate civil engineer and are pursuing a law degree. That is an excellent combination. If I ever decide to come back to Kentucky on a business venture, I will look you up. Now, George, if you will take me to the Middlesboro airport, I will go back to Boston. I am very glad to have had the opportunity to meet all of you. If you are ever in Boston, look me up," Pat said.

About five minutes after George and Pat left, the phone rang again and Gerry answered. It was Bige Napier.

"Mrs. Deane, this is Bige and I wondered if I could speak to Rebecca?"

"Why certainly, Bige," Gerry said as she handed the phone to Rebecca.

"Hello," said Rebecca.

"Rebecca, this is Bige Napier and I just wanted to thank you again for being so nice to me. I wonder if I could come talk to you for a little while. You made me feel so much better the other day that I would like to talk some more."

"I would love to, Bige, but G T, Mr. Deane and I are going up Red Oak Creek to look about a permit. We should be back by six o'clock," she said, not thinking that she shouldn't tell anyone where she was.

On the way to Middlesboro, George and Pat talked about the White Pines mines and the customer, Electrique Internationale. Pat began. "Kurt Holtz is a good man to do business with. He is honest and plays fair, but he is hard nosed when it comes to business dealings. We have been his supplier for five years and we negotiated a new contract just last year. He has escalators and de-escalators put in the contract, which is contrary to the way utilities in this country try to deal. He will listen to you if you have problems and will escalate if you prove the need. By the same token he will expect you to de-escalate if he needs it done. I think that you and Frank will enjoy doing business with him. As you know we have been sending all of his coal to a mine in China. He is an electric company entrepreneur and I have a feeling he has his eyes on a company in this country, Public Service of Kentucky to be exact. I'm just going by what I have heard, but I believe he would buy the controlling stock in PSK if it ever got ten percent below its present market value. Holtz also has indicated that if he could acquire PSK, he would go on and buy controlling interest in Commonwealth Electric and Gas since they are intertwined with PSK's transmission lines. He definitely wants to come into the American market and he has the money to do it with. I also heard just before I came down here that he had hired the vice-president of fuel purchases away from PSK and I believe her name is Rogers," said Pat.

"We know Ms. Rogers very well," George nodded. "When we bought Golden Star from Ed Durham, we also got the PSK contracts. Frank's wife, Sarah, who you have met, is our marketing person. She called on Ms. Rogers and came away feeling that we were in good shape with her. We have yet to find out who took her place. We hear that it is a young man from western Kentucky who worked underground for a few years, but has little experience in buying," George said turning into the Middlesboro Airport.

"One more word of caution about Jason Strick," Flannery offered. "I think he is extremely dangerous. He appeared to be angrier with Miss Holton than anyone else. I honestly believe that would kill her if he got the chance. Well, good bye, George. I have really enjoyed doing business with you and Frank. The two of you are coal miners and know how to make money at it. My people and I aren't and we didn't know how to cope with what Jason told us," Patrick said as he shook hands with George and climbed aboard his plane. George couldn't help but notice how Patrick scraped the mud off of his shoes before climbing into the co-pilot seat.

George watched as the plane took off and then he started home. He had gotten two hard hats and two cap lamps the day before, so he went home to get G T and Rebecca. They were waiting on him to go to the Strick Silver Mine, as G T called it. G T hadn't forgotten how to set timbers so he had put a chainsaw and a miner's ax in the back of George's truck. Looking at his watch, it said 10:00AM. On their way to Red Oak Creek, George stopped at Golden Star Mine #3 and got about twenty mine props. He also loaded three bundles of cap boards and six rough sawed cross collars. They drove as far up the left fork of Red Oak as they could and then they walked the remaining one hundred yards or so. G T called George's attention to the tire tracks that were in the soft ground where they had parked.

"These look like they were made today," he said.

"Who would be up in here?" asked George. "Maybe somebody sanging. Other than that I don't know."

G T carried about four or five props and said he would come back for the rest of them if they were needed. Rebecca carried the ax and the saw, while George carried the cap boards. When they got to the mine, they noticed that someone had been there recently. The bushes in front of the opening were mashed down and there were foot prints in the soft mud. Smooth drag marks scoured the opening, as though some one had dragged a sack of meal or sugar in recently.

"I guess that we should crib this up to do it right, but I believe the best thing to do is be real careful and not touch the roof. If we start setting props and try to shore it up, the whole thing might come in. It will hold long enough for us to see if Strick's Silver is in there," George said as he winked at Rebecca. And stay clear of that pile of rocks that look like they are holding the roof up. They may be doing just that," George told G T.

George turned on his cap light and crawled in the opening. Going about fifteen feet, he called back to G T to come join him. George again cautioned G T to not disturb the crib of rocks that was sitting on the left side. The mine widened out to about ten feet as it got further back. G T crawled up beside George.

"Look over here, G T," George said.

Shining his light ahead of George, he saw a man's shoe. Looking a little farther, he saw a man's body.

"Who is it, Dad?" G T asked.

"I think it is Jason Strick," George answered.

"Is he dead?" queried G T.

"To the best I can tell, he is," said George, feeling for a pulse in the man's leg.

Crawling up a little ahead of George, G T shined his light on the face of the man. "It is Jason Strick all right," G T said. "Wonder what happened?"

"I don't know," said George,

"There are bloodstains on his shirt and pants like he has been shot more than once, and the size of the wounds looks like a .38 or larger up close. The stains are still wet so it didn't happen too long ago. We need to get out of here and let the police see to this. Look over there, Dad," G T said shining his light to the left of Strick's body.

"What is it, Son," George asked.

"There is another body beside Strick," answered G T, "and a skeleton on up ahead of them. Someone has been in here lately because they have dug into this pile of silver coins"

"Do you recognize the other body?" asked George.

"No, but it looks like an Asian man," said G T, "and he's been shot at least twice with what looks like a pistol or a rifle."

"Let's get out of here. Be careful of that rock pile on up ahead of you near the entrance. It looks like it was put there for a purpose," said George shining his light ahead of G T.

Turning around, G T crawled out and waited on George. Rebecca was sitting on a nearby log. "I'm glad to see you all," she said, "It's spooky out here by myself and I keep hearing noises like someone is up there in the woods. I don't like this place."

"I'll stay here while you take Rebecca home and call the sheriff or state police," said George.

"Do you think it's safe?" asked G T. "Whoever killed Strick and the other fellow may still be around."

"I'll crawl back inside out of sight. If they want me they will have to come and get me," said George.

G T and Rebecca started walking toward George's truck when another truck pulled up beside it. It was Bige.

"I was wanting to see Rebecca again before you all left and she had said that you all were coming up here, so I just drove up to see if you were still here," said Bige with a bashful look on his face.

"You are a life-saver, Bige," said G T. "I need you to take Rebecca back to Mom's and then go get the sheriff or Jacob Gibson, whichever is quickest, and bring them up here. There are two dead men in that little mine."

Rebecca didn't seem to mind at all switching partners. She climbed in Bige's truck just like she belonged there. Maybe she did. G T went back to the mine where George was getting ready to go back inside.

"Bige drove up just about the time we got there," GT explained to George. "He took Rebecca home and will go on and get the police." Looking at his watch, G T noted that it was 11:00 AM. "I hope Bige gets ahold of Jacob," he thought.

CHAPTER 25

Lieutenant John Talbert had spent three days sitting outside Wing Fu's door at the hospital. Betty had spent the same amount of time in the room with her. It would have taken a pure fool to try to get into her room. John screened every nurse who went in and Betty did the same in the room. It had been some time since Betty had used her martial arts experience, but she hadn't forgotten how. Dr. James had ordered the baby to be kept in the room with her mother after John Talbert explained the circumstances to him. He told Wing Fu and the Talberts that he had never had a patient that was as responsive as Wing Fu had been. He was proud of the way she had endured the obvious hardships she had undergone and yet kept the baby from harm.

"You are as tough as a pine knot," he told her as Betty interpreted.

Wing Fu smiled and said, "Thank you," in English. Betty had spent the three days teaching her some easy English phrases and she was happy to get the chance to use one of them. Wing Fu had stayed in the Pineville Community Hospital for three days and Dr. James was amazed at how fast she had recovered. The baby was beautiful and the nurses couldn't get over how well both had done.

With the baby now three days old, the time had come for Wing Fu and the baby to be moved to Thelma Durham's house. John called her and asked her if it would be all right for them to bring the baby and Wing Fu that night.

"Any time is fine with me," Thelma said.

To keep anyone from knowing what was going on, John and Betty donned surgical scrubs, complete with hats and masks. Instead of the usual wheelchair, they put Wing Fu on a gurney and she held the baby next to her under the sheet. They put a scrub cap and mask on Wing Fu, then moved mother and child from the gurney to an ambulance cot. Dr. James drove the ambulance to Thelma's home where she and Jemjelf were waiting for them. Thelma had asked Jemjelf to come help her with the baby because it had been so long since she had been around a small one.

When Ed Durham had the house built, Thelma had demanded a separate bedroom downstairs complete with bath. That was her room and she slept there all the years they were married. After Ed died, she made a guest room out of his room. It, too, had a complete separate bath. She and Jemjelf changed the sheets, the bathroom linen, and put various lotions and powders in the bathroom for Wing Fu. Thelma had gone out and bought a crib, diapers, lotions and baby powders, and several baby gowns for Alberta when she found out that Wing Fu was going to be with her for a while. She also bought a small tub for Wing Fu to bathe Alberta in. Betty and Jemjelf put the crib in the room where Wing Fu could watch her at night. They had put a rollaway bed in Wing Fu's room for Betty. She had to stay with Wing Fu all of the time since Betty was the only one who could understand what she was saying.

Thelma and Jemjelf had cleared the second car space out so that Dr. James could get the ambulance in and the garage doors down. Once they had Wing Fu in the house with the baby, Dr. James took the ambulance back to the hospital, got his car and returned to Thelma's. Wing Fu was overcome with the attention she was getting. She kept telling Betty how nice everyone was to her, and how she wanted all of them to come see her when she got back to her home.

John called Governor Martin and told him that all was well. Albert told him that Ching Lee and her running mates were all in the Peary County jail. She had tried to bluff her way out of it by claiming diplomatic immunity, but to no avail. They finally let her make one phone call which went to the Chinese Embassy in Washington. Since all of the conversation was in Chinese, the jailer couldn't make out what she was talking about, but she acted real distressed when she hung up. She asked the turnkey to let her talk to the three men, which he shouldn't have done, but did. She told them that a fourth member of their group, Lin Chou, who was supposed to meet a contact from the embassy, had not made any appearance. His function was to negotiate a new price with the mine manager, for the marijuana that was being grown on White Pines property. She didn't know that the property had been sold and "the honeymoon was over."

CHAPTER 26

Sam Eldridge looked at his watch, not for the time, but for the date. The *Lexington Journal*, of which he was the editor, had finished up its coverage of the Olivia Napier trial with a story about her suicide that Sandy sent in. "Those girls have been gone five days. That's enough time to cover the end of the world, although, they did a beautiful job. No other paper, TV station or tabloid had done as well as Sandy had," he mused to himself, "but it's time they got back here to cover other stories."

Picking up the phone he called the number that Sandy had given him. Isabel answered.

"Is that you, Isabel?" he asked, "This is Sam Eldridge."

"Yes, Mr. Eldridge, it's me. Do you want to speak to Sandy?"

"You'll do," he answered. "I just wondered when you girls were coming back."

"We planned to come back tomorrow, if that is all right," she said.

"That will be okay. There is a big story about to break in Frankfort. It seems that some pregnant Chinese woman worked her way into the governor's office and then left with another woman and a state trooper. A couple of days ago, a special envoy of the Chinese government went to see Governor Martin. He threw them out of his office and had them escorted to the interstate. The next day the governor's helicopter took off from the capitol and was followed by another one. No one seems to know where either of them went, but the governor came back alone," Eldridge said. "It's got all the indications of being an international incident and I want the two of you to cover it. There was also a bad wreck on I-64 two days before that. I don't know if it had anything to do with the Chinese woman or not."

Sandy, Isabel, Chris and Bill had been sitting out on the Morgan's patio when Eldridge called. Isabel had come in and answered it. When she hung up she went back out with the others.

"That was Sam Eldridge and he wants to know when we are coming back. He says that there is a big story about to break in Frankfort," Isabel said and she finished telling them what had gone on.

"Do you remember me telling you about a tip we had received from our head office that there was a renegade Chinese woman trying to take refuge in the State of Kentucky?" Bill asked Isabel.

"Yes," Isabel said.

"Maybe we ought to go to Frankfort and check into this," Bill said to Chris.

"That would be a good idea. We could leave the rental car at the Lexington airport when we got ready to leave," answered Chris. "Going back to Lexington, you could ride with Isabel and Sandy could ride with me."

"That would be more interesting," said Bill, laughing.

"What time do you all want to leave tomorrow?" asked Sandy.

"I'll go when the wagon goes," said Chris.

"There are some people I need to see before I leave," said Isabel, "I would like to make it about two o'clock. That would put us into Lexington by around four. Would that suit everybody?"

All agreed.

In the morning before they left, Isabel told Sandy that she needed to go see some people. Isabel invited Sandy but she demurred, saying she would get her things together, and maybe she and Chris would leave a little earlier than Bill and Isabel.

Isabel went to the Pretty Posey flower shop first. She told Emma Caldwell how pretty Olivia's casket piece and the flowers at the funeral were. Emma was very pleased that her work had satisfied everyone. She told Isabel that Jeremy was doing real well at Western Kentucky University where he was studying to be a math teacher. He was to graduate next spring. Isabel told her to give him her love when she talked to him. Emma got tears in her eyes when she tried to thank Isabel for the banana box of food she and G T left on her porch in Wallsend Hollow the night before Thanksgiving years ago. She gave Isabel a big hug and told her how much she meant to Jeremy and her.

Next, Isabel went to see Rosemary Gibson. She liked to go to Rosemary's house because it always smelled so good. Today wasn't any different, although Howard was home. Isabel gave both of them a big hug and asked about Jacob. They told her that he had finished up at Southeast in June and would go on to UK from there. He planned to get a degree in accounting first and then go on to law school. He had met a Tennessee state police detective who was a beautiful girl, and was going to Knoxville every chance he got to see her.

"It sounds serious," said Isabel.

"I think it is and I am glad. We really like her," said Rosemary.

She took Isabel back into the kitchen where she was making a rum cake. Talking in a whisper, she told Isabel that PSK was forcing Howard to retire. He didn't want to, but it was that or move to western Kentucky. They didn't want to leave Pineville, so he opted to retire.

"He has been home for two weeks now and he is like a caged animal," said Rosemary, "He doesn't want to go back into contracting because he is too old and he feels that he is of no use to anyone. He has to find something to do. He's applied for a job as a security guard at the hospital, but so far nothing has come of it."

"What happened?" asked Isabel.

"They hired some new guy to be the personnel man and he has set about getting rid of as many of the good, faithful employees as he can. Evidently Howard was at the head of the list. The new fellow fired Roy Seevers, the manager at Barmore, and Roy knocked his teeth out. It's all a great big mess and I am glad that Howard is out of it except that I wish he could find something to do."

Giving Howard and Rosemary a big hug, Isabel left, asking them to give Jacob one for her. From the Gibsons' she went straight to Golden Star's office where she caught Frank, George, Gerry and Sarah sitting in George's office drinking coffee. Unannounced, she stormed into the office.

"As long as you all have been in business, I have never asked you for anything. The only thing G T ever asked for was a job for Bige and that paid off. Now it's my turn," she said with tears welling up in her eyes.

"What's the matter with you?" asked Frank.

"I need a favor," she said, half crying.

"You've never asked for one that you didn't get it, have you?" said Frank. "What is it?"

"Some dirty bastard at PSK has forced Howard Gibson to retire and he can't find anything else to do. He has tried several places, but he hasn't had any luck. He is a good man and when good people get down, other good people need to lift them up. I am asking you all to hire Howard. With his know-how and the addition of White Pines, it looks to me like you all need someone like him."

Frank looked at George like he had been hit by lightning. "Why didn't we think of Howard?" asked Frank.

"It never occurred to me. I didn't know he had left PSK," said George.

"Tell us what you are talking about," said Gerry.

"Yes," said Sarah," We are part of this too, you know."

"With the acquisition of White Pines, we are going to have somewhere in the neighborhood of fifty miles of power lines to keep up. In addition to that, we will be opening new mines from time to time and we need someone to do that when we want it rather than having to wait on a contractor. We have been trying to think of someone we could hire to take care of all of this and we never thought of asking him. A man like Howard would be invaluable with his experience and knowledge. I vote that we hire Howard right now," said Frank.

"I second the motion," said George, handing Frank the telephone.

"Aye," said Gerry and Sarah in unison.

When he called the Gibsons', Frank asked Rosemary to let him speak to Howard. When Howard came to the phone, Frank explained briefly what they wanted and asked Howard if he could come talk to them.

"When?" asked Howard.

"Now," said Frank.

"I'm on my way," he answered.

Fifteen minutes later, Howard pulled up in the Golden Star parking lot and went in the office where the foursome was still sitting. Isabel had left them with Howard Gibson as a project.

"Howard, we have bought White Pines and we are looking for someone to look after the power end of Golden Star and White Pines," Frank said. "We would get him all of the equipment he needed and someone to work with him that had similar experience. We heard that you had retired from PSK and we wondered if you would be interested."

"I certainly would be interested. I know a fellow who is younger than me, but he has a lot of experience. For the equipment, I can buy retired vehicles from PSK since I am a retired employee," said Howard, who had played over in his mind what he would do if they hired him. Thinking for a minute, he asked if it was a "make work" deal just because he had been retired from PSK.

"No way," said George. "We really need you. We have a pretty good idea what you make at PSK and we will top that by five thousand."

"When do I start?" asked Howard.

"Would tomorrow be too soon?" asked Frank.

"You all don't know how much Rosemary and I appreciate this," said Howard with his voice choking up.

"We have a truck that will be yours. Get Rosemary to bring you out tomorrow and she can take yours back home. Gerry will sign you up," said Frank. "We sure are glad to have you aboard."

When Howard got home from talking to Frank and George, he was a different person.

"What happened?" asked Rosemary.

"They hired me to take care of all their power lines and they are starting me at five thousand more than PSK was paying. They have a retirement plan, hospitalization and all the other benefits. I can go to the retired truck sales that PSK has and being a retired employee, I can buy whatever equipment I want. I am to do that next week. They said that I would probably need some help and I could start off by hiring another person. I told them about Roy Seevers and they said to get him."

Thinking for a minute, he asked Rosemary if she told Isabel about his problem. Rosemary confessed that she did and asked him why.

"She was leaving their office as I drove up. Knowing Isabel, I'll bet she told them about me," Howard said.

"Bless her heart," said Rosemary.

When Isabel got back home, Sandy and Chris were ready to leave, but they had waited to tell her that Chris would be at Sandy's apartment and she could let Bill out there.

"You have feathers on your mouth," said Sandy,

"What do you mean?" asked Isabel.

"You look like the cat that ate the canary," said Sandy. "Where have you been?"

"Out picking up news leads. Did you know that PSK is laying off a lot of good employees and replacing them with contractors?" she asked Sandy.

"No, but we will look into it," said Sandy as she got in the car with Chris.

"You all be good and we will see you in a couple of hours," said Isabel.

"You know me," said Sandy.

"That's why I said 'be good'," Isabel quipped

The trip to Lexington was uneventful for both couples. It was a good time to get to know more about each other. Chris Evans was originally from Rochester, New York. His father was an insurance salesman and had done quite well. His mother was a housewife who said that was her only talent, but she was very good at it. There was always a hot meal on the table at supper time, the house was kept immaculate and there were always clean clothes to wear. That might not have seemed like a lot to some people, but there were many husbands and children who didn't get that good a treatment. Chris and his sister, Clara, were raised in a loving family. Chris was a 5'9" wiry young man with straight blonde hair and hazel eyes. He had graduated from a high school in Rochester as salutatorian of his class of two hundred-fifty students. He was a superb tennis player and had earned a scholarship at Yale University as a result of his tennis ability. He had elected to study journalism because he loved to write and his best subject was English. He had also studied Russian and could converse fairly well in it.

Sandy had become enamored with him during the short period of time that she had known him, but was questioning herself as to whether it was a bona fide attraction or rebound from her split with Marc West. His intelligence seemed to be the primary draw. On the way to Lexington, they played a game where one would say a word and the other would have to build a sentence around it. It sounded like a simple thing to do, but it could get complicated. At one of his turns he had told her to make a sentence using the word "love." She had faltered on it and her face got red. She suggested they play something else. She wasn't quite ready to commit to the use of the word in the way she wanted to.

They went to her apartment when they got to Lexington and Sandy asked him to come in and wait on Bill. They continued their conversation along the lines of "where do we go from here?"

Isabel and Bill interrupted them putting an end to the week of work and play. From there, Chris and Bill went on to Frankfort, leaving Isabel and Sandy to get back to the daily grind of the *Lexington Journal* and school.

CHAPTER 27

As soon as he returned from Bern, Jack Colbert called an emergency board meeting of the directors of PSK to tell them about finding Pete Kelly. Once the board had convened, he told them that he had received an anonymous tip that Pete was in Bern, Switzerland. He had gone there and found Pete. He admitted that he took a pistol with the sole purpose in mind of killing Kelly, but cigarettes had saved him the trouble, or so he thought. Jack said that he expected to hear that Pete had died any day. He showed the board the letter and told them that he had ordered a check for $10,000 to be sent to the Special Olympics. None of the board evidenced any knowledge of who had blown the whistle on Pete, but Joe Barnes and Harry Baker both knew. However, they were not about to say.

The new personnel director was not at the meeting. Unknown to Colbert, Al Jamison was having some dental work done. After the board meeting, Colbert went into Jamison's office to see why he wasn't at the board meeting.

"What happened to you?" he said after viewing Jamison's cut lip and swollen mouth.

"When I fired that damned manager from Barmore, he assaulted me. I'm going to sue him," said Jamison through his busted mouth.

"You'll do no such thing. We will catch enough flak over this reengineering as it is. Leave it alone, your hospitalization will pay for it," Colbert said. "Continue with your program and get it over with as fast as possible before the public gets wind of it."

"I have another group coming in tomorrow morning for the 'buy-out or get-out' offer. That ought to cut things down to about two-thirds of the original number of people and send expenses down and dividends up," said Jamison.

The group that came in the next day after the board meeting was not nearly as docile as the previous groups. Candace Bingham had done a good job of firing them up against Jamison. His mouth was sore and he looked worse than usual. The word had gotten around that Roy Seevers had knocked him flat and everyone was jubilant about it. They kept whispering to each other about it and he knew what was going on. He finally lost his cool and told them just exactly why they were there. They had nominated Claude Pembroke to speak for the group. He stood up and unloaded on Jamison.

"This group represents no less than four hundred years of service to this company, and they are not going to sit still and see you and Jack Colbert tear it apart. You and Colbert don't know anything about working all night in the rain and snow to restore service to people who are freezing. You and Colbert don't know anything about wading water up under you armpits to help people get out of their flooded homes. You and Colbert don't know anything about fighting forest fires all day and night to keep them away from transmission lines that are about to be burned down. You are just what Roy Seevers called you, a fat ass, bandy-legged bastard. Go ahead and fire me if you dare. I have tape-recorded this entire meeting and the lies you have told, and when I leave this building I mean to give it to a reporter for the *Lexington Journal.*

"Not only that, we have a list of stockholders and we are going to call each of them about what is going on, that you and Colbert are rigging this company for bankruptcy. We've got a telephone campaign started by calling every representative and senator. Elmer Bingham is going to the governor again. We have called on all the council members of towns where offices are being closed to increase the franchise tax and look into the possibilities of the city purchasing the entire facilities. We also have a secret plan that we will reveal later on," Claude said as he sat down. The group clapped and whistled until Colbert came in to see what was going on.

"What's all the cheering about?" asked Colbert.

Before Jamison could get his sore mouth open, Claude again took the floor and delivered just about the same message to Colbert. When he sat down, the group cheered him again as Colbert stalked out the door. Then everyone got up, shook hands, and left to go back to their hometowns. Jamison skulked back to his office. As soon as he reached his desk, Colbert summoned him to his office.

"Who was that man that did all of the talking?" Colbert asked him.

"That was some guy named Pembroke from Maryville," answered Jamison.

"I want him fired," said Colbert.

"That was what I was in the process of doing when he started talking," said Jamison.

"You have a mess started. How are you going to get it settled down?" asked Colbert.

His intercom buzzed and his secretary told him it was Mr. Carson with Commonwealth Electric and Gas.

"Hi, Bill," Colbert said as he picked up the phone.

"Hi, Jack. What have you got going on? I am hearing all kinds of bad things about what that new man is doing," said Carson.

"We are doing a little shuffling around and some people are dissatisfied, but you know how that goes," said Colbert gritting his teeth. "It won't bother our plans, though."

“Let’s hope not. Some of my people have expressed concerns that this might spill over on us, but I have assured them that it won’t,” said Carson.

“I’ll call you in a couple of days and we’ll talk,” said Colbert hanging up.

CHAPTER 28

Isabel and Sandy met with Sam Eldridge first thing the morning after they got back to Lexington.

"You girls did a fantastic job on the Olivia Napier trial. Your articles were so real that I almost felt sorry for her. Her funeral must have been a real tear-jerker from the way you described it and the people who were a part of it," said Sam.

"I'm sorry Mr. Eldridge, but Sandy is the one who did the story. I was so emotionally involved that I wasn't thinking straight. I'll try to do better next time," Isabel said.

"Nonsense, child, you were at a disadvantage, but we all knew that. How come neither of you ever turned in an expense report?"

"We stayed with Isabel's parents and they wouldn't let me pay a dime for anything. I tried to take them out to dinner one night and they both almost whipped me," Sandy said. "Have you ever been to Pineville, Mr. Eldridge?" Sandy asked.

"No, I am ashamed to say that I haven't," Eldridge answered.

"If you ever get the chance to go, do it. It is the most tranquil setting I have ever been in. The people are wonderful to you. They make you feel like you are a native. I loved every minute of it. I should pay the paper for sending me instead of accepting my salary," said Sandy.

"Are you now working for the Pineville Chamber of Commerce?" laughed Sam.

The receptionist buzzed Sam's office and asked for Sandy, telling her that she had a call on an outside line.

"Hello, this is Sandy Deiss," she answered.

"Miss Deiss, my name is Claude Pembroke and I have a tape recording of a meeting that was recently held at PSK. I was discharged as a result of my part in the meeting and if you listen to the tape, you will hear why. I would like to give this tape to you to use in any manner you see fit. I promise you that the corporate management of PSK is not going to like it. I am fixing to leave Lexington and I will bring it by the *Journal* offices as I go out of town," he said.

True to his word, Claude Pembroke appeared at the *Lexington Journal* offices forty-five minutes after he had talked to Sandy on the phone. The receptionist buzzed Sandy and told her he was in the lobby. Sandy came out to the lobby and introduced herself.

"I am Sandy Deiss and you would be Claude Pembroke," she said.

"Yes ma'am and up until today I was the PSK manager at Maryville. I guess they will close the office next week and retire, relocate or discharge all of the employees there. The tape will tell you all about it. They hired a big sack of wind for a personnel director and he is reengineering the company. That is a big word for getting rid of a lot of people so the expenses will go down and the corporate management will get great big bonuses for their efficiency. Nobody ever says anything about the decrease in public relations and efficiency that will follow this laying off of people.

"When I went to work there eighteen years ago, it was a good place to work. The pay was good, the hours were good, the benefits were good and if you did your job and kept your nose clean you had a job for life. I don't know what happened to it, but it seemed like all of a sudden, everything changed. I know a couple of people on the board of directors and they never appeared greedy to me. I think the fault lies in Jack Colbert wanting to be bigger than he is. It's a known fact that he is queer and that fellow who ran off with two million dollars was his boyfriend. I'm not telling you anything that isn't common talk around the company. Listen to that tape. Here is my card if you want to call me and verify any of it. If you want to use my name, feel free to do so," Pembroke said as he shook Sandy's hand and left.

Going back to her office, she buzzed Sam and Isabel and told them she had the tape. Sam told her to bring Isabel and the tape and come to his office which she did. After listening to the tape, Eldridge couldn't believe his ears. He had always been a PSK supporter and so had the paper. It was unbelievable what Jamison, at Colbert's direction, was doing to the company. Eldridge told Sandy that the story was hers, but he cautioned her to hedge her terms and refer to all of her sources as being anonymous. Next, Isabel told them about Howard Gibson, how he had been treated and he was just one person. She also told them what Rosemary had told her about Roy Seevers knocking Jamison flat and breaking his bridge. Sam sent them both off to work while he mulled over the change that had taken place in one of his favorite companies.

Sandy pondered the rest of the day on how she should word the headline of her article. She finally decided on, "What's happening at PSK?" Going from there she launched into the facts as she had heard them related on the tape Claude Pembroke gave her. Following her early training as an investigative reporter, she began a background check on Al Jamison. As she progressed in her search for information, she was astounded by his track record. He wasn't a reengineering specialist, he was a wrecker. He had left four other companies that had almost closed their doors because of a lack of employees. Those that could had retired early, while those that couldn't had gotten jobs at other places. He was a menace and should be locked up, according to the word she got from one of the PR people at a gas company located in Rhode Island. She carefully worded her article to avoid saying anything libelous. When she had finished it, the day after she got the tape from Pembroke, she took it to Sam. Reading it cautiously to be sure that she had stayed in the guidelines of good journalism, he approved it and sent it to be printed.

Her article hit the fan big time. People from all over the state were calling in to PSK to find out what was going on. Members of the state legislature were being hassled to call a special session to look into the matter. The state public service commission switchboard stayed lit up. Jack Colbert called Sam, wanting to know where Sandy got her information. Sam wouldn't tell him a thing. Colbert was almost unintelligible. Throughout the company, employees couldn't get anything done for answering the phone and discussing among themselves what was going to happen.

The stock had closed at 24 the day before. By closing time the day of Sandy's article it had fallen to 20. Kurt Holtz had put a buy order on it if it went below 22. His brokerage firm bought all it could find in big blocks. Before the day ended he had purchased forty-eight percent of the PSK common stock. In essence, he owned PSK.

The board of directors of PSK were all on the phone with each other discussing what to do. Joe Barnes was leading the charge. He called a special meeting of the board for the next day. All of the board members said that they could be there and they were. Quite deliberately, they excluded Jack Colbert and told him so. Colbert was livid. When he told Joe that no board meeting could be held without the president there to chair it, Joe's retort was: "Watch me."

CHAPTER 29

From the mine site, Bige took Rebecca back to Gerry's in order to call the police. On the way, they talked about each other. Rebecca told him about her father and his injury.

"I really think it was his fault, but he is my father and I'll back him no matter what," she said.

"I felt the same way about Mama. I know what she did was wrong and I can't find anyway to make it right, but I loved her and I always will," he said as he began to sniffle.

"I guess we have a lot in common," said Rebecca.

"Are you and G T serious about each other?" he asked.

"Nah, we are just friends. We started off hating each other, but he was nice to me and I came to like him. He is a nice fellow, but he's so crazy about Isabel that he can't think about anyone else. "

"They've been awful good friends to me," Bige said. "G T saved my life when we got caught in the cut-in and then he got me on at Golden Star and she backed me all through Mama's trial. I've known them both since grade school. I wish they would settle down and get married."

When they got to Gerry's, Bige went in with Rebecca. G T had asked Gerry to stay home in case they needed to send Rebecca back, which they did. "Could I use your phone, Mrs. Deane?" he asked.

"Why certainly, Bige, if you'll call me Gerry like all of G T's friends do," she said.

Since it was Saturday, Bige called the Gibson house looking for Jacob. Rosemary answered the phone and Bige asked her for Jacob. It just so happened that he was there so Jacob came to the phone.

"Jacob, this is Bige Napier. G T wanted me to call you. He and his dad found two dead men in an old mine in Red Oak Hollow. I'm at Mrs. Deane's house now. I'll wait on you at the mouth of Holly Tree to show you where they are," said Bige.

"I'm on my way," Jacob answered. Turning to Howard, he told him what Bige had said and asked him if he wanted to go along.

"I guess that now that I am an employee of White Pines/Golden Star that I had better go along," said Howard getting up from his easy chair.

When Jacob got to Holly Tree, he slowed down and let Bige pull out in front of him. Bige turned off at Red Oak and took the Left Branch road when he got to the forks of the road. He pulled up and stopped next to George's truck and got out. Jacob and Howard followed suit. When they got to the mine site G T and George were waiting for them.

"How come anytime there is a murder, you always show up in it somewhere, G T?" Jacob asked jokingly.

"It's a talent I have, Jake," answered G T.

"What have you got in there?" asked Jacob.

"One of the fellows is Jason Strick. The other one is an Asian man that I don't know. They are back in there about fifty feet. Dad and I didn't mess around them because we didn't want to disturb any clues that might tell who did it. I'll take you in and we can bring the bodies out." said G T.

"I'll go with you," said Bige, who had brought Rebecca's light with him.

Giving Jacob a light, George cautioned them to be careful. The mine roof looked shaky. He hadn't intended to go in and out of the mine this many times. He also warned them about the pile of rocks that was an obvious deadfall.

G T, Jacob and Bige crawled back in the mine to where the two bodies were. Jacob crawled around behind them looking for anything that might tell him who had killed the two men. There was nothing tell-tale around the scene. The Asian man had been shot three times with a pistol or a rifle. The bullet holes were close together and there were powder burns on his clothes. Jason Strick had been shot twice, apparently with a weapon similar to the one used on the Asian man. It looked like the two men had been shot by the same person, or at least by the same gun. There were knee prints on the dusty floor where someone had been kneeling, evidently when they pulled the bodies into the mine. The knee prints went further back into the mine. Jacob shined his light back in the mine and saw two skeletons lying side by side.

"Look at this, G T," he said shining his light on them.

G T and Bige crawled back to where Jacob was. Together, the three of them moved on back to the skeletons. There were small pieces of blue cloth lying near the former bodies.

"Look over here," Bige said pointing at an old Union army belt buckle.

Moving a little closer, G T pushed away the dirt that had settled where the skeletons lay, uncovering a pile of silver coins. There were several brass buckles lying in with the coins that had been used to fasten the bags carrying the silver.

"We have found Strick's Silver Mine," said G T.

Jacob had called the ambulance service on the way to meet Bige and told them that he had two bodies to be retrieved. He also told them that someone would be waiting at the mouth of Red Oak to show them the way in, so he had asked Howard to take his cruiser and go to the mouth of the hollow to meet the ambulances, which he did. The ambulance driver had two body bags, but once on the scene, he called the dispatch and told them to send two more for the skeletons.

Taking the body bags to the entrance of the mine, the driver called inside and told Jacob that he was going to throw the bags inside as far as he could but he wasn't going to crawl back in the mine to get the bodies. Rolling each bag into as tight a bundle as he could get it, he heaved the first one into the mine opening. G T had his mouth open to tell him to be careful and not hit the dead fall rocks. As luck would have it, the driver threw the bag against the pile of rocks, which tumbled over. A deafening roar exploded in the mine entrance as the roof fell in, trapping G T, Jacob, Bige, two dead men, two skeletons and a treasure trove of untold value.

George reacted immediately. Waiting until the dust had cleared away, he then called out for G T but got no answer. He remembered that the rocks which supported the roof had been piled close to the entrance. George figured and hoped that the three of them were not caught by the fall. Running to his truck, he called the office and got Frank. He told him briefly what had happened and that he needed a rescue team fast. Frank called the #3 mine where Fred Tinsley was the superintendent.

"Fred, we've got three people trapped in an old mine on the Left Branch of Red Oak Hollow. Put together a team and come there as soon as you can. Bring your people out to help with the rescue," Frank said. He then called Sarah, telling her to get Gerry and bring her to the site. He reminded Sarah that Rebecca might be with Gerry and if she was, she could show them the way.

Howard had ridden to the site with Jacob and didn't have any transportation. He told George he wanted to go home to get Rosemary, so George told him to take his truck, which he did. Howard and Rosemary returned to the mine at about the same time that Gerry, Sarah and Rebecca got there.

CHAPTER 30

Whitley got up at the regular time, showered, fixed her hair and dressed. She really liked her work at EI, as it was referred to by its employees. Kurt Holtz had really nice to her, taking her to dinner again after another concert and she thoroughly enjoyed it. The rest of the time she stayed at home and studied. The French course she was taking was a little harder than she had anticipated, but she thought she could master it in time. On her every-other-day trips to the supermarket she had looked for Pete, but she had not seen him again since that first time. She hoped he hadn't picked up on her presence. She doubted that he had done that, because the one time she saw him he looked so bad that he didn't seem to care who anybody was.

One morning, a short time after she had seen Jack Colbert out in front of Pete's apartment, she was going to work when she saw an ambulance and a police car in front of the condo where Pete lived. She was consumed with curiosity to the point that she had to stop and see what was going on. Pulling into the curb, she parked and got out. Walking over to the small crowd that had gathered around the ambulance, in very broken German she asked a man standing there what had happened. He couldn't understand her, so she tried again very slowly. He finally shook his head that he understood.

"A man in that apartment died. He had been dead for three days so the police were called in. He died of syphilis," he said.

Whitley caught most of it, especially the part about the disease. That's why everyone was wearing surgical masks and rubber gloves. She continued on her way to work, mulling over in her mind how she should report this to Colbert. She finally decided to send him another patchwork letter. That night when she got home, she got an old magazine that she had brought with her and cut out the letters and words to make the letter. It said, "Pete died today of syphilis. Bet you have it too. Ha Ha."

Addressing the letter, she got her coat and started to go out the front door when the door bell rang. Looking through her peephole, she saw two policemen standing at the door. One was tall and good-looking with a faint mustache, the other short, bald and fat. Leaving the chain lock in place, she opened the door.

The tall officer addressed her in perfect English with a slight western drawl. "Are you Ms Whitley Rogers?" he asked

"Yes, I am. What do you want?" she quizzed.

"Please unlock your door. We must talk to you," he answered.

"Show me some form of identification," she demanded.

Both officers produced IDs that satisfied her and she released the chain lock.

"We have a warrant for your arrest, Ms. Rogers," the tall officer said.

"For what?" screamed Whitley.

"Please come with us with out any trouble. It will be so much easier," the short one told her.

She became completely unstrung. Grabbing her purse, she went with the two officers to their car. "You are making a bad mistake," she said.

"We will discuss this with you at the police station, Ms. Rogers," the tall one said.

The Bern Police Station was the same as a lot of other police stations: dimly lit, dirty and cold. When they got in the station, the officers led Whitley to a room marked "Interrogation" in German. Seating herself in a straight-back chair, Whitley asked them what this was all about.

"The man who passed away at 1728 Montmarte Street died of a venereal disease known in your country as syphilis. Before he died he wrote a letter and addressed it to our attention. He implicated you as the carrier of this terrible disease and said that you infected him. He also left a letter addressed to you which we will now give you. You may read it, but we must also read it," said the tall one, giving her the letter. Asking for a pair of rubber gloves, Whitley put them on and opened the letter:

"Dear Whitley, I saw you in the supermarket several weeks ago and I realized that you knew who I was. I know that you are the one who turned me in to the FBI for embezzlement and told Jack where I was, so I have left a letter for the Bern police telling them that you infected me with this venereal disease. Turn about is fair play. Ha! Ha! Your old friend, Pete."

Handing the letter to the short officer, Whitley told him to read it. "I want to be tested for syphilis and when I am shown to be negative, I want an abject apology from both of you and your chief," she said.

The short one handed Pete's letter to the tall one. After reading it, they both left the room and conferenced outside the door. Returning to Whitley, the tall one said, "We feel that you have been wrongly accused and we apologize. The letter seems to indicate that you have been the victim of a cruel hoax. If you insist, we will have you tested, but our laboratory doesn't open until 8:00 AM and it is now 10:30 PM. You are free to go unless you elect to stay until the lab opens."

"If you will take me home, we will call this what you said it was, a cruel hoax, and forget the entire matter. What disposal will be made of Mr. Kelly's body?" she asked.

"Our laws require cremation in instances of death from a communicable disease. The ashes are usually turned over to a kinsman or a friend. If no one claims them, they are put in an urn and buried in an unmarked grave. Do you want them?" the tall one asked.

"No, thank you. I will give you the address of the next of kin and pay to have them sent to the United States, if you will not identify me as the sender," said Whitley.

"If you will give us the address, we will ship them," he answered.

After writing Jack Colbert's address on a form, Whitley handed it to the tall man and asked him to take her home. On the way back to her condo, Whitley's curiosity got the best of her and she began to ask the policeman questions. As a result she found that his name was Gary Brown, born and raised in Enid, Oklahoma. He joined the army as a choice between that and going to college, when he graduated from high school. He had been a military policeman and had served three tours of duty in Germany, two in Stuttgart and one in Munich. He had become accustomed to the European way of life and after his third hitch, he resigned and took a job with the Bern Police Department. He was not married and was not really interested in anyone.

"You have had a very interesting life," she said.

"And what about you?" he asked.

She told him about her time spent at PSK and why she left. She also told him about Pete Kelly and Jack Colbert. She admitted blowing the whistle on them.

"Have you met many people since you have moved to Bern?" he asked.

"Only those where I work. I am studying French and that takes up a good deal of my time. However, it does get a little boring on the weekends," she answered, dropping a hint that she was available.

When they had gotten to her condo, Brown got out and opened Whitley's door for her. Escorting her to the door, she thanked him for being so nice to her.

"I would be glad to show you Switzerland some weekend," he said picking up the hint.

"I would love that," she said, giving him her business card with her home address and phone number. "Please call me."

Opening the door for her, he bade her good night and left. Whitley had found him quite entertaining and looked forward to spending a weekend seeing Switzerland with him.

She decided to rewrite the patchwork letter to Jack Colbert so she set about cutting up another magazine. She added another sentence to the letter that said, "He was cremated and his ashes will be sent to you."

On her way to work the next day, she mailed the letter.

CHAPTER 31

The gist of the conversations among PSK board members on the day of Sandy's article was to discharge Colbert and put someone else in. Joe Barnes had kept a copy of Colbert's contract when Colbert was made president. He got it out and read it over. He thought he remembered correctly the conditions necessary to ask for Colbert's resignation, and misfeasance was one of them. Another clause in the contract stated that if misfeasance was proven, Colbert would leave with no remuneration and, in addition, would forfeit all stock he had acquired during his tenure as president. This stock would go on the open market for sale to the highest bidder, the employee retirement fund being the beneficiary of the transaction. Any stock Colbert obtained before his elevation to the presidency could not be touched. Joe had talked the matter over with Harry Baker, Mary Elizabeth Chandler and Jon Williams. They were all in agreement that Colbert should leave.

Jamison's actions had scattered employees like dust on a windy day. Some of the upper management had jumped ship just like the rest of the employees. Robert Michaels, the senior executive vice-president who was the heir apparent was no different than the others. He had lined up a job as a marketing vice-president at one of the local banks and had been waiting on an opportune time to leave. The uproar from Sandy's story did the trick. He called the bank president the day after the article appeared and told him he could come any time. The same day he applied for early retirement.

The next most logical candidate was the vice-president of engineering, Royce Langford. Royce was a graduate of the University of Kentucky with a degree in electrical engineering and an MBA from the University of Louisville. He had spent his professional life at PSK, having gone there after he got his MBA. He stood about 5'8" with a weight that matched. His hair had been dark brown before it turned gray. His eyes were a dark hazel and his very dry sense of humor made then twinkle when he told a funny story. Royce was a quiet man who seldom crossed Colbert unless he tried to tell him how to do his job; then he became a lion. He was highly respected and liked by employees throughout the company, and would be a complete change from Colbert's arrogant ways.

James Weller, owner and publisher of the *Pennyrile Chronicle* and a PSK board member from Princeton, Kentucky, had picked Sandy's story up from the Associated Press wire. He had been afraid from the beginning that Jamison was going to trigger something like this and for his part, Colbert could pay the price. He went along with Joe and the others. He called Sam Eldridge and bragged on Sandy for having the guts to write such a story.

David Walton, another director and owner of Walton Farm on Old Frankfort Pike, was a little stand-offish about coming down on Colbert. They belonged to the same country club and had a standing engagement for a golf game on Thursday of each week. He told Joe that he would have to back Colbert. Joe told him that it was his privilege, but the rest of the board was going to can him.

The last board member contacted was Larkin Downey. He was a retired PSK meter man who had won a bundle of money on the lottery and put the whole works into PSK stock. Colbert had always looked down on Downey because he had been an hourly employee and, most of the time, Downey went along with what Colbert wanted to do. This time, Downey's true opinion of the president came out. When Joe called and told him what they were going to do, Larkin told him that he was with him one hundred percent.

Joe called the meeting to order and explained to all the members the conditions of Jack Colbert's contract as president of Public Service of Kentucky. Harry Baker made a motion that Colbert be replaced with Royce Langford. Mary Elizabeth seconded the motion. Harry then made another motion that Colbert be discharged from PSK. Mary Elizabeth seconded that motion. Both motions carried unanimously. David Walton had seen the light, and after he found out that the rest of the board was in favor of canning Colbert, he voted yes. Joe then buzzed Colbert's office and requested his presence at the meeting. When he came in the room, he was white as a sheet. He was mad and scared. He had just gotten word that Pete Kelly had died of syphilis and that his ashes had been sent to Jack.

When Joe read him the board's decision, Colbert cursed the entire group and said that he would take it to court. Joe told him to vacate his office immediately, and as he went out to tell his puppy dog, Jamison, that he was no longer employed at PSK and to get off the premises. Colbert was to also tell Jamison that any agreement made between the two of them regarding money or benefits was null and void and that included repairing his teeth.

Joe next buzzed Royce Langford and asked him to come to the board room. When he came in, all of the board members stood up and clapped. Royce was unaware of what was going on, but when Joe yelled, "Hail to the Chief," it finally dawned on him. The room finally settled down and Joe explained the proceedings to him. Royce thanked the board for the show of confidence in him and he promised to do the best job possible.

The first thing Langford did was fire Scott Senters, who had become Colbert's toady in the short time since Whitley left. Senters didn't have anything in the retirement account and hadn't been there long enough to become eligible for insurance. He moved out the same day that Colbert was fired and went back to western Kentucky. He got a job with a small engineering company and counted his time at PSK as experience, but he didn't ask for a recommendation.

CHAPTER 32

The next morning at the *Lexington Journal*, Sam Eldridge buzzed Sandy's office and asked her to come with Isabel to his office immediately. This scared Sandy, who thought that her PSK story had caused a problem. Getting Isabel, they went to Eldridge's office.

"Sandy, I thought that you said that Pineville was a quiet, serene place," he said, not smiling.

"It is, Mr. Eldridge. What is the matter?" she asked.

"We have an agreement with our carriers who deliver our paper to people's homes. They get a bonus depending on the weight of the story they tip us to. This morning, our carrier in Pineville called to say that there was another double murder at an abandoned mine near Pineville. A state policeman together with two other fellows was trapped inside the mine by a rock fall."

"Did he name the people who were trapped?" asked Isabel with fear in her voice.

"No, he didn't give me any names. He said that to the best of his knowledge, rescuers had not made contact with the men who were trapped. I want both of you to go pack enough clothes to last four days and then come straight back here. I am going with you. Now, scat," Sam said as they left him.

It took them exactly thirty-two minutes to pack their bags and come back to the paper.

"You know the territory, Isabel, so you drive," said Sam. "While you all were gone, I called to get more information. The three men trapped were G T Deane, Bige Napier and Kentucky State Police Trooper Jacob Gibson. As yet there has not been any contact made. The Department of Mines and Minerals has organized a rescue team that is on its way. Golden Star Coal Company has already got a rescue team on the site. The present plan is to drill an air hole through the eighty-five feet of sandstone and shale, and proceed from there with a rescue attempt."

Isabel turned ashen when Sam said that G T was trapped, but she called on reserves she didn't know she had as she backed her car out of the *Lexington Journal* parking lot. The normal trip from Lexington to Pineville is usually about an hour and forty-five minutes, if the 65 mile per hour speed limit is observed. Isabel set the cruise control on eighty, weaving in and out of traffic like a NASCAR driver. She was good and she knew it. The entire time, she was praying that all three of her friends were all right. Sandy and Sam smalltalked all the way, but Isabel had her mind on G T.

When the journalists arrived at the mine site, they were met by George, Gerry, Frank and Sarah, plus Rosemary and Howard Gibson. In addition, the site had started to collect a gathering of people offering to help. George explained to all of them what had happened.

Late the previous afternoon, Fred Tinsley, the captain of the Golden Star rescue team, told George and Frank that they needed a hole drilled into the area where the three were in order to provide communication and good air. Frank drove to the strip job on Golden Star that abutted Red Oak Hollow. Climbing on a D9 Dozer, he started across the property line and headed down the hollow toward the accident site, cutting a road in the side of the mountain as he went down. He made the road wide enough and properly graded to accommodate the blasthole drill, if the driver took his time, but the job lasted through the night. Frank was still pushing dirt as hard as he could when Isabel, Sandy and Sam Eldridge drove up. Isabel was almost crying as she hugged Gerry, Sarah and Rosemary.

"Have you all heard anything?" she asked.

"No, there hasn't been any sign," said Gerry.

"How long have they been trapped?" Isabel asked.

"It happened yesterday afternoon about four o'clock and it's ten-thirty in the morning now. That makes almost nineteen hours," said Gerry who had kept a vigil all night along with Rosemary and Sarah.

"Where is Daddy?" Isabel asked Sarah.

"He's pushing a road for the blasthole drill. They are going to drill a hole at about where George thinks G T, Jacob and Bige are. George is staying here to direct Frank," said Howard.

"Where is the drill operator?" she asked.

"Frank had somebody trying to locate him the last I heard," said Howard.

Getting into G T's truck, she scratched off out of the hollow and up Straight Creek to the road that led to the White Pines strip job where a blasthole drill was parked. Pulling up to it, she checked the fuel gauge. The operator had followed customary practice and fueled up before he left. He had also left the keys in the ignition. Isabel clambered into the driver's seat and started the engine, praying all of the time that she remembered how to set up and drill. When the engine started, she shifted into tram gear and the rig moved. Slowly she followed the tracks of Frank's dozer.

Memory flashes kept coming to her as she followed the dozer tracks. A squirrel hopped across in front of her and she thought about the time she and G T went squirrel hunting with their broom stick guns. She even remembered the blue jay that had scolded them from up in the oak tree. How quiet and peaceful it had been! She remembered the time that G T squished, as she called it, the copperhead. He had saved her from getting bitten. She could still see him sitting in the chair that Howard had made, holding the dead snake in one hand as the other lay limp across his knees. She started crying again. He had saved her life, now it was her turn to save his.

When she saw a pickup truck parked near the edge of the slope, she didn't pay it any mind. Coming to the edge of the berm where Frank had started his road, she down-shifted the drill into its lowest speed and started over the brink. Isabel could smell the sassafras roots that Frank had dug out making the road, and the fresh smell of the newly cut dirt gave her hope for some reason, but she didn't know why. It brought back memories of the summer days that she and G T had spent working for Golden Star. Her praying was audible. She was talking to God, asking him to please let G T, Jacob and Bige come out of this uninjured. She asked Him to let her get the drill rig down to the bench so she could do something to help them.

Isabel could see her father ahead of her. He had finished making a bench for the drill to sit on and had moved the dozer to the end of the bench, out of the way. Slowly she eased down the side of the mountain on the newly cut road. He had gotten the bench leveled off and was ready for her. She brought the drill into position as if she were driving a crate of eggs, looking down at George who was signaling to her. When she came to the place that he thought was about right, he gave her a thumbs-up sign. She put the drive transmission in neutral and engaged the drill gears. Hopping out of the cab, she set the leveling jacks and raised the drill into position. Slowly she set the drill on the ground and started its drilling rotation. Thinking back to the days that she and G T had run equipment on the strip job and how much fun they had, she began to cry again. She remembered him telling her that she was spacey because she liked to watch the drillings pile up around the hole. Isabel was scared.

Frank walked up about then and couldn't believe it was Isabel. "Where did you come from?" he asked her, as he put his arm around her.

"Oh, Daddy, I'm scared. I had to do something to help, and when Howard said that they couldn't locate the drill operator I had to try it," she said.

"You were always one of the best. I'm going to leave the dozer here. If you need me, wave at me. I'm going to go see about getting some lights down there. We didn't have any last night," Frank said.

"I believe someone has beat you to it," said Isabel pointing to Howard Gibson who had pulled up to the accident scene driving George's truck and escorting a truck carrying a portable generator with several banks of lights.

"I wonder where that came from," said Frank. "We don't own one."

"Looks like you do now," said Isabel.

Howard was reeling power cable off of the back of the truck and another man, whom nobody knew, had started pulling it up the mountain toward Isabel. When he got to her bench, he stopped and caught his breath.

"I'm Roy Seevers. Howard Gibson told me that you people might want me to come to work for you. I used to work for PSK," he said.

"I am Frank Morgan and this drill operator is my daughter, Isabel. Howard told us about you and you are hired as of yesterday," said Frank, extending his hand to Roy.

"I'm pleased to meet you, Frank. Howard said that you were up here. I appreciate the job," said Roy.

"We are pleased to have you and Howard," said Frank. "Now tell me where the generator came from."

"A contractor that Howard knew was in here a few years back, and he left the generator and the lights at the warehouse. He owed Howard some money, so he gave Howard the keys to the truck and told him he could keep all of the equipment and use it until he came back and paid Howard what he owed him. Howard had hidden the keys outside the warehouse, so he called me and told me where they were. I went by the warehouse and got them, then he met me out at the mouth of the hollow and showed me the way in. It's a 500-KW machine so we will have plenty of power. I'll go back and get a set of floodlights because Isabel will probably need them. I guess I'd better bring them around in a truck. The people down at the site are calling her 'the beauty queen who can run the machine' and I believe it. I'm proud to know you people," said Roy.

++++++

When the roof fell in, all three men were in the clear, although it scared them. When the dust had finally settled, G T told the other two that he thought it best if they turned out their lights, which they did. G T was reminded of something an old miner had once told him. "It's not dark underground, it's dark dark," the old man had said.

"Let's all get as comfortable as we can," G T said, trying to bolster the other two's spirits as well as his own. "Dad and Howard were outside and they have called in help by now. Fred Tinsley is the captain of the rescue team and he is one of the best. He has worked several bad falls where people were trapped and he really knows what he is doing."

"How will they go about this, G T?" Jacob asked.

"I hope they put an air hole down while they are removing the rock. The air in here is not good and I hope we don't have to stay in it too long," G T told him.

"Where will they drill the hole?" Jacob asked again.

"I don't know. The hillside is pretty steep and a road will have to be graded to it and that will take a while. On top of that, it will take some expert driving to get the drill in place, not to mention taking a real pro to set the drill up. I'd say that they will get Lonnie Howard to drill it since he is the best around here," G T answered.

About 22 hours had passed since the cave-in, when G T heard the sound of the drill above them.

"Somebody is drilling," he told them. "Well, I'll be damned! That's Isabel on the drill."

"How do you know?" Bige asked.

"You can tell by the way the drill is bumping. She is really putting the down pressure on it. I wonder how she got that drill down the mountain," he said, half-talking to himself.

Another two hours later the drill sound had changed.

"That's Lonnie Howard drilling now," G T told them. "We'll get good air in just a little bit."

++++++

Sam Eldridge had watched Isabel with his mouth open. Turning to Sandy he just shook his head.

"She's really something, isn't she," said Sandy.

"I can't believe what I am seeing," answered Sam, "Did you see the way she brought that machine down that steep hill? I would have never believed it could be done."

"She's running scared. She has a part-time fiancé and two childhood friends in there, so she will do what ever it takes to get them out," said Sandy.

While Sandy was talking to Sam, Bill Minter and Chris Evans drove up. Sandy had called Chris and told him where she was going. It sounded like a good story so he and Bill drove to Pineville. They asked a service station operator how to get to the accident site and he gave them real good directions. They like everyone else couldn't believe what they were seeing: the beautiful Isabel with her hair pulled back in a pony tail, her jeans, blouse and shoes covered with dust and oil as well as smudges of grease on her face, running a blasthole drill. The drill operator from Golden Star, Lonnie Howard, had heard about the accident and had come to the site to see if there was anything he could do. When he saw who was running the White Pines drill, he couldn't help but laugh. He remembered showing her how to change steel and how to blow the hole out every so often. George came up to him and thanked him for coming to help.

"I don't believe you need me, George," Lonnie said, pointing up the hill with his head.

"Yes, we do. I would appreciate it if you would go relieve her. She is good, but not as good as you are. She has put down two joints of pipe and I figure it will take another three to get to them. We haven't heard any sounds out of them since this happened. The rescue people have been working on clearing out the rock, but it is a slow process. It was fortunate that the rock fell in such a way as to bridge the creek, so there shouldn't be much water buildup. I just hope we can get to them in time," said George.

Lonnie backed his truck out to where he could turn around, then hurried up Straight Creek to the road leading up on the White Pines strip job. He parked it near the newly cut dozer road and walked down it to the drill. When Isabel saw him, she started crying and hugged him.

"Don't worry about it, Isabel, we'll get them out. I'm glad to see that my years of teaching you were not in vain. You have set the drill like the professional you are. I'll be glad to take over if you want me to," Lonnie said.

"Thank you, Lonnie. I really do appreciate it. I think I'll go back down the hill if you don't need me," she said.

"You have already done all of the work. All that's left for me to do is sink a couple more pieces of pipe. When this is over, you'll have to come back and take the rig back up that road. I'm scared to try it," Lonnie said laughingly.

"The Lord got it down here for me. Maybe if you are good, He will take it back up for you," she said as she started down the mountainside. When she got halfway down the path to the site, the crowd that had gathered started clapping. She hadn't heard that kind of sound since she came out of her last high school basketball game her senior year. She was embarrassed.

Clyde Napier had just gotten back from his daily train run to Norton when he heard about the accident. He drove to the site and George explained to him what happened. The rescue team was in the process of cribbing up the entrance and clearing out the rock. It was a very slow process. Gerry had introduced him to Rebecca. Clyde stood around for a few minutes and then left. He returned about an hour later with a small Bobcat end-loader on a trailer behind his truck.

"I thought this might make it easier for them to move that rock out," he told George as he unloaded the machine. "I borrowed it from the railroad maintenance people."

"That was good thinking," George answered. "They can use it."

Rebecca walked over to Clyde and put her arm around his waist.

"Bige will be all right, little girl," Clyde told her putting his arm around her. "He is a survivor. His mother made him be one."

CHAPTER 33

The Kentucky State Police Commissioner called John Talbert to tell him that Jacob Gibson, the trooper he had worked with on the Durham-Atmore murder case, was trapped in an underground mine with two other men. He asked John to check on Jacob and offer any assistance necessary to get the three of them out. John had called the Harlan Post that Jacob worked out of and told the post commander what had happened. The commander, in turn, assigned three troopers to handle traffic and keep sightseers away from the worksite. They did allow a local TV cameraman to go to the site and film for the evening news. Among the shots the cameraman took was one of Isabel bringing the drill onto the bench and setting it up. The commentator explained that her fiancé was one of those trapped. Later after she came off the mountain, he got a good close-up of her.

John had instructed Thelma, Betty and Jemjelf not to let anyone in the house while he was gone.

"We aren't stupid, John," retorted Thelma. "And please get our little boy out of that place. Keep us up to date on what is going on."

John drove to the site where cars were lined up on both sides of the road. The trooper directing traffic recognized him and let him through. Parking alongside George's truck, he got out and walked up to the site. Fred Tinsley was one of the rescue team and he spotted John, who he knew from Thelma's ordeal.

"How's it going, Fred?" John asked.

"It's awful slow," said Fred, who was loading rock into the Bobcat bucket.

"How much longer do you think it will take to get an air hole to them?" asked John.

"He's on his fourth piece of steel so it shouldn't be too much longer," said Fred.

Going over to Rosemary Gibson, John put his arm around her. She was about to cry, but she knew that Jacob would quit speaking to her if he found out. While he was talking to Rosemary, Lonnie Howard yelled to George that the drill had gone through into the mine opening. The mine rescue team was on hand with a telephone that they let down into the hole for communication and the telephone company people had brought a compressor and hose that they used to ventilate their underground cable installations when they worked on them. They immediately put this to work, pumping fresh air down the hole.

Dark had come on again before anyone knew it. Howard Gibson fired up his generator and Roy Seevers switched on several banks of lights.

Everyone held their breath waiting for Frank to tell them what the conditions were, when he started to laugh.

"G T says that they are all three okay, and so are the bodies and the skeletons. The roof fall was between them and the mine mouth. The water is not building up very much. They have waited this long, it won't hurt to wait a little longer until the mine is cleared up, but to hurry. He said that Jason and the Asian are beginning to stink."

Jacob got on the phone next, telling Frank to order the ambulance driver to set up to take four bodies to the funeral home. He wanted an autopsy performed on the two who had recently been killed, and he wanted the two skeletons sent to Frankfort for the forensics people.When Bige got on the phone, he asked Frank if Rebecca and his daddy were there. Frank told him that they were. He said that was all that mattered to him.

CHAPTER 34

The Peary County Jail was an old structure that had been built in the early thirties by WPA. It was a pretty building, if you could call a jail pretty. Locally cut stone had been used to construct the walls and the roof was covered with corrugated tin. A concrete block furnace room for heat was attached to the back and accommodated a stoker-fed coal furnace. The heating system was steam with radiators. During the winter months the prisoners all complained about the air being too hot or too cold. Window air conditioners were used in the summer and no one ever griped about it being too cold. Toilet facilities were scanned by the closed circuit TV which brought comments about privacy from some of the prisoners. The fiscal court had appealed to the Justice Department for funds to build a new one and had finally gotten approval to start. The new jail was to be at a new location and would have facilities for keeping federal prisoners.

At present, the men and women prisoners were kept on the same floor. Only "make do" remodeling had been done. Instead of adding to the back of the building, the fiscal court had added on to one end, making the jail a long narrow building with women on one end and men on the other. There was a wall separating the two with closed-circuit TV scanners mounted on both sides, facing down the halls. Ching Lee's cell was the one nearest the wall. Her companions' cell was nearly halfway down the corridor.

Feigning illness, Ching Lee called the turnkey. She had vomited and was gasping for breath. The turnkey opened the cell door which was a bad mistake. Giving the guard a karate chop, she grabbed the cell door keys. She had watched the closed-circuit television scanner until she had it timed pretty well. She had dropped the guard with one lick and pulled him into the cell. Waiting for the scanner to turn away from her, Ching Lee ran out of the cell, and stood in the door between the cell blocks. It wasn't locked. Once more watching the scanner that played on the men's section, she picked a time and ran to open the cell door of her comrades. The four of them made a rush for the front of the jail. Another guard sitting at a desk next to the outside door was supposed to be watching the scanner, instead of reading a girlie magazine which was what he was doing. Before he knew what had happened, one of the Chinamen dropped him. Grabbing the keys to the jailer's car, Ching Lee and her gang ran out of the back door, got in the car and left, grabbing a portable police scanner on the way.

They drove out of town and were headed back toward Interstate 75 when the scanner came on. It was Governor Martin calling John Talbert, asking him about the accident. Talbert related all he knew. When he told the governor that one of the bodies was that of an Asian, Ching Lee immediately surmised it was Lin Chou. She knew that he was supposed to meet with the White Pines mine manager so she figured that Talbert was in the Pineville area. That would also mean Wing Fu was close by. Ching Lee was a lot of things, but stupid was not one of them.

Pulling into a shopping center, she told one of the Chinamen to steal a car while she was inside diverting attention. She also told him to be sure it was full of gas. Going into one of the mall stores, she started looking at dresses. She was still wearing the old gray suit she had worn the day they got thrown out of the governor's office. From the dress rack, she moved over to some slacks that were on a hanger. From the slack rack she could see her cohorts peering into car windows. How stupid could they be? Anyone who happened to be watching them could figure out real quick what they were doing.

After selecting a pair of black pants, a blue blouse and a pair of gym shoes, she went to the pay counter. Giving the clerk cash for the items, she asked if she could change in the store. The clerk showed her where the change room was. Ching Lee slipped into her new clothes, grabbed her gray suit and shoes, and hurried out of the store. Her companions had selected an old model Buick that was easier to hotwire. Seeing her come out of the store, they pulled out of the parking space and picked her up in front of the store. They had made their getaway cleanly. It so happened that the car they stole belonged to a security guard who was patrolling the back of the mall, so the car wouldn't be missed for a while. It was only 8:30 PM by the clock in the mall when they left.

The road from Haggard to I-75 was not heavily traveled so they didn't meet many cars on the way to the interstate. Ching Lee made the driver keep below the speed limit. She didn't want some state trooper to pick them up for speeding. Reaching I-75, they turned south toward the intersection of I-75 and US25E. When they came to 25E, she told the driver to turn south and go to Pineville. She had planned the escape to come off around dark so that the stolen car would not be as noticeable. Following the road signs, they arrived in Pineville around 11:00 PM. She had to figure out where Wing Fu and the baby were, so she had the driver pull into a fast-food restaurant drive in. There Ching Lee ordered the driver to let her drive. Pulling around to the pick up window, she ordered hamburgers and fries with a soft drink for all four. After paying for their food, she pulled into a dark area of the restaurant lot where she parked facing traffic.

She started going over in her head all that Lin Chou had told her about the marijuana deal and Wing Fu. First, Ching Lee figured that Wing Fu had delivered the baby and would be looking for diapers since she was "Americanized." The closest place to find those was a grocery store. Second, Lin Chou had told her that the pot was being grown on a mine site near a place called Straight Creek, so it was a good guess that if he were the dead Asian, he had been killed somewhere on Straight Creek. Getting out her map of the state of Kentucky, she scoured it for a place near Pineville named Straight Creek.

Driving out of the restaurant parking lot, she started to go up Straight Creek when she spotted a grocery store on the left side of the street. Pulling into that parking lot, she again parked facing the street. She didn't think Wing Fu would come in for diapers, but that woman she took up with or her husband, that policeman, might. Ching Lee had the Chinese gift of patience, so she looked hard at every car that went by and bided her time.

CHAPTER 35

During the four-hour wait after Lonnie Howard put the air hole in, G T, Bige and Jacob tried to put together who had killed Jason Strick and the Asian and why they had done it.

"The treasure in Confederate coins appears to be the most obvious reason," said Jacob.

"Did they all come in the same vehicle?" asked G T. "If not, then how did the two of them and the person or persons that killed them get here?"

"Maybe they all came together," said Bige.

"Maybe Strick killed the Chinaman and someone else killed him," posed G T.

"Maybe it was the other way around," said Bige.

"How would the Chinaman know about the treasure? I think he was here for another reason," said Jacob. "Let's think about it. What would draw someone like him to a place like this? The only thing he could have been interested in would be drugs."

"We don't know that," said G T.

"Can you think of a better reason?" asked Jacob.

"Maybe he was going sang hunting," joked Bige.

"Have either of you ever been up on this part of White Plains strip job?" asked Jacob.

"I have," said Bige.

"What's it like?" asked Jacob.

"It's beautiful," said Bige. "They have reclaimed it to where it looks like a garden."

"Did they grow anything on it?" asked Jacob.

"Yeah," said Bige, "they had it planted in sugar cane and some kind of plant that I had seen but couldn't remember where. Funny thing that they planted sugar cane with it."

"You made a permit for them, G T. What do you think it was planted in?" asked Jacob.

"I specified autumn olive, but I didn't see it after they had reclaimed it," said G T.

"What are you getting at, Jake?" asked G T.

"I was just thinking it might have been a pot field," said Jacob.

"Surely they had more sense than to try to raise pot right out in the open," said G T.

"Maybe it wasn't out in the open, maybe it was camouflaged by trees or sugar cane," said Jacob.

"I never thought about that," said G T.

"We have come up with a possible motive, but who do we have to suspect?" said Jacob.

"Are you in there, G T?" asked a familiar voice as a miner's cap light lit up the area where they were.

"Is that you, Fred?" asked G T.

"We will have you out in about another hour and then I'm gonna bust your tail for going out from under supported roof. I've already given George a good lecture about it," Fred said. Then he asked if all three were okay. G T told him they were and he would take the tail-busting for doing what he knew was wrong.

Backing out of the way, Fred let the Bobcat loader scoop up the rock. Going back into the crowd, he told the mothers, fathers and girlfriends that they were okay.

When the crew finally got the rock cleared out, Jacob said he wasn't going to leave until he saw that the two corpses and the two skeletons were properly taken care of.

"If you don't go, then I don't go," said Bige.

"Well, I'm not going to be the first one out," said G T.

"How about sending us those body bags," said Jacob.

"I'll bring them to you," said Fred.

Placing both corpses and both skeletons in the bags, Fred called for some help in getting them out to the ambulances. When Fred told them that all was taken care of, Jacob suggested that they leave and they finally crawled out, the crowd that had gathered started cheering. Isabel hugged G T until he thought she would break a rib. Rebecca and Clyde hugged Bige together; then she kissed him.

"I'm glad you are safe," she said, "I wouldn't want anything to happen to you."

Jacob went to Rosemary and Howard and hugged them, then he saw a familiar blonde head behind them.

"Hi, Jennifer," he said.

"Hi, Jacob," she answered. "I hear you have another double murder on your hands."

"There were also two skeletons in there and some old Civil War relics," Jacob said. "Where did you come from?" he asked.

"I'm here to help you in the investigation," replied Jennifer with a twinkle in her eye.

"What interest does the Tennessee State Police have in this?" he questioned.

Rosemary and Howard were both about to laugh, but they held it in.

"They don't. I was going to tell you, but you got yourself caught in that mine so I just waited. I joined the Kentucky State Police last week. They let me transfer from Knoxville to Harlan Post 10. KSP has been looking for a woman detective for some time and your friend, Lieutenant John Talbert, told them about me. They recruited me and here I am with a little help from Lieutenant Talbert and Sergeant Martin Wallace. I am now assigned to Post 10 at Harlan and I have an apartment in Pineville that your mother helped me find. You are not going to get away from me so you had just as well give up," she said standing on her tiptoes and kissing him.

"Was that you on the drill?" G T asked Isabel.

"How did you know?" she responded.

"You always did go heavy on the down pressure and made the bits jump and thump," he said laughing and looking up the mountain to where Lonnie Howard was getting ready to take the drill back up the road Frank had graded.

"Who moved the drill in place for you?" G T asked.

"I moved the drill myself and if I had known that you were going to be so critical, I would have let the rabbit sit and let you stay in that damned place where you had no business going in the first place," she answered, pretending to be huffed up.

"Thank you, Isabel, for saving our lives," G T said as he hugged her again, "I was just kidding. You are one of the best and I would be the first to admit it. You are also a very beautiful woman, even if you do have a dirty face and greasy hands."

"Your face is dirty, too," she answered.

Sandy, Chris Evans, Bill Minter and Sam Eldridge had been standing back out of the way while the rescue operations were in process. Bill had taken several photos of Isabel as she drilled the airhole. All four had taken notes to make items for their various publications.

Isabel walked over to where they were standing and thanked them for their support.

"I have never seen anything to match your handling of that drill. You evidently have had considerable practice at it," said Sam Eldridge.

"G T and I used to work summers for our dads. He liked to drive a haul-back or push a dozer, but I preferred the drill. I was running scared, too. Please don't put anything in any of the papers about it. I would be terribly embarrassed," she said.

John Talbert walked over to where Rosemary, Howard, Jennifer and Jacob were standing. "Looks like you might have a new partner, Jacob," he kidded.

"What about you pulling this off and not telling me," Jacob said.

"All I did was tell the Commissioner that I knew where he might find a really good woman detective for Harlan Post 10. The rest is history," John said.

"Thank you for the compliment and the help, Lieutenant Talbert," said Jennifer. "I like the partnership."

"I know someone who might be able to identify the Asian body, but we need to keep this very quiet. Once the coroner gets them to the morgue, we need to get this person to look at him," John said.

CHAPTER 36

Two weeks after Royce Langford became president of PSK, Kurt Holtz buzzed Whitley's office and asked her to come to his office, which she did.

"How would you like to go back to Kentucky for a visit?" he asked.

"I would enjoy that," she answered.

"As I told you, our coal supplier, White Pines, has come under new ownership. I believe that you told me that you knew the people at Golden Star who had bought White Pines."

"I am acquainted with their coal marketer, Mrs. Frank Morgan, but I have never met the owners themselves. From what I have always heard, they pay pretty close attention to their business and stay in Pineville most of the time," Whitley answered.

"How about Public Service of Kentucky? Its stock fell drastically a few days ago and I bought as much as I could. Electrique Internationale now owns forty-eight percent of PSK. I would like to go to their general offices in Lexington and meet some of the people there," Kurt told her.

"I'm not trying to tell you how to run your business, but I hope you get rid of Jack Colbert. As I told you before, he wants to run PSK into bankruptcy so that it will have to merge with Commonwealth Electric and Gas and he can become president of both," Whitley answered.

"That has already been taken care of. The board of directors, under the leadership of your friend Joe Barnes, ousted Mr. Colbert along with his new personnel director," said Kurt.

"Who did they put in Colbert's place?" asked Whitley.

"The engineering vice-president, a Mr. Royce Langford," answered Kurt.

"That was a good move. He is well liked by the employees and is smarter that Colbert ever thought about being. He will do you a good job," said Whitley.

"CEG's stock is falling also. It is presently at 23 and I have put a buy order on it if it goes as low as 21. If we can acquire it, we will merge the two and that will give us a good foot hold on the power market in the United States," said Kurt.

"When do you plan to go to Kentucky?" asked Whitley.

"If you can get ready today, we will go tomorrow," he answered.

The corporate offices at EI were no different than those in a thousand other corporations around the world. The gossip about Kurt and his new coal person was all that any of the office personnel could talk about. When the word got out that they were going to the United States, the tongues really wagged. Whitley was aware of this and reveled in it. She had worked hard at her job at PSK and had played the game the way she thought it should be played, regardless of what the rules were. Now that she was in the big time, she was going to enjoy it as long as she could.

The plane trip to Lexington was uneventful. The company jet made the trip, stopping only in Lisbon, Portugal to refuel before crossing the Atlantic Ocean. They flew straight into Lexington, Kentucky where Kurt rented a car to expedite their visits to PSK and at least one of its power plants. Holtz had reserved rooms at the Marriot for Whitley and himself, where they went from the airport. Checking his watch and briefly converting from Bern time to Lexington time, he realized that it was nearly five o'clock in the afternoon. Telling Whitley this, he suggested that they freshen up, have dinner and then turn in for the night. She was agreeable. She was not accustomed to jet lag as he was and it had her physical clock all messed up. He took her bags to her room, set them on a baggage rack and went to his room. Kurt gave her an hour and then buzzed her. She was ready. During the short time Whitley had worked for him, she had found that he was always on time and expected everyone else to be. She had suggested that they go to dinner dressed casually. He appeared in jeans and a sport shirt with cowboy boots. She couldn't believe it. She had on a pair of designer jeans and a soft flannel shirt.

The dinner was a typical Bluegrass dinner of county ham, corn pudding and spring peas with a combination salad. The dessert was Derby pie. Whitley suggested decaf coffee rather than wine to drink with the meal. The entire menu was new to Karl. He loved the country ham and asked Whitley where he could get more of it. He said that the Derby pie was sinful, it was so good. Whitley enjoyed the meal because it gave her a menu to use when they got back to Bern. She had a recipe for Derby pie that she thought was better than what they were served.

The next morning for breakfast, she ordered country ham with biscuits and red gravy and sunny side up eggs. Karl had fallen under the spell of country ham and he ordered it again. Finishing breakfast they went back to their rooms, freshened up and brushed their teeth. Whitley then called Joe Barnes and told him she was in town. He was delighted to hear from her and made her promise to come by and see him. She also told him that she had Kurt with her, who wanted to meet some of the board members.

Kurt called her room and asked if she was ready. She said that she was and would meet him in the lobby, which she did. Since she knew Lexington better than he did, he let her drive. She told him that the first stop was to see Joe. When they entered Barnes' office, Joe got up from his desk, then came around it and hugged Whitley until she thought she was going to faint. After introducing Joe to Kurt, he offered the two of them chairs and they all sat down.

"Do you feel comfortable with the ownership of Public Service of Kentucky being in the hands of a foreign company?" asked Kurt.

"To be perfectly honest with you, Kurt, I'd rather not have it that way, but there is nothing that I can do about it now. The board of directors dropped the ball when they didn't wise up to what Colbert was doing. We went to sleep at the switch and the train ran off the track. He was a conniving scoundrel and getting rid of him was one of the nicest feelings I ever had. We have a man in there now who is an electrical engineer and understands the electric utility business. The biggest mistake PSK made was putting an accountant in as president. They know how to juggle dollars and make things look good, but they don't know beans about getting electric service to people. I don't always trust their figures, either. You asked me and I told you."

"I appreciate your being so candid with me, Joe. Whitley told me that you would be," said Kurt. "Now I will be the same with you. I intend to acquire Commonwealth Electric and Gas if it has not already been done. I want to get EI into the American utility market. I believe that it is a growing industry in this country and I think that the location of the two utilities makes a sensible combination. They have competed with TVA for many years and have still maintained their rates below those of their neighbors. This tells me that the companies have had good management and good employees in the past, in spite of a man like Jack Colbert. I admire your handling of his discharge and the installation of his replacement. I agree with you about accountants. I am an electrical engineer myself and I would never let an accountant be in charge of any of my companies."

"I believe I am going to like you," said Joe extending his hand for a handshake. "How about we go meet Mr. Royce Langford, the new president of PSK?"

Whitley had always liked Royce Langford. He was very polite, removed his hat in the elevator and always referred to the women in the office as 'ladies'. His trademark was gray. He always wore a gray tweed sport coat, a gray suit or a jacket with gray pants, and a gray hat. All of his shoes were black, and his socks were either gray or black except on Saint Patrick's Day, when he wore the only pair of green socks that he had. In the winter he wore a gray overcoat.

Since the mailroom people were always the first to know any gossip, somehow they had picked up on Whitley and Kurt and had made a mountain out of a molehill. Some said they were secretly married while others said that they were just living together. Either way, they were glad to see her because she was the one who had begun the downfall of Jack Colbert. Royce Langford was just as glad to see Whitley as Joe was. He, too, hugged the breath out of her. When she introduced Kurt, Royce gave him a hearty handshake and offered all three a chair.

Kurt asked Royce the same question he had asked Joe and he got the same answer, more or less. Royce had no problem with the acquisition of CEG and the subsequent merger. In fact he thought it should have been done years ago. However, he didn't like the way that Colbert went about it; he felt that it could have been done without making the stock almost worthless or laying off a host of employees. Kurt told Royce that he would like to see one of the power plants and Royce offered to take him through the one named Grant that was on the Ohio River.

When the conversation lulled, Whitley asked Royce where Scott Senters was. He told her that they discharged Scott. He had approached a coal supplier for University of Kentucky football and basketball tickets first and then for cash money. Colbert was told about it, but for some reason he didn't act. The first thing Langford did was fire him and told him not to ask for a recommendation.

The Grant plant, a ninety-minute drive from Lexington, was the largest and newest of the five PSK plants. It was located on the Ohio River and its coal came in by barge. It was a very efficient arrangement for bringing in coal. Each barge had a high speed auger that ran the entire length of the coal containment area. The auger ended in a feeder that was part of a conveyor that was put aboard the barge when it came into position for unloading. The auger was electrically driven and unloaded a barge in record time. Kurt was impressed with the unloading facility. Although plant personnel had only two hours to prepare for his visit since Langford called them, it was as clean as a hospital operating room. Holtz was better acquainted with the generation end of the utility business and had spent a good part of his learning career in a plant at Hamburg. He was fascinated by the sound of the generators. With the least change in it he wanted to know what was wrong. The generators in the Grant plant were all four humming at the right rhythm. To Kurt, this signaled good operating procedures.

Leaving the Grant plant, which was near Carrolton, they went on into Carrolton to see Mary Elizabeth Chandler. Kurt was very impressed by her knowledge of the electric utility business. She was outdone with Colbert, who had let the stock go down. Kurt assured her that her stock would be back at its pre-Colbert value in a short time.

On the way back to Lexington, Kurt said to Royce, "Having met Joe Barnes and Miss Chandler, I believe that I have a pretty good feel for the quality of your board of directors. It is my intention to leave everything as is, at least for the time being."

"We appreciate that very much. We would like to get the company back on its feet before there are any major changes in management. Colbert had that Jamison fellow fire a lot of real good people. We intend to bring them back. They have always been the backbone of this company and I would like to get back as many as possible," Royce told him.

Once in Lexington, Kurt and Whitley bade Royce and Joe goodbye and promised to come back again soon. Turning their rental car in, they boarded the company jet and took off for Knoxville since the airstrip in Middlesboro was too short for the high speed company plane. Landing in Knoxville, they went through the same procedure that they had gone through at Lexington. Kurt rented a car and the pilot stayed in Knoxville while Kurt and Whitley drove to Pineville.

They arrived at the Golden Star offices, unannounced, three days after G T, Bige and Jacob had been rescued. The excitement of the accident had died down and Jacob was awaiting an autopsy report. He, Jennifer and Lieutenant Talbert had gone back to the site to look for clues to the murders. Sarah and Gerry were in the office, but George and Frank were at the mines. Sarah recognized Whitley.

"Why Ms. Rogers, what a pleasant surprise. We heard that you had moved to Europe," Sarah said in her best coal-marketing style.

"How are you, Mrs. Morgan? It is a pleasure to see you again," she said, turning to Kurt.

"I would like for you to meet Mr. Kurt Holtz, president of Electrique Internationale and the newly acquired Public Service of Kentucky," said Whitley.

"I am very pleased to meet you, Mr. Holtz," said Sarah extending her hand to shake.

Taking her hand in both of his and bowing low at the waist, he kissed it. "I am charmed to meet you," he said.

Gerry came out of her office about then and almost popped.

"Let me introduce the two of you to Gerry Deane, wife of the other partner, George Deane," Sarah said.

Gerry got the same treatment that Sarah had gotten and she blushed a bright red. Trying to think of something to say, she blurted out, "Oh, Mr. Holtz, my hands are dirty."

Both Sarah and Whitley laughed.

"Mr. Holtz wanted to meet the new owners of White Pines and discuss contract provisions with them," said Whitley.

"Let me call them on the radio," said Sarah going out to the radio on the front desk. Calling Frank, she told him that Kurt Holtz and Whitley Rogers were in the office. He responded that he and George were in the parking lot, and would be right in.

Whitley had never met either of them so Sarah did all of the introductions. George and Frank both told Kurt that they were glad to meet him. He told them that his chief concern was whether or not White Pines could meet the contract requirements. They assured him that they could. They explained that the permitting process had been held up due to some problems that they believed had been taken care of.

"Would the four of you join Ms. Rogers and myself for dinner this evening? We have reservations at your Pine Mountain Lodge," said Kurt.

"We would be delighted to have dinner with the two of you, only if you will be our guests. The dress will be very casual," said Sarah, exhibiting her marketing manners.

"We accept, Mrs. Morgan," countered Kurt.

"Would seven be acceptable to you and Ms. Rogers?" asked Sarah.

"That would be fine," said Kurt. "Now if you will tell us how to get to this place we will see you at seven o'clock."

Frank gave very detailed instructions on how to get to the Lodge, then Kurt and Whitley left.

"I like the Golden Star people. They seem very down to earth and business like," said Kurt as they passed the Wasioto Winds golf course on their way to the Lodge.

"During the time that I was at PSK, we never had any trouble with quality or delivery," said Whitley in very hesitating French.

"Ha," said Kurt, "you are showing off your newly acquired skills. Bravo."

"That looks like a beautiful golf course. I would love to play it some time," he continued, "Do you play, Whitley?" he asked.

"No. I'm ashamed to say that I never learned," she answered again in French.

"Then I will have to teach you," said Kurt.

"There are some things I would like to teach you," thought Whitley.

Going into the lobby at the Lodge, Kurt registered for both of them and got the keys to their separate rooms, taking Whitley's bag into her room and putting it on the baggage rack at the end of the king-size bed.

Looking at his watch, he remarked that it was almost five o'clock and they had two hours until dinner. "I will meet you in the lobby at six and we will discuss our plans for Golden Star and Public Service of Kentucky," he said as he went out and pulled the door closed behind him.

Forty-five minutes later they met in the lobby of the Lodge.

"It is my intention to continue with the contract that we had with Garbon Ltd.," said Karl, "but I will wait and see what their plans are."

"Do you want to continue to use them as a supplier for PSK?" asked Whitley.

"If they did the job that you say that they did, then I see no reason to change," he answered.

CHAPTER 37

The morning after the rescue, Jacob, Jennifer and John met at the dispatch center to plan how to go about finding who had killed Jason and the other man in the cave.

"We need to go back to the site and see what we can find. Let's take your cruiser, Jacob," said Lieutenant Talbert.

Thirty minutes later, they reached their destination. "There was nothing inside the mine that offered any evidence at all as to who might have killed them." said Jacob as he, John and Jennifer walked from where he parked his cruiser to the accident site. "There was evidence that someone had been in the treasure pile because the dust had been blown off of it and some of the coins looked almost new as though they had been covered up away from the mine dust. There were a lot of knee prints where we had crawled on our knees, but I couldn't make out any foot prints in the dust and there was not a weapon any where that we could see and we all three looked for one."

"Could I make a suggestion?" asked Jennifer.

"We are all ears," said John.

"Why don't we sit down at the mine site and see what each of us knows about the Strick man and the Asian John Doe?" she asked.

"That sounds smart to me," said John.

Using some of the crib blocks that were left over from shoring up the accident site, they all three got comfortable. Jacob started by telling the other two how Rebecca had been threatened over the permit, about the Camry wreck on I-64 and the burned up Marquis outside of Frankfort and about the cache of silver coins that was still in the mine. Jennifer, who was taking all of this down in shorthand, posed the question as to whether or not this was related to Jason Strick or the other man.

"I don't know," Jacob replied, "but G T told me a tale about there being a treasure buried somewhere in these parts that was referred to as Strick's Silver Mine. That was what we found. While we were trapped, we discussed the fact that maybe Jason Strick didn't want the permit approved, because G T had designed a hollow fill to go in this area as soon as mining started. It would have covered the mine up and the treasure would have never been recovered. We believe that was the reason Rebecca was given such a hard time about approving her part of the permit." He went on to explain about the Group and how they had put pressure on Rebecca.

"What is a hollow fill?" asked Jennifer.

"When the dirt that covers the coal is removed, it has to be put somewhere. The best place for it is in an abandoned hollow. If there is a spring or some other source of water in the hollow, then large boulders are laid in it to allow drainage. The dirt is hauled in and spread in fifty foot lifts. There are drainage ditches on both sides of the fill and in some cases, another one down the middle. For every fifty feet of height, a bench is put in to provide a channel for rainwater that runs off into the drainage ditches on the sides of the fill, and to limit the possibilities of large slides. When the hollow fill is completed, it is sowed in grass and other vegetation. This provides food for wild animals such as deer and elk," explained Jacob.

"Thank you," said Jennifer. "I've heard the term used, but I never knew what it was."

"While we are at it, we need to arrest someone in the Division of Permits for complicity in an attempted murder scheme," said Jacob.

It was now John's turn to add what he knew about the circumstances. "I have an informant who told me that there was an Asian staying in a Lexington trailer park who was supposed to meet with the manager of this mine to renegotiate the price he was getting for the pot being grown on the reclaimed strip jobs. According to my source, the pot was being harvested by a White Pines employee and put up to dry in an old house on the creek. He implicated a fellow named Smith that we interrogated during the Durham-Atmore investigation."

"That would be Carl Smith. He's the one that blew the whistle on Olivia," said Jacob.

"Maybe we should bring him in for questioning," said Jennifer.

The three of them were sitting in a semicircle, with Jennifer facing the mine and Jacob and John sitting on either side of her. Tearing a sheet out of her notepad, she wrote a note saying, "There is someone in the mine." Passing it to the other two, she continued talking about Carl Smith.

"That sounds like a good idea," said John getting up from his crib block seat.

Walking out of the hollow to Jacob's cruiser, they got in, except that Jennifer got under the wheel, John got in the front seat and Jacob walked around as though to get in the back seat on the blind side of the car. Easing into the brush beside the road, he squatted down in a laurel thicket with his pistol in his hand. He had a clear view of the mine entrance after Jennifer backed out to turn around. He had his portable radio turned off so there would not be a give-away.

Jennifer and John drove out of Red Oak Left and went up Red Oak Right where they found a burned-out car. They got out and checked what was left. The license plate had been removed and the trunk rifled. There was no visible identification of any kind. John got a lug wrench out of the trunk of Jacob's cruiser and pried the open the driver's door. There was an ID tag inside the door, which he copied down. It had to be Lin Chou's rental vehicle, but they would have to go over it after it was towed in. John called dispatch and told them to have Roland's garage send a wrecker to pick it up.

Jacob waited about fifteen minutes before he saw a miner's cap light flashing in the mine entrance. The man who came out had a gunny sack that he was dragging. Coming out of the mine, he turned and started up the path that Roy Seevers had made going back and forth while the drilling was in process. Calling out to the man to halt, Jacob fired one round in the air. He called on the man to halt a second time and when he didn't stop, Jacob fired into the ground ahead of him. The man stopped and put down his sack.

"Pick up that sack in both of your hands and come back down to the mine entrance," he said, holding his gun on the man. "I am a state police officer and you are under arrest."

Calling Jennifer and John on his portable radio, he told them he had made a capture. He had no sooner pocketed his radio than Jennifer came flying up the road in Jacob's cruiser. Skidding to a stop, she bounced out of the cruiser with her pistol drawn.

"We heard your shots. Are you all right?" she queried.

John was cracked up laughing. "We were over in the next hollow and when she heard those shots, she scratched off and split this hollow wide open," laughed John. "She's going to take care of you."

Handcuffing the man, Jennifer asked him who he was.

"My name is Jerry Hoag and I have a perfect right to be here. I am an employee of the Division of Mine Permits. I had investigated this area for permit violations in the past and I discovered this old entry. I thought it might be interesting to explore sometime and I was in the area checking on a complaint, so I had a look. To my surprise there was large amount of old Civil War Confederate money stashed away in there. Realizing that this would be a real treasure for the Civil War museum at Frankfort I gathered up some of it. Now if you will please remove these handcuffs, I will go on about my business."

"We are placing you under arrest for suspicion of the murder of Jason Strick and an unidentified Asian man who we are calling John Doe," said Jacob. "Jennifer, will you please read this gentleman his rights."

"You don't seem to understand. I haven't killed anyone and I have no idea what you are talking about," said Hoag.

"Let's make this easy. Just come get in the cruiser and we will talk more about this," said John.

"I will have all three of your badges when I get back to Frankfort," growled Hoag as they walked to the cruiser.

"Just get in the car and hush," said John.

"What were you driving and where is it parked?" asked Jennifer.

"I was driving my personal truck and it is parked up there on the White Pines strip bench," answered Hoag.

"I believe we need to impound it," said John.

"Is it locked?" asked Jacob.

"Yes," answered Hoag.

Handing Jacob the keys, Hoag got in the back seat of the cruiser and John got in the back with him. Jacob got in beside Jennifer

"Let's take him and lodge him, then come back and get his truck," suggested John.

Just as they were getting ready to leave, the wrecker pulled up to get the burned-out car in Red Oak Right. They followed the wrecker out of the hollow and on into town. The officers didn't discuss the burned-out wreck.

All the way to the jail, Hoag didn't say a word. Once Jennifer pulled into the secured entrance of the Bell County jail, Jacob took Hoag up to be booked and jailed. When he got back to the car, Lieutenant Talbert suggested that they go check on Thelma after they got Jerry Hoag's truck.

"I guess that Carl Smith is where he always was before, right, Jacob?" asked John.

"I'd say you are right and I would say he will stay there until we get to him," said Jacob as Jennifer pulled out and headed back up Straight Creek. On the way up the creek, they told Jacob about the burned-out car they had found on Red Oak Right. It might lead to the murderer.

When she got to the road up to the White Pines bench, Jennifer downshifted and eased up it. The road was in a good state of repair and had been freshly graveled. Getting up on the bench, they could see Hoag's truck up ahead near the road that Frank had made.

"Why don't we walk from here?" said John.

They all got out. Then Jacob opened the trunk, got out a camera, checked to see that it had batteries and film, and hung it around his neck.

"I've often wondered what a strip mine bench looked like," said Jennifer. "I've heard about them all my life and now I have seen one."

Nearing Hoag's truck, John stopped the other two. "Look at these tire tracks that lead up to his truck and these two sets of cat tracks leading to that drill over there. The ones to his truck are under the cat tracks to the drill, and yet the drill was moved when Isabel drove it down the mountain. In addition to that, Frank brought the dozer from Golden Star over to make the road to the drill site and the tire tracks are under the dozer tracks."

"What you are saying is that Hoag's truck was parked here before the accident," said Jennifer.

"Exactly," said John.

"And G T said that the blood on Strick's clothes was still wet when he and George went in the first time," said Jacob.

"Right," said John.

"Then Hoag must have either committed the murders or very possibly seen them committed," added Jennifer.

"I'll take some pictures of the tracks crossing over," said Jacob.

"But why was Hoag here? Was he here to get the treasure or was he here for some other reason such as murdering those two men?" asked Jennifer.

"Let's go ahead and impound the truck, go check on Thelma and Wing Fu, and then talk to Hoag without letting on that we know about his truck being parked here before the accident," said John.

"I'll drive the truck and follow you, Jennifer," Jacob said.

John hadn't seen Ching Lee when they passed the supermarket on the way back to town and wouldn't have known who she was if he had. But she saw him sitting in the front seat as Jennifer drove past on her way back from the mine site. She only got a glimpse, but she was sure it was him.

"Get your eyes open. We are about to find out where Wing Fu is," she said.

Jennifer drove up Log Mountain to Roland's garage where Jacob parked the truck alongside the burned-out car in a space designated for impounded vehicles. Jacob, Jennifer and John then drove to Thelma's and parked. Going to the door, John rang. Jemjelf opened the door after she made sure who it was.

"Well, if it isn't my little coal mining trooper," kidded Thelma as the three officers came in.

Hugging Jacob she fussed at him, "I'm glad you are safe. You need to quit going in places like that." Then she hugged Jennifer, welcoming her to Pineville and the Harlan Post 10.

Jennifer knew everyone except Betty and Wing Fu. John introduced her to them."This is Jacob's new partner," said John, "I think it may be for life."

Jennifer turned beet red as she asked Thelma and Jemjelf how they were after their ordeal at Curtis' hideout.

Wing Fu had Alberta in her arms and Jennifer went to her.

"What a beautiful baby," said Jennifer, which Betty interpreted to Wing Fu.

"Thank you," said Wing Fu in one of her few English phrases.

They were all standing in the entranceway and Thelma offered them a seat.

"We just came by to check and see if every thing is all right," said John, putting his arm around Thelma and Betty.

Everyone was getting seated when the doorbell rang. Looking through the peep hole, Jemjelf saw a tall Asian woman. Asking what she wanted, Ching Lee said that she had a message for Wing Fu. Not questioning how the woman knew that Wing Fu was there, Jemjelf told her to hand it to her when she opened the door. Being sure that the chain was in place she opened the door. Before Jemjelf could shut it back, a set of bold cutter-jaws snipped the chain and the door burst open, knocking her to the floor. Standing in the entrance to the living room with a drawn pistol, Ching Lee ordered her flunkies to take Alberta away from Wing Fu, but to not harm either the baby or its mother. She had it all figured out except for one thing: she didn't know Jennifer or her background.

Jennifer had been standing in front of Wing Fu admiring Alberta, who was smiling and cooing at Jennifer, when the intruders appeared. The Chinaman who came over to get the baby never knew what hit him. Karate chopping him in the Adam's apple, Jennifer dropped him with one lick. Jacob took on one of the other two while John collared the third one. Betty reacted as fast as or faster than John and Jacob. Knocking the pistol out of Ching Lee's hand, Betty threw the other woman to the floor and landed on top of her. Pinning her left arm behind her, Betty calmly asked John for his handcuffs, which she put on Ching Lee's wrists. Jacob had cuffed his prisoner and Jennifer had cuffed hers, but John was left with no cuffs thanks to Betty.

"Hold him where you have him, John, I'll be right back," said Thelma going into her bed room. Returning to the "action arena" she handed John a set of cuffs that she had brought with her from her encounter with Curtis.

Soon Jemjelf had revived and began apologizing for letting Ching Lee and her accomplices in.

"It certainly wasn't your fault," said John. "I'm just glad that they were dumb enough to try this while we were here."

"I don't have the slightest clue who these people are and where they came from," said Jacob. "Will someone please let Jennifer and me in on what is going on?"

"Let's get these four to the jail and when we come back, I'll cut you in on what is happening," said John.

Putting Ching Lee and one of the men in his cruiser, Jacob and Jennifer took them to the Bell County jail. John and Betty took the other two in his car and followed them.John told the jailer that the prisoners had escaped from the Peary County jail so he should not take any chances with them. The Bell County jail was more modern than the Peary County one and it had a lot better security. The women's cells were completely away from the men's. The cell doors opened into a hallway that was secured at both ends. The release mechanism was electrically operated with a portable generator in case of a power failure. The closed-circuit TV was monitored in two places and the emergency power served it also. Guards were kept at both locations while a third guard sat at the release console. They changed positions every half-hour so that no one got too tired. It was a good system.

The cell blocks were on the second floor. Prisoners were taken into a secured garage where they were then transported to the second floor by elevator. Once the car bearing the prisoner entered the garage, the opened door closed before the car doors could be opened. It was a virtually inescapable setup.

After depositing Ching Lee at the jail, the officers returned to Thelma's and sat down in the living room while John brought Jennifer and Jacob up to date on Wing Fu and Alberta. For lunch, Jemjelf had fixed chicken salad and served it over a fresh tomato with crackers. She had also made her famous pineapple upside-down cake that she served everyone along with a big dollop of ice cream.

After finishing their lunches, John suggested that they go question Carl Smith about the murders. Parking in front of the pool room, the three policemen went through the front of the restaurant to the back part where the pool tables were located. Sure enough, Carl was playing nine-ball as usual.

"Hi, Jake, who's the good looking broad?" asked Carl.

Ignoring his comment, Jacob put his hand on the cue stick and kept Carl from shooting. "We want to ask you what you know about the murder of Jason Strick and a Chinaman that was with him," said Jacob.

"How come every time there is a murder, you come to me?" Carl asked in righteous indignation, "I've got me a good job now at White Pines Coal Company and I don't need you hustling me, understand? Now turn my cue stick loose or I may break it over your head," Carl threatened.

Grabbing Carl's arm, Jacob pulled it up behind his back and walked him out to the cruiser. Jennifer opened the back door and Jacob shoved him in, then she then read Carl his rights. John got in beside him and Jennifer got in up front. Jacob then drove around to the jail where they took Carl to an interrogation room.

"I'm getting tired of you people rousting me every time somebody gets a parking ticket. Like I told you, I am a hard working man that never misses a day's work. I don't want it on my record that I was suspected of killing somebody," said Carl.

"What is your job at White Pines?" asked Jacob.

"I told you that I did the reclamation work," snarled Carl.

"Who hired you?" asked Jacob.

"I want a lawyer before I answer any more questions," said Carl.

"There's the phone. You can make one call," said John.

When he dialed a number, Carl got an answering machine. Slamming the phone down, he dialed another number. This time he got an answer. "This is Carl and three state cops have me down here at the jail and they are asking me questions. I'm not going to answer any until you get here," he barked into the phone.

After he hung up, Carl reported to the officers, "That was Beecher Hewl, my lawyer, and he said that you all could cool your heels until he got here."

All four sat around in the interrogation room to wait. Jennifer read a magazine she found, John and Jacob played cribbage on a board that Jacob got from the jailer. Carl tried to look intelligent as he thumbed through an old magazine he found, but most of the time he was ogling Jennifer. Fifteen minutes after Carl had made his call, Beecher Hewl showed up. He stood about six feet and weighed in at about 140. He was thin and spindly, with gray hair and a two-day beard. His eyes were blue when they weren't bloodshot. He didn't have a very savory reputation among the local lawyers. He had been caught in a real estate scam some years ago and his law practice had suffered the consequences. Hewl supposedly sold out his partner on the real estate deal and the partner got five years in prison. The word on the street was that he was a crook and you took your chances using him.

"What are you people trying to do to my client, Mr. Smith?" he asked Jacob.

"We have been informed that Mr. Smith is part of a marijuana ring that is cultivating the drug on the property of White Pines Coal Company. The former manager of White Pines was found murdered day before yesterday. We want to know what Mr. Smith knows about the murders."

"Just because Mr. Smith is an employee of White Pines doesn't mean that he is a drug dealer. That is a libelous statement that you have made there, and you can rest assured that I will counsel Mr. Smith to bring you before the bar of justice for making it," said Hewl.

"We have enough evidence to bring Carl to trial for the murder of Jason Strick and an Asian John Doe. Now if you want to counsel him to take the Fifth Amendment, then that is his constitutional right. It is our duty and responsibility to bring to justice the perpetrator of these crimes and we can lock him up on what we have proof of," bluffed John.

"I would like privacy with my client," said Hewl.

"That is also his privilege," said John. "We will be out in the hall. When you are ready to cooperate, then call us."

It was difficult to keep from overhearing the conversation between Carl and his attorney, but all three moved to where the voices were indistinct. Ten minutes later, Carl's lawyer, such as he was, came to the door and told John that Carl was ready to talk to them. Going back into the interrogation room, they seated themselves around Carl with Jacob sitting next to the door.

"I'm ready to cut a deal," said Carl.

"I don't know if we can do that," replied Talbert. "This is a murder investigation and we don't cut deals with someone who may be tried for murder. The best we can do is to tape your story and ask the judge to hear it in confidence. If what you say is true and it can be proven as such, then we will play the tape for him in his chambers with your attorney present and let him decide if you should be given any consideration." Talbert was giving Jacob and Jennifer a good lesson in running a bluff.

"Okay, get your recorder out and let's get on with it," said Beecher.

Jennifer had gone out and gotten the tape recorder while they were waiting on Carl and Beecher to make up their minds. Plugging it in, she laid the mike in front of Carl and turned it on.

"State your name," said John.

"Carl Smith," said Carl.

Turning off the mike, John told Carl, "Say that you are making this statement without any duress or influence from us and that we have not made you any promises."

Turning the mike back on, John nodded his head at Carl for him to start.

Carl made the preliminary statement and began his story. "I've done some bad things in my life, but I ain't never killed nobody. Back about two year ago, old man Jason Strick come in here in the poolroom one day and told me to come outside, that he wanted to talk to me. I went outside with him and he told me he had a job that he thought I might be interested in. I told him that I wasn't going back underground for nobody, no matter what they paid. He said he didn't want me to go underground, but that he had a big piece of property that had been reclaimed and he wanted somebody to put a crop of pot on it. I told him that I wasn't interested, on account of the Aser Land Company had a man that didn't do nothing but patrol their property for pot fields. He used to be a deputy sheriff and had shot at a couple of fellows who had a crop at another place. Strick said that I didn't have to worry about that on account of his company had bought the property. He told me that I would be an employee of White Pines and wouldn't have to go underground or nothing. All I had to do was raise the seedlins and plant them, keep the pot watered during hot weather, and when the crop come in, to cut it and spread it out to dry in that old Neddles house up the road. I told him I didn't have no truck or way to get around and he said he would give me a truck. I ain't never owned a truck or had a steady job since that bastard Bradley Durham fired me, so I took him up on it.

"Well, I took the job. I had me some pot seeds and I hot-housed them in the Neddles place. I got me about two hundred of them little seed things that you put seeds in and some of them sunlight tubes for light fixtures. I made tables out of plywood and sawhorses, screwed them light fixtures to the bottom of the plywood, and laid the board on them horses with the lights shining down. The house had electric in it so I ran me some circuits to the lights. Now you people think I'm dumb, but I figured all of that out by myself and built it by myself. I set the tables against the wall and hung black plastic around the other three sides. That way the plants could get air, but the light wouldn't shine out at night.

"I had some of the prettiest seedlins that you ever seen. I was afeerd that they would get too big to transplant, but they didn't. Come spring, I set them out. I did it all by myself. I didn't have no helper. Well, sir, I had the prettiest pot patch that you ever seen. I planted sugar cane in with it and they growed up together. I've heerd that you people can spot pot in a corn field so I used cane. They come in about the same time, so I separated them as I cut them. Strick give the cane to somebody and they made sorghum out of it. That crop put me in the big time. You don't mind working if you get paid for what you do. Strick tried to slip-shuck me on the pot, but I told him I would quit and he couldn't get nobody else, so he backed off and give me my fair share.

"I didn't have no trouble with people nosing around. He had the field fenced before I put the crop out and we kept the gate locked with a Keep Out sign on it. I run three strands of barbed wire along the top of the fence and put one of them cattle shockers on the top wire. That Fuson feller come nosing around one day and I told Strick about it. He must've sat down on Fuson on account of he never come back, at least that I knowed of.

"After the pot dried, I stripped the stalk and put the stuff in old steam-cleaned oil drums. I had it bagged in little plastic bags and put some boxes of rocks in with it to make it weigh heavy. I sealed them drums up and welded the lids on, then I marked the drums COAL SAMPLES. I put the drums in my truck and took them to the coal loadout. Nobody knowed the difference. I asked Strick where it was going and he told me I was better off not knowing. I ain't no rocket scientist, but it didn't take long to figure out that it was going to China on account of that's where the coal went. That was the first year that I raised it and I done a good job if I do say so."

"Did anyone know about this beside you and Strick?" asked Jennifer.

"I don't know if they did, but Strick come in one day with a feller I think was a Chinaman and showed him the whole operation. He seemed real pleased with it. Then Strick come by the other day with a different Chinaman. He showed him everything and then they began to talk money. The Chinaman was trying to make Strick cut his price, but Strick wasn't gonna budge. They got pretty hot at each other and Strick told him they needed to go somewheres else to talk about it. I didn't care what Strick got for the pot on account of he had me on a flat salary of two hundred a week, but that Chinaman had a satchelful of money and he wasn't going to turn loose of it until him and Strick saw eye to eye. From where I stood, that looked like it was a long time off.

"What were they driving?" asked Jacob, not wanting to be outdone by Jennifer.

"They was in a car that I guess was rented by the Chinaman," answered Carl. "They took out of here and went back down the road. I never knowed where they went and to be truthful with you, I never cared."

"Did you ever know an inspector named Jerry Hoag?" asked John.

"I can't say that I did. I never had much truck with inspectors on account of I didn't want them to find out about my pot field," answered Carl.

"How did you keep them away from inspecting the fenced area?" asked Jennifer.

"They never come around it, so I never had no trouble keepin' it a secret," said Carl.

"Why didn't they inspect it?" asked Jennifer.

"Like I said I never had no truck with them and I never knowed why they didn't at least look at it. Now that you mention it, when I started to put them first seedlins out, I asked Strick about inspectors. He told me to not worry about them, that he would take care of it," Carl answered.

"I don't have anymore questions. Do either of you have any?" asked John.

"I don't. What about you, Jennifer?" asked Jacob.

"I don't have any more right now," said Jennifer.

Turning to Beecher Hewl, John told him that he, Jacob and Jennifer were going to step out in the hall, but they wouldn't be long. Once they were in the hall, John asked the other two what they thought.

"I believe what he says," said Jennifer. "He had no motive to kill either one or both of them. Strick was his livelihood and he didn't even know Asian John Doe."

"I agree," said Jacob. "He steered us right on Bradley Durham and Veronica Atmore. It was his tip about Bige's truck that put us onto Olivia. I vote that we let him go and forget about the pot charges. Golden Star owns White Pines now. As soon as Frank and George find out about the pot field, they will destroy it, so we really don't have any proof that Carl did what he said he did, other than that tape which he can refute whenever he wants to".

"Do you vote to let him go, Jennifer?" asked John.

"Yes," said Jennifer.

"That makes it unanimous," said John. "Let's go back in." Back in the interrogation room, Talbert gave Carl the news. "We have decided to let you off the hook, Carl," said John, "provided your attorney does not bill you for his attendance here."

"I swear I've told you'uns all I know and I guess I'm out of business now," said Carl.

"We will forget about the pot patch if you'll swear not to get back into the business. However, if we catch you growing that stuff again, we'll come down on you like the white on rice," said John.

"You have my word," said Carl.

After Beecher and Carl left, Jennifer suggested that they question Jerry Hoag, who was upstairs in the jail. Going upstairs to the turnkey, they told him that they would like to take the prisoner down to the interrogation room for a while. The turnkey went to Jerry's cell and got him, turning him over to the three troopers.

When they got to the interrogafion room, Hoag told them that he had called his superior, Edwin Lee, and informed him that he had been arrested for inspecting a surface mined area. Lee had hit the ceiling and told Jerry to not say a word until he got the department's lawyer to come to Pineville. The department attorney was a young man named Joseph Stowe, who left for Pineville right after Edwin's call. He had arrived at the jail not too long before John, Jennifer and Jacob got there. He was in the turnkey's office when they announced that they wanted to question Hoag, so he accompanied them.

Joseph was a graduate of the University of Cincinnati and had recently passed his bar exam. He was a typical young lawyer, wearing a Harris tweed coat and dress khakis, soft lime green shirt and a figured silk tie. All of this draped over a six foot-180 pound frame. His thick brown hair was cut short as was the style of the day and he was cultivating his facial hair into a beard and mustache. He had grown up in Frankfort so it was almost natural for him to come back to practice.

The questioning began by John filling Stowe in on the circumstances surrounding Jerry Hoag's arrest. He told him about the double murder, the cache of silver coins that was in the old mine and how Jacob caught Hoag coming out of the mine. Talbert also told Stowe about the burned out car that was up in Red Oak Right. "We feel that we have sufficient evidence to hold your client on suspicion of murder," said John.

"I don't feel that you have any evidence at all, except the fact that Mr. Hoag was seen coming out of the mine entrance with a sack of old coins. You haven't told me how you will prove that Mr. Hoag had that sack of coins. Trooper Gibson could have just as well brought the coins out when he was rescued. Mr. Hoag is an employee of the Department of Natural Resources and has every right in the world to inspect the White Pines mine site. I demand that you either place him under arrest on suspicion of murder or release him. I must warn you that if you place him under arrest and it is proven that he is innocent, you will face a civil suit for infringing on his civil rights," said Joe Stowe.

"We are going out in the hall and conference," said John. "Stay here until we get back."

Going out into the hall, they moved some fifteen feet away from the door.

"We really don't have anything, do we?" noted John.

"How did he know that money was in there?" questioned Jennifer.

"I wondered the same thing," said Jacob. "He's bound to have been in there before, but why did he go the first time?"

"If we could find that out, we might find out a lot of things," mused John.

"Let's let him go until we find out more about him and the old money," suggested Jacob.

"I agree," said Jennifer.

Going back into the interrogation room, John told Jerry and his lawyer that they were going to release him, but they might want to talk to him again. Acting on a hunch that he could catch him off guard, Jacob turned to Hoag.

"How did you know those coins were in there?" he asked.

"I have an old map," Hoag answered before his attorney could shut him up.

"Where did you get it?" Jacob asked.

"This conference has ended. My client will not answer anymore questions," growled Stowe.

"This is a murder investigation and we can get a warrant requiring Mr. Hoag to produce the map, which we will do immediately," said John.

"I want to confer with my client," Stowe said.

"We will leave the room," John said as he ushered Jennifer and Jacob out of the room.

"You have put yourself in jeopardy," said Stowe, once the room was clear.

"I have an old map that my great-grandfather gave my father when he was a little boy. So what? That doesn't mean that I killed somebody," said Jerry.

"Do you have the map with you?" asked Stowe.

"No. It's in my truck that they impounded," said Jerry.

"The best thing for us to do is to get that map and give it to them without them having to get a warrant. This would show that we want to cooperate and you are not involved in any murder," said Joseph.

While the officers let Stowe talk to his client, John had complimented Jacob on his flushing out the map. "You've got you a smart one, Jennifer," he told her.

"That was a work of art in finessing," said Jennifer, looking at Jacob like she could eat him up.

Sticking his head out of the door, Stowe told them that he and Jerry were ready to talk to them. "My client is innocent of any murder complicity and I think the three of you know that. In an effort to show that we want to cooperate, we will produce the map. It is in Mr. Hoag's truck, which you all impounded," said Stowe in a voice of accusation.

Turning to Jerry Hoag, John told him that if he would produce the map, they would allow him to go free, but to not leave the state. John rode with Stowe and Jerry Hoag while Jennifer rode with Jacob. Both cars drove up to Roland Chevrolet on Log Mountain. Hoag's truck was parked in the impoundment area near the body shop. Going inside, Jacob got the keys and all five persons went to Hoag's truck.

Opening the truck, Jerry reached behind the driver's seat and got a briefcase. Setting it on the tailgate of the truck, he opened it and got out the map. He had encapsulated it in plastic when he first got it and it had held up pretty well. There were some bloodstains on it that Cyrus Hoag must have gotten there after he dragged Samuel and Ezekiel into the mine.

The only writing on the map was "strait crick" that was scripted along what is known as the Left Fork of Straight Creek. There were no other names on any of the creeks or tributaries. There was a rude sketch of the mine opening showing the stack of rocks, with a skull and crossbones drawn under them. Curiously, there was a circle drawn at the head of the left fork of Dog Star Hollow. Even a person knowing the area such as Jacob did would have trouble finding the mine opening using this map. It was no wonder that Cyrus Hoag had gotten confused when he came back, because Dog Star Hollow was the spitting image of Red Oak. Over the years that Jerry Hoag had been a reclamation inspector, he had searched the Straight Creek watershed for the hollow. Since Red Oak and Dog Star looked so much alike, he had searched the left branch of both hollows but had still missed the opening.

"What is the story behind the map?" Jacob asked.

"It's a long story and is not particularly nice about my kinfolks," Jerry said.

"We need to go some place where we can talk," John said, looking at Jacob.

Going back in the garage, Jacob called Rosemary to see if they could use her kitchen again. She told him he could, but John would have to go get Betty and Jennifer would have to stay for supper. Meanwhile, Rosemary prepared a menu of meatloaf, fried okra, and macaroni and cheese. She had a congealed salad of lemon jello with grapefruit, crushed pineapple, mandarin oranges and slivered almonds that she knew John would like.

"Mom said that we could use the kitchen table," Jacob said.

"Let's go," said John.

All five sat down at Rosemary's table. She served each a glass of iced tea and put a plate of cookies on the table. Jennifer plugged in the tape recorder and began taping every word. Jerry Hoag told about his great-grandfather being a guerrilla during the Civil War and how he was almost captured and hung. He really struck a nerve when he told them that the leader of the group was Jason Strick's great-grandfather, Burl Strick.

"Did Strick have a copy of this map or a map like it?" asked Jacob.

"I think he did, but I never talked to him about it," said Jerry.

"Did he ever get any of the treasure?" asked Jennifer.

"I don't know," said Hoag. "Old Cyrus Hoag came up here from Tennessee one time after the Civil War and searched the hollow above Red Oak. He followed his own map, which was wrong. When he didn't do any good, he gave up and went back home where he drank himself to death. The map was handed down from father to son through each generation. My old man talked about looking for it, but he never did. When he gave me the map he said that it was a wild goose chase, but if I wanted to look for it, I was welcome to do it.

"I didn't have any intention of looking for it when I first became a reclamation inspector, but one day I came here to walk a permit and I remembered the map. I brought it along and tried to figure out where the mine was. However, I didn't have much luck. Sometime after that a permit came through that had been done by G T Deane. I remembered him from when he worked for Golden Star in the summer. When I saw a hollow fill designed to go in Red Oak Left, I thought about the map and I came down here to see about it. I didn't make it to the mine until it was too late. That cave-in caught you three fellows and I figured you were dead, along with the treasure. I heard a radio account of the rescue so I came back down here again from Frankfort to see about the treasure. After all of the excitement died down, I drove up on White Pines and walked down the drill bench road. I had just gone in the mine when you three drove up. I decided to wait until you left. That's when you arrested me. That is my story and I will stick by it."

"I don't believe we have any grounds to hold you on, Mr. Hoag. As far as I am concerned you are free to leave, but we may be in touch later," said John.

As they were leaving the jail, Jacob got a call from dispatch that the coroner was trying to get up with him. Going to the funeral home, Clifford told them that he had finished the autopsy. Both Strick and the Asian had died of gunshot wounds. Strick had been shot four times with what appeared to have been a .38 caliber pistol. Clifford had retrieved the slugs and gave them to Jacob. The Asian had been shot twice with very possibly the same gun.

John told Jennifer to come with him and they left Jacob with the coroner. They returned in about fifteen minutes with Wing Fu and Betty. John told Betty to explain to Wing Fu that they would be looking at a dead man and to not get too upset. Clifford took them into a refrigerated room with drawer-like compartments in the wall. Opening one of the drawers, he pulled out a long tray with a body on it. When he pulled back the sheet, John told Betty to ask Wing Fu if she knew the man. She replied that she did. It was Lin Chou, the man who had accompanied her to the United States and then deserted her. Thanking her, John took Betty and her back to Thelma's. Wing Fu expressed relief that Lin Chou was dead. She feared for Alberta as long as he was on the loose.

Clifford also told Jacob that he had prepared the two skeletons for shipping to Frankfort and would send them off in the morning. He apologized for the fact that the bones had come apart, but he had numbered the joints as best he could and he believed that a good forensics scientist could put them together in the proper way. He almost said "like new."

CHAPTER 38

Frank, Sarah, George and Gerry arrived at Pine Mountain Lodge at about 6:45 PM. They entered the lobby where Karl and Whitley were sitting. Looking at her watch, Sarah asked if they were late. Karl said that they weren't and all six moved to the dining room. Sarah asked the waitress if they could have the table in the window corner where windows were on two sides. They sat alternately man and woman, with Kurt and Whitley seated where they could look up the Big Clear Creek valley.

"Your beautiful countryside reminds me of the area at the foot of the Bavarian Alps. It is so restful and picturesque. It makes you feel like the world is at peace," said Karl.

"We love it," said Sarah.

The waitress came to take their orders. As usual, the four local people ordered the fried catfish and highly recommended it to their guests. Karl was torn between the catfish and the country ham, but settled for the catfish.

Sarah pointed out to Whitley that Ed Durham was born on the other side of the ridge on the left.

"He was truly a nice man," Whitley said. "Doing business with him was a real pleasure."

"I have heard of Mister Durham," Karl said. "Why did he get out of the coal business?"

"There was a cut-in at one of the mines and an employee drowned. Ed called us and said that he had lost his stomach for coal mining and he would like to sell to us," said Frank.

"May I ask why Garbon wanted to sell to Golden Star?" asked Karl.

"Their production had fallen off dramatically and they had missed some shipments. Pat Flannery felt that they had violated the conditions of their contract with you, and that you would be asking questions as to what they were going to do about it. He admitted to us that the company was not fulfilling their part of the agreement and he had no answer for it," said Frank.

"Do you have an answer for it?" asked Karl.

"We feel that we do. The problem with the approval of the permit has been worked out and we plan to put a strip section to work on the property by the middle of next week," Frank responded.

"What is your projected production?" asked Karl.

"We can ship 40,000 tons a week by working two shifts, six days a week. We would like to do this for the period of time that it takes to eliminate the deficit of 100,000 tons that has accrued over the last year. Once we have achieved that goal we would go to working six- and five-day weeks alternately. We can assure you that we will not fall behind on our agreed amount and, at the same time, we would continue to supply PSK with their requirements. With scheduled production from both Golden Star and White Pines, we would have the versatility to have one help the other such as the case may be. We also have plans to open a two-section double-shifted deep mine in the Haggard #8. That would increase out productivity considerably. The former owners didn't try to develop deep mines so that is where we feel we can pick up the slack. We doubled our loadout capabilities at Golden Star and we plan to do the same at White Pines," said Frank.

"It appears to me that you and George have the matter well in hand. We would like to continue our contract with you and possibly increase our demand in the near future, provided that you can handle it," said Kurt.

"We would be glad to discuss the future with you at some later date. At the present we would like to prove our ability to live up to the present contract," said Frank.

"Shall we go to the salad bar?" asked Sarah.

"That sounds good to me," said Whitley getting up from the table.

All six filled their salad plates and then returned to the table.

"I understand that your son had a very narrow escape recently. I hope he is in good health," said Whitley to Gerry.

"I think he is in good shape. It shook him a little, but on the other hand it may have been a good lesson for him," said Gerry.

"The account I read in a Lexington newspaper showed a beautiful young woman running a blasthole drill. I believe her name was Isabel Morgan. Is that your daughter, Frank?" asked Whitley, full well knowing who Isabel was, but feigning ignorance.

"Yes. I am proud to say that it was her," answered Frank.

The meal was excellent as usual. Kurt agreed that the catfish was a real delicacy, but he still wanted a country ham to take home.

CHAPTER 39

Charles Iveson, the chief engineer at Golden Star, was glad to get the job security with the acquisition of White Pines, and he could handle the work. The only problem was, he was going to have to have some help. He had planned to talk to George and Frank about it, but the accident had put that off. He decided to approach them at the first opportunity and that came a week after the accident when everything settled down.

Charles, Frank, George, Sarah and Gerry always had a cup of coffee the first thing in the morning while they discussed the plans for the day. They were sitting in Frank's office the morning that Charles made his case. Frank told Charles about the meeting they had with Kurt and Whitley and about how well it went. Charles didn't know that Whitley had gone to Electrique Internationale. After he found out, he counted this as a plus because she knew their track record and if she was honest about it, she would tell Kurt.

"Acquiring White Pines is great, but you all know that they contracted out all of their permit work while we do all of ours in-house. I can handle the additional work with the mines, but I'm going to have to have someone to do the permits. I would hope that we could hire a person who had a background in permits and the route they take through Frankfort. I have racked my brain and I can't come up with anyone," Charles said.

"Maybe we should advertise in the *Lexington Journal*," said Frank.

Motioning to Sarah, Gerry got up and went out in the hall. "What about Rebecca?" Gerry asked her.

"That is a stroke of genius, Gerry," Sarah said.

Going back in the office, Frank asked them where they had been.

"We had a conference and we have a suggestion to make," said Gerry.

"Let's have it," said Frank.

"We think that Rebecca Holton would be a good choice to solve Charles' problem. She is a licensed professional engineer and knows her way around Frankfort. Checking permits is her job right now, so she would have to know how to do all the calculations required in one. What do you all think?" asked Gerry.

"Why is it that you are the one that always has the solution?" asked Frank.

"We think about other things while you all just think about running coal," said Sarah laughingly.

"Do you think she would be interested?" asked Charles.

"We could ask her and see," said Gerry. "She and G T went back Friday and they seemed to think that the danger to her had passed. They are both convinced that Jason Strick was the one who was having the pressure put on her. With his death, things should loosen up."

"Why don't you call G T tonight and see if he thinks she would be interested?" asked Frank.

"I will and give you all an answer tomorrow morning," said Gerry.

Gerry called G T and put the proposition of Rebecca before him. He liked it. He said that she was very astute and even when they were quarreling over the White Pines permit, she evidenced knowledge of the permitting process. Gerry asked him what he thought they should offer her in the way of money. G T said that he would find out about that and also whether or not Rebecca wanted the job. He also told Gerry that he would call her back.

Calling Rebecca at home that evening, G T told her about the offer. She was delighted. She was so excited that she began to cry, then she got concerned about the paper that she and her father had signed. G T told her not to worry about that, that he would take care of it. When she asked him how he would do it, he told her the job was hers if she wanted it and not to question how he was going to get the contract back. When he asked her what her salary was, she told him. In his estimation she was grossly underpaid.

G T called Gerry after he hung up from talking to Rebecca. He told her that Rebecca wanted the job, but that she and her father had signed a paper that obligated her to follow the Group's instructions. He then asked Gerry to let him talk to George. He explained about the paper Rebecca had signed. George told him not to worry about it, that the company would buy it back if she owed money on it. When all of the telephoning was done, Rebecca was hired and would go to work in two weeks after she tendered her resignation, which would be the next day.

She typed up her resignation, signed it and gave it to Phil Banks who seemed upset that she was leaving.

"Where are you going, Rebecca?" he asked.

"They asked me not to say," she said.

"It is necessary that I know where you are going and why," Phil pressed.

"I am going because it is a better job, but where I am going is of no concern to you," she said, getting a little tired of being pushed around.

"What about the work promise you made when you went to school?" he asked.

"What do you mean?" Rebecca asked, beginning to put two and two together.

"You know full well what I mean. You told me that you and your father signed a paper that you would work for the Group as an environmental activist if they paid your way through school," Banks said.

"That was just a tale I told you to keep my job," Rebecca said, realizing that Phil was part of the problem, but she wanted to tell G T before Banks got spooked and ran off.

"I'm going to tear up this resignation and I will expect to see you at your desk tomorrow and the day after, until such time as you are released from your promise to those people," he said.

"I have a little vacation left, and I want to take two days of it tomorrow and the next day," she said.

"Okay, but you'll be back here after the two days if you know what is good for you," he threatened.

Leaving the office, Rebecca went straight home and called G T. She told him about her conversation with Phil Banks. He said that he would be right over and for her to pack a bag to go back to Pineville, where he should have left her in the first place. He also told her to call her parents and tell them to get what valuables they had together and put them in her father's truck, lock the door and leave. Rebecca still didn't catch on to what G T was telling her and he finally told her that if the Group lost their hold on her they might try to make an example out of her. They had threatened her and her family once before and there was no reason to believe that they wouldn't carry it out. He reminded her of the Marquis that sat out in front of her apartment, the Camry that wrecked on I-64, and what Jacob had said about the Group being dangerous.

When they got back to Gerry's, G T explained what had happened and called Jacob. "Jake, this is G T. I believe this thing is beginning to unravel," he said.

"What are you talking about?" asked Jacob.

G T went into a brief explanation over the phone and Jacob told him to stay where he was that he would be there in about fifteen minutes. Jacob and Jennifer showed up in record time. Jacob had called John and told him that they might have a lead, so John also came out to Gerry's.

With all three officers present, Rebecca repeated her story about Phil Banks.

"He definitely has something to do with the Group," said John, "but right now it is your word against his and he is your supervisor. He could concoct a story about your resignation that would be more believable than the one you are telling. I feel like he is getting his orders from someone else, possibly Hoag."

"I think we need to question Hoag again and brace him about where his truck was parked," said Jennifer.

"We might throw a scare into him if we tell him that Phil Banks tried to threaten Rebecca about quitting," said Jacob, agreeing with Jennifer.

"I have a feeling he hasn't given up on the treasure," said John. "I wouldn't be at all surprised if he wasn't up there right now. What is Hoag's number, Rebecca? I'll call Frankfort and see if he is there. If he isn't it might pay us to go back to Left Branch and check."

Dialing the number that Rebecca said was Jerry Hoag's extension, John waited for it to ring six times and then hung up."What is the receptionist's number?" John asked.

Rebecca gave him that number and John dialed it. When the receptionist answered he asked for Jerry Hoag.

"I am sorry, but Mr. Hoag is out in the field," she said.

"May I ask what area he is in? It is very important that I get in touch with him," said John.

"He signed out to be in the Bartel District," she answered.

John hung up the phone and told the others what the receptionist had said.

"Pineville is in that District," said Rebecca.

"Let's go have a look," said John to Jacob and Jennifer.

"Rebecca, you stay in here until we get this thing wound up. You can call Bige to come stay with you if it is all right with Gerry," said John.

"That would be fine with me," said Gerry.

The three officers left in John's unmarked car and went to Left Branch. They parked at the last curve before they got to Left Branch and walked the rest of the way. When they rounded the curve they saw Hoag's truck parked at the path that led to the mine. Quietly easing up to the mine, they could see a miner's cap light flicking back and forth inside the mine. Waiting at the truck, their patience was finally rewarded with Hoag coming out of the mine and walking to the truck. He didn't see the officers who had hidden behind the truck until he started around to throw the gunny sack full of Confederate money into the truckbed. It was too late then. He reached for a pistol he had on his belt when John told him to put his hands in the air, which Hoag did. "Mirandize him, Jennifer," John said, which she did.

"You have saved us a trip to Frankfort, Mr. Hoag," John said.

"I won't say anything until you let my attorney be present," Hoag growled.

"That's fine with us. We want him to hear about Phil Banks threatening Rebecca Holton because she was quitting and was going to default on her loan from the Group," John told him.

"Wait a minute," said Hoag. "I don't have anything to do with that outfit. Their tactics are too strong for me."

"I don't think you should say anymore until you have an attorney," said John.

Back to the Bell County jail, they lodged Jerry Hoag again and impounded his truck at Roland's garage again. They took his cargo to the bank and had it locked up in the vault. Joseph Stowe finally showed up and the turnkey called John. He radioed Jacob and Jennifer, and they all met at the jail. Once more taking Hoag to the interrogation room, they settled in to question him. Jennifer had a tape recorder and a note pad that she used for backup shorthand.

John started the questioning by asking Hoag what he knew about the group. "You are Phil Banks' supervisor so you obviously were aware of his association with this outfit known as the Group. Why don't you open up and tell us about the whole affair beginning with the lie you told about how long your truck had been parked on the White Pines strip bench before the mine accident," directed John.

"Before he does that, I want to have a conference with him," said Joseph.

John, Jacob and Jennifer left the room and settled outside in the hall. Then Stowe turned to Jerry and asked him what John was talking about.

"There is an environmental organization that is very clandestine and radical. They have been accused of murders, although none have ever been proven on them. They have infiltrated our office and though I am suspicious of who is in it, I don't know for sure. The EPA is full of them, but definitely does not approve of their tactics. We have a young lady in our permit section who is evidently a member of this group and she has quit, which according to what I have heard, you can't do," said Jerry.

"Okay, I'll let the troopers back in and you tell them the gospel truth. If they ask you something that is self-incriminating, look at me and refuse to answer, but whatever you do, do not lie to them. Do you understand me?" Stowe said in a very positive voice.Going to the door, he called to John, Jennifer and Jacob, telling them that they were ready to talk.

John asked the first question. "Are you a member of an organization known as the Group?"

"Absolutely not. I have never been, nor will I ever be," answered Jerry in a very adamant tone.

"Are there people in the Division of Permits who are members?" he asked.

"I can't say positively that there are, but I believe there are. Who they are, I don't know," Jerry responded preempting John's next question.

"When did you park your vehicle on the White Pines strip job prior to the accident?" John asked.

Hesitating for a short time, Jerry Hoag remembered Stowe warning him not to lie.

"What I am going to tell you is the truth. I have lied to you before, but you obviously know that my truck was parked there before the accident, so I will make a clean breast of the whole affair. One of the inspectors called in the office and told me that Jason Strick had been fired. Realizing that this might be my last opportunity to get any of the treasure that my ancestor had hidden, I decided to go to Pineville and get what I could of it before the permit was approved that would allow a hollow fill to cover it up.

"I came up Left Branch road and when I got to the last curve, I saw a truck and a car parked at the mouth of the path up to the mine. I backed down the road, turned around and went out of Red Oak. I went on up to the road that turned up to the White Pines strip job and drove down close to the berm until I was just above the old mine. I parked, got out and walked over to the berm. Then I crouched down behind a tree and watched as best I could. There were three men standing in front of the old mine. I recognized Jason Strick and I believe one of the other two was Bryan Fuson. The third man I didn't know and I don't believe I had ever seen him before. I don't know how they got there. I couldn't see down the path to where they would have parked. They were arguing about something, but I couldn't make out what it was. Suddenly the man I think was Bryan Fuson pulled a pistol and shot Jason Strick. He then turned the gun on the other man and shot him. I don't know how many times he shot either of them, but he kept clicking the pistol after it was empty.

"Evidently Fuson was afraid that he would be caught at the scene, because he dragged both bodies into the mine and then left. Not long after he walked out of the hollow I heard an explosion and saw some smoke come up from what looked like Red Oak Right. I waited about forty five minutes and then started down through the woods when I heard voices. I stepped behind a tree and waited until they were close enough to see and I peeked around the tree. There were George Deane, G T Deane and Rebecca Holton coming up the path to the mine. I waited until George and G T went underground and then I eased back up the hill. Rebecca must have heard me because she looked up toward where I was, but the bushes blocked her view.

"I watched the whole rescue operation. Once I started to go down and help clear up the entry, but then I would have had to explain why I was there and that could have gotten sticky. I had a couple of sandwiches and a bottle of water and I slept in the truck. I'm surprised that no one saw me, especially Frank or Isabel. I will give that girl credit. She sure knew what she was doing with that drill. That is the truth, so help me."

"Are you sure the man who did the shooting was Bryan Fuson?" asked Jacob.

"No. I couldn't swear to it, but he favored him," said Jerry.

"You can return to Frankfort, Mr. Hoag, but you are a material witness in this crime so do not leave the Frankfort area," said John.

Going to the turnkey, John advised him that they were removing the charges against Hoag and he was free to go.

After they left Hoag and Stowe, Jacob, Jennifer and John were right back where they started from so they decided to question Bryan Fuson.

CHAPTER 40

Jason Strick was a coarse, crude, pig of a man who didn't give a tinker's dam about being fired. He had a foul mouth and delighted in telling dirty jokes in mixed company. Over the period of time that he had worked for White Pines, he had hooked and crooked enough to put him at ease the rest of his life. His wife had left him for the last time and he was glad. She gave the reasons as irreconcilable differences. He laughed when he saw the papers. The only reconcilable thing between them had been his giving her enough money to fritter away. She had been hitting the bottle pretty heavy lately and he could use that in the divorce action. Margaret Strick had been a pretty girl, with long auburn hair. Her hazel eyes were attractive, but in the last couple of years they had taken on a look of sadness. Jason Strick was a hard man to live with. Being frustrated with her marriage and its failure, she had started spending more time in the Lexington bars. She had started picking up younger men who she thought would alleviate her frustration, but it didn't work. She even picked up a bagboy at the supermarket, but he was too young to know what she was talking about so she let him go. Jason and Margaret were actually sad and pitiable for the misery they had brought themselves and each other.

When Pat Flannery fired Jason, he also demanded Jason's keys to the company truck, leaving Jason with no transportation. Margaret was out of town, as usual, so he had to figure a way of moving around. Bryan Fuson had been sick for a week so he didn't know anything about not having a job. Jason decided not to tell him, but to use him as a taxi service. Jason had one thing in mind and that was to recover the Confederate money in the old doghole mine at the head of Red Oak Left. It had become an obsession with him. He needed to get it to prove to himself that he was a better man than any of his ancestors. Burl Strick would have been proud of Jason because he was cut more like Burl than any of his other ancestors. But Jason was still afraid to go in the mine and get the money, while at the same time he didn't trust anyone to get it for him. He had pondered on this since Pat Flannery had discharged him. It suddenly came to him that he would get Lin Chou to retrieve the treasure. He wouldn't know the value of it and Jason would give him half of the pot money Lin Chou was supposed to pay him. He had planned a meeting with Lin Chou for the day after he was fired to settle up on the last pot shipment, so he would get the Chinaman to go in and get the silver.

Strick got Bryan to take him to meet Lin Chou at Helen's Grocery, at the mouth of Red Oak Hollow. Then he sent Bryan on a wild goose chase to get the maps showing the mine development in Red Oak Left; in reality, there were no maps and there was no proposed mine. Jason went in the grocery where Lin Chou was drinking a pop. He told Lin Chou to get the money and they would go someplace and count it. They headed to Lin Chou's rental car and Jason showed him where to go up to Red Oak Left. Jason didn't tell Lin Chou that this was his last trip and the pot field would probably be destroyed. He led him on as though they would continue to do business. He apologized to Lin Chou for arguing with him when they were at the old Nettles house. He was so nice to Lin Chou that he was almost unctuous.

Jason explained to him about the treasure that was in the mine and how he wanted Lin Chou to retrieve it for him. The Chinaman realized that there was no way for him to capitalize on it so he went along with taking half of the pot money and agreeing to get the old money out of the mine.

++++++

Bryan Fuson lived in subdivision outside of Pineville. Jacob knew where he lived, so he and Jennifer could go get him for questioning. John said that was fine with him, that he needed to get back to Thelma's and see what Betty wanted to do. She was pretty well locked in to taking care of Wing Fu since neither Thelma nor Jemjelf could talk to her.

Driving out to Bryan Fuson's home was the first time that Jacob had been alone with Jennifer for any period of time. He told her that he was glad that she had changed jobs and he would like to have her as a partner until he went to UK to law school. After pulling into Fuson's yard, he and Jennifer got out, rang the doorbell, and waited to be answered. A nice-looking older woman answered the door. Jacob explained to her what they wanted and she let them in. Calling to Bryan, she left them in the living room and retreated to the kitchen.

Coming into the living room, Bryan spoke to Jacob who he knew. Jacob in turn introduced Jennifer.

"We would like to ask you some questions, Bryan," Jacob said, "and it would be to your best interest to have an attorney present."

Jennifer read Bryan his rights and told him to go with them back to the jail. He called to his wife and told her he was going into town with the troopers but that he would be back in a little while. Also before leaving, Bryan called Jeff Cawood and asked him to meet him at the jail, which he did. Conferring with Jeff for a few minutes, Bryan told Jacob that he would be glad to answer their questions. Jennifer set up the tape recorder and got out her shorthand pad.

"Did you kill Jason Strick and or a Chinaman named Lin Chou?" asked Jacob.

"No. I did not," said Bryan.

"Do you know who did?" asked Jacob.

"No. I do not," said Bryan.

"Were you with Jason Strick and Lin Chou on the morning of the accident in Red Oak Hollow?" asked Jacob.

"Yes, I was with Jason. I don't know a Lin Chou," replied Fuson.

"Will you explain to us what the nature of the meeting was?" asked Jacob.

"I had been off for a week with the flu and I wasn't aware that Jason and I had been terminated. The morning of the accident, I went to work as always. Jason was already in the office when I got there. He seemed to be in his usual bad humor so I didn't talk to him too much. He told me that he had a meeting with the coal buyer for Electrique Internationale and he wanted me to take him to Helen's Grocery at the mouth of Red Oak Hollow, where he was supposed to meet the man. He said he was going to show the buyer where he planned to open a deep mine in the Haggard #4 at the head of Red Oak Left.

"I didn't know that we were no longer working for White Pines and he didn't tell me. I still had my company truck, but Pat Flannery had taken Jason's keys away from him and that was why he wanted me to drive him to the meeting. We met the coal buyer, who was Chinese, at Helen's Grocery as planned and Jason told me that he would get the Chinaman to take him back to the office. But Jason had forgotten the maps showing the proposed mine and he sent me back to the office to get them. As I went back down Straight Creek, I passed someone driving Jason's truck. That was the only vehicle I passed. When I got to the office, I found a locksmith in the process of changing all of the locks and a security guard with him. I still didn't know what was going on and I told the guard that I needed to get some maps, but he refused to let me in. He said that his orders were to keep everyone out and that meant everyone.

"I went back to Red Oak to tell Jason that I couldn't get the maps. As I passed Helen's Grocery, I noticed that the Chinaman's rented car was not in the parking lot. I didn't think anything about it, but as I turned up Red Oak I was passed by an ambulance with its lights flashing. When I got to the mouth of Red Oak Left, I found a crowd of people. I recognized George Deane and spoke to him, but he didn't answer me and I doubt now that he even saw me. I am not one for crowds, so I left. As I went out of Red Oak I met several vehicles, but I didn't recognize any of them. I went on home because I figured that someone would call me if it were something that pertained to the mines. When I got home, my wife told me about the accident. I still didn't know that Golden Star had bought White Pines and I didn't have a job. In a sense, after I found out, I was relieved because I didn't like living here. I have always planned to go back to Richmond, Virginia where I came from and this made it possible.

"I went back to Red Oak to find out what was going on. The state police turned me back after telling me what happened. When I got home I tried to call Pat Flannery to tell him, but his secretary told me that he was en route from Middlesboro to Boston, and when he arrived he would return my call. I waited all day and finally about nine o'clock that night he called me. I told him that there had been an accident on White Pines property and he said that that was not his or my problem, that Garbon had sold White Pines to Golden Star and he had fired Jason. I told him that I would have met him at the Middlesboro Airport if he had let me know he was coming. He said that George Deane met him and lent him the use of his truck while he was here. He told me that I would be transferred to another branch and to not worry about it. That was how I found out. That is all I know, Jacob."

"Who is Pat Flannery?" asked Jacob.

"He's the president of Garbon, Ltd., the mother company of White Pines," answered Bryan.

"Did you know that Jason had a large pot field on the property?" asked Jennifer.

"I knew he had an area fenced off and had hired a man named Carl Smith to reclaim it. He said that he was raising sugarcane and he had fenced it off to keep out the deer and elk."

"Was there anything unusual about Jason meeting Lin Chou?" asked Jacob.

"I don't know. We have been doing business with that power company for several years and just last year was the first time we had been visited by a coal buyer. He was Chinese, but it was not Lin Chou. I only met him, Jason squired him around, and he was only in the office one time," responded Bryan.

"Who was driving Jason's truck when you passed it?" queried Jennifer.

"I don't know. It looked like Pat Flannery, but I didn't know he was even in town and I didn't know what he would be doing driving Jason's vehicle.

"We appreciate your coming in and talking to us," said Jacob. "We ask that you not leave the area, since we may want you as a material witness."

After taking Bryan home, the two officers went to Thelma's to talk to John. Jacob told him about their interview with Bryan Fuson while Jennifer played with Alberta.

"I think we need to sit down at Rosemary's table," said John.

CHAPTER 41

Following their dinner at the Lodge with George, Gerry, Frank and Sarah, Kurt and Whitley sat in the lobby at the lodge and discussed their coal providers.

"I will be up-front honest with you, Kurt," Whitley began. "Those people are straight arrow if such a thing exists. I liked Ed Durham and he was a pleasure to be around, but every now and then he would want a favor of some sort and it was up to me to provide it. He was very loose with the football and basketball tickets for the University of Kentucky games and those come at a premium, but these people will never ask you for a thing and they do not expect you to offer them anything. They stay very close to home."

"Before I hired you I looked into all of those things and I was waiting for you to tell me about it. My confidence in you is growing every day. And now I think we had best turn in, as you Americans say it. George and Frank are going to show us over the property starting at eight o'clock and it could be a long day," said Kurt.

Getting up at six-thirty, Whitley showered and dressed in jeans, blouse and hard-toed boots. She packed all of her belongings and met Kurt in the lobby at seven. Kurt again had country ham for breakfast with two eggs, biscuits, grits and red gravy. Unbeknownst to Kurt, Whitley had purchased a country ham that she slipped out and put in the trunk of the car.

After breakfast, they each returned to their rooms to brush their teeth and freshen up before they left the Lodge. Arriving at Golden Star at 7:45, they found all four of the Golden Star people ready to go.

"Gerry and I felt that it wasn't fair to subject you to listening to three men so we decided to go along," said Sarah. She and Frank got in the rear seat of George's suburban, Gerry and Whitley sat in the middle seat and Kurt rode up front with George, who drove.

The trip started with a drive to Golden Star Mine #3 to tour through the processing plant. They saw the raw coal washed in a washer that had been converted from a jig washer to a heavy media washer. This cut down on the amount of slurry that had to be disposed of and made the refuse easier to handle. Going through the lab, which was connected to the plant, they saw how the samples taken from the raw coal were tested.

"We also test our clean coal to see that the plant is producing what we want," said Frank, "From that we can adjust our washing process to get nearer to the product that you want. The three large concrete silos that you see are where we stockpile the clean coal for loading. The clean coal from the plant is conveyed up to the top of the silo and dropped into it. As the silo fills up, the coal exits through the windows you see in the sides of the silo and builds up around the silo. From there it is conveyed underground to the load out where it is again conveyed into the load out hopper. The hopper holds one hundred tons which is what a gon will hold. We have two load outs with an operator in each one. They load coal from the same stockpile. Ed Durham had all of this in place except the second load out which we put in."

Outside the plant, they walked to one of the loadouts where the coal was loaded into railroad cars known as coal gondolas or 'gons.' As luck would have it, a train was in the process of being loaded and all six went into the control room where the loader operator was talking to the train engineer, telling him when to drop the full cars.From the plant, they rode to Golden Star Mine #6 in the Haggard #8 coal seam. Kurt and Whitley demurred on going underground although Fred Tinsley had coveralls, hats, rescuers and lights ready for them.

"Thank you very much, Mr. Tinsley, but I think I will put that tour off until another time," said Kurt.

Bige Napier's strip section was next. George introduced Bige as one of their most valuable employees. "He is a natural strip operator and we couldn't do without him. He has a girlfriend who is going to work for us next week as our permitting engineer. She is a natural also."

Bige's face turned scarlet.

Returning to the office, they went into Frank's office where everyone had a soft drink.

"Do either of you have any questions about our way of doing things?" asked Frank.

"I believe you have shown us that you have the capabilities to provide our plants with the contracted amount of coal," said Whitley.

Looking at his watch, Kurt told Whitley that he believed they should be moving out, since they would be flying in the dark all the way they needed to get started.

"This jet business has my internal clock all confused," said Whitley. "It will take me a week to get back on schedule."

Before saying their goodbyes, Kurt called the pilot in Knoxville and told him that they would be at the airport in about two hours and to be ready to leave. The road trip to Knoxville was uneventful and when they turned the rental car in, the pilot got their bags and stowed them on the jet. Whitley and Kurt then boarded and the plane took off for Bern. They stopped in Lisbon to refuel and finally landed in Bern. Whitley was worn out and slept most of the way. Kurt, who was used to the trans-oceanic travel, studied his notes on the way home. Once they landed, Kurt took Whitley to her condo from the airport. In addition, she managed to retrieve the country ham without his discovering what it was. It had been put in a box and when Kurt asked her about it, she told him it was a memento of Ed Durham's that Sarah and Gerry had given her. Whitley chuckled to herself: little did he know the ham was means whereby she meant to seduce him.

Kurt had told her to take the day off after they got back to Bern so that she could catch up on her sleep. She slept ten straight hours without moving. She was exhausted and the rest brought her up to speed once more. Getting up at three in the afternoon, she made some coffee and checked her mail. There were several pieces of junk mail, but nothing important. She next checked her caller ID. There were three calls on it from Detective Gary Brown of the Bern Police Department. While she was going over her calls, the phone rang and it was Detective Brown.

"Good afternoon, Ms. Rogers, I have been trying to get in touch with you. We have Mr. Kelly's clothes and other personal effects and we would like to dispose of them. Do you have an address where we could send them or should we just burn them?"

"I would suggest that you burn the clothes, but I would be glad to go through the personal items to see if I recognize anything of value for his friend to whom you sent his ashes," she answered.

"We would appreciate that. When would be good time for you to do this?" he asked.

"I am available almost any afternoon after five. In fact I have the rest of this day left. If you would come get me in about thirty minutes, I would be glad to sort through Pete's things," Whitley offered.

"Thank you, Ms. Rogers. I had hoped you would say that. I have just one more request. Would you have dinner with me afterwards?" Gary said.

"I would love to," she answered, baiting the trap for Officer Brown.

Three-thirty that afternoon found Gary Brown ringing her door bell. Answering it, Whitley invited him in."I would offer you something to drink, but you are on duty. Maybe after dinner we could come back here for a snifter of brandy," she said drawing him further into her web.

"That sounds like a good idea," he answered.

Pete's effects were little or nothing of value. There was an address book that Whitley kept. The rest of it was a wallet with no money and two credit cards, a driver's license and a photo of Jack Colbert. A key ring had several keys on it, one of which was to the front door of PSK. Whitley asked if she could have those and Gary told her she could. The whole process took about an hour. Afterward they went to dinner at a small restaurant in downtown Bern. The meal was more along the lines of German fare. The kraut and polish sausage were delicious as were the boiled potatoes. The dessert was a piping hot strudel covered with ice cream.

"It's not like the usual first date meal," said Gary, "but it is good solid food."

"I needed this after the last few days. I am tired of rich food and this breaks the monotony," she said.

Small talk at dinner consisted of describing their backgrounds, which they had been through before, but didn't reveal anything new. It was almost eight o'clock when they left the restaurant and returned to Whitley's condo. True to her word she poured each of them a snifter of brandy, turned the lights down and the rest is history.

Shortly after Gary left about six o'clock the next morning, Whitley got up, showered and went to work early. Kurt was already in the office when she came in.

"Are you rested from your trip?" he asked.

"Yes, I feel wonderful," she answered.

"That is good. Our next project is to see what we can find out about the Shuai province and its availability. Would you research this and give me a report?" he asked.

"Yes. I will be glad to," she answered.

At the Bern library, she went through the entire section on China, to no avail. She searched the history section and still found nothing. Returning to the office late that afternoon, she told Kurt that there was nothing in the library about Shuai.

"The city of Nanik is near the entrance to Shuai and has a small airport. I have an appointment in Moscow about the mines in Russia and I believe you are well enough versed in our requirements to check out the Shuai province by yourself. I have an interpreter who speaks their dialect that I will send with you if you feel that you can handle it alone," said Kurt.

"I feel confident that I can handle it," answered Whitley.

Kurt made all of the arrangements for her trip. She went home and packed her bags for another long journey. Before she left, she called Gary Brown and told him she was going to be away for a few days, but she would call him when she got back.

This time she went in a small twin engine plane that the interpreter flew. It required their landing at several places on the way to refuel, but at least they weren't crossing the ocean, which had given her an uneasy feeling.The interpreter was an expatriate of the Shuai province. He told Whitley all about the Bear and the Butterflies, which she took with a grain of salt. He said that he would show her the way into the Valley of Shuai, but he wouldn't enter. He was afraid of the butterflies, but she said that she wasn't. They landed at the small airport near the valley entrance and he negotiated the rental of two horses from a native who lived near the airport. The landscape was very stark. The plant life was primarily sage brush type flora.

The corresponding fauna was almost nil except for a few rabbits and gophers. It reminded her very much of west Texas without the cactus. The population of the village, Nanik, was about one thousand. The airport had been built by the communists to use as an access to Shuai. After losing four helicopters in attempts to fly into the village, they abandoned the idea, but kept the airport in hopes for the death of the Butterfly Princess that would gain them admission to the valley.

The Shuai province entrance was only five miles from the village so Whitley and her interpreter reached it in a short time. The entrance was a blowhole that had developed over centuries of winds in and out of a small fissure in a wall of massive sandstone. It was about fifteen feet wide, sixty feet in height and one hundred fifty feet long. Alighting from the horses, the guide held them while Whitley took pictures of the entrance. Looking through the entrance she decided that it was no more than a long tunnel. She could see daylight at the other end and it appeared that the sun was shining. There was nothing that she could see that was forbidding, so she told the guide that she was going to go through the tunnel. He told her again about the butterflies, but she ignored him. Mounting her horse, she started into the entrance. The horse balked on entering the tunnel, but she finally overcame his stubbornness with her own and went into the tunnel.

CHAPTER 42

Jacob called Rosemary to ask if the three officers could once more sit down at her kitchen table to talk. She told him that he knew that he and his friends were always welcome and to come right on. She had just taken a butterscotch pie out of the oven and they could eat it before Howard got home. Seating themselves around the table, John suggested that Jennifer keep notes in her laptop computer. She agreed.

"How many suspects do the two of you think we have?" he asked.

"Carl Smith, a Pat Flannery, Jerry Hoag, Bryan Fuson and Mr. X," said Jacob.

"Who is Mr. X?" asked Jennifer.

"That's the unknown suspect who may be out there somewhere," said John.

"Can either of you think of anyone else?" asked John.

Both Jacob and Jennifer shook their heads, "No".

"Why do you suspect Carl Smith, Jacob?" asked John.

"He saw that Lin Chou had a satchelful of money. That's a motive. Strick said that they were going somewhere to talk. He could have followed them. That's an opportunity. Knowing Carl, he could have had a gun and since we haven't found one, that's a possible weapon. Dragging the bodies into the old mine wouldn't bother Carl, who has worked underground. He could have torched the car and driven out in his own truck, but then that holds true for any of them.

"What about this Pat Flannery, Jennifer?" asked John.

"The only thing we have on him is the fact that Bryan Fuson thought he passed him coming out of Straight Creek. I don't think we can make that stick. I say that we pass over him for right now," said Jennifer.

"How do you both feel about Jerry Hoag" asked John.

"He is my number one suspect," said Jacob.

"I agree," said Jennifer.

"How do you feel about Bryan Fuson?" asked John.

"The one thing that counts Bryan out is the fact that he is claustrophobic and will not go underground," answered Jacob. "That is common knowledge around Pineville. He could have killed them, but I don't think he would have dragged them underground. Carl had worked underground and it would not have bothered him. The same thing for Jerry Hoag."

"Why do you suspect Jerry Hoag?" asked John.

"The motive could have been money or the treasure. He and Strick were the only ones who knew about the treasure. We heard him say that he watched what went on so that tells us he was there by his own admission.

Hoag could have walked up on them while they were arguing and taken them by surprise. He wanted the treasure for the same reason Jason did, to prove that he was a better man than his ancestors. Jerry said that he thought he saw Bryan Fuson, but he must not have known that Bryan will not go underground," said Jacob.

"That leaves Mr. X who has the money and the murder weapon," said John.

"Let's go back to the site and look for the money and the gun," said Jennifer.

"That was next on the things to do," said John.

As they left Rosemary's and drove back up to Red Oak Left, all three were quiet while each studied about where he would put the money and the gun.

"The logical thing to do would be to get rid of the gun at the same time you get rid of the car," mused John out loud.

"It seems to me that the logical time to get rid of the gun would be when you first got out of the car," said Jennifer as they reached the site.

Jacob opened the trunk of the cruiser and got a crescent wrench. Walking to the place where Lin Chou's rental car had been parked when it was burned, he positioned himself about where he would be if he got out of the car on the driver's side. Pitching the wrench underhand, he told the other two to watch where it went. Since the open car door would have blocked his throwing it toward the front, and throwing it to the rear would have taken longer, Jacob threw it in a direction almost perpendicular to the car. All three pushed aside the brush and went to where the wrench had landed. Then spreading out from the wrench, they began to search.

Fifteen minutes after they started, Jennifer yelled. Going to where she was, they saw what she had found, a .38 caliber pistol. Picking it up with a pencil in the barrel, Jacob put the weapon in a plastic bag.

"We'll run this for prints," said John as they got back in the cruiser.

"That just proves that three heads are better than one," said Jacob.

"I need to go back to Frankfort tonight anyway," said John, "and I'll get the lab to run this for prints. I should be back some time in the morning and hopefully we can make an arrest. " On his way out of town, John stopped by Thelma's to ask Betty if there anything she needed from Frankfort. She told him that there wasn't, but she would sure like to sleep in her own bed for a change.

CHAPTER 43

Isabel and Sandy had finally gotten back to normal at their jobs a week after the accident. On the way back to Lexington, Isabel had driven and thought about G T. Sandy and Sam Eldridge chit-chatted about things in general. It had been a good opportunity for Sam to learn more about his fledgling reporters. They sure know how to stir up the news, he thought. Sandy was going to be an ace. Even though the accident had more or less fallen into her lap, she had done a bang-up job of reporting it. She had definitely increased circulation by her story about PSK. At no time did she let her emotions get in her way. Isabel was going to be different. She was obviously made of high-grade carbon steel from the way she handled the drill rig, but she was also easily touched by the troubles of others. That could impair her ability to report accurately. Time would tell about that.

After giving them time to settle down, Sam called them into his office one day.

"I want to compliment both of you on the way you handled yourselves in Pineville. I was very proud of you. Sandy, your reporting was excellent. There was an opportunity there for you to get maudlin about Isabel and her friends, but you didn't let it get to you. You are going to be a world famous journalist one of these days and I want to be able to say that we worked together at one time. When the job offer comes that will take you away from here, don't hesitate about accepting it. I will be glad to counsel you about it, but I will not try to dissuade you.

"Isabel, you are a different case. You have more guts than a government mule. Your knowing what to do and how to do it was the reason those three fellows are alive today. I am an old man by your standards and I have been around quite a bit, but I have never in my life seen anyone, man or woman, who had the poise, know-how and determination that you exhibited. You also are going to be famous. I'm not too sure it will be in the field of journalism, but it will come to pass. You are an exceptionally beautiful woman, and that's from an old married man. I look for you to be an actress or a model or maybe a truck driver, who knows. I will one day say that I knew you and we worked together. The pleasure is all mine. Now both of you get back to work. Scat!" Sam said as he shooed them out of his office.

They were both walking on air when they came out of his office and went to their separate desks. Isabel's buzzer sounded right away and she picked up her phone. Answering it, a voice said, "Miss Morgan?"

"Yes?" Isabel said.

"My name is Don Parker and I am a talent agent. I have several companies that are interested in putting you under contract and I would like to talk to you about it," he said.

"I don't know, Mr. Parker. At the present time I am employed and working on my master's degree in journalism. What do these various companies want?"

"The story of your part in the rescue of three men trapped in an old mine appeared in 'A Week in the World,' a worldwide publication, along with some beautiful photos. There were several shots of you on that drilling machine that you were running. One company wants to use you to advertise their outdoor wear. There would be photos of you sitting on a bulldozer and that sort of thing."

"I don't want to be rude, Mr. Parker, but I am not at all interested in capitalizing on the mine accident. I thank you for calling and may you have a good day," she said as she hung up the phone.

When they went to lunch, she told Sandy about the call.

"I'm not a model and I'm not going to pose for photos on a bulldozer or other piece of equipment. It wouldn't be right for me to use that accident for publicity," she said.

"Isabel, you are a real ding-a-ling. You wouldn't have to pose for anything you didn't want to pose for, but you ought to look into it if for no other reason than to satisfy my curiosity," Sandy told her. "If that guy calls back, apologize and ask him to come see you."

The next day, Don Parker called again. This time Isabel did as Sandy said and apologized to him. She agreed to a tentative date for two days later to discuss a contract. That night, she called G T and told him about it. He told her he would sit in on the discussion if she wanted him to.

"That's why I called you," she said.

Sandy was on pins and needles until Don Parker showed up at Isabel's apartment. He was in his early thirties, a nice-looking young man about 5'11" with crew-cut sandy hair. He had a dimpled smile that was very infectious. His teeth were clean and even and his blue eyes were very deep. His dress was casual with an open at the neck light blue shirt. His pants were khaki in color, but expensive in appearance. Isabel introduced him to G T and Sandy, not telling him that one was a budding lawyer and the other a reporter.

"I have been contacted by a sportswear outfit that wants you to pose for them along the lines of sports such as golf, fishing, swimming and boating," Parker said.

"Before we go any further, Mr. Parker, I will not pose nude or semi-nude. I will not pose for clothes made outside the United States and I will not pose for hunting photos," she said.

"You drive a hard bargain, Miss Morgan. I'll have to go back to these people and give them your criteria, but I will be back with you. These people pay big bucks for calendar type photos," he said.

"Not meaning to be rude, Mr. Parker, but you called me, I didn't call you. I would enjoy posing for fishing, camping, football, or that sort of thing, but not anything degrading. I don't have to," she said.

"I've enjoyed talking to you and your friends. It is refreshing to find someone with your ideas and principals. I'll be back in touch," he said as he left.

CHAPTER 44

Jacob and Jennifer checked in at the Harlan Post 10 as usual. There were no new assignments, so they went back to Pineville to work on the Strick-Lin Chou murder case. It had occurred to both of them that they didn't know anything about Pat Flannery. They were pretty well-versed in the other suspects, but they had passed over him.

"Let's go talk to George Deane about Flannery," said Jacob.

"That's fine with me," said Jennifer.

Pulling into the Golden Star parking lot, they went in the office. Gerry came out into the reception area to see what they wanted and Jacob told her they would like to talk to George. Gerry took them to George's office and told George that they were there to arrest him for not paying a speeding ticket. George, who never drove over fifty miles an hour, got a big laugh out of it. Showing them a seat, Gerry asked if she could get them anything to drink, but both thanked her and refused.

"George, we're trying to track down the person or persons who killed Jason and Lin Chou. We were discussing the people who might have been involved and Pat Flannery's name came up. You and Frank are the only people we know that know him or anything about him," said Jacob.

"I don't really know that much about him, Jacob. He is the president of Garbon, Ltd., which owned White Pines. He is a very affable fellow. He called us about buying White Pines. Frank and I found the money and together with Sarah, went to Boston to cut a deal. Afterwards, he came in here and fired Jason Strick. I met him at the Middlesboro airport and let him use my truck while he was here. I took him back to the airport the morning of the day that you, G T and Bige got trapped. His plane came in and he flew back to Boston. That's about all of the association I had with him. He did have a flat tire on my truck and must have crawled under the truck to fix it, because when he came to the house to get me to take him to the airport his knees and shoes were all muddy."

"Did you have the flat fixed, Mr. Deane?" asked Jennifer.

"Honey, nobody calls me Mr. Deane. You'll have to be like G T, Isabel, Jacob and all the other young people around here and call me George," he answered.

"Okay George, did you have the flat fixed?"

"No, I've been meaning to and I haven't let the shop have my truck long enough to fix it," he said.

"May we look at it?" asked Jacob.

"Sure thing. It's out here on the parking lot. Come on, I'll show you," George said getting up from his chair.

The three of them walked out to George's truck that was on the parking lot. Checking the spare tire, they found that if it had been flat, it had been fixed. Jennifer dusted the lug nut that held the tire in place and took a print of it.

"Thanks again, George. We appreciate your help," said Jennifer with twinkle in her eye.

Leaving the Golden Star parking lot, Jacob spoke first. "Now what do you think?" he asked Jennifer.

"I think we need to contact the Boston Police Department and get them to get Pat Flannery's finger prints," Jennifer answered.

Going to the dispatch center, Jacob called John Talbert and told him about their talk with George Deane.

"The lab ran prints on the gun and there were some real good ones. I'm on my way back to Pineville and I'll tell you about it when I get there," said John.

CHAPTER 45

Jerry Hoag was still upset about losing the treasure and he was blaming Phil Banks. He knew that Banks was a member of the Group, but he couldn't prove it. If Banks hadn't leaned on Rebecca Holton so heavily, she might not have quit, and that would have kept the permit from being approved so he could have retrieved the treasure. He kept asking himself who else in the Department was a member of that Group. Maybe the best way to find out was to collar Banks and beat it out of him. Waiting for an opportunity, he finally caught Phil in the men's room that afternoon and shoved him up against the wall.

"Tell me real quick and don't lie. Who is in that Group with you?" Hoag demanded.

"I don't know what you are talking about," said Phil.

"Yes, you do and if you don't tell me now, I'll get your ass fired," snarled Jerry.

"You better lay off or the same thing will happen to you that happened to Jason Strick and that Chinaman," said Banks.

"What does that mean?" asked Jerry.

"You'll find out. Now let me go and get out of my face or it'll happen before you know it," Phil retorted.

Leaving Banks in the washroom, Jerry went back to his office and began to play over what Phil had said. Dialing information, he got the number of the dispatch center in Pineville. Dialing that number he asked for Jacob Gibson. Jacob wasn't there so Hoag left numbers for him to call both at the office and at home.

Quitting time had come around and Jerry was getting ready to leave his office when his phone rang. It was Jacob. Jerry Hoag went through the entire conversation he had with Phil Banks. Jacob took all of this down on a tape recorder after telling Jerry what he was doing. Playing the tape back to Jennifer, they called John on the radio and asked where he was. He was just outside of Pineville and would meet them at Rosemary's in about fifteen minutes.

"Whose prints are they?" Jacob asked.

"We don't know. They aren't Carl's or Jerry Hoag's. Both of theirs are on file so that leaves Pat Flannery and Bryan Fuson," said John.

"We found Mr. X," said Jacob.

After playing the tape for John, the threat was enough to bring Phil Banks in for questioning, which John said he would do. Calling the office in Frankfort, he got a trooper to go pick up Phillip Banks and hold him until John could get there. Then he got back in his car and went back to Frankfort.

Phil Banks had been lodged in the Franklin County jail and John went straight there to question him. Joseph Stowe was already there when John went to get the turnkey to let him question Banks. Taking Banks to an interrogation room, John read him his rights.

"What did you mean when you threatened Jerry Hoag by telling him that the same thing would happen to him that happened to Jason Strick and the Chinaman?" asked John.

"I was just kidding him," said Banks.

"No you weren't," said John. "Now listen to me. I am going to fingerprint you, and if your prints match those on that gun that was used in their killings, then you are in deep trouble."

"I didn't have anything to do with those killings," said Banks.

"Then who did?" asked John.

"I'm not telling you any more," said Phillip.

"Then I am going to book you for murder," said John.

"If I tell you all that I know, will I get off?" asked Phillip.

"I can't cut you any deal, but you will be a lot better off if you tell me the truth," answered John. Joseph Stowe agreed. John hooked up a tape recorder and turned it on.

"Oliver Barton, the attorney, is my superior in the Group. He called me one day and told me that there was a permit for White Pines Coal Company that I was to delay for at least a month. I gave it to Rebecca Holton who I knew was under the Group's influence. It went along fine until she and G T Deane, the engineer who prepared the permit, went to Pineville to review it. She came back from that and began to balk on holding it up. I leaned on her as hard as I could, but she wouldn't budge.

"I called Jason Strick one day and told him I was having trouble. He was real snotty about it and told me to tell my superior, who would have Holton disposed of. I told Oliver and he said he would have her put away. The people who were supposed to take her out had a wreck on I-64 and were both killed. Strick then called Oliver and threatened him with exposure if he didn't get the permit held up for at least a month. Oliver called me, and told me that he and I needed to go to Pineville so I went with him. He somehow knew where Strick and the Chinaman were and we went up a hollow called Red Oak Left.

"There was a car parked in the road so we stopped. Oliver got out and walked up a path that went out of sight. I followed him, but made sure he couldn't see me. Strick and the Chinaman were talking. Oliver walked up to them with a pistol in his hand. He told Jason that he had lived out his time and he shot him four times real fast. Then he turned and told the other man that he had lived out his time and shot him twice. I had seen all I wanted to see so I high-tailed it back to the car.

"Oliver came back down the path in a few minutes and told me to drive the other car up the other hollow, which I think is called Red Oak Right. He handed me the pistol and told me to get rid of it. I drove the car up the adjacent hollow and when I got out, I threw the pistol up in the brush. Oliver had walked up the hollow behind me. First, he wadded up some papers he found in the car and set them on fire in the front seat. Then he uncapped the gas tank, stuck a folded up piece of paper in it and lit it.

"We ran back to our car and Jason started driving out of the hollow. We heard an explosion not long after we left. I asked him what went on, because I didn't want him to know that I knew. He told me that he had completed some business that he should have completed a long time ago. When we got home, he let me out and went on to his apartment. I read about the murders in the paper the next day. That's how I found out what the Chinaman's name was. If you found the gun, it had Oliver's prints on it as well as mine."

"I will have to book you as an accessory to murder, but if you turn state's evidence like you are saying, it should get you a lighter sentence," said John.

CHAPTER 46

Jemjelf answered Thelma's phone after the second ring, which was her general practice. That gave her an opportunity to see whose name was on the caller ID. She recognized the area code as being Frankfort, but she didn't recognize the number. "Durham's residence," she said in her soft low voice.

"This is Governor Martin's office calling. Would you please ask Mrs. Durham to hold for Governor Martin?" the caller asked in a very crisp voice.

"Yes, I will," answered Jemjelf, then called Thelma to the phone.

"Mrs. Durham, this is Albert Martin and I am calling to ask a favor of you," said Albert.

"Why I'll be glad to oblige if I can, Governor Martin," Thelma answered.

"I have gotten word from the Chinese Embassy that Wing Fu is free to go back to her province without any more trouble. I have also made arrangements for my friend, Abdullah Savig, the owner of Oasis Farm, to negotiate with Wing Fu for the sale of at least fifty of her horses. I would like to have a party at the Convention Center at Pine Mountain State Park for Wing Fu, the three young men who were trapped in that old mine, and the state troopers who collared the drug people who were after Wing Fu and her daughter. My problem is this sort of thing is hard for me to do. If I have such a party and someone is left out, then I have lost a friend. I would like to ask you if you would put on such an affair and I will pay for it personally. You know who should be included and the number is of no consequence."

"I greatly appreciate the chance to do this and I would also like for it to be my party. I will pay for everything and all that you have to do is show up," Thelma answered.

"I can't let you do that," Governor Martin answered.

"Let's have the party and then fight over the bill after it is over," said Thelma. "This is your idea so you pick a date and time. I'll do the rest."

"How about two weeks from this coming Saturday?" he asked.

"That suits me," said Thelma.

"Now may I speak to my assistant, Betty?" he asked.

"Yes, you may," answered Thelma, motioning Betty to the phone.

"Good morning, Governor Martin," Betty said.

"I told Mrs. Durham this and I am sure she will tell you, but I wanted you to hear it firsthand. Wing Fu is free to go back to her province. The Chinese Embassy called thanking John and the others who captured the drug dealers who were after Wing Fu and Alberta. Mrs. Durham is going to have a party to honor Wing Fu, and I am going to bring Abdullah Savig and Dr.

Tao Chang to it. Abdullah wants to buy fifty of Wing Fu's horses and Dr. Chang wants to meet his daughter and granddaughter."

"How did you know about Dr. Chang?" Betty asked.

"Sarge let it slip, but don't tell him that I told you. Abdullah said that he would like to fly Wing Fu and Alberta back to their home. He has chartered a twenty-seat plane which you, John and Thelma Durham are to be the first to board. I will see you in about two weeks," Governor Martin said.

CHAPTER 47

"Miss Morgan, I have a company named Arcan that specializes in sportswear. We want you to model and endorse a line of their product. It would be primarily jeans, sweaters, blouses and shoes. Their bathing suits are one-piece, but by a number of standards are very demure. They have six plants in this country and buy no materials that are not produced in this country. We are talking about a six-figure, three-year contract with annual openers for renegotiating length and dollar amount. Are you interested?" Don Parker asked.

All that Isabel had done was answer the phone. He started talking before she could ask who it was.

"I am not being coy or difficult, Mr. Parker, but I would like to talk this over with my attorney. Will you please mail me the contract so that he can look at it? I will be back to you in a few days," Isabel said.

She called Sandy right away to tell her what Don Parker had said.

"I knew it would happen. Where do you go to be photographed?" asked Sandy.

"I don't know. I'll know more after I get the contract."

Next she called G T and told him all about it, asking him if he would please review the contract. He was very excited for her, although he knew that it meant that he might lose her. After talking to G T, Isabel called Frank and Sarah. They were like G T; they were excited for her, but they hated for her to get too far away.

The contract came in the next day's mail. As soon as she got it, Isabel called G T and told him. He came to her apartment after work and they went over the contract together.

"It looks like a pretty general contract. They pay all expenses, insure you for one million and provide you with health care. I like the name 'Isabel's Items.' That has a nice ring to it," G T said. "If you want to sign it, I will witness it."

"Do you want me to sign it?" she asked.

"I want you to do what you want to do. If you are ready to get married and settle down, I'm ready. If you want to sign on for this for three years, I'll be glad to wait. It's your call, Isabel. You know that I love you and always will. I hope you will sign this and become a world-famous model. I will always be here when you need me," G T said.

Isabel started crying as she signed the paper.

"I will always love you and I'll come back to you," she said as she hugged him and kissed him.

CHAPTER 48

John called Jacob and Jennifer to tell them that Phillip Banks had spilled his guts, which led to Oliver Barton's arrest for the murder of Jason Strick and Lin Chou. That closed most of the file on the murders. Then Jacob and Jennifer went to George and Frank to ask what they proposed to do with the treasure. They said that they hadn't given it any thought, but whoever retrieved it was welcome to it. Since Jerry Hoag had been instrumental in the cracking of the case, Jacob called him and told him what the owners of White Pines had said. He showed up the next day. Jerry told Frank and George how much he appreciated it even if his ancestor, Cyrus, had been a murdering thief.

Thelma's and Governor Martin's party was a real bash. Sam Eldridge came and brought Sandy. Isabel had gone to Phoenix, Arizona to pose for a new sweater line, but Arcan had agreed to have her back in Middlesboro, via the company plane, for Sarah to pick her up and get her home in time to get dressed and go to the party. It seemed that about half of the Golden Star-White Pines staff showed up. Howard and Rosemary brought Roy and Debbie Seevers, then introduced them around. Bige brought Rebecca Holton and his father, Clyde. Rebecca had gone to work for Golden Star/White Pines the week before. The Natural Resources Commissioner had apologized to Rebecca for the treatment Phillip Banks had heaped on her and offered her a promotion, which she gracefully turned down, explaining that she might have a housewife offer in the near future. Governor Martin also apologized to Rebecca and assured her that the Group would not bother her or her father. A purge of the Natural Resources complement had revealed two other members of the Group, who were immediately arrested. G T had come to the party with George and Gerry, but he had saved Isabel a seat next to him. She came in with Frank and Sarah who were seated next to George and Gerry.

Wing Fu still didn't know what was going on since Governor Martin had sworn Betty to secrecy. Betty had explained to her that she was safe and would soon be going home, so there was no reason to not bring Alberta. As soon as they came in, Jennifer went to Alberta who started cooing and smiling. Jennifer asked Betty to ask Wing Fu if she could hold Alberta and Wing Fu was glad to oblige, remembering that Jennifer was the one who started the resistance against Ching Lee.

A good-sized crowd had gathered when the governor's helicopter landed in the parking lot. Along with Governor Martin and his wife, Margaret, were Dr. Tao Chang, Abdullah Savig and his wife, and Trooper David Wilson. Albert Martin had flown the plane to Pine Mountain to keep his hand in. The crowd had all gotten seated when the Governor's party entered the room. Thelma herself escorted them to the front table. Governor Martin introduced Thelma to all in his party and thanked her for "having this little get-together," as he called it, and inviting them.

After everyone had finished eating, Governor Martin stood to the microphone and gave a short talk. "I want to thank Mrs. Durham for asking Margaret and me and our friends to this most elegant affair. I have several things I would like to do. First, I want to introduce Dr. Tao Chang to his daughter and granddaughter, the Butterfly Princesses," he said turning to Wing Fu and Dr. Chang who was sitting on one side of her. Betty was sitting on the other. When Betty told Wing Fu what Governor Martin had said, she turned to Dr. Chang and hugged him. When Jennifer brought Alberta over to meet her grandfather, the baby smiled and cooed for him as Jennifer handed her to him. Dr. Chang kissed Alberta on the forehead, handed her back to Jennifer and wiped the tears out of his eyes.

"Next, I want to introduce Mr. Abdullah Savig, owner of The Oasis farm outside of Lexington. Mr. Savig wants to return to the Shuai province with the Princess in order to buy fifty or more horses," he said. Betty told Wing Fu what he had said and Wing Fu became ecstatic. She turned to Betty and hugged her as she began to cry for joy.

Governor Martin handed Wing Fu a letter from the Chinese president, which she read and handed to Betty to read, and then to Dr. Chang. It was very flowery in its content, but basically it said that the People's Republic recognized that all Chinese should be free to live as they wished. Therefore the people of the Shuai Province were free from any governmental interference. They were to be their own government.

Next, the governor told the crowd how thankful he was that G T, Bige and Trooper Gibson had been rescued. He commended the rescue team led by Fred Tinsley for the great work they did and he asked Fred to say a few words. He introduced the other members of the rescue team and thanked Clyde Napier for the use of the Bobcat. "Rescue work of that type is tough and tiresome. You are working against time and you are never sure what you will find when you get the fall material out of the way. It's even tougher when you know the people who are trapped like we knew G T, Jacob and Bige. One of the fellows said that he knew Jacob because he had ticketed him for speeding three times, but never turned them in.

"That's the way it was with us. We were tired and wanted to take time out when we saw that little blond-headed girl drive that drill rig down that hill. A fellow working next to me said, 'By damn, if she can do that, then I can pick up more rock. She has really got guts.' Isabel, you inspired us and we salute you. You are the beauty queen who can run the machine and you are tough."

Fred's talk brought on a standing ovation for the crew members and Isabel whose face turned scarlet. Lonnie Howard, who was sitting behind her, leaned over and hugged her. She started crying. The party ended on that note. People crowded around Isabel to congratulate her on her new line of business. Even Governor Martin and his wife congratulated her. Margaret Martin pointed out to Isabel that she was wearing an Arcan blouse herself. As the crowd thinned out, Isabel sought out Fred Tinsley. She hugged his neck and fussed at him for embarrassing her. Jemjelf Tinsley, who looked like a model even after having four children, also had on an Arcan outfit.

Finally, Isabel found Sam and Sandy. They both told her that they missed her at the paper, but they were glad she was doing well. She assured them that she was going to finish the course and get her Master's degree in journalism. Sandy said that Chris had called her almost every day since he and Bill left. He told her that Bill was surviving, but his time with Isabel was something he would never forget. Isabel thought to herself that she would never forget him either.

She rode home with G T who had driven his truck to the party.

"I'm proud of you, Isabel. You not only saved my life, but you are fast becoming a household word. Please don't forget me as you become a famous person," he said.

"I expect you to be a famous person and I ask that you please not forget me," she countered.

"I meant to tell you that the old house that Emma and Jeremy lived in at Wallsend Hollow burned a while back," said G T.

"I'll be home for Thanksgiving," she said. "How about we pool our resources and get Valerie Arnett to arrange for us to buy clothes and shoes for all the poor children in the first six grades. We could keep our names out of it and just be around to watch."

"I like that," said G T as he got out, went around and opened her car door. Taking her arm, he helped her out, walked her to the door and kissed her.

"Goodnight, Isabel. I love you," he said.

"Goodnight, G T. I love you," she responded.

PEOPLE

Abdullah Savig	Owner of Oasis Farms
Adam Lawson	Commissioner Natural Resources
Albert Martin	Kentucky governor
Anne Quinlan	Betty's supervisor
Arcan	Sportswear company
Augusta Harp	Savannah's cousin
Austin Martin	Governor's son
Avaline (McGill) Fuson	Wife of Bryan Fuson
Bacon County	Home county of Elmer Bingham
Barmore	County seat of Bacon County
Barry Foreman	Permit reviewer at Natural Resources
Beecher Hewl	Carl Smith's lawyer
Bill Carson	President of Commonwealth Electric and Gas
Bill Minter	Reporter for Reporting Service International
Bryan Fuson	Vice President White Pines
Burl Strick	Ancestor of Jason Strick and civil war guerrilla
Calvin Marks	Piedmont Bank
Candace Bingham	trouble maker at PSK
Carboones	Store in mall where Veronica worked
Caroline Moss	Court reporter and Jeff Cawood's girl friend
Caron Dell	Commonwealth's Attorney
Carson Napier	Dorothy's husband and Bige's father
Ching Lee	Wing Fu's half sister and special envoy
Chris Evans	Reporter for Reporting Service International
Claude Pembroke	PSK manager at Maryville
Clyde Napier	Olivia's husband
Curtis Bradley	Bradley Durham's father
Cyrus Hoag	Rode with Burl Strick
Daniel Winston	Employment company that contacts Whitley
David Walton	PSK board member Walton Farm
David Wilson	Copilot trooper with governor
Deborah Haley	Lawyer in Curt's office
Dorothy Dillon	Olivia's sister & Bige's mother
Dr. Alvin Carnahan	Psychiatrist who examined Olivia
Dr. Ralph West	Frankfort obstetrician

Dr. Tao Chang	Professor of Asian History at UK
Edwin Lee	Assistant Commissioner Natural Resources
Elmer Bingham	Local politician in Bacon County
Emma Caldwell	Jeremy's mother and Pretty Posy operator
Father Jerome Hogan	Priest in Pineville (check in Fogs for correct name)
Fred Tinsley	Jemjelf's husband
Harry Baker	Sarah Morgan's first husband-Whitley Rogers lover
Harvey Stone	Curt's chalkeye
James Weller	PSK board member from Princeton-Pennyrile Chronicle
Jason Strick	President of White Pines Coal Company
Jeff Cawood	Olivia's attorney
Jemjelf Tinsley	Thelma's housekeeper and friend
Jennifer McComb	Tennessee detective
Jeremy Caldwell	Southeast student
Jerry Hoag	Permit Section Supervisor
Joan Carter	Woman who worked with Veronica
Joan Ripples Constanza	Judge Constanza's wife.
Karla Matheson	Governor Martin's receptionist
Kelly Carr	Manager of PSK at Barmore
Kurt Holtz	Whitley's new boss and president of Electrique Internationale
Larkin Downey	PSK board member from Pineville
Larry Spang	Caron Dell's assistant
Lin Chou	Wing Fu's escort
Mabel Jones	Veronica's supervisor
Marc West	Sandy's former fiancé
Margaret Martin	Governor's wife
Margaret Perkins Strick	Jason Strick's wife
Martin Wallace	Tennessee detective
Mary Ann Taylor	Foreman of jury trying Olivia
Nanik	Village near entrance to Shuai
Oliver Barton	Environmental Law Professor at UK
Patrick Flannery	President of Garbon, Ltd.
Paul Nolan	Randy's replacement
Pete Kelly	Jack Colbert's boy friend and treasurer of PSK
Percy Hatfield	Bailiff in Constanza's court
Phillip Banks	Rebecca's supervisor
Rebecca Holton	EPA at Natural Resources

Robert Michaels	Executive vice president at PSK
Roy Seevers	PSK manager at Barmore
Sam Eldridge	News editor at Lexington Journal
Sandy Deiss	Isabel's sorority sister & good friend
Savannah Dillon	Olivia Napier's mother
Scott Senters	Brad's replacement.
Joseph Stowe	Natural Resources attorney
Thomas Wilder	Scott's friend at UK
Theo Shawitz	CRG lawyer
Timothy Patterson	Head hunter for Daniel Winston
Will Hoskins	Whitley Rogers' brother
Wing Fu	Chinese refugee

ABOUT THE AUTHOR

Jim Roan is a seventy-eight year old Electrical Engineer who works for a Southeastern Kentucky coal company. He retired from the position of Division Engineer after thirty years with a statewide electric utility. He has lived seventy-three years in the City of Pineville, Kentucky which is the locale of his books. Except for three years aboard the submarine USS Queenfish during WWII and three years at the University of Kentucky.

He consults with his wife, Gerry, on various characters.

This is the second of his weather/month book series. The first was *The Fogs of August*.

At present he is working on *The Rains of October*.

Printed in the United States
1208900005B/58-282

The Mists of September continues the adventures of G T Deane and Isabel Morgan who grew up together as brother and sister. As they attend the trial of Olivia Napier a Chinese refugee comes into their lives. Whitley Rogers leaves PSK.

G T and two friends get trapped in an old mine where they find two murdered men and two Civil War skeletons and a treasure of Civil War currency. Isabel assists in the rescue as the murderer is sought.

ISBN 1-4107-2665-7
90000
9 781410 726650